# The Knights of Dark Renown

No historical episode leans so close to fiction as the Crusades.
The world of Bohemond and St Louis, of Saladin and
Richard the Lionheart still appears as highly coloured and
dramatic as it did eight hundred years ago. The people are
still, somehow, larger than life; their virtues brighter, their
vices blacker than the world of everyday. The sheer
improbability of the whole undertaking still astounds;
both its heroism and its villainy seem to transcend reality.

In this novel of the Crusading Kingdom of Jerusalem,
Graham Shelby has found full scope for his remarkable gifts
of story-telling and characterisation. The speed and
violence of events is balanced by an eye for light and colour
and a curiosity about human motives. Churchmen, barons,
knights, courtiers, their wives and mistresses, are seen in
sharp outline against a hard, dry, dangerous landscape
commanded by huge castles and roamed by mounted
soldiers. The code of chivalry chimes in hideous dissonance
with massacre and cruelty, personified most memorably in
Reynald of Chatillon who knew neither fear nor mercy. It
is indeed the story of his monstrous exploits culminating
in the famous battle of the Horns of Hattin that Graham
Shelby has taken for the theme of this most exciting book.

# The Knights of
# Dark Renown

*Graham Shelby*

The Book Society

*For Ann*
*and*
*MAW, BZM, DCH,*
*and many others*
*with the gift of*
*encouragement*

Published by
The Book Society
4 Fitzroy Square, London, W.1.
by arrangement with Collins Publishers
© 1969 Graham Shelby
Printed in Great Britain
Collins Clear-Type Press: London and Glasgow

# Contents

# The Factions within the
# Kingdom of Jerusalem in 1183

REYNALD OF CHATILLON *Lord of Kerak*
STEPHANIE OF MILLY *Lady of Oultrejourdain, Chatelaine of Kerak*
HUMPHREY IV OF TORON *son of Stephanie, step-son of Reynald*

BALIAN OF IBELIN *Lord of Nablus*
MARIA COMNENA *widow of King Amalric I, Lady of Nablus*
ISABELLA *Princess of Jerusalem, daughter of Maria; step-daughter of Balian*
FOSTUS *Constable of Nablus*
ERNOUL *Squire to Lord Balian*

KING BALDWIN IV OF JERUSALEM
AGNES OF COURTENAY, *ex-wife of King Amalric I, mother of King Baldwin IV and Princess Sibylla of Jerusalem*
JOSCELIN OF COURTENAY *Seneschal of the Kingdom, brother of Agnes*
AMALRIC OF LUSIGNAN *Constable of the Kingdom*
HERACLIUS *Patriarch of Jerusalem*
PASHIA DE RIVERI *draper's wife*

RAYMOND III OF TRIPOLI *Lord of Tiberias*
ESCHIVA OF BURES *Princess of Galilee, Countess of Tripoli*

GUY OF LUSIGNAN *brother of Constable Amalric*
SIBYLLA *Princess of Jerusalem*
BALDWIN *son of Sibylla*

BALDWIN OF RAMLEH *brother of Balian of Ibelin*
WALTER OF CAESAREA
REGINALD OF SIDON

ARNOLD OF TOROGA *Grand Master of the Temple*
ROGER OF LES MOULINS *Grand Master of the Hospital*
GERARD OF RIDEFORT *Templar*
ERMENGARD DE DAPS *Hospitaller*

## The Force without

SALADIN *Sultan*: Salah ed-Din Yusuf, al-Malik un-Nasir
AL-AFDAL *Saladin's eldest son*: Ali, al-Malik al-Afdal
KUKBURI *Emir of Harran*
TAKEDIN *Emir of Hamat*: Al-Malik al-Modaffer Taki ed-Din
    Omar
LULU *Egyptian Admiral*: Husam ed-Din Lulu

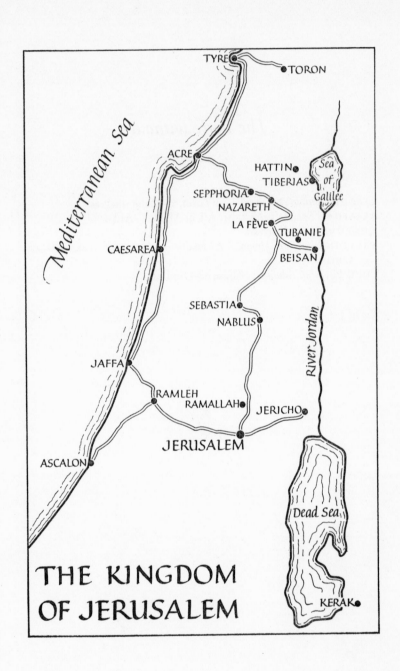

# THE KINGDOM
# OF JERUSALEM

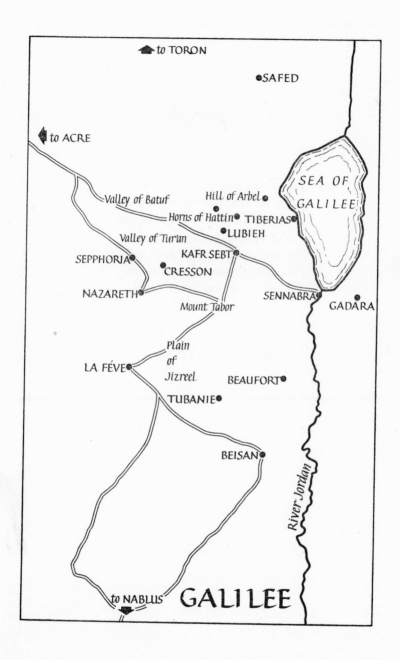

# Epigraph

*Tell of the Lord, tell of the Lady,*
*Tell of the King with his robe and crown;*
*Tell of the Dancer, tell of the Juggler,*
*Tell of the Knight of bright renown.*
*Sing out, speak out, link hands and run,*
*The daylight's gone and supper's on,*
*The fire's alight and winter's come.*

CHILDREN'S SONG

# CHAPTER ONE

# The Red Sea

## *April 1183*

From a distance the long war galley looked deserted. The pine masts were bare, the twin rows of oars dipped, unmoving in the water. It was as though the crew had lowered the heavy linen sails, bound the rudder bar, filed out of the rowing benches and dived overboard, leaving the vessel to the vagaries of wind and current.

But from a distance it was not possible to see the open decks below the bulwarks, or the benches that traversed the mid-section of the ship, or what lay beneath the small canopy draped across the bows. For a more detailed assessment of the galley's fate the curious sailor or fisherman would have to move closer. However, at this time, in the dawn of one of the last days of April 1183, there were no other craft in the vicinity. The galley was alone, isolated by choice somewhere in the northern expanse of the Red Sea.

She had neared her present position an hour earlier, having run all night before a fleet of high-prowed Saracen *butas*. Through a combination of great good fortune, the cover of darkness and the desperate skill of her captain and crew she had eluded the enemy warships and limped north into the day.

Although there were no signs of life aboard, the crew were still there. They were sprawled flat on the decks, slumped over the benches, huddled against the bulwark rails. Eight of the sixty rowers were dead, but no-one had dared tip the bodies over the side for fear they would float and mark the passage of escape. The five-strong team of steersmen had been reduced to three, while the contingent of armed men who crouched between the midship benches had lost a quarter of their number. The captain, a thin-faced Sicilian pirate named Camini, was alive and nursing the crudely bound stump of a severed wrist. Throughout the latter part of the chase he had laughed bitterly to himself, since it was one of his own men who had swung a short sword too wildly and chopped off Camini's left hand. The man had been killed during the subsequent hours of the pursuit, so the Sicilian's sense of justice was satisfied.

The *butas* had come upon the galley at dusk and attempted to drive it east toward the coast of Arabia. Camini had anticipated the manœuvre and the galley had broken free heading north. The chase had continued in that direction for several hours, while the Moslem ships clung tenaciously to the wake of their prey. The Saracen archers fired hundreds of black-feathered arrows, some tipped with iron, some with lumps of flaming tar. Twice the stern of the galley was set alight, and twice members of the crew swarmed over the huge rudder to hurl vinegar and sand on the flames. In this way, standing unprotected, they had presented the archers with an easy target, and most of the casualties had been incurred there.

Eventually, taking advantage of the approaching darkness, Camini had ordered that the dun-coloured sails be lowered and extra men sent to the rowing benches. He commanded his own archers to hold their fire, while all aboard the galley were told to maintain the strictest silence. He made his way round the stern, knelt once to cut the throat of a wounded soldier who would not stifle his moans, and whispered directions to the steersmen. The galley moved north-west, then north-east, then due west and round again in a wide northward arc. The *butas* fanned out and the Saracen bowmen fired blazing naphtha high in the air in an effort to trace the fleeing vessel. The harsh white flares illuminated a ship ploughing east from Nubia, but by the time the Moslems recognised it as a merchantman, the galley had vanished.

Now she lay silent, a fire-scarred nest of shame and fury.

Despite Camini's profession, the galley was not the property of some common corsair. Her name had been erased from the prow and she carried no insignia, yet the Saracens had committed their entire first fleet to the pursuit of this single ship. They had learned who she was and, more important, who beside Camini rode aboard her. This knowledge strengthened their resolve to capture the vessel and to treat those who survived the fight with the vicious disgust usually reserved for poisonous yellow scorpions, or the hairy spiders called *tarantes*. The Saracen navy regrouped and continued the search.

The vessel they were so determined to destroy was the Crusader war galley *Ter e Mer*. She was the flagship of a sixteen galley fleet, all of which had been constructed in the Christian countries of Moab and Ascalon, test-sailed on the Dead Sea or the Mediterranean, dismantled and carried hundreds of miles overland to the Gulf of Aqaba. There, they had been re-assembled, armed and crewed, then sent south in search of the black devils of Islam. For three months *Ter e Mer* and the other fifteen had served as floating castles, from which the Crusaders issued forth to burn and pillage the coastal towns of Arabia and Nubia, to make landward sorties against merchant caravans and to threaten Mecca itself.

The man they sought to destroy was now asleep under the bow canopy. He was the Frankish suzerain, Reynald of Chatillon, Lord of Kerak of Moab. Known to his friends as Prince Reynald and to the Saracens as the Red Wolf of the Desert, he was regarded by his Christian allies as the most dangerous man in Palestine.

He lay on his side, his spine pressed hard against the oak planks that curved round to the prow post. In one hand he held a broad stabbing knife. The other was curled over the pommel of his massive sword. Because he could not swim, and would rather risk taking an arrow in the chest than falling overboard, he had stripped off his full-length ring-mail hauberk. Now he wore only a long-sleeve leather gambeson, a broad, stained belt and sword-hanger and high felt boots with sewn-on leather soles. His flat-topped helmet—again too dangerous to wear as it would drag him head first under water—a cross-bow and a sackful of quarrels were piled near him under the brown canopy.

He had fought ferociously, not only during the past hours, but almost without respite since early February. He had personally killed more than seventy Moslems, men, women and, on five occasions, children. So, whenever he slept, he enjoyed the tranquillity of mind that comes to a man who has done his work well. Yet he slept in the shallows and as Camini advanced in silence toward the prow he came awake and twisted to a crouch.

'You,' he snarled, 'don't you play the dancer with me.' He made a sharp sideways movement with the knife, then pointed it at the pirate's bandaged stump. 'Creep up on me like that again and you'll hold your wine mug with your feet. You understand? Well, what news?'

Camini, who had earned himself a reputation as one of the most ruthless men in the eastern Mediterranean, had been forced into second place by Reynald of Chatillon. The corsair had responded to Reynald's call for good pilots, men who knew the Red Sea and were not afraid to trespass on it, and he had presented himself at Kerak in January. By the time the Crusader's raiding column had swept south from the fortress and captured Aqaba, Camini realised that he was hardly more than an apt pupil in Reynald's school. When the port had been taken the two men had disagreed over some trifling detail and Reynald had used his sword pommel to club in three of Camini's teeth. Since then the Sicilian had limited his observations to nautical matters and Reynald had left him alone.

Now the pirate held up his good hand, gestured to the Crusader to hold his temper and said, 'We are well clear, Prince.' He whistled through the gaps in his teeth, and it amused him to see Reynald smile. When he killed the Lord of Kerak, as he had promised himself he would, he hoped to devise a way of death that would also make Reynald whistle.

Reynald nodded and pushed himself to his feet, stooping until he had moved clear of the canopy. He sheathed his dagger and asked, 'How many men have we lost?'

Camini shrugged. 'Until they wake I cannot tell the living from the dead. Twenty-three I know of, but more may have died in the night.'

'You did well to get us free, Sicilian. At one time I thought we would be taken.'

'Yesss,' the captain sibilated, 'when they made the circle round us.' With sadistic care he added, 'On the subject, Prince, have you heard the news of the others in your fleet?'

'What news? I know we still have a ship off Aqaba.'

'Yesss, that's so. But I mean the others, those you sent south. Did you know Lulu has them?'

'What? In God's name, cut-throat, who's Lulu?'

'In the Name of Mohammed.' Camini corrected, his eyes bright with malice. 'He is the Egyptian Admiral. Husam ed-Din Lulu. Saladin sent for him to take command of his new navy. Ah, yesss, did you not know? It was launched some days ago. Did you not think it strange that Emir Saladin could afford to send an entire fleet after us and risk leaving your other ships at liberty? He now has two fleets, an old and a new. And has destroyed yours, I hear.' He paused to let Reynald assimilate the first part of the report, and carried out an inspection of his grotesque wound.

They both knew that the Moslem leader, Salah ed-Din Yusuf had been as stunned as his people by the savage efficiency of the Red Sea raids. But he had recovered quickly and thereafter matched Reynald move for move. Where the Lord of Kerak had had ships built and dispatched from Moab and Ascalon, Saladin had commissioned his own fleet and had had it transported from Alexandria and Damietta.

Unable to secure the support of his fraternal overlords, who were deeply shocked by his boast that he would raze Mecca, holy place of Islam, Reynald had been content to hire bloody profiteers like Camini. For his part, Saladin chose the highly-trained sailors from Maghrib to man his ships, and Admiral Lulu to command them. In this way he was able to send a competent and disciplined navy against a pack of sea wolves, whose only advantage, surprise, had long since evaporated.

'You say this Lulu has them?' Reynald thundered. 'All of them?'

'Perhaps one or two escaped. He surrounded them near al-Hawra. It's said he sank five ships and seized the rest. Before long Saladin's two fleets will become three, because he will use our own galleys, your galleys, against us. It would seem wise to return quickly to Aqaba, yesss?'

Reynald felt the devil's talons bury themselves in his neck.

He was a large man for the age; heavy-set, with sagging shoulders, bowed legs and thick, corded arms. He had red hair on his head, jaw and upper lip, and his face and body were stitched with the jagged scars of combat, or drunken misjudgement. His mouth was filled with teeth the width and colour of his thumb-nail. He was not a man to be shaken easily, but he shook now, jerked this way and that by the invisible claws, his spine twisted by the pressure of the satanic force. But if one did not believe that the Prince of Demons could find the Lord of Kerak where the Saracens had failed, then Reynald's contortions equally well fitted a man who had been fed poisoned salt.

Camini needed no explanation. He had seen many men dance like this, some with pain, some with anger, some because they had been born with a snake in their intestines. Whatever the cause, they were all dangerous. He drew back and slid his hand inside the folds of his robe. He felt safer when his hand closed round the hilt of the Turkish dagger he wore slung across his chest.

Blood trickled from Reynald's mouth as he gasped, 'All save two? *You say we lost all but two!*'

The captain allowed the pain of his severed wrist to dictate his expression. Piously he said, 'The report may be exaggerated, but you have heard what I have heard.'

'And when did you hear it? What proof have you?'

'None, save that we know our ships *were* near al-Hawra. I also heard that many of the captives are to be given in sacrifice at Mecca and Cairo.' He pushed words about in his mind, hunting for a way to repeat that they were Reynald's men and that al-Hawra was Reynald's defeat. Nobody, not even the Lord of Kerak, could snap Camini's teeth with impunity.

Then suddenly, a voice from the stern screamed, 'Captain! Oh, sweet Christ, Captain! See behind us, in plain sight!'

The pirate spun round. Reynald spat blood and moved beside him. They stared beyond the waking mass of oarsmen and soldiery, beyond the littered stern deck and high scarred rudder to where, moving toward them from the horizon, was the silhouette of a three-masted ship. There was no wind, so the scarlet and yellow sails hung limp, but the long, double banks of oars drove the vessel steadily closer. Even if she were not moving on a pursuit course, the colours marked her as a Saracen craft.

Camini leapt to the rail that separated the forward deck from the rowing pit. By now most of the oarsmen were awake, pushing their companions to see if they had survived the night, or shouting at the steersman who had first raised the alarm, or at Camini, or at the men-at-arms who crowded the central gangway, or at each other with growing panic. Some rose from the benches and decks to see for themselves the approaching vessel. Others reached for oars, spears, cross-bows, then gesticulated angrily, indicating the corpses that lolled in the pit.

'Tip them out!' Camini shouted. 'Clear the decks! Down there, help on the benches!' He caught the attention of the three remaining steersmen and commanded them to set a course due north.

Reynald moved level again and said, 'No, we will not run. We will take this ship.'

'Are you insane? Take it with what? You see the size of it. It will have catapults, hook ladders—Look at it! It sits twice as high ——'

'I said we'll take it. Turn the galley.'

Camini dragged down the corners of his mouth and shook his head with finality. 'Ah, no, Prince. I will not turn. I command Ter e Mer. It is why you brought me from Sicily. That may well be a warship, with Lulu himself at the helm——'

'Just so,' Reynald grated, his lips stained with blood. 'Lulu, the man you say destroyed the Christian fleet, my fleet. You think I would not take my chance with him?'

'What chance? We have no chance. He will crush us with his upper oars, pour fire down on us, run across us and——' He stopped and let the air whistle through his broken teeth as he felt the blade of Reynald's knife against his spine.

'Turn the galley, Sicilian. If you don't like the way it goes, swim to Aqaba! Make haste and give your orders. Do it now!' He jabbed the point of the blade into Camini's back. 'Now, I say! We must face them before they reach us.'

The captain winced with pain. 'Cover your blade,' he hissed. 'You'll get your way. Our deaths too, for the same price.' He wrapped his handless arm in a fold of his soiled robe, then leaned forward against the rail. The corpses from the previous skirmish had been dumped overboard, their places taken on the benches by sullen men-at-arms. He told the steersmen to pull the rudder hard over, then gave the order to row. A wave of protest rose from the exhausted crew. It was one thing to use the last of one's energy in a bid for freedom, but quite another to expend oneself rowing toward certain destruction. Camini breasted the wave of complaints, then drew his own curved knife and repeated the order. Even with his left hand slashed away he was too dangerous to cross.

The oarsmen waited while one of their number set the rhythm, then pushed forward and down. They brought the dripping blades clear of the water, pulled back together, let the blades slice back into the sea and heaved on the long poles. The corpses that still floated were driven under or washed alongside the hull. *Ter e Mer* began to move. The galley came round in a wide arc, then turned more tightly as the starboard rowers reversed their stroke, while their counterparts kept the steady forward rhythm. The Saracen ship was less than a mile away and holding its course.

Aboard the Christian galley the soldiers ranged themselves along both sides of the forward deck. The bow tent was pulled down. Boxes of sand were stacked in the centre of the deck and against the bulwarks. Jars of vinegar were uncorked and roped to the rails, ready to combat a naphtha attack. While Reynald of Chatillon took command of the archers and men-at-arms, Camini moved along the central gangway to con the ship from the helm. Reynald found his cross-bow, wound it, then laid it at his feet. He had regained full control of himself, licked the blood from his lips and now stood braced against the prow post. He did not know how they would tackle the huge Saracen vessel; *Ter e Mer* had been engaged in no actual naval conflicts, save last night's running skirmish. But so long as there was a chance that Admiral Husam ed-Din Lulu was aboard, Reynald vowed he would find some way to scale the steep sides of the *batseh*.

By the time the distance between the ships had narrowed to half a mile the Crusaders had forgotten their fatigue and were impatient to loose the first bolts and arrows. There was no sign of activity aboard the Moslem ship; it held the same course, the same speed, as though convinced that *Ter e Mer* would soon move aside. The red and yellow sails still hung limp, perfect targets for the fire arrows. Reynald smiled. If Lulu was in command, he obviously believed that the Christian galley would make an easy victim. If the *batseh* had some other captain, the over-confident Moslem was in for a shock.

The Frankish archers had already positioned two braziers on the forward deck. A few moments more and they would dip their pitch-tipped quarrels into the burning charcoal, raise the flaring barbs and send them arcing across the water. A few moments more, a few more yards, a few strokes of the oars . . .

One of the sailors had scaled the bare pine stern mast for a better view of the approaching craft. He reached the castellated lookout tower and clung, one leg hooked over the low wooden wall, unwilling to believe what he saw. Then, because he was a superstitious man, he gabbled a prayer before howling at Camini.

'Captain!'

Camini squinted up at him.

'Captain! It's no warship! There are no soldiers! Captain, do you hear me?'

Camini thought he'd heard the sailor say it was not a warship, but that was impossible, he must have misheard.

'What? Say it again!' he called, then changed his mind and waved the man down. 'Here. Get down here.'

The sailor slid down the pole, stumbled as he reached the deck and spoke before he had gained his balance.

'It's—it's no *batseh*,' he gasped. 'Captain, I swear to you, it's not even armed. The decks—they're full of people, but there are no soldiers. I saw what I saw and——'

'Then by hell's teeth, what are they, troubadours? A ship of that size. No cargo vessel would take passengers. Unless——'

'Yes,' the sailor nodded, 'unless the cargo were pilgrims. It must be a pilgrim ship! They are all standing there on deck, in the open. And Captain, I don't believe—I mean, from what I saw——'

'Yesss?'

'I don't believe they know us! *Captain, I don't think they know who we are!*'

At that moment the Sicilian realised why his reputation could never match that of Lord Reynald's. Camini was happy to plunder caravans, torture civilians for amusement, murder children if he must. Without hesitation he would rape women, burn crops and houses, leave innocent villagers destitute or dying. But, in the manner of the time he, too, was superstitious, obedient to the laws and signs of that godless religion. He could not bring himself to harm accredited pilgrims, however foreign their beliefs. He accepted that he must have killed some pilgrims at one time or another, such things were inevitable, but he knew that if he murdered these men in cold-blood they would take the form of eagles and peck his eyes and testicles and feed off his liver.

He glared at the sailor, hoping that his nerve would fail and that he would admit he was mistaken. But the man's story fitted too well with the innocent progress of the vessel, with the hanging sails and the general air of unpreparedness.

'You say this on oath? Your life is forfeit if——'

'I do, Captain. God save me, I do!'

'Would you say as much to Prince Reynald?'

'If I must, I suppose, but——'

'You must. Come with me. Hurry, or we are all damned!' Cradling his bandaged stump he strode along the gangway and climbed on to the forward deck.

Reynald turned, grinning.

'Look at the sheets, Sicilian. Could we find a better bed for our arrows? Our work is done for us. I tell you——'

'Tell me nothing, Prince. Listen to this man. You may not care to go ahead when you hear what he has to say.' He nudged the sailor. 'Spit it out!'

The terrified observer made his report. Camini nodded as he spoke and glanced anxiously at the shrinking channel that separated the vessels.

As Reynald listened his smile dissolved to nothing and he began to prod the luckless sailor, driving him back toward the gangway steps.

'You've been hoodwinked, pirate,' he snarled. 'This man has no stomach for a fight. I remember him from the previous struggle. He would have us all be cowards, wouldn't you, hmm? Hmm? Take him away before I dim his faulty eyes for good.' He used his knife to herd the sailor down the wooden steps.

Camini said, 'Coward or not, I believe him. It agrees——'

'And I don't.'

'Prince, I ask you. Stop this while there's time. We cannot risk it. We must first find out if there is any merit in the man's story. I'll take the galley round to one side——'

'Oh, no. I want *them* to turn, not us. Leave things as they are.'

'But they may be pilgrims!'

'So this blind worm would have us think.'

'I'm turning the ship.'

'Stay still, Sicilian. You've played your part.' He hefted his knife.

Camini held his own Turkish dagger. The two men stared at each other. The sailor stood at the foot of the steps, looking up at them. Then the corsair sighed and lowered the curved blade.

'As you say, Prince.'

The next instant he brought his arm up again and stabbed wildly. Reynald, with a lifetime of distrust to warn him, leapt back. Camini's dagger had slit the Crusader's gambeson and drawn blood from his stomach. It was the last injury the pirate would ever inflict. Reynald laughed with shock, stepped forward and drove his knife into Camini's throat. Camini whistled as he reeled away and collapsed against the foredeck rail. The Lord of Kerak left him to die in his own time and turned away, one hand held over his stomach. The wound was not deep and he decided to let it mend itself. The sailor had already fled to the farthest part of the ship. Reynald looked round for him, then laughed again. He did not feel vindictive, so allowed the blind and lying coward to escape.

Under the command of the Red Wolf of the Desert, the crew of the war galley *Ter e Mer* engaged those aboard the pilgrim ship in hand-to-hand combat. Undefended, the sides of the ship were not difficult to scale. Partly to assuage his fury at the news of Admiral Lulu's victory near al-Hawra, and partly because he saw the opportunity to climax his Red Sea expedition with an act that Islam would long remember, Reynald of Chatillon set the pilgrim vessel alight and, for the loss of eleven Crusaders, killed in excess of three hundred Moslems. If any survived they did so without his knowledge, because *Ter e Mer* made two circuits of the blazing hulk, while he directed the attention of the archers toward anything that moved in the water.

By midday the pilgrim ship had burned down to the waterline and the Christian galley was moving northward again, heading for the Gulf of Aqaba and the disembarkation port at the northern end of the Gulf. Throughout the voyage, Reynald was comforted by the thought that Mohammed would have difficulty in pulling his scorched and water-logged believers to Paradise by their hair.

# CHAPTER TWO

# The Dead Sea

## *June 1183*

The road dipped, levelled, then dipped again. The horsemen who moved along it had travelled eighty miles in three days, though they were still two days short of their destination. They had now reached the western shore of the Dead Sea, the lowest place on earth.

The leader of the group raised his hand and motioned to the others to dismount. He could have called to them, but he was awed by the utter stillness of the scene and by the absolute silence. He had visited the place many times before, but each time was like the first. In truth, he was frightened that if he had voiced an order, no sound would have emerged from his mouth. His companions were grateful that he had not spoken, and climbed from their horses without a word.

They sniffed the salt air and stared at the turgid surface of the water. There were no fish in this narrow, inland sea, so no birds settled on its shores. A few bleached and stunted bushes dotted the otherwise barren rocks, while stiff reeds struggled for survival in the mouth of an occasional dry wadi. Nothing moved, save the shimmering waves of warm air that sucked the water with greedy lips.

The men watched each other, their eyes half closed against the white glare of the rocks and the flat deposits of salt. They frowned to mask their fear, but made no effort to break the silence. Then one of them tried to stifle a cough and failed, and they all heard the sound and laughed noisily. They moved their arms, took tentative steps along the beach, slapped their horses to make them stir. The man who had coughed forced himself to do it again, to remind his fellow knights that it was he who had made the first sound. Somebody spoke, commenting on the heat and then they were all talking unafraid.

There were fifteen of them, each dressed in a long surcoat, worn over a ring-mail hauberk. Since leaving Jerusalem they had been tracked by a merciless June sun, which grew in strength as they moved southward. Their bodies continually ran with sweat. To combat the discomfort they had interrupted their journey twice a day, stripped naked and let the sun dry their skin and clothes. Then, temporarily refreshed, they had pulled on their leather gambesons, mail tunics and linen surcoats. Each time they shed their clothes they risked dehydration or a sudden chill, but the damp, slippery leather became unbearable and they welcomed a few moments respite from the heavy suits of mail.

Three of the fifteen might have dispensed with armour, but the other twelve had no choice. They were Knights of the Order of the Hospital of St John at Jerusalem. Known as the Knights Hospitaller, they were acting as escort to the three lay Crusaders. At any time the group might come under attack from a Saracen raiding party, or marauding Bedouin, so the Hospitallers rode ready-armed. Each protected his mail suit as best he could from the sun's rays with the black surcoat of his Order, on which was stitched a white, split-pointed cross. In contrast, the lay knights wore white coats emblazoned with the straight scarlet cross of Christendom.

While half the escort stood guard, the rest helped each other out of their armour, then unbuckled the sodden gambesons. They turned the garments inside out and moved naked along the shore. One of the younger Hospitallers, who had not heard about the unique properties of *Mare Mortuum* looked at his companions for approbation, then strode into the water. They laughed as he floated on his back and waved to them. The water was so buoyant that he lay quite still, unable to sink. He stayed there until he was sure all his brother knights had seen him—Sir Guibert the Swimmer—then waded ashore, cool and pleased with himself.

Before he reached his clothes his skin turned white. His face and body were coated with salt, his eyes stung, his throat seemed to contract. Gasping, he ran for his water-skin. The Hospitallers roared with mirth; young Guibert would know better next time.

The trio who were not members of the military Order stripped off with the first members of the escort. The tallest of the three was well-proportioned, with thin, sandy hair. His face, neck and arms were burned brown by long years in the Palestinian sun. He had lately indulged in the fashionable pastime of 'sunning', so his legs and torso were also tanned. The other two were unevenly brown, since they did not share his passion for rooftop exposure. One was short and slim, the other built like a fairground wrestler. Where the slim one was almost hairless, his powerful companion was covered with a hirsute black mat.

The first of the trio was Balian of Ibelin, Lord of Nablus and husband of the dowager Queen Maria Comnena, widow of the late King Amalric I of Jerusalem. Balian was also the younger of the respected Ibelin brothers. The elder, Baldwin, held the Seigneurie of Ramleh, some thirty miles south-west of Nablus. Their father had died a few years earlier and the family fortress of Ibelin had been given into the custody of their allies, the Hospitallers. But Baldwin had retained Ramleh, while Balian was content to govern his wife's territories north of Jerusalem. The Ibelins, and in particular Balian, who kept a cooler head than his brother, were loyal to the reigning King of Jerusalem—a young leper, also named Baldwin—and to the Christian cause. This alone set them against many of the Frankish overlords, who saw something shameful in paying homage to a twenty-two-year old monarch whom they regarded as nothing more than a diseased idealist. Paramount among these disaffected Crusaders was the man Balian was on his way to see, Reynald of Chatillon, Lord of Kerak.

The second, slim one of the three was Balian's squire, a young, native-born Frank named Ernoul. He was a witty and intelligent observer, and would be remembered by history as an authoritative chronicler of his times. However, this was in the future. For the moment he was content to toss chips of salt into the saline water.

The last was the Constable of Nablus and Balian's personal body-guard, Fostus. He was forty-five years of age, a descendant of Cornish peasants and Welsh mercenaries, and as hard as iron. He was, in all, the barbican gate to Lord Balian's keep. To stand within a sword's length of the Lord of Nablus was to have first gained the confidence of his massive protector. For twenty years Fostus had guarded the Ibelin family. The fact that they had risen from obscurity to occupy a deserved position as one of the leading houses in Palestine was in part due to the unceasing vigilance of Constable

Fostus. But he, too, had relaxed momentarily and was teasing
Ernoul by hurling huge lumps of rock farther than the squire could
throw his chips.

'Go on,' he growled, 'put your shoulder to it. What does that
piece represent, a bird's egg?'

Ernoul shrugged and attempted to make the stone skim the water.
It was not flat enough and sank without bouncing. Fostus decided
it marked the limit of the young man's strength. He shook his head
in despair and sent his own rock spinning far out to sea.

'No competition,' he grumbled, moving away to challenge the
Hospitallers.

Balian came down to the water's edge. Ernoul pointed to a high
plateau beyond the far shore and asked, 'Is that where we're going?'

Balian nodded. 'I forgot. You've not been to Kerak before.'

'No. And from what I've heard of it I would have no wish to go
there alone. Too many, they say, have gone in and never been seen
again.' Looking round, he added, 'It's small wonder that Lord
Reynald thinks himself a king in his own country. He's so far from
the centre of things.'

'In body, perhaps,' Balian said, 'but if you were to light a fire
back there—' he jerked his head in the direction of Jerusalem—
'say on King David's Tower, it would be seen from the walls of
Kerak.'

'But that's—it must be forty miles!'

'Nearer fifty. But how else do you think he could summon the
royal army so promptly when the Saracens threaten? Still your
impatience for two more days and you'll allow Lord Reynald his
self-deception. Any man who was made master of Kerak would feel
like a king. Even you, I daresay, skin-and-bone. It's in the nature of
the place. The fortress alone is the size of a city.'

'It's possible,' Ernoul admitted dourly, 'but Lord Reynald is not
a monarch and is unlikely—God preserve His Kingdom—to become
one. Master of a city-castle or not, if the reports about the pilgrim
ship are to be believed—and King Baldwin appears to believe them,
then Reynald is no better than the pirates he employs. Does he really
think that God would countenance such an action?'

'I doubt if he consulted God,' Balian said. 'God rules in Heaven.
Mohammed rules in Paradise. We have the courageous Leper King

to rule us in Jerusalem. Reynald rules—well, these days where he pleases. He would only accept God's blessing if it came with a consignment of weapons.'

'If he ruled where he pleased he should call himself a Bedouin and not a Crusader.'

'Be cautious,' Balian murmured. 'Don't find fault so readily with those who take the Cross. Very few could draw a clean sword; certainly not I.'

'That may be so, my lord. But you must grant that Reynald of Chatillon goes beyond the pale of normal human failings. I'm not talking about a petty grudge, or an open act of war. I mean the way in which he murdered hundreds of innocent pilgrims.'

'It's alleged. We've yet to prove it.'

'Oh, everybody knows it. He himself makes a poor secret of it. And how many hundreds did he—is he alleged to have slain? Two? Three? Five?'

'The Arabs claim three and a half hundred. They usually prove to be reliable.'

'Three and a—You see! That's no normal failing. He murdered them because they were easy prey and because by then he must have heard of the defeat of his fleet. There can be no other reason for it. He used bitterness as an excuse for mass slaughter. The man stains us all.' He picked up a lump of salt, glared at it, then threw it to the ground.

Balian turned away, so his squire would not see him frown. However much he sympathised with Ernoul's indignation, he hoped the young man would not make so free with his opinions when they reached the Red Wolf's lair.

'Another thing,' Ernoul stated, worrying the problem. 'You should not have to make this arduous journey. I don't mean you are physically, uh——'

'Yes?'

'I mean, it was Lord Reynald's duty to present himself at court in Jerusalem as King Baldwin demanded. Any subject must. But it seems that not only does Lord Reynald imagine himself a monarch, but already a greater one than Baldwin. I intend no disrespect, my lord, but on this mission you are no better than an emissary. It reflects sadly on our state when the rightful king is insulted by a truce-breaker, and one of his most respected leaders takes the part of a messenger.' He noticed Balian's frown deepen with anger and stopped abruptly.

'Well, well, Ernoul, that's enough.'

'My lord, I——'

'No, you have a grievance. I need not have made you ride with me.'

'God forbid, that's not what I wished to say. I am honoured to be with you. You must not think otherwise.'

'So. Then you in turn must wait until we hear what Lord Reynald has to say. There are two sides to the coin.'

'Oh, you're too fair, you're too fair!' Ernoul erupted. 'You know Bloodhead for what he is. Why do you give him so much benefit?' He stamped away in a cloud of youthful temperament, snatched another stone from the beach and hurled it furiously across the water.

Fostus saw it and called, 'That's better. You're using your shoulder.'

Balian thought, is that what they call him now, Bloodhead? Is the Red Wolf a dated term among the young men? Without hesitation he acknowledged that Bloodhead was more explicit, but these days so were Reynald's actions.

The Commander of Knights came up to announce that his men were ready to leave. Balian nodded and the trio reclaimed their dried-out clothes. A few moments later the column rode up the steep incline from the beach and turned south along the narrow coast road.

They camped for the night in one of the gorges below Mount Masada. The twelve hundred foot peak stood opposite a flat white promontory on the eastern shore called Halashon, the Tongue. To the south of the Tongue was Reynald of Chatillon's private port at the mouth of Wadi Kerak. When darkness had settled over the water and the distant mountains of Moab, Balian gazed across to where he was sure he could see lights from the port. The Lord of Nablus had known the Lord of Kerak for more than twenty years, but Balian was not prepared to hazard even a guess at the meaning of the lights. They could be marking the position of the port for some late-in-the-day visitor, or illuminating the work of hired ship-wrights who were busy constructing another fleet of war galleys. Or perhaps there were no lights at all, just splinters of sun that had lodged in his eyes.

He yawned, stretched his arms above his head, then let them fall slack at his sides. When he looked again there were no signs of light on the eastern shore. He grinned wryly, aware that he was as sus-ceptible to Reynald's magic as any other Crusader. So many rumours flitted like bats around Kerak that it was often impossible to separate truth from falsehood. Nobody had really believed that Reynald would denude vast tracts of forest, build his own ships, then send them in wagons and on camelback across some of the most inhospitable country in Palestine. Yet he had done it, as he had once ravaged the entire island of Cyprus, as he had survived sixteen years in the Saracen prison at Aleppo. He had grown more power-ful with the years, until, as Lord of Kerak and master of Oultre-jourdain he bore out Ernoul's description. He regarded himself as an autocratic ruler, greater than the king. And, sealed in his massive fortress, he looked down on enemy and ally alike.

It was time, Balian thought, that Reynald's fellow overlords took his threats as seriously as they bemoaned his subsequent actions. Past time, since, as a result of the Red Sea expedition, Saladin had vowed swift and dreadful retribution on the Christian kingdom. This was the message Balian carried to Kerak, along with a plea from King Baldwin that Reynald would avert total war by making restitution to the inhabitants of the Red Sea coast and the families of all those aboard the pilgrim ship.

Balian scuffed his feet on the floor of the gorge and turned his back on the water. In the silence of the night he could already hear Bloodhead's reply, while the echoes of his laughter blew chill across the salt sea . . .

The horsemen rode out of the gorge before dawn. In the afternoon they passed the villages of Sedom and Amora, sparse habitations that were thought to have once been the accursed cities of Sodom and Gomorrah. They rode in silence and, remembering the Scrip-tures, none glanced back.

A few miles farther on the riders made an error of judgement.

Eager to cover as much ground as possible, and thus bring Kerak within a day's march, they started across the glaring salt pans that marked the southern shore of the Dead Sea and the northern end of the vast Arava valley. The immolating heat crushed their shadows into grotesque black lumps. By the time they had reached the centre of the valley they had lost all semblance of military bearing. The Hospitallers gritted their teeth as the heat seeped under their skulls. They covered their heads with spare surcoats, towels, even the wide Arab kerchiefs called *kafiyas*, but the cotton might as well have been metal. Young Guibert and one or two others cried openly, but when they moved to wipe the tears from their faces they dragged dry hands across dry eyes. The sun had already purchased the juice of their agony, leaving salt in payment.

The column faltered. Balian was presented with a harsh choice. If he increased the speed of advance the horses would sweat and lose water more quickly, then weaken. Yet if the heavy Norman palfreys retained their present pace they would take too long to reach fertile country. He cursed himself for having allowed the precipitate crossing and waved the Commander of Knights alongside.

'We must hasten on, Sir Conrad. I take the blame for this, but I want the situation resolved in our favour.'

The Hospitaller twisted round in his saddle, saw the pitiful condition of his men and nodded mutely. Then he turned his horse, trotted back along the line and snarled at the swaying riders.

'Get on! Move! Martin, prick your mount! Herve, don't shame me, sir! Move on, move on! Back there, you, Guibert, what ails you? Why do you shiver, is it so cold?' He pulled level with the sobbing knight, snapped at the riders ahead and waited for them to draw away. Then he took an inlaid dagger from his belt.

'You see this?' he hissed. 'You see this piece of bone set in the pommel? Well, do you see it, sir?'

Guibert blinked and nodded.

The Commander nodded with him. 'What do you think of it? Say out, man! God gave you breath, didn't He?'

'It's pretty,' Guibert croaked, letting his mouth hang open as he gasped for air, any air, however hot, however salt.

'Pretty, yes, but do you know whose bone it is?'

The young knight rolled his head. He didn't care. The sun was carving lines in his face, tapping holes in his head. He didn't care if it was man bone or animal bone. Why should he know what——

'It's from the precious body of our blessed St John. Yes, our patron. How's that, Guibert?'

'St John?'

'Just so. Now listen to me. Eh, straighten your horse! Take a grip. That's better. Now listen. You ride to the head of the column ——,'

'What? I cannot. I—I can't——'

'Of course you can. You do it and reach the front and this knife is yours. I'll make you a present of it. You have my word on it.'

'Would you really part with——'

'Don't doubt me, boy,' Conrad snapped. 'Take the lead and you've earned it. Will you do it?'

Guibert strained every muscle in his face and managed to close his mouth. There was nothing of greater importance to a true Hospitaller than his faith in St John. And to possess a particle of his body—this was a man's greatest reward.

The Commander of Knights had not made the offer lightly. He, too, set great store by holy relics, but he had heard so many claims, seen so many splinters of bone that in his more cynical moments he wondered if any saint had been allowed to rest in peace, and to rest in one piece. The word joke was popular among those who doubted the authenticity of certain well-known religious tokens, and Conrad was prepared to admit that he had no way of knowing if the bone in his dagger was truly a segment of John the Evangelist. He wanted it to be, and had sufficient faith in the word of the man who had sold it to him to be able to offer it to Guibert in all honesty as a holy relic.

Guibert found fresh strength and echoed, 'The head of the column?'

'Yes.'

'For—for St John?'

'For St John, yes. Will you do it?'

'Yes. Ah, yes, I will. With our sweet saint to aid me, I'll do it! St John and the Hospital!'

He forgot the heat, hunched forward and drove his single prick spurs into the horse's flanks. His cry was flattened by the heavy air and thrown to the ground. The palfrey started, sank its hooves into

the salt crust and broke into a canter. Guibert shouted again, then
kept his breath for riding. He saw Edouard de Cavanne and
Matthew of Dorset, spurred his mount and passed them at the
gallop.

Guibert had been told by more than one priest that if he did
something true and pure and did it in the name of God and his
patron saint he would see the Evangelist in the company of angels.
He passed Denys, then three shrouded figures he didn't recognise,
then Thomas the Wanderer. Salt and sand flew from the horse's
hooves. Guibert rode with his eyes wide open, waiting for St John
to reveal himself. He drew level with Cesarini the Italian, who called
out to him, but Guibert heard only the pounding of his heart and
the roar of blood in his ears. He passed the Italian, overtook two
more Hospitallers and galloped towards Ernoul and Fostus and
Lord Balian. Everything was dry, so dry, white and dry and burning with an arid salt flame. He knew he would soon see John.

Ernoul saw the knight, scowled and pulled his horse aside. He
glimpsed the drawn white face, the salt-filmed eyes, blood and foam
on the palfrey. Then Guibert had moved ahead, thundered between
Balian and the Constable and was riding free, out across the valley.

Far behind, the Commander of Knights roared, 'Catch him! He's
a boy! Will he guide you all?'

The line bunched, stretched again, then broke apart as the horsemen responded to the challenge and gave chase. Conrad rose in his
stirrups, squinting through the haze as his Hospitallers urged their
mounts towards the distant foot-hills. Satisfied, he touched the
dagger. Guibert had done well and had earned the reward.

But the young knight had not yet seen St John. Clearly more was
required of him. He had never ridden so hard in all his life, yet he
knew he must ride harder. He jerked his feet away from the horse
and slammed them back, the heels turned inward. The single metal
spikes stabbed deep into the animal's flanks and it screamed and ran
with pain. Guibert's mouth hung slack. His eyes bulged as the salt
dust swirled around him. Blinded, his inner eye saw the Evangelist
ahead of him. Deafened, in his mind he heard John calling:

'Come then, true knight. Here, take my hand. Yes, Guibert, yes,
yes, I am here now. Ride forward to me.'

The first riders overtook the Hospitaller while he was still a mile from the hills. His horse had slowed, because the young knight lolled in the saddle and so had not continued with the spurs. His face was as white as when he had emerged from the Dead Sea. His mouth was still open, strictured in a smile. Fostus and Ernoul rode up on one side, Cesarini the Italian and a knight named Ralf on the other.

Cesarini gasped, 'Well run, Swimmer,' while Fostus leaned over to take the loose reins. Then they saw that the smile was fixed and that Guibert was dead. His eyes were blocked open, staring at something none of them could see. Fostus and Ralf, who were stronger than the Italian, held Guibert in his saddle and led his horse across the last mile of the Arava valley.

Two and three at a time the escort reached the welcoming tree-line and slid from their mounts. Some collapsed immediately, while others sank to their knees and gave rasping thanks to God, St John and the knight who had inspired them, Sir Guibert the Swimmer. They laid his body in a grove of oaks and oleanders and stood watch over it throughout the day and the following night. They prayed for the salvation of his soul, though they knew it to be assured. The Commander of Knights placed the dagger on Guibert's chest, where, for all eternity, he could glance down at it and reach for it easily, if he should ever need it. But they knew, too, that he would only use it to show to the angels and his new-found friends.

Next morning the Hospitallers laid the body on a makeshift stretcher and took it in turn to carry it up the winding path that ascended three thousand feet to the Moab plateau. They followed the path north to Wadi Kerak, then east toward the fortress. It was cooler on the plateau, so those young knights who wept were not robbed of their tears.

# CHAPTER THREE

# Kerak

## *June 1183*

Stephanie of Milly reclined on a plain red couch, enjoying the final rays of the sun that streamed through the wide, stepped window. One of the jongleurs had just left the solarium, after performing a *chanson de geste* based on a story by the popular French poet-composer, Chretien de Troyes. The song described the amorous and military adventures of a knight errant called Yvain. However, the troubadour who had adapted the story, and the jongleur who performed it, were both careful to give Yvain red hair, like Stephanie's husband Reynald, and a fierce disposition, matching Reynald's, and a sword incribed IN NOMINE DOMINI such as Reynald carried.

She had rewarded the jongleur with a bolt of Damascene silk, told him to cut a generous length from it and pass it on to the troubadour, then dismissed him and relaxed under the window. She remembered some of the lyrics, kept them in mind while she hummed the simple melody, closed her eyes and let the sinking sun warm her face.

The chatelaine of Kerak was thirty five years of age, though it would take another woman to know. Following the fashion set by the ladies of Jerusalem and the coastal towns, Stephanie had begun painting her face with cosmetics. She had noted the disastrous results some women achieved and learned from their mistakes. First, she had sent to the capital for a wide variety of ingredients; then, alone in her chambers, she had experimented cautiously for several days. She had tested this colour against that, compared this bright stain with something less vivid. The final balance was quite pleasing and she knew she looked younger than her years. She had a strong face, with light hair that was occasionally brushed through with cinnamon, dark green eyes and a figure that was neither all bone, nor all flesh.

She had every reason to feel self-satisfied. As the mother of two children, and now married to her third husband, she had worn remarkably well. It was even more remarkable when one knew something of the three men.

The first was, perhaps, the least outstanding. He was Humphrey III of Toron, son of the great warrior constable who had earned the admiration of Christian and Moslem alike. Unfortunately, few of the constable's juices ran in the veins of his offspring. Humphrey III was an uninspired nobleman and an ordinary mortal. Stephanie was fifteen when she married him and, during the five years they were together, she gave birth to a son, naturally named after his father, and a daughter. Then, in the bitter winter of 1168, Humphrey III succumbed to pneumonia and died.

Although a mother and a widow, Stephanie of Milly remained one of the most eligible women in the kingdom. She was still young, physically attractive, and so far untainted by gossip. She made commonplace conversation, unleavened by a sense of humour, yet most men were happy to overlook this essential dullness. She did not need wit or wisdom when her greatest attribute was to have clung successfully to the desolate frontier fief of Oultrejourdain, with its capital at Kerak. Along with her heart and body she offered the right man one of the greatest fiefdoms in Palestine, and the power that went with it.

Sadly, she did not choose the right man.

She chose instead an ambitious French knight, originally from Champagne, the Seneschal, Miles of Plancy. As steward of the Christian Kingdom he expressed an extremely high opinion of himself, boasting that even if his enemies crept up on him while he slept—the only way they would dare attack him—they would not find the courage to disturb him. An egoist, de Plancy.

Since Stephanie's father had, at one time, held the position of Grand Master of the Temple, the Seneschal gained the support of the Templar knights. But he was actively disliked by the rival Order of Hospitallers, and by the native-born barons. How many times, they asked wearily, would such opportunists be allowed to reap the harvests that other, lifelong Crusaders had sown? How many more would arrive, men like de Plancy, exert their stored-up charm on some bereaved dowager, then presume to tell third and fourth generation settlers how to run the country? What did they understand, these *novi homines*, who came east because they were acknowledged failures in their own lands? What right had they to shout from the hilltops of Palestine in the nasal accents of Europe?

The sun sank below the window. The coolness that followed fitted well with Stephanie's wandering thoughts...

She had felt no warmth for Miles of Plancy; he was too busy drawing heat from the banked fires in Jerusalem to bother with a home, or a family. He was the Lord of Kerak and Oultrejourdain, but he had never intended to live there. If his wife wished to visit him at court, well and good. If not, she could run the affairs of the castle, while he performed his duties as Seneschal and played his part in the ceaseless struggle for power.

Stephanie did visit him, two or three times a year for four years. She saw the changes that strain and frustration wrought in him; he had not advanced himself far, nor lessened the enmity of the local barons. It seemed that he would soon crack and retire from the field.

Then, in July 1174, King Amalric I of Jerusalem died of dysentery and attendant complications. He left only his thirteen-year-old leper son Baldwin to succeed him. Nobody disputed the youth's right to the throne, but he was too immature and infirm to govern, so the kingdom would be placed under the control of a regent. There were several candidates for the vacancy, and near the head of the list came Miles of Plancy, backed by the Templars.

Another serious contender was the realistic and reliable Count of Tripoli and Lord of Galilee, Raymond III. He laid claim to the regency on the grounds that he was Amalric's cousin and was also a great deal more trustworthy than the interloper de Plancy.

The Seneschal made a desperate bid for power. A council of barons was convened and, accompanied by the Grand Master of the Temple, Arnold of Toroga, Miles of Plancy entered the chamber to present his case. He found himself confronted by Raymond of Tripoli; the Grand Master of the Hospital, Roger of Les Moulins; Baldwin of Ramleh, Balian of Ibelin, and even Stephanie's one time father-in-law, Constable Humphrey II of Toron. All these and more were rigidly opposed to de Plancy and they made it clear that they wanted Raymond and only Raymond as their Regent. The Seneschal withdrew. For the first time in four years he left Jerusalem and rode south to Kerak to lick his wounds and formulate a fresh course of action.

Stephanie hardly recognised him. He had fought and lost and become an old man. She pleaded with him to remain at Kerak and govern the great fief. There was much to be achieved in Oultrejourdain, she told him. If Jerusalem had no need of him, he had no need of Jerusalem. Stay, she said, and be your own master here.

He responded by railing at her and accusing her of trying to immure him in the castle. Time after time he assured her that he still had friends. He would go to the ports and coastal towns and recruit help there. He was not finished yet, whatever she and others might think.

So, a month later, he went to Acre. He had been there less than a week when he was attacked in the street, cut down and stabbed to death by unknown assassins.

Again Stephanie of Milly was a widow. And again, because she had kept a firm, if solitary hold on Kerak she remained an enviable prize.

She shivered as the first waves of cold evening air swept across the Moab plateau and entered the chamber. She left the couch, returning with an embroidered cloak, lined with soft, grey miniver. For a while she gazed out of the window and watched the sky bleed over the rounded hills. When the colours had run together and dimmed she sank back on the couch, her body warmed by the skins of thirty Siberian squirrels.

Ah, yes, she remembered, at that time it was true. I was the prize, much sought after. And those who were free to court me were envied by those who were not. Each day brought another landless Crusader, his hands and feet washed clean, his lips moving as he rehearsed his pretty speech. They did not think the journey to Kerak was too long then. They talked of it as though they had crossed the street to meet me. The Arava valley? A dry mud patch in the road, my lady. Were your castle on the lip of the world I would have come to share your sorrow and pay my respects to the Lady of Oultrejourdain, the widow of my friend, sweet Miles. And, though they did not say it, to cast a convetous eye over the tapestries and granaries, to gauge the strength of the garrison and the thickness of the walls.

She had married Humphrey of Toron and he had failed because, all his life, he had moved beneath the shadow of his warrior father. She had married Miles of Plancy and he had failed because too many recognised him as an upstart immigrant whose ambitions outstripped his abilities. This time, she decided, she would marry a man who did not know what it was to fail. So she received her suitors, listened patiently to their overtures, encouraged them to speak of their past life, then sent them away to await her decision. None satisfied her until she was visited by one, older than most, who had just emerged from the Saracen prison at Aleppo. His wife, Princess Constance, had died while he was still a prisoner, and with her had been buried his future as Prince of Antioch. Stephanie was flattered that a prince should seek her hand, and she found him quite magnetic, with his forceful manner and red hair. He told her how, twenty years ago, he had subdued the island of Cyprus. Indeed, she smiled, go on. He described how he had sliced off the ears and noses of Cypriot priests, sacked the Greek churches and driven the entire population of several villages over cliff tops into the sea. I am the friend of friends, he stated, but the enemy of enemies.

She entertained no more visiting knights. She might have waited longer and chosen an honourable champion and made a match that would have been of advantage to the Christian kingdom. But she could not do so now, for she had fallen under the spell of Reynald of Chatillon.

They were married in 1176. To-day, seven years later, Stephanie acknowledged that with all the Moslem nations and half the great houses of Palestine turned against him, Reynald was still accounted a success. And, at the third attempt, she, too, had succeeded, for the Red Wolf of the Desert had made its lair at Kerak.

It was almost dark when the horsemen reached the fortress.

They had been sighted an hour earlier and a detachment of cavalry had been sent out to meet them. As soon as the Lord of Nablus and the Hospitaller escort were identified, two of the garrison cavalry wheeled their horses and galloped back to relay the news. The Captain of the North Garrison loathed the black-and-white men of the Hospital, and he was pleased to hear that they were bringing a dead knight with them. He gave orders for the visitors to be contained in one of the outer courtyards, then remembered something and gave a more explicit command. Balian and his party were to be brought in by the north-west gate and left in the courtyard there.

He waited on the wall until the horsemen entered Wadi al-Frangi, then smiled to himself and went to alert Prince Reynald. The Captain of the North Garrison was named Fulcon. Like everyone else at Kerak, Fulcon addressed Reynald as Prince. Embittered by the loss of his lands in Antioch, Reynald had refused to relinquish his royal title. Those who wished to remain in his favour called him Prince and asked no questions. Some extremists, like Fulcon, believed that this chosen title was too mean; he should be called King.

The horsemen made their way along the floor of the wadi and up the steep, curving path to the castle. In the fading light it was impossible to judge the extent of the defences, though it seemed to Ernoul that wherever he looked he saw a fresh looming mass of fitted limestone blocks. He had already accepted what Balian had told him; there was no doubt that the fortress had the dimensions of a city.

They turned off the path and clattered across a wide drawbridge. The young squire made a mask of his face so that the gatehouse guards would not think he was overawed by the length of the bridge, or the depth of the fosse beneath, or the arm-thick chains that hung from grooved apertures above the entrance. They rode in pairs under the teeth of the portcullis and past the great double gates. A short walled passage led towards another arched gateway, and then they were through the arch and turning in an enclosed yard. They heard the chains rattle as the bridge was raised and they reined in, gagging and coughing.

The stench was unbearable.

Ordure and excrement were heaped along three sides of the yard and smeared over most of the floor. Although cold air now rolled across the plateau, the heat of a full day was trapped with the riders in the deep stone box. Before the Hospitallers could rally, the garrison cavalry bowed forward over their mounts and urged them

through a second, smaller gate in the inner wall. With an angry roar
Fostus and others spurred after them, pulling up sharply as the gate
was swung shut.

It appeared that the Lord of Nablus and his party were to wait on
a dungheap.

The foetid air filled their nostrils and clawed at their throats.
Ernoul felt beads of cold sweat on his face and neck. He rode to the
rear of the group, slid from his horse and stumbled into a corner of
the yard. Praying that he could not be seen, he vomited, then leaned
weakly against the wall. He was used to the everyday smells of men
and animals, to the sweet smell of blood and the sour odour of urine
and stale sweat. He had grown up with the acrid fumes of wet wood
and the sulphurous clouds of burning pitch. But this foul effluvium
that rose from the ground, then sank again in his lungs, this was
more than he could take. He stayed where he was until he had
stopped shaking, then shuffled back to his horse, his head bowed. He
mounted with difficulty and sneaked a glance at his companions.
They were waxy-faced and sweating and he felt a little better.

The Commander of Knights approached Balian to suggest that
they break down the inner gate.

'If we stay long here, lord, we'll grow too faint to move.
Christ, what a smell. My men would be as well employed at the
gate as sitting sick on horseback.'

Balian thought about it, then shook his head.

'When we were met on the road,' he queried, 'did you notice any
omission in the order of things?'

'Their manners were missing, if that's what you——'

'They were, Sir Conrad, but I mean something more essential.'

'Well, they brought no water with them.'

'Exactly. They had been told to deny us any refreshment. Now,
did your men admit they were thirsty?'

It was the Hospitaller's turn to shake his head. 'They know
better,' he said vehemently. 'They wouldn't tell the hellhounds of
Kerak if they were——'

'—if they were dying of thirst,' Balian concluded. 'And nor will
we tell them when we choke on their perfume. We'll not knock on
their door just yet. But rest assured, good Commander, we have all
marked their sins. The hours and days now move against them.' He

looked round at the exhausted knights. All, save Sir Guibert, had endured the heat of the valley, the arduous ascent to the plateau, the long ride eastward to the castle. They had breathed the salt air of the Dead Sea and the thin air of the heights, and now they must breathe the putrid air of the yard. They deserved a respite, but they could not take it yet.

Balian said, 'Draw your men into two lines, so that they find us in good order. Do we have any water left?'

'Not enough for a taste apiece. I scarcely thought even the men of Kerak would refuse us water.'

'Nor I, though it's a lesson to us. Well, if we can't make a drink out of it, we can at least cool our lips. Pour what there is on to a towel and we'll pass it around.' He had seen Ernoul stagger into the corner of the yard and added, 'If there's a drop left give it to the weakest here.'

Conrad nodded. He collected the water skins from his men and shook the last drops on to a cloth. Then he took Sir Guibert's flask, with an inch of water in it, and passed it to Ernoul.

'Here, young squire. You got on well with the Swimmer. Drink this and pray for him.'

The escort had formed ranks and stared ahead, closing their ears to the sound of swallowing.

Ernoul hesitated, rubbed a thumb against the damp leather stopper and tasted the vomit that stained his throat. God, how he would like to wash that taste away. Perhaps with just half the water, just enough to——

He pressed down with his thumb, sealing the skin, then rode from the rear of the lines. He asked for the cloth and when it was passed to him he uncorked the flask and poured the water on to it. The knights yelled approval and for a moment the sound seemed to drive the stench from the yard.

It also sparked some activity among the garrison. As though in response to the concerted cheer four guards pulled open the inner gate. Captain Fulcon emerged smiling, but the smile shrank as he saw the waiting lines. Recoiling from the smell, he called:

'Lord Balian, Prince Reynald has made time for you. You arrived here unannounced, but our gracious prince——'

'Step forward!' Balian snapped. 'Stand before me! Who are you, to call from the dark like a peddler of flesh? What are you, Kerak, a soldier or a catamite?'

Fulcon gasped with anger. He had expected to find the visitors half dead. The yard had been heaped with filth at dawn, when Reynald wished to lower the price of some quarried stone he needed. The salesmen had arrived and asked so much, and he had offered so much less. Then he had shut them in the yard to think about it. An hour later they had staggered out, the colour of parchment, ready to settle at any price.

But these black-and-white men, who had already suffered the rigours of the Arava valley, then completed a full day's ride, these devils had not even dismounted. As for Balian the king-lover, he was still fit enough to make speeches.

'You know me,' Fulcon retorted. 'I am the Captain of the North Garrison.'

'So you say. Advance as such, so we can be sure. Move! Plough through your dirt and reach us.'

As he moved away from the door, Fostus rode past him. When the Constable was between Fulcon and the guards he turned his horse, barring the captain's escape. The four men-at-arms glanced up at him, then at each other. One of them mouthed the word no. They had heard of Fostus. They believed what they'd heard.

'Ah, yes,' Balian said, 'I recognise you now. You *are* the Captain of the North Garrison——'

'I told you who I——'

'——so the riders who met us on the road were your men——'

'Yes, naturally they——'

'——and it was on your orders that they denied us water——'

'You are in no position to demand——'

'——and at your command that we are cooped up here. Your name is Fulcon, I remember. Well, Fulcon, you rancid man, I hold you responsible.' He pointed down at him. '*You.*'

It was not just the smell that made the Captain of the North Garrison blanch. He had tried to weaken the Lord of Nablus and his constable and squire and escort and he had failed. They were not weakened, though they were holding him responsible for the attempt. What Balian had said was not *you*, but *I, or my Constable, or my squire, or any of my escort will wait until the opportunity presents itself, then kill you.* So Fulcon blanched.

He retreated along the edge of the yard, keeping well clear of Fostus. His boots, leggings and cloak were caked with filth. He had been humiliated in front of his own men and promised death by Prince Reynald's enemies. His body was clammy with sweat and he was ready to be sick. He suddenly felt great sympathy for the men who had come to sell their quarried stone.

They followed Fulcon through the inner gate and along a four hundred foot tunnel to an extensive underground stable. The captain knew that Reynald was waiting in the Great Hall, but Balian had demanded that before all else the horses must be fed, watered and stabled, while his men were given water, wine and cold meat. Later, they were to be fed properly, then offered the warmth of the nearby guard-room, or a fire of their own. A priest was to be found and arrangements made for the burial of Sir Guibert. Was all this clear?

Fulcon signified that it was.

While they waited, the Hospitallers stood under the great air shafts that opened in the roof, letting the night wind blow down through the mountain and drive the smell from their clothes. When the food came they gave some to the four garrison guards—in case it was poisoned—then consumed the rest and raised their mugs in salute to Lord Balian. They were strong men and quickly overcame the effects of the yard. When they had finished, the Commander of Knights selected four of them, and, with Balian, Fostus and Ernoul, the five Hospitallers followed Fulcon from the stable.

He took them deep into the mountain on which Kerak stood, through a series of galleries that twisted upward through the rock. They passed bakeries and corn mills, olive and wine presses, dormitories and a smithy and an armoury that was stocked with enough weapons to equip half the Crusaders in Palestine.

Ernoul estimated that they had covered half a mile before they emerged at ground level. It was too dark to see much, but he gained a vivid impression of walls beyond walls, distant flaring torches, darkened archways and, on every wall-walk and battlement, the silhouette of a guard or a passing patrol. He was glad the Hospitallers were with him. He was no coward, but he was haunted by the thought that each unlit portal marked an entrance to a subterranean maze. It was like a snake-pit, except that the writhing bodies were frozen in stone, while the mouths gaped open, showing iron-bound teeth. He stationed himself between Fostus and Sir Conrad and stared ahead, concentrating on staying in step with Balian.

Without warning Fulcon stopped, pointed to a flight of shallow steps and muttered, 'Up there. The doors at the top lead to the Great Hall. I don't wa— there's no call for me to go in. The guards there will not impede you. I, uh, I was acting on orders, you know. I hold no personal grudge against you, Lord Balian. No, nor against the Hospital.' He laughed feebly. 'We are all soldiers. Orders must be obeyed, isn't that so? Sir Conrad? It's so, you must agree.' He cleared his throat and glanced down at his soiled clothes. The Crusaders waited, pitiless. Then Fostus growled, 'You stink, vermin,' and knocked him aside. He retreated into the night and the men gripped their sword hilts and climbed the steps.

Stephanie approached the Great Hall from another direction. She hoped that the meeting would not end in bloodshed. But at the same time she was thrilled by the possibility that Reynald might lose his temper. Her first husband, Humphrey, had never shown much emotion, while Miles of Plancy had shown none at all. A man, if he was a real man, should not be frightened to unleash his passions and let his feelings run like hunting dogs in pursuit of his quarry. Diplomacy and sugared words were all very well for the Royal Court at Jerusalem, but here, in her castle, she liked men to behave like men. She, herself, of course, would remain quiet; a gentlewoman must never raise her voice. But a man should let the wide world know he was alive, yes, and let his woman know he was a man.

In a state of high excitation she entered the Great Hall.

# CHAPTER FOUR

# Kerak

## *June 1183*

He leaned on the massive *table dormant*, waiting for his tardy callers to reach him. The table stood on a high dais and ran most of the forty foot width of the hall. There were other tables in the body of the hall, and these could be knocked down and stacked against the walls when more space was required for trials, dances, or debates. But the *table dormant* was a permanent fixture, dominating the room as he dominated its occupants.

In preparation for the meeting, some of the trestle tables had been dismantled. Those that remained were bare of everything but wine stains. Guards were stationed at ten yard intervals round the tapestry-covered walls. They wore the long, ring-mail hauberks, plain iron skull caps or Norman 'acorns' complete with neck guard and nasal bar. Each man carried an eight foot spear of ash or apple wood and curled his left hand over the top edge of a kite-shaped shield. The shields were turned from elm, banded with iron or boiled leather. All had a raised boss in the centre, though there was no uniformity of design. The guards stood with their feet slightly apart and tried to ignore the draught that blew through the leather-curtained windows.

Flames curled from a stone pit in the centre of the hall, and Reynald peered through the firesmoke, searching for Fulcon. He wanted to know why he had been kept waiting; why so much time had elapsed between Fulcon's departure to release the visitors from the dung yard and their arrival here, in the Great Hall. He wanted to know, too, why men who should be thoroughly nauseated approached him with long strides, their shoulders back and heads erect. The Captain of the North Garrison had failed him somewhere and he wanted to know why.

But Fulcon was absent, so the explanations would have to wait. The man was clearly incompetent, but he would be given the chance to speak for himself at his trial. His excuses might yield some information that would later prove useful to whoever took his place. Something of value could be garnered from every trial, and some example set by every subsequent punishment. But all that could wait until to-morrow. The advancing Crusaders were of more immediate concern.

He recognised Balian, and the hairy ape Fostus, and Sir Conrad of the Hospital. He had heard that in the event of the death of Roger of Les Moulins, Sir Conrad might succeed him as Grand Master of the Order. So there seemed little point in offering the Commander of Knights a well-paid post at Kerak. Anyway, Reynald accepted, once they had taken their vows of poverty, chastity and obedience they became deaf to the blandishments of the world. Well, to hell with them; he had never trusted the Hospitallers.

He pushed himself away from the table and threw an arm over the leather back-rest of his chair. The weight of his arm dragged the sling down and strained the thongs that bound it to the chair posts. On his right sat Stephanie, then three visiting knights from the other great Moabite fortress of Shaubak. On his left sat his seventeen-year-old step-son, Humphrey IV of Toron, and beside him Captain Azo of the South Garrison.

The knights from Shaubak were confused about something. One of them leaned across to ask their host if the squat arrival was Fostus, bodyguard to the House of Ibelin.

Reynald nodded, then said, 'What of it?'

'Nothing, Prince,' the spokesman hurried. 'We had heard—' He shrugged, sorry that he had asked.

'Ah, no, you don't stop there. What have you heard, Sir Aime? Do you have some sneaking regard for that stunted figure?'

'I—no, not at all. We—I thought he was dead, that's the sum of it. I heard rumour that he had been killed near Sebastia.'

'Would you hasten his death?'

'Well, I—I have no direct quarrel with him.' He glanced at his companions, but they were busy looking elsewhere. Unwilling to pursue the subject, he coughed noisily, giving the visitors time to approach the dais.

Balian recognised the red-haired Lord of Kerak, and the Lady Stephanie, and young Humphrey of Toron. He knew none of the knights from Shaubak, nor the Captain of the South Garrison, but he smiled wryly to himself because Humphrey was so out of place in their company. They were all thick-set, florid men, while Stephanie's son had a thin face, thin nose, and the swollen lips of a girl. Balian had last met him a year ago, in Jerusalem, and remembered that he spoke softly and used his thin hands and thin fingers to illustrate what he said. This was a nicety, because Humphrey used words well—when Reynald allowed him to speak—and was readily understood by all save the most ignorant Crusaders. He also spoke fluent Arabic and had already acted as interpreter between Christian and Moslem. Reynald of Chatillon must have looked twice when he first met Humphrey, knowing that when he married Stephanie of Milly he would get the frail linguist for a step-son.

Seated beside Reynald, Stephanie looked composed and attractive in a white silk gown embroidered with gold and blue thread and laced at the bosom. She wore her hair loose and, because she was a long way from the fire, she kept her squirrel-skin cloak around her shoulders. Aware that a gentlewoman must not show her true feelings, she kept her hands below the table and twisted them together with excitement.

Balian had met her, too, on previous occasions, though not by choice.

When her second husband had been struck down in the streets of Acre, the Frankish kingdom was ready to accept his murder as the outcome of a private dispute. De Plancy was known to be mean of purse and arrogant of manner, and they guessed that he had died for the price of a pair of shoes. But his widow had thought otherwise. De Plancy had been out-voted on the question of the regency. Where most men would concede defeat, he had taken it in bad grace and sworn to continue the fight. He had then gone to Acre to curry support for his cause. News of his activities must have reached Raymond of Tripoli, and the new regent might well have been worried by such durable opposition. This was how Stephanie had seen it, believing that nothing was more natural than that Raymond should wish to silence his rival once and for all. She had therefore laid her husband's murder at his door. And, suspecting that Raymond would have first conferred with his friends, she had named as his accessories the Knights of the Hospital and the Ibelin brothers, Baldwin and Balian.

So for the last nine years the members of Kerak and their allies had drawn apart from those of Tiberias, Ramleh and Nablus. Now when they met it was by accident, or through absolute necessity.

But apart from the mutual hostility that existed between the families, Balian had his own reasons for avoiding the chatelaine of Kerak. Attractive though she was, Stephanie enjoyed only two topics of conversation—herself, or Kerak. If a man would stop and listen to her while she chattered about the colour of cloth and the price of rugs, then more fool he, but at least she would regard him as a friend. And if the subject was not drapery or cooking, it would be Kerak. She had fought so long to hold it, lived so long in it that it had become her world and her way of life. She knew every step and stone, rat hole and bird's nest, shadow and sun trap. She knew Kerak and its furnishings, but precious little else. It was ungallant to remark on it, but Balian knew that there were times when Lady Stephanie waxed exceedingly tedious. He had watched her in conversation with her 'friends' and seen them stiffen with boredom. Even more irritating was her divided wish to be surrounded by raucous, virile men, and yet to hold their attention with talk of filigree work and sweetmeats. Balian sighed, grateful that his own wife Maria Comnena was so very different.

He stopped a few feet from the table, bowed to Stephanie and offered a courteous greeting to the assembled family.

Humphrey said, 'It's good to see you again, Lord Balian. Have you come directly from Nablus?'

'From Jerusalem.'

'Well, either way it can be a ferocious journey at this time of the ——'

'Where's Fulcon?' Reynald interrupted. 'It'll fall badly on you if he's come to harm.'

'We left him well,' Balian said. 'He fouled his clothes, releasing us from your recreation yard, but he would not change until he had seen us fed. As you say, Sir Humphrey, a ferocious——'

'Fed?' Reynald pressed. 'He gave you food?'

'A gentle man, your Captain Fulcon. Hay and water for the

horses, meat and wine for the men. I think he would not want us to appear before you in a state of exhaustion. It's well known that men need their wits about them in your presence, Lord Reynald.'

'I am called Prince here.'

Balian smiled, said nothing, then turned to Humphrey. He had no quarrel with the delicate young man, which was as well since he was betrothed to Balian's step-daughter, Isabella. This incredible arrangement was the result of an attempt by the leper King Baldwin to reconcile the houses of Ibelin and Kerak. Baldwin was the son of the late King Amalric I and his first wife, Agnes of Courtenay, while Isabella was the daughter of Amalric and Maria Comnena. The young princess was therefore the king's half-sister and answerable to him. On the death of Baldwin's father, Maria had married Balian, and Baldwin had insisted on the betrothal. There had been no reconciliation, of course, but the arrangement stood and Humphrey and Isabella were to be married at Kerak later in the year.

Laying this problem aside until the appropriate time, Balian said, 'Where were we? Ah, yes, you asked about the journey. You know the extent of the Arava valley.'

'I do,' Humphrey nodded. 'A playground for scorpions and devils.'

'It is indeed, and sadly we lost a good companion there. This young knight, Sir Guibert was——'

'We have heard of the corpse you brought with you,' Reynald intruded, 'but I am more interested to learn what else you carry. I issue few invitations to the flies at the court in Jerusalem, yet they wing their way here. Do you bring a message from the leprous Baldwin, or have you been in council again with your fellow barons? You meet every week, I should say, by the weight of grave conclusion that falls on our ears. What fresh threat of disaster betokens our downfall? Are we lost yet again to Islam and the satanic powers?' He gazed wide-eyed, as though he believed his fears, then glanced left at Humphrey and Azo, and right at his wife and the knights from Shaubak.

'Only your fleetest horses will save you now,' he warned them. 'Our good Lord of Nablus has made a—what was it—a ferocious journey, risking all to alert us.'

The ingenuous knights hesitated, unsure whether to laugh, or take him seriously. Reynald enjoyed their discomfort and let Balian see how Shaubak looked to Kerak for guidance. Then he lurched forward, slammed his fist on the table and roared with laughter. The knights joined him in chorus. The kingdom lost to Islam? Satan stalking their fleeing horses? How absurd. Of course it was funny.

Azo laughed with them, while Stephanie smiled demurely, inwardly confused. Why would Reynald talk of flight? That was the coward's way, and not at all in his character.

Humphrey caught Ernoul's eye and looked away again, embarrassed. He had heard of the young chronicler and, although he had read none of his writings, he wondered if Ernoul would record his step-father's coarse display.

Balian waited for the laughter to subside, then said, 'You have answered your own question truthfully, Lord Reynald. I do indeed bring the threat of disaster.'

One of the knights blurted, 'Saddle the horses!' and erupted at his own wit.

'What disaster?' Humphrey asked. 'The truce with Saladin is still in force. Unless you mean the encroaching illness of the king; is that it?'

'No, the king struggles bravely. But you were close to it when you mentioned the treaty of peace we held with the Saracens.'

'I was among those at Jerusalem when it was signed. You were also there, I recollect.' He frowned suddenly. 'You said *held*. Why, do we not still hold it?'

'Until a short while ago, yes, in writing. Though in point of fact it was lost the moment Lord Reynald set sail on the Red Sea.'

'But that was a scientific expedition!' Humphrey protested. 'How could that affect the treaty?'

Balian stared, genuinely astonished. 'Is that what you heard? A scientific expedition? Is that the story here?'

'Certainly. And everywhere else, so far as I know.' He turned to his step-father. 'It was, wasn't it?'

Reynald studied the vaulted roof. 'It was intended as such,' he said, 'and as such it started. But during the first week our ships came under attack. We had no choice but to defend ourselves. If the truce was broken, it was not by us.'

K.D.R.

D

'Your memory fails you,' Balian commented bitterly. 'We have eye-witness reports——'

'Paid raconteurs.'

'—among them survivors of al-Hawra.'

Reynald shrugged. 'Where, or what is al-Hawra?'

Beside him, Humphrey was worried. He had heard rumours of a great Saracen sea victory, and it had been linked with that very name. He had also heard of a pilgrim ship that had been sunk with all hands, though the information was sketchy and he had discounted Reynald's presence on the scene. On the other hand it was rumoured that the Mediterranean would rise in the autumn and flood the Holy Land, and that an Italian physician in Tyre had discovered the secret of eternal life. The days would be too long without rumours to set the mind turning, but they were not all to be believed. He was worried, yet exercised caution as he echoed, 'Yes, Lord Balian, what or where?'

'It's where, Sir Humphrey. The place at which, two months ago, Lord Reynald's fleet was routed and destroyed by the Saracen navy——'

Stephanie said, 'But you told me the ships had been sold at Aqaba.'

'So they were,' Reynald insisted, thinking of *Ter e Mer* and the one other that had been left to guard the port. 'So they were.'

'—under the command of Admiral Lulu,' Balian concluded. 'That alone might, or might not have brought about the present state of affairs. However, it is what follows that causes us the greatest concern.'

'Everything causes you concern,' Reynald told him, 'and you cause me concern when you try my patience. If you have a message, deliver it and return home. But I warn you, Ibelin, those things that trouble you most may leave me cold. I do not answer to the wailings of Jerusalem. I am too far removed from that nervous city.'

'You're miles from it, I agree. But you are still part of the kingdom. You have certain respon——'

'No, I do not! Not to you, nor the leper you helped crown, nor any of your timorous companions-in-arms. I live on these lands and defend them and govern them well. I——' He broke off, felt the fury rise within him and pushed himself to his feet. They were off the subject of naval battles now. For a change they would discuss

the long-time rivalry between him and the jealous king-lovers of
Jerusalem. Or rather, he would speak, while the rest of them kept
silent.

He pounded the table with his fist again and snarled, 'You listen
to me, Balian of Ibelin. I came to this country thirty years ago. I've
visited every city, every town, every windswept hamlet. I've ridden
on every road, crossed every ford between Cilicia and Egypt,
climbed all the hills and scaled most of the mountain ranges. I was
Prince of Antioch when your family were still digging for a name.
I subdued Cyprus in less than a month, returned to lead a force to
the very gates of Damascus, and drove the enemy from my own
lands. I held those lands and would be holding them yet if I had not
been tricked into an ambush.' He snapped his teeth together and
stabbed a calloused finger at his visitors.

'Now mark this,' he went on, 'and mark it well. They dragged
me behind a horse, tied a rope round my neck and dragged me to
Aleppo and threw me into prison. They thought I would die there.
None of my frail allies made an attempt to ransom me, something
I am unlikely to forget. So I was left to my enemies, who thought
to break me, or age me, or reduce me to nothing. Some here know
how long they tried. Some may not. You!'—pointing at Ernoul—
'You skinny creature who clutches Lord Balian's skirts, do you
know? Think of it as I say it. Think what sixteen years in prison
would do to you. Yes, boy, sixteen years! And all that time they
tried to break me and they failed and I watched and waited and
kept a whole mind. I dodged death at the hands of those black pigs,
and I came away from that prison, and now I am Prince Reynald
again, and Lord of Kerak. I am master of all the land between the
Jordan and Arabia, as far north as the Zerka and south to the Red
Sea. I've fought my way from nothing, not once, but twice. I
have earned my place here, and I do as I wish on my own lands.
I am Oultrejourdain! And by God's eyes I will not be told by
you!'

His voice reverberated round the walls, so that the men-at-arms
seemed to chorus his claim; *I will not be told by you, not be told by you,
told by you, by you, you, you* . . .

The echoes died away and for a moment there was only the creak
of leather and wood, and the hiss of the wind edging past the cur-

tains, and the spit and crackle of the deep, central fire. Humphrey stared down at the table. Stephanie sat with her eyes closed, trembling with excitement. Captain Azo and the knights from Shaubak gazed straight ahead at the visitors.

Then Balian nodded assent.

'Yes,' he said, 'you have earned your place. And so long as it is not to the detriment of the kingdom, you have the right to do as you wish in your own fief.' He sensed Ernoul glance sharply at him, but ignored the squire and continued, 'However, your lands stop short of Aqaba and the Red Sea. It is Arab territory, defined by the treaty, where you least of all may move freely. Do as you wish in Oultrejourdain, Lord Reynald; we have no wish to curb you here. But we are all bound to observe the same treaty of peace, and not even you——'

'Aah, you timid creature! That was your truce, not mine. I signed nothing. The Moslem pigs have pushed their snouts against Kerak before——'

'Never in time of peace.'

'—and they'll do it again. What do I care for your truce? You use whatever methods you like to oppose them, but leave me mine. I have sixteen years to erase, and I'll do it on the Red Sea, or in Mecca, or in Cairo, or wherever I see fit. Do you understand me, courtier? I make the laws here. What you or your king says is of no moment. In Jerusalem, yes. Under the drooping palms of Nablus, yes. But in this hall, in Kerak, in Oultrejourdain, no! No, dusty Balian, no, and finally, no!' He shook, then braced himself, his heavy hands pressed flat on the table.

'Believe me or not,' Balian said, 'I have some sympathy for you.'

'Keep your sympathy.'

'You hold a difficult fief.'

'Made more difficult by you.'

'Whatever the causes, you have held it secure. The kingdom looks to you to safeguard this border county.'

'Does it? Well, I look to the kingdom for nothing. I would that all Palestine were under the shadow of my sword.'

'I can believe that, and you are not alone in this desire for unity. But with your sea raid all you have succeeded in doing is to unite the Moslems, Saladin has vowed personal vengeance on you——'

'And I on him.' He grinned at his allies from Shaubak. 'Now we are equal,' he told them. It brought a laugh from the knights.

Doggedly, Balian continued. He had a message to deliver. He could not answer for the way it was received.

'Saladin has vowed vengeance on you, swearing to seek you out and slay you with his own hand. It is a rare thing for him to say, but he has announced it publicly.'

'And do you in turn seek to terrify me?' Reynald laughed. 'Am I to clap my knees together in front of my wife? Must we again take flight?'

One of the knights repeated the joke he had made earlier. 'Saddle the horses! Quick, saddle the horses!' His companions applauded, aware that 'saddle the horses' would become a standing joke among the garrisons of Shaubak and Kerak.

Silent until now, Fostus snarled, 'We did not ride this far for such petty entertainment. Now, will your humour keep, or shall I show you other diversions?'

The men-at-arms stiffened and looked towards Captain Azo. The Hospitallers marked the position of the garrison guards, while Azo glanced at Reynald. The visitors were out-numbered, but any group that boasted Balian of Ibelin and Fostus and Sir Conrad and four Knights of St John could not be judged by number. Reynald knew this and traded force for sarcasm.

'We are terrified enough, Constable Fostus. There is no call for you to frighten us further. Your good lord has already raised the spectre of the worldly Saladin. Is there more, Nablus?'

'Much more,' Balian told him. 'I did not expect you to heed the personal threat, and if it were that alone I would not have troubled to relay it. But the emir has gone beyond that singular promise. You sank a pilgrim ship while you were being chased north——'

'Is that what you heard, that I was being chased?'

'It is. We heard it from an oarsman who was aboard your flag-ship, *Ter e Mer.*'

'You personally spoke to him? The Lord of Nablus in con-versation with a base galley-hand?'

'I did. And this base galley-hand also told us that you had killed your captain, a pirate named Camini. That's of no consequence, and we're probably well rid of him, but when Saladin heard that you had burned and sunk an innocent ship he revoked the truce.'

'Your truce,' Reynald repeated. 'Why must you involve me?'

For the first time since he had entered the Great Hall, Balian showed that he, too, had a temper. He strode forward, pulling a roll of parchment from his surcoat. The parchment was tied with a blue cord, from which hung the heavy red wax seal of Jerusalem. He tossed the letter on to the table and thundered, 'You are involved! Like it or not, you are party to the truce! The question is not why we bring you into our affairs—you are already in them—but why do you drag us into yours? Why must you involve *us*, Reynald of Chatillon? You have broken the treaty, filled your cellars with the profits of senseless murder, and dishonoured yourself and us with you. You dare say you are not involved?'

Reynald started to speak, but Balian called, 'Hold silent! I've not done!' He indicated the letter. 'You will read there that Saladin has formally revoked the truce and declared war on the Christian Kingdom of Jerusalem. He is at this moment gathering his troops near Ajlun. There are signs that he will invade the seigneurie of Beisan within the month.'

'He must invade somewhere,' Reynald shrugged. 'Send me word when it happens and I will take up arms as readily as anyone.'

'You fool! Do you still not see? Until your so-called scientific expedition, we were at peace with Islam. You have always been ready, more than ready to take up arms, but the kingdom is not. We are not ready for war!'

The Lord of Kerak glared down at him. Spacing his words carefully, he said, 'Tell me this, Righteous. Were you ever ready? Hmm? For all your councils and decorative speeches, were you ever prepared to fight?'

'Sweet God,' Balian breathed. 'You choose this time to taunt us? You who drove us into this bloody trap?' His voice hardened. 'Yes, we were once ready. When we believed in what we were doing. When a Crusade was not merely an excuse to escape the hangman's noose in Europe, or to seize land here, regardless of right. When we came as part of God's army, to liberate His Holy City and to free His Kingdom on earth. When we came so that His peoples— pilgrims, Chatillon, much like those you slaughtered—so that all men of prayer might journey in safety to worship Him in His own house. Oh, yes, we were ready then. Before you and those like you tore us apart.'

Stephanie found herself nodding agreement. For the moment—thrilled by the novelty of Balian's anger and his obvious sincerity—she forgot that Kerak did not side with Nablus. She knew that what Balian said was true; men were no longer fired with religious fervour. Now each knight fought for himself, or at most for his family and friends. Times had changed, there was no disputing it. And Balian was emerging as a much more attractive emissary. Perhaps after Humphrey and Isabella were married, she might encourage his friendship and——

Reynald rounded on her and she stopped nodding.

Balian pointed to the letter. 'Emir Saladin is more generous than we deserve at this time. He doesn't want war any more than we do, and he offers you the opportunity to avert the conflict. He has informed King Baldwin, and the king now informs you, that if you will make full restitution——'

'What!'

'You cannot bring dead men to life, or raise a sunken ship, but if you send two million dinars to Damascus——'

'*What!*'

'—and undertake to remain within the frontiers of the kingdom ——'

Reynald dragged his sword from its scabbard, raised it above his head and brought it crashing down on the table. The planks bucked with the force of the blow, while the parchment jumped apart, neatly sliced in two. The knights from Shaubak rose in their chairs, and Stephanie put a hand over her face. Below, in the hall, Fostus watched the sword, ready to bar its path if Reynald threw it. The *table dormant* bore a long, deep scar, edged with raised splinters.

Gasping noisily, so that the words themselves were hacked into segments, the Red Wolf howled, 'Send him . . . I will send him noth . . . You tell your king . . . the leper, take this message back . . . if he wish . . . void a war, let *him* send the dinars . . . *him* do it . . . dertake whatsoever he choo . . . long as he understands that I . . . my lands as he does on his . . .' His mouth open, he stabbed at the bisected letter. One piece rolled within reach. The other, bearing the royal seal, fell from the table, fell again from the edge of the dais and rolled to Ernoul's feet.

Reynald threw his sword on to the table, snatched his half of the parchment and tore it to shreds. They all watched the display of uncontrolled savagery, all except the young squire and Humphrey of Toron. Ernoul stooped, collected the bound tube and slipped it under his surcoat. Humphrey blinked, acknowledging that his step-father's behaviour would not only be reported to the court at Jerusalem, but probably recorded by the chronicler so that all the world might learn what kind of man Reynald of Chatillon was. But, of course, when the world did learn of it, it would be far too late. If there was a war, it would have come and gone and been stitched into the fabric of history, a blood-stained thread that marked a thousand or ten thousand graves, the deepest and widest of which might contain the disfigured corpse of the Christian kingdom in the East.

Reynald allowed the Hospitallers to bury Sir Guibert at night, outside the castle walls, but refused them permission to use the garrison chapel. Then he dictated a letter to King Baldwin, formally rejecting Saladin's offer.

Immediately after the meeting in the Great Hall, Stephanie of Milly retired to her chambers, her mind spinning with noisy fantasies.

Next morning, with Reynald's letter in his saddle-bag, Balian led his party back the way they had come, through Wadi al-Frangi, then through Wadi Kerak toward the Dead Sea.

While the Hospitallers were navigating the twists and turns of the descent, Reynald had the Captain of the North Garrison brought before him. He accused Fulcon of having given aid and sustenance to a potential enemy. Fulcon made his plea, then was found guilty and taken to the south-east tower, where he was made to look down into Wadi as-Sitt, several hundred feet below. His arms and legs were bound, a wooden box was fitted over his head to prevent him losing consciousness, and he was thrown out from the top of the tower.

Captain Azo recommended his cousin, Aegelric, for the vacant post, and the young soldier was given trial command of the North Garrison.

Saladin did not invade Beisan within the month. In the sincere, though naïve belief that the Frankish overlords would somehow make Reynald see reason, he returned to Damascus. But no money or word of contrition was forthcoming from Kerak. Other nobles were sent to Reynald. Their efforts were rejected out of hand. The Moslem leader waited three months, then lost patience and re-assembled his forces. On September 29th, 1183, he led the army of Islam across the Jordan and entered the seigneurie of Beisan.

But his misplaced trust in the honour of his foes had given the Crusaders time to prepare for the conflict. They assembled at Sepphoria, thirty-five miles north-west of Beisan, then moved south to intercept the invaders at Tubanie. The Christian kingdom, could, at last, rebut Reynald's accusation; this time they were ready for war.

# CHAPTER FIVE

# Sepphoria, Tubanie

## *September, October 1183*

Among the fourteen hundred knights who rallied to the royal standard at Sepphoria were many who wore borrowed armour. Some had only recently arrived in the Holy Land and had yet to earn a place for themselves. Others had fought for thirty years or more, and had nothing to show for it but the scars. There were those who had lost a limb, or an eye, or merely all sense of personal ambition. They had suffered military reversals, imprisonment, starvation and disease, yet they fought on for a hundred different reasons, or for no reason at all.

And among the fourteen hundred were those who had prospered. Some had grown too fat, or too rich. Others had combined a Crusading career with political advancement. They had risen from obscurity through their own endeavours, or inherited a distinguished past with which to pave the future. They, too, fought for a hundred reasons, for there are a hundred routes to aggrandisement.

Lastly, there were the lucky ones. They had no particular abilities, or talents; they were who they were, and it was enough. Fate smiled upon them and led them by the hand. There were very few purely lucky ones, but of these the most fortunate was a fawn-haired Frenchman named Guy of Lusignan.

To his credit, he was handsome. But he was also petulant, spoiled and irresolute. It was quickly learned that he could be swayed by whoever blew hardest upon him, and that the voice to which he listened most carefully was the last voice he heard.

He was the younger brother of Amalric of Lusignan, a clever, ruthless Poitevin who, in 1179, had foresaken France for the Holy Land. On his arrival, Amalric had married Baldwin of Ramleh's daughter, Eschiva, then, before long, foresaken her for a woman twice her age. Politically it was a shrewd move, since the woman was Agnes of Courtenay, mother of the leper King, Baldwin IV. Agnes also had a daughter, Sibylla, and although Amalric and Agnes did not marry, they conspired together to find a suitable husband for the king's sister. Sibylla had been married before, but her husband had died, leaving her to give birth to a sickly son, also named Baldwin. So, whoever married her would become the brother-in-law of the present king, and the step-father of the future one.

Even though he, himself, could not marry the young widow, Amalric saw a chance to further the fortunes of the House of Lusignan by presenting his younger brother for her approval. He spoke glowingly of Guy's handsome appearance, of his kindness and gallantry, and of his desire to give love and receive it from a woman as beautiful as she. Then, before the effects of this panegyric could wear off, he summoned Guy from Poitou and hustled him before the ardent Sibylla.

She found him as attractive in the flesh as in her dreams. Amalric and Agnes congratulated the young pair fulsomely, then directed their efforts at King Baldwin. Mother badgered son, and sister worried brother until the leper gave his weary blessing to the union. Guy was not the man he would have chosen for his sister, nor as a brother-in-law, but he realised that Sibylla could not be dissuaded. Moreover, he reasoned, it was better to have a compliant vassal like Guy than a troublemaker like—well, like so many others.

This well-intentioned indulgence may have pleased his immediate family, but it angered the local barons. Once again a princess had been squandered on an interloper. Amalric of Lusignan was the Constable of the kingdom, and he had the king's mother as his mistress. But these two achievements had not earned him the right to place his kinsmen in bed with royalty.

Nevertheless, Guy and Sibylla were married in the spring of 1180, and Guy was awarded the coastal counties of Ascalon and Jaffa.

Prospects seemed bright for the Lusignan-Courtenay alliance. Agnes's brother, Joscelin, had obtained the post of Seneschal and was engaged on a course of wholesale embezzlement, using his authority to divert money earmarked for the treasury at Jerusalem. His close friend, Reynald of Chatillon, had made a successful transition from the prison at Aleppo to the fortress of Kerak. Amalric remained unchallenged as Constable, and manipulated the strings that worked his brother. Sibylla was completely enamoured of Guy, and lived a mindless, fairy-tale existence in Ascalon. She ignored her feeble child, so that he grew in years, though not in strength.

By the end of 1180 the senior members of the alliance were all in their place, waiting for one more event to occur, an event that would open the way to absolute power. They waited for the leper king to decay.

They held themselves in readiness for nearly three years until, in February, 1183, the twenty-two-year-old monarch fell gravely ill. This courageous ruler, who knew he would die, yet refused to acknowledge his infirmities, was forced to concede that he could not govern the kingdom single-handed from a sick-bed. He would need a Regent, as Raymond of Tripoli had been Regent during his infancy.

As before, Raymond came forward, supported by those who had helped him nine years earlier. But this time they could not out-vote a single upstart like Miles of Plancy. Now they faced the concerted opposition of Seneschal Joscelin, Constable Amalric, the king's mother, Guy and Sibylla, Reynald of Chatillon and the Knights of the Temple. Agnes and Sibylla allowed none of the Tripoli faction near the ravaged king. Instead, they poisoned his mind against his former Regent and convinced him that there was only one man worthy of his trust, the one man Agnes said they would all be happy to follow.

They persuaded him to place the regency in the uncertain hands of Guy of Lusignan.

Baldwin the leper still found the strength to advise his court and dictate letters, demanding that Reynald make restitution for his Red Sea foray. He travelled about the country on a litter, exhausting himself in his efforts to keep abreast of monarchic affairs. But by September he could no longer lead the army, so the fourteen hundred knights, together with six thousand foot soldiers, moved south from Sepphoria under the inconstant leadership of their new Regent.

Guy wiped the rain from his face and struggled to hold his horse in check. The morning had been cool and overcast, and the army had made good progress through the fertile valleys that lay between Sepphoria and Nazareth. They had passed groves of olive trees and thick stands of carob, from which the soldiers had gathered the sweet, locust beans. They had eaten bitter oranges, poor cousins of those that grew around Ascalon and Jaffa, and at midday they had balanced their diet with the meat of wild black goats that roamed the area. Then, as the vanguard started up the steep hill of Nazareth, the first fine veils of rain drifted across from the dim hump of Mount Tabor.

The leading section was composed of three separate contingents, each of which answered to its own commander. The Grand Master of the Temple, Arnold of Toroga, rode at the head of one hundred and twenty Templars. Joscelin of Courtenay led two hundred lay knights and eight hundred infantry, while a further two hundred horsemen and five hundred men-at-arms followed the banner of Constable Amalric.

These three leaders had been joined by a fourth—Reynald of Chatillon. He had come alone to Sepphoria, having left his step-son to follow with a detachment from Moab. If all went well, young Humphrey of Toron would make contact with the main body of the army at Tubanie.

The vanguard reached the crest of the hill without incident, and Amalric glanced back as the next section toiled up the slope. He saw his brother at the head of a strong force of Poitevins and waved to him. But the rain had made the ground slippery, while the animals and men who had already climbed the hill had turned it to mud. Guy's horse slipped and plunged, and he ignored Amalric's greeting. He was not a particularly good horseman, not good enough, any-way, to control a slithering mount with one hand and wave with the other. Moreover, he was in no mood to be fraternal. He hated the responsibilities Amalric had forced upon him. If he was a poor equestrian, he was a worse strategist. Yet he was expected to lead more than seven thousand Crusaders to victory against an unknown number of Moslems, and to do so over country with which he was unfamiliar, in the rain. God, how he hated the rain.

His horse dug its hooves into the churned ground and advanced another ten yards up the hill. Cold water blew in his face and flattened his linen surcoat against the ring-mail tunic. All around him the men of Poitou fought for a foothold, or threw themselves out of the path of skidding wagons and nervous destriers. Farther down the incline, drivers thrashed the baggage mules to make them move. Some did move, but others stumbled, spilling their loads, or kicked out at their torturers. Guy spat water and mouthed obscenities at the louring sky. It was not enough that Amalric and his fellow barons had made him play Regent and general; now he was supposed to shoulder the added responsibility of baggage-master. One way and another, he groaned, his brother had a lot to answer for.

During the last two days the Saracens had attacked the Greek monastery on Mount Tabor, destroyed the surrounding villages and undermined the walls of the castle at Forbelet. They had threatened the cities of Beisan and La Feve, and ridden within arrow-shot of the great Hospitaller fortress of Belvoir. Unimpressed by the speed with which the Christian army had assembled at Sepphoria, the lightly armed Moslem cavalry had pounded through the twisting valleys of Lower Galilee, driving off thousands of sheep and cattle, firing houses and barns and spreading panic among the scattered population. They rode in groups that ranged in size from fifty to five hundred, pinning their faith on horses that could turn on a cloak.

Now, as Arnold of Toroga led his Templars down the southern slope of the hill of Nazareth and on to the floor of the valley, two such groups swept westward from the shadow of Mount Tabor and attacked the head of the column. Each group contained between two and three hundred horsemen, armed only with iron-tipped reed spears, light bows and either maces or extravagantly decorated scimitars. Some wore the curved swords at the waist; others carried them in a shoulder sling. Spurning Western-style armour, the bearded horsemen contented themselves with small circular or heart-shaped shields and with leather caps that they wore concealed under their turbans. What use was armour, they gibed, against an enemy that was too ponderous to catch them?

One group turned to engage the Templars, while the second streamed across the face of the vanguard, then wheeled sharply and charged Amalric's contingent.

The leaders of the van had expected an attack somewhere *en route*. But the incessant wash of rain had made them at first irritable, then sullen, so that they were moving with heads bowed and shields slung when the Saracens struck. The Templars had reached flat ground and were advancing in good order, but Amalric's hundred foot soldiers were strung out along the contours of the hill. They did not see the Saracens until it was too late. A hundred at a time, the black-feathered arrows thudded into the line. Amalric screamed at his knights to skirt the bewildered infantry and get between them and the Moslem archers. The Crusader captains heard his orders, then interpreted them in their own way. Their desire to retaliate overcame any concern they may have felt for the brutish men-at-arms, and they led the knights straight down the hill, smashing through their own lines to reach the enemy.

Within a matter of moments they had inflicted more unintentional damage on their pedestrian companions than the Saracens had achieved with their murderous volleys. More than sixty men lay dead or wounded on the lower slopes. The cries of the wounded were flattened by the rain, their bodies crushed into the mud. Those who were too badly injured to move suffocated in the mire, or lay facing the sky, waiting for the torrents of water to block their nostrils and fill their lungs.

The impetus of the charge carried the weighty Norman horses away from the base of the hill. The Moslems held their ground until a clash seemed inevitable, then turned and fled, luring the Crusaders after them. Amalric's captains made a desperate attempt to re-group the men, but the temptation to give chase was irresistible. Roaring 'Saint George!' and 'Holy Sepulchre!' the hotheads thundered on into the overcast.

Few returned. The Saracens had seized the initiative and the opportunity to prove once more that they were adept at cutting broken formations into even smaller pieces. Hidden by the drifting curtains of water, they out-rode and out-manœuvred the Frankish horsemen, vanishing in one direction, only to appear an instant later from another. Of the two hundred knights who spurred down the southern face of the hill, almost half allowed themselves to be drawn into the valley. Of these, nine were slain, a further twenty wounded, and thirty or so unhorsed and taken prisoner. Given the choice, a Moslem preferred to capture rather than kill his mounted adversary. A living knight could be held to ransom, whereas a corpse could only be stripped of his armour and mutilated. There was some emotional satisfaction to be gained from the latter, though every Moslem soldier knew that Balian of Ibelin's brother, Baldwin of Ramleh, had once been ransomed for 150,000 dinars. On another occasion, the Hospitallers had promised 80,000 dinars for the safe return of their friend Raymond of Tripoli. The fact that the Hospitallers had broken their word and sent Raymond's captors less than 60,000 dinars did not deter other hopeful bounty-hunters. When an Egyptian horse soldier earned the equivalent of three dinars a month whilst on active service, he would not complain if the Christians short-changed him.

While Constable Amalric's lay knights were being cut down in the open valley, the Templars, aided by Reynald of Chatillon, were acquitting themselves well on the left flank. They had learned to resist the taunts and temptations of the enemy and to ignore the crooked finger that beckoned them into a trap. They closed ranks, charged together, reformed, then charged again. The Saracens were unable to break the iron line and, although they killed three Templars and wounded eight or nine more, they withdrew in earnest, leaving forty slashed bodies on the field.

A round-faced knight named Edouard became the object of attention when he approached Arnold of Toroga, grinned and indicated the seven ostrich-feathered arrows that had lodged in his mail tunic and boiled leather boots. Such a sight was not uncommon, and one of his brother Templars was quick to recollect that, a few years earlier, at the battle of Montgisard, he had seen a horseman wearing ten arrows, plus the broken shaft of a reed lance. This tactless comparison angered Edouard. By the devil's arse, he raged, what did he care about Montgisard? He was showing them seven arrows, here, now, not reminiscing about past wonders. But then, the sour-tongued Sir Ranulf could always be relied upon to belittle a hero.

Fearing that the men would come to blows, the Grand Master interposed, 'We have all witnessed others, Sir Ranulf, but there is no question that Sir Edouard rode deepest into this fight.' He rested a hand on Edouard's arm and ignored Ranulf's muttered aside about fat men making easy targets. Somewhat mollified, Edouard called to his friends and they rode over to pluck the souvenirs from his armour.

A few moments later they heard that Amalric's men had charged through their own lines and been broken apart in the valley. The Templars sneered at the news, united again in their disdain for the Constable's imitation warriors. God knew, the Hospitallers were a tiresome enough Order, though they at least would close ranks in battle. But these others—who made few vows and kept none of them—they were worse than useless. With the exception of Reynald of Chatillon and Joscelin of Courtenay and one or two more, the lay knights were a sorry crew. It was the Templars, and though they would not admit it, the Hospitallers, who, time and again had turned the tide of battle and staved off disaster. And if the recent skirmish was any indication of the way things would go, the salvation of the kingdom rested firmly in the mailed fists of the Temple and the Hospital.

The army continued south.

Amalric's decimated contingent was withdrawn from the van and replaced by a force of Italian and Sicilian mercenaries. Guy and his Poitevins retained the second position, followed by a rambling, ill-disciplined group of volunteers from the coastal towns under the competitive command of a dozen minor nobles.

Balian of Ibelin took charge of the centre, assisted by his impetuous brother Baldwin and two of their allies, Reginald of Sidon and Walter of Caesarea.

The rearguard comprised one hundred and fifty Hospitallers led by their Grand Master, Roger of Les Moulins, plus a powerful detachment from Galilee and Tiberias, responsible to Raymond of Tripoli.

The rain pursued the army as far as La Feve, then lifted as the Crusaders advanced on to the Plain of Jizreel. There were no more surprise attacks, though the patrols reported that the Saracens were encamped between Tubanie and Beisan. The Frankish scouts suffered from their usual inability to estimate numbers, so that some swore they had counted less than five thousand heads, while others insisted that they had seen at least seventy-five thousand, may God blind them if they lied. Since the invaders had pitched their tents in a wide arc across the plain the higher estimates were the most popular. The encampment looked impressive, so the estimates were made to match. The Christian army was apparently out-numbered by as many as ten to one. Torn by indecision, Guy of Lusignan called on his leaders for advice.

They responded quickly, each eager to make his voice heard. Balian and his brother rode back to consult with Raymond of Tripoli and the Grand Master of the Hospital, then accompanied them to where Guy's scarlet tent had been hastily erected. From the head of the column came Reynald, Joscelin, Amalric and the Grand Master of the Temple. The two groups gathered at opposite sides of the tent, eyeing each other. The air smelled of wet leather, sweat-soaked wool and scoured metal. Amalric and Baldwin had bad teeth. Arnold of Toroga suffered from heat sores that would not heal. The Lords of Sidon and Caesarea arrived, and Reynald immediately sent for two of the more vociferous Italians to redress the balance. They hurried in, and, six a side, they turned to their irresolute Regent.

From the comments and estimates that had passed between the assembled barons it was clear that there was already a divergence of opinion. Guy had feared as much and glared angrily at his brother. Ah, Amalric, he groaned to himself, did you have to uproot me from France to bring me here for this? In truth, brother, what am I in the scheme of things but a palisade to be torn down, first from one side, then the other?

He shook his head and murmured, 'God save us, nobles, if the fate of the kingdom must rest on my strategies and my brother's ambitions.'

Standing near him, the tall, sallow Joscelin of Courtenay asked, 'Did you speak, Lord Guy?'

'What? No, I—Yes, I asked for your views on the reports. If the enemy are indeed in such strength, we must avoid a direct, man-to-man——'

'What strength?' Reynald bored. 'My horse has a better head for figures than these rabbit-hearted scouts. You could show them an empty city and because they saw streets and houses they'd tell you

that fifty thousand armed men were hidden within. Spit of the ser-
pent, I reject their reports. What did they really see? I'll tell you;
rows of tents. That's all, just long rows of tents. And another thing.
How many of them returned wounded, or failed to come back at
all? None. Which shows you how close they ventured to the
enemy. Aah, the black pigs have no strength.'

Guy mumbled, 'Well, we cannot assess the strength of an army
from its tents, I grant you that. But, on the other hand——' He
glanced at Raymond of Tripoli, praying that the dour, former
Regent would fill the other hand.

Raymond said, 'My Lord Guy. We know the Saracens have
entered Beisan and Galilee. The vanguard itself came under attack a
few hours ago. I therefore suggest we take a defensive position and
hold it until we have made a more accurate appraisal of their
strength and intentions. Time is on our side, since the——'

'Oh, he goes on!' Joscelin complained. 'Accurate appraisal.
Strength and intention. Eh, Balian? You have a squire who writes
don't you? You should sit him with our Lord of Tiberias here; they
could write a book on military strategy for us. Meanwhile, we will
ride on unhindered to fight the battles!' He roared with angry
laughter. His supporters joined him, while Guy struggled:

'I don't know about a defensive—I mean, we're not sure what
they will do.'

'Exactly!' Raymond snapped. 'We are sure of nothing, so what
good can come of advancing blindly toward a waiting enemy?
There may only be five thousand of them——'

'If that,' Reynald commented.

'—but there may be ten times that number. Great God, we cannot
fight a battle on guesswork! I repeat, we must first defend ourselves,
then test their strength.' He stared at Guy, but the despondent
Regent had already foundered.

Balian said, 'Lord Raymond makes more sense than all of you.
Constable Amalric, would you care to tell us once more how
your knights fared when they rode off into the blindness of the
rain?'

'Say what you like,' Amalric glowered, 'we drove them off.'

'At what loss?'

'We drove them off, that's enough.'

'So are we now to chase them from Beisan and lose the entire army in the process?'

Guy shook his head again. He wanted to scream, *why do you argue, why do you argue*? Even now the army was waiting, leaderless, because its generals could agree on nothing. And what if this very tent was the object of a sudden Saracen attack. What if five hundred Moslem horsemen were, at this moment, pounding toward the scarlet cone? Every man inside would be trampled and crushed, hacked down, stripped and—and——

'Stop!' he shouted, his thin voice rising. 'I will not have you arguing around me. I want a decision from you. Discuss it if you must, but you are my commanders and I—I *demand* an answer. Yes, I demand it.'

Reynald glanced at Amalric as if to say, your brother is more woman than man; we must stop before he weeps and stamps his foot. The Constable shrugged, and the two groups turned in on themselves, leaving the handsome young Frenchman isolated and frightened.

While he waited, a messenger was admitted to the tent. The man edged between the huddled groups and whispered something to Guy. He jerked forward, gripped the man by the sleeve of his damp hauberk and made him repeat it. Then he nodded once and the messenger ducked out beneath the sagging canopy.

Reynald noticed the intrusion and the wan expression on Guy's face. He inquired brusquely, 'Are you ill, Lord Regent? If you need rest, we can be safely left to decide this policy for ourselves. We'll tell you the orders when we've——'

'No, I'm not ill.' The barons turned to face him again as he continued:

'Lord Reynald, is it true that you were expecting your step-son to join you at Tubanie with men from Kerak and Shaubak?'

'I still expect it. What of it?'

'Then there must be some truth in the report. I have just heard that he was ambushed somewhere along the eastern slope of Mount Gilboa. His force sustained heavy casualties, though happily Humphrey escaped and is on his way——'

Reynald instinctively disputed the report. Speaking more to himself than to the Regent he said, 'It's not possible. He has Azo with him, and Aegelric, and twenty as capable. He couldn't have led them—they wouldn't allow him such latitude.' Then he caught sight of Amalric and acknowledged that the Constable's decimated contingent had also been composed of capable men.

'Damn him!' he railed. 'I hope the enemy catch up with him yet and cut his manhood, if they can find it. Damn him! Damn Humphrey for a delicate——'

'I'm sorry,' Guy offered. 'It's a severe blow to you, to all of us.'

'Sorry? I don't want sorrow! I want men. Those fancy, waving hands, I should never—I should have set him knitting with the women. Damn his soul!'

'We are all sorry,' Raymond of Tripoli commented, earning a weak smile of gratitude from Guy. 'However, it supports our case. We dare not move now. If we venture farther east we risk being cut off by those Saracens who surprised us near Mount Tabor, and by the others who will be moving north from Gilboa. And without the force from Moab to protect our right flank——'

'You speak out of turn!' Amalric snapped, grasping his opportunity. 'They were my men who engaged the enemy below Tabor—' He looked at Reynald and grunted as his friend caught the drift of the argument.

'—and mine at Gilboa,' the Lord of Kerak concluded. 'We have a greater debt to settle now. I say we must move quickly to Tubanie.' He had adopted a belligerent, hunched forward posture, and found it easy to substitute Humphrey for the malleable Regent. They were too much alike, these paltry girl-men. If one was not available the other would serve.

'I say we go without further delay. I say we move now.'

'I understand your feelings, Lord Reynald. Any man who has lost——'

'My men are unbloodied,' Joscelin inserted, 'yet I agree with the Constable and the Lord of Kerak. I, too, say we advance.'

'And I,' from Arnold of Toroga.

'Yes, we strike them hard, before long,' from Reynald's Italian allies. 'If not, we take our men against them, alone.'

Raymond, Balian and others started to protest, but Guy had had enough.

'We'll go on,' he piped. 'We are too vulnerable, stuck here.

We'll go on in formation as far as the springs at Tubanie. Then we'll see. That is all. Thank you. Assemble your men.'

On October 3rd, the Christian army reached Tubanie. Having agreed to come this far, Guy hesitated, then refused to go farther. He had managed to please, and so displease both factions. Reynald and his supporters hammered away at him, while Balian and Raymond presented him with reliable reports, in which the Moslem forces were estimated at between twelve and twenty thousand. They did not press the scouts for greater exactitude, but merely reminded Guy that, if it were twelve or twenty, Saladin would be forced to withdraw within a few days. His army could not live indefinitely off the countryside, whereas the Crusaders could keep open several supply lines to the coast. And, so long as they stayed where they were, within reach of water, they blocked the plain and prevented the Moslems moving westward.

Guy was tempted to vacillate, but he knew he dare not face the consequences of a defeat. Nevertheless, this enforced inactivity soured the army. The volunteers threatened to return to the coast. The Italians vowed to attack unaided, and never again to follow his banner. The greater mass of the army branded him a coward. Reynald and Joscelin raged at Amalric, demanding to know whether or not the Constable was able to influence his brother. Humphrey of Toron arrived with forty men—the remnants of the detachment from Moab—and drove his step-father to fury by siding with Raymond and his defensive policy.

The Saracens tried every trick to make the Crusaders break ranks and stream out across the plain, and Reynald's party worked hard to grant their wish. But Raymond and his allies hung on, refusing to be drawn. The army held its line, while its leaders stormed between their own sections and the scarlet tent. Those soldiers who heeded the defensive policy brawled with those who clamoured for action. Knives were drawn and on one occasion arrows flew in the Christian camp. By October 7th, the army was ready to disintegrate.

Then, unaware that he was camped opposite a schismatic force, Saladin chose the night of the 7th-8th to withdraw his men from the seigneurie of Beisan. There seemed little chance of enticing the Franks from their position, or, he believed, of making an impression on the unified body of mounted knights. He accepted the situation philosophically; there would be another time. The Christians had been in Palestine for a hundred years. He could afford to wait a hundred hours, or a hundred days.

The royal army remained encamped throughout the next day. Patrols probed north-east toward the Sea of Galilee, east to the Jordan and south-east through the swamps that surrounded Beisan. One patrol roamed south and came upon the bodies of Humphrey's column. They saw immediately that the leopards and wolves had been there first. There was no sign of the Saracens west of the Jordan. The army was free to stand down.

Amid sighs of relief and groans of frustration, the barons collected their men and led them back toward Jerusalem, or Tiberias, or the coast. Guy and Amalric rode together at the heads of their sections. As they were passing through the camp someone sang out:

> 'Brother and brother,
> Brother and brother;
> A Lusignan coward
> And a Courtenay lover.'

The last referred to Amalric's mistress, Joscelin's sister Agnes of Courtenay.

Guy clenched his fists and half turned in his saddle. 'Why?' he hissed. 'Why didn't you leave me be in Poitou? I am not the kind you want, Amalric. You and I, we are alike in nothing. Why did you have to choose me?'

Staring straight ahead, Amalric replied, 'Hold your tongue, brother. You'll do. You're one of the luckiest of us all.'

'Oh, I thought so, too, once. But less and less with every day. Don't you give thought to it? I don't *want* to be Regent. Nor commander of this splintered army. I want to be left alone.'

'Aah, shush. Your pretty features and corn hair have bought you a piece of the world. Be thankful and keep silent. Even fate can be intolerant of fools.'

# CHAPTER SIX

# Jerusalem

## *October 1183*

Pashia de Riveri waited impatiently for her lover. She paced across the mosaic floor, circled the reception chamber in the great house in Jerusalem, then threw some cushions on to the tasselled Persian rug and crouched down before the stone fireplace. She watched the flames curl·round the spitting pine logs and marvelled at her new-found constancy. Or rather, that she had remained constant for so long. She was thirty-three years old and for the past six years she had lived and slept with only one man. She supposed that, before she had met her present lover, she had been bedded by eight or ten others. She remembered three of them clearly, and like most women she could pinpoint the date and place of her initiation into the rites of love; the bloody, painful moment of defloration.

She had just turned fifteen, though she had been physically ready a year earlier. Her father was a fletcher in a village near Toron; three days before Easter a group of soldiers had arrived, one on horseback, three in a heavy baggage-cart. The horseman had introduced himself as Baldric, the steward of Thierry of Alsace, Count of Flanders, and Champion of the Christian Right. He had brought bows to be mended, cross-bows to be re-sprung, and an order for as many arrows and quarrels as the fletcher could supply. Baldric said that the fortress at Banyas was being besieged by a Saracen force under the command of Nur ed-Din, Emir of Aleppo, and that Count Thierry was on his way there with a strong counter-force of Crusaders.

Her father had busied himself with the repairs, then had called to his daughter to help him carry the bundles of arrows and mace-head bolts to the cart. Baldric had stopped him, taken him aside and told him that the soldiers would carry whatever was necessary.

Looking back across the years, Pashia was sure her father knew why Thierry's steward wanted her released from the work benches, but at the time she had thought Baldric the most perfect gentleman she had ever met. Ignoring the sly glances of the soldiers, he had taken her by the hand and walked with her, amusing her with jokes and word pictures of his fellow Crusaders. She was still giggling to herself when they reached the food-store behind the house.

She was a country girl, so she was not entirely ignorant of the sexual act. But the Baldric who led her into the storeroom, then closed and barred the door, was not the Baldric who had charmed her and impressed her father. Then he was a man, now an animal.

He ripped her dress, dragged off her thonged boots, caught her by the hair and forced her head back while he kissed her face and throat and naked body. Then he pulled her down and fell on her and penetrated her and clamped a hand over her mouth to stifle her screams. While he worked himself deep inside her and let his shuddering passion run its course, she gazed up at the rows of smoked meat, the boxes of salt, the piled sacks of vegetables and the casks of boiled figs and pomegranates. Carelessly, he had unbuckled his belt and thrown it and his knife on to the ground beside him. She could have reached for the knife, dragged it from its sheath and plunged it into his back. She could have clawed his face, or kicked him, or waited until she was free of him, then shot him with one of her father's arrows.

She did none of these things because, when it was over, she was sure her heart had melted, sure that she was in love with him.

She never saw Baldric again, though she heard a rumour that he had been burned to death at Banyas.

A year later she was married to a merchant in Nablus. She thought him a dull and stupid man, more interested in his ailing drapery business than in her. He made her work the daylight hours in the shop and paid her a pittance. If she took a fancy to any of the stock she had to buy it, like any other customer, and he made a profit on the sale. One day she took some dark green silk, omitted to pay for it and made herself a dress. De Riveri discovered the theft and beat her, blaming her for his own mis-management of the poorly-lit establishment. This was not the first time he had lacerated her skin, but she vowed it would be the last. She waited until he was asleep

that night, then crept from the house and walked through the darkness to Sebastia, a few miles away.

There she met an attractive young harness-maker, named Lambert. She told him the truth, that she had been married for almost
five years and had eventually run away from her husband. She
explained what de Riveri had done to her and showed him the
fresh weals on her back. If he would let her stay with him she promised to cook and clean house.

Before a week was over they were in love. They lived together
above the harness-shop for more than six months.

Then, incredibly, four out-of-work Crusaders turned up, told her
they knew who she was and that her husband had employed them
to trace her and return her to Nablus.

'Don't deny it,' they said. 'You're a whore, but you're also Pashia
de Riveri and you're going back to your husband.'

'How long?' she gasped.

'How long have you been a whore, missy? That's for you to say.'

'No, I mean how long have you been searching for me?'

'A month or so. Where's your man friend? Lammer? Lammert?
Some such name.'

'He's out at—Why do you want to know?'

'We want to tell him——'

'Ask him,' another of the Crusaders corrected.

'Yes, we want to ask him not to do it again. Where is he?'

'I don't know. Only a month? Why—If he wanted me back why
didn't he do something about it before? Why now?'

'He couldn't afford it before. He told us how you used to steal the
money. It's funny, but he's been saving up for you, missy. He can't
be blamed for that. You look as though you'd tuck up nicely. Oh,
don't worry, we'll find your friend. Now pack your things, you've
had your last of him.'

She tried to run. One of them caught her round the waist and
sent her sprawling in a wide leather chair. Lambert had made the
chair for himself; it was his chair and she felt guilty being in it,
even like this. One of the Crusaders stayed to guard her while the other
three went in search of the harness-maker. They met him on his way
back from the nearby stables. When the Crusaders returned to the
house they had blood on their hands and clothes.

Pashia screamed, then sobbed over and over again, 'You need not have hurt him, you need not have hurt him.'

Indignant that she should think they were not well-disciplined, they said, 'We were paid to take you back and teach him a lesson. Now, pack what you can carry. What do you think we are? No need to hurt him? Get along, missy, you're going home.'

She went home to Nablus and the draper. The Crusaders had exaggerated de Riveri's sense of sacrifice. Nablus was expanding as a city and business had picked up. In the six months that she had been away, her husband had put on weight and developed a taste for civic responsibility. Unfortunately, this outward conformity did not prevent him from thrashing her in the privacy of his own home. While he punished her he called her a whore, then forgave her and insisted that she share his bed. She stayed three nights and three days, then fled with his savings to Jerusalem. Because he had called her a whore and made dull, obese love to her she decided to make him pay for his entertainment. He had told the Crusaders she was a thief, and now she had earned the title. And because he had caused Lambert to be maimed she left a small fire burning against the thin stockroom door. De Riveri escaped with his life and wrung his hands amid the smoking ruins of his future.

Pashia lost herself in Jerusalem. At first she lived off her husband's savings, then as the mistress to a succession of well-to-do business-men. Through them she came into contact with members of the king's court, and it was in this way that she met her present lover.

He was deeply attracted to her, took her to live with him in his sumptuous house, and showered her with jewellery and fine clothes for which she paid not one besant.

His name was Heraclius.

He was not a well-to-do businessman.

There were those who said he had no right to keep a mistress, since he was the Patriarch of Jerusalem, and thus the Head of the Latin Church in the East.

Ernoul followed Balian and Fostus into the city of Jerusalem. They entered from the north, through the Gate of the Column of St Stephen, and rode across the paved square to where two main streets started into the city.

Balian waited for his squire to draw level with him, then said, 'One hour, after which time I'll have need of you. I know an hour is not long enough in the presence of a beautiful woman, but if you insist on seeing her now——' He shrugged resignedly.

'It's time enough my lord. I only want to tell her, well, one or two things.'

Fostus guffawed. He loved Ernoul, as he loved Lord Balian, but there were times when the young man seemed little more than a boy. And this boy had now found himself a girl, a herbalist's daughter who worked in one of the narrow covered alleys opposite the Hospital of St John. That was fine; perhaps she would feed him herbal concoctions to keep up his strength, while he read aloud to her from his own immortal writings. But this girl had worked her way under his skin so that, instead of waiting until his day's work was concluded, Ernoul had asked leave to visit her the moment they reached Jerusalem. Lord Balian had warned him he would be required at the Royal Palace, but he had pleaded so eloquently that he had been granted one hour's release. By the time the lovesick young man had battled his way through the crowded streets to Rue des Herbes, then along that to the herbalist's stall, he would have to tell his girl that he would be back later, then dash away to rejoin Balian at the palace. Still, Fostus admitted, if Ernoul thought it was worth the pushing and jostling, then it probably was.

'You'd better be on your way,' Balian said.

Ernoul nodded and, because he thought it was expected of him, mumbled, 'If you would rather I came with you now——'

'No, no, you go on and see your lover.'

'She's not my lover!'

'Oh?'

'Of course not. I mean, well, I've known her less than a month. Now I'm not saying she wouldn't——'

'Have you asked her?' Fostus growled. 'Perhaps I should come with you. If the words stick in your throat I could ask her for you. I'll put my hands on her here and here—no, lower, there—and then —hell's claws, I'll keep you company.'

'No, you won't!' Ernoul retorted. He knew he sounded immature and undignified and made an effort to lower his voice.

'That won't be necessary. Thank you, but I am quite capable of managing my own affairs.'

As soon as he'd said that he regretted it, but Fostus had already pounced.

'Affair, eh? What affair? You told us it hadn't started yet. She might say no. She might be married by now, have you thought of that? A lot can happen in a month. She might already have a lover. If she's a nice girl she won't have room for two of you.'

Ernoul's face reddened with protective anger. 'You have no right to speak like that! I ought to—' He stopped as Balian nodded toward the entrance to St Stephen's Street. Angry though he was, Ernoul was glad that Balian had dismissed him. He did not want to trade blows with Constable Fostus. He admired the hairy Crusader too much to fight him; and anyway, Fostus would lick him with his eyes closed and one hand behind his back.

Still suffused, Ernoul dismounted and led his horse along the congested street.

When he had gone, Balian said, 'You taunt that fine young man mercilessly. Were you always so sure of yourself with women?'

'Always,' Fostus stated. 'They're simple creatures, so why should they cause me any confusion?'

'You have a poor opinion of them, in general?'

'You know otherwise, sire, but no man's a god, so where's the sense in treating a woman like a goddess? They're good for bed and giving a man sons and running the kitchens, but I don't worship them for it. And I don't trust them, either.'

'Bed, birth and board. Such sensitivity. Ernoul could obviously learn much from your methods.'

Impervious to sarcasm, Fostus agreed immediately. 'He could. And when he's willing to learn, I'll teach him.'

Balian grinned and shook his head. He knew his stalwart bodyguard far too well to be taken in by his callous façade. Fostus had risked his life more than once to save a servant girl from rape, or to prevent a Jewess from being vilified by drunken Franks. He was not one for affairs of the heart or the romantic trappings of love, but he respected women—all women, save perhaps Agnes of Courtenay and Guy's wife Sibylla—and it was evident that, though no man would ever dominate him, the right woman might.

'Come on,' Balian said. 'Now that you've voiced your shaky creed, let's find out why the king requires us.'

'It's probably his mother,' Fostus commented, making another clumsy stab at humour. 'Agnes has told him she wants to be proclaimed a goddess.'

'That's incautious talk,' Balian reminded him quietly. 'If I were you, I would not repeat such notions here. Agnes has too many long-eared reporters in her employ. Come on.' He jerked his head toward where the second main street entered the square.

They rode along the Street of the Spaniards, crossed Via Dolorosa and continued through the Street of the Furriers toward the Wailing Wall and the entrance to the great Temple Enclosure. This paved and lead-sealed area was more than two thousand feet long and seven hundred wide and contained some of the holiest of all Moslem and Christian shrines. Also known as the Noble Sanctuary, it housed the Mosque of El Aqsa, with the Royal Palace attached to its south-west corner. Four gates—the Gate of Paradise, the Golden Gate, the Gate of Grief and the Beautiful Gate—all led in to the Temple Enclosure, while in the centre of the open area stood the magnificent Dome of the Rock. This white marble edifice, with its gold octagonal dome, boasted more than fifty windows, each filled with sixty square feet of coloured glass. The building stood one hundred and forty feet high on a wide, raised platform, and the dome itself acted as a shimmering beacon to the faithful.

They came because it was here that Mohammed had conversed with Jesus, Moses and Abraham, and from here that the prophet of Islam had leapt to Paradise, leaving his footprint on the rock. It was here that the Ark of the Covenant had stood; here that Solomon had built his temple; here that Abraham had made ready to sacrifice his child, Isaac. The Angel Gabriel had visited this place, and, on the Last Day, Allah would gather the faithful together in the Cave of Souls below the rock.

Fostus had seen the building many times and did not give it a second glance.

The two men dismounted by the Beautiful Gate and made their way alongside the west wall of the Temple Enclosure. They passed groups of pilgrims and sight-seers, the Moslems dressed in striped robes and kafiyas, the Frankish pilgrims in ragged cloaks and wide skin hats. Most of the Christians carried a long staff curved at the top to take their pathetic bundles of food and clothes. What little money they possessed was contained in a leather scrip that swung from their belt. Some groups chanted quietly to themselves, or murmured together in prayer.

Balian slowed the pace, watching them and comparing their way of life with his. However hard-fought a battle, however chilly a bed-chamber or a river crossing, the life of a noble, or even an ordinary soldier, was not harder than that of a pilgrim.

Before a man embarked on his pilgrimage, he and his possessions would be blessed by a priest. Then, where the soldier was cheered on his way, the pilgrim would leave alone, often unnoticed. Throughout the time he was away he would purchase only those things that were essential to him—cheap food, a new pair of sandals, another staff to replace the one that had snapped or been stolen. Months, and sometimes years later, he would return home, unrecognisable. His hair would be lank and unkempt, his clothes rotting on his back, his face blistered and darkened, his body a mass of cuts and bruises. And yet, belying his abject poverty, this far-travelled pilgrim would be strung with evidence of his journey. He would wear this evidence proudly; it was his religious insignia.

Over the years, having met and conversed with pilgrims of every type, Balian had learned the significance of these treasured objects. They were like souvenirs of battle, some more impressive than others. He knew, for example, that a pilgrim who returned to London wearing a flask, or small, flattened bells gained less respect than one who carried a picture of St Peter or St Paul. The ampulla might contain the blood of St Thomas Becket, showing that the pilgrim had visited Canterbury, whereas the pewter effigy of St Peter proved that its owner had reached Rome.

Now, here in the enclosure, he could tell which of the pilgrims had bathed in the Jordan and which had travelled south, having worshipped at the shrine of St James of Compostella in Galicia. The first carried palm branches, or wore them tucked into their hats, and were known as palmers; the second had sewn scallop shells to their clothes and possessed a chip of bone, purporting to be from the body of St James. A few wore shells *and* lead medallions *and* palm leaves. These were the true pilgrims, who did little else with their lives but travel from one Christian shrine to another. They were the object of awe among their fellow pilgrims, and they earned money for themselves by giving advice on conditions abroad, or by supplying crude maps and the addresses of sympathetic inn-keepers.

There was another way in which a pilgrim might make money. He could sell his religious tokens to those who wanted the evidence without the toil.

The Lord of Nablus had once met such a salesman in Jaffa. The shameless pilgrim had shown him a muslin sack stuffed with effigies and crossed keys. He had bought them in Rome, caught a ship south from Naples and was about to re-sell them for profit in Palestine. Palestine, he said, was a good market, and anyway he intended to buy a farm in Antioch with the proceeds. Balian had been tempted to snatch the sack from him and throw it in the harbour, but he dared not destroy tokens of such a holy nature. So he voiced the hope that God would strike the man down, then let him go.

He had heard of others who filled ampullae with sheep's blood and who made their own clay impressions of genuine medallions, but he knew it was impossible to stop men from spitting in the face of God. Religion was like any other calling: some heard a voice, some the chink of coins.

He and Fostus reached the El Aqsa Mosque, walked past the white marble columns and entered the small Royal Palace. They blinked as they moved through the dark, tapestry-hung entrance hall, and for a moment they did not see the figure who stood at the far end of the room. But when he spoke they immediately recognised the rich, sonorous voice and then the big-bellied person of Patriarch Heraclius.

'I saw you from the window, Balian Ibelin. I thought: "He has incurred some injury, to be dawdling so." We expected you before this.'

There was no love lost between these two men. Heraclius had had almost no formal education, stated the fact proudly and often commented that 'a man must teach himself about God and the World'. He had done just that, linking arms with the sacred and secular, and using his florid good looks and resonant tones to gain the peak of clerical achievement in Palestine. He had become the protégé of the Courtenay family, and, with their help, had advanced from local priest to Archdeacon, then to Archbishop, and finally to Patriarch of Jerusalem. Power brought him money, and he used the money to realise greater power. Nobody denied that the churchman was avaricious and sybaritic, with the morals of a dog. His mistress, Pashia de Riveri, was know as Madame la Patriarchesse. The cynical title amused him; it proved that the common people feared God's senior servant too much to call his woman a whore.

Balian said, 'If I had known you were loitering in anticipation—' then shrugged. There was nothing to be gained from a dispute with Heraclius. The one was everything the other was not. The two could not be joined; not even in spite.

He asked, 'How is the king?'

'How else, but dying? But he is waiting for you, as we have all been waiting for you. I was not loitering in antici——'

'Who is in there with King Baldwin?'

'—pation. What? Regent Guy, the Grand Masters, the Lords Courtenay and Tripoli.'

'Why are we summoned, Patriarch?'

'You'll learn that soon enough.' He made as if to lead them through into the palace, then said, 'Do I know your man?'

'Which m—? Who? Constable Fostus? Of course you know him; you've met him more than—' He frowned, suddenly suspicious. 'Patriarch, are you deep in some private game?'

'Not so. But there has been talk of assassination.'

Whose, Balian thought, yours or the king's?

'Baldwin is guarded at all times. Though now that I see your, ah, Constable Fenus, I accept that we may have met on occasion.'

'Fostus,' Balian corrected. 'And now that you've played the watchdog you may lead us through.'

'I am not a watchdog, and nor am I a servant, save only of God. I am His humble——'

Something was wrong. Balian knew it, but did not yet see the reason for it. He snapped, 'I thought we were late. You know who we are. Let's get on with it.'

'—and obedient servant, and proud to be so. You must leave your weapons here.'

'Spit on the fire! You know who we are!'

While Heraclius explained that he was merely relaying the wishes of Regent Guy, Fostus whispered something to Balian.

'You're right,' Balian said, 'and I'm a fool not to have—Heraclius! You have not been true with us. You were not out here waiting to greet us; you're here to delay us. Now lead us through!'

'First, your weapons.'

'Damn you, churchman! God knows what your friends are cooking in there——'

They were too late.

The sound of angry voices echoed along the corridor. They heard:

'. . . a poor exchange . . . plan to reseat you among your enemies . . . every right to be wary, Lord Regent . . . clear as water what Baldwin wants . . . demented by his sickness . . . itself a gift of the devil, I wouldn't wonder . . .'

Then Guy of Lusignan, Arnold of Toroga and four or five others strode into the entrance hall and through it and out into the sunlight.

Balian crashed a fist against his open palm. 'Hell's gorge, now what?'

Heraclius started to make an appeasing gesture, caught Balian's expression and stopped. Fostus glanced at the Patriarch as though he were a diseased animal, then plunged after his lord, treating the priest with the same contempt he had shown for Reynald of Chatillon's garrison captain. The men of Nablus headed along the narrow corridor and turned into the throne room—in which the throne was a leper's pallet.

They saw Roger of Les Moulins and Raymond of Tripoli, who started toward them. They saw Baldwin's bed hung round with gauze curtains, and, inside the opaque canopy the hideous skeletal frame of the young King of Jerusalem. They saw the six man guard, composed of one Templar, one Hospitaller, one of Constable Amalric's men, one of Raymond of Tripoli's, one of Guy of Lusignan's and one from the king's own household. Balian was disturbed by this political arrangement. The Temple, Amalric and Guy represented one camp, Tripoli, The Hospital and the royal guard another. If a would-be assassin were to approach the bed there was no guarantee that all six men-at-arms would leap to

Baldwin's defence. It was indicative of the situation in the Christian kingdom that the dying monarch sought refuge from his unseen enemies inside a ring of faithless friends.

The Lords of Nablus and Tiberias greeted each other, then Balian and Fostus crossed the patterned floor, moving through bars of early winter sunlight, and knelt before the filmy tent.

Baldwin lay on a jumble of tasselled cushions and silk pillows. His face was dreadfully eroded. He had lost the use of his hands and legs and within three months would be completely blind. He lay still as cooled wax and mouthed, 'Who is it? Is that you, Courtenay? Regent Guy, is it you? Are you back to shout at me again?'

'There will be no shouting, King. It's Balian of Ibelin.'

'Ah, yes. But I heard two men.'

'My constable is with me.'

'Old Fostus? That grizzly warrior? Fostus, let me hear that quarried voice of yours.'

Fostus could think of nothing to say, so cleared his throat, hoping it would suffice. Balian saw Baldwin smile and asked, 'Have we reached you behind time, Lord King?'

The smile faded and the young leper replied, 'I fear so, loyal Balian. Did you see Guy and his band?'

'They passed us in the hall. We were held in conversation with the Patriarch.'

'Held by him, you mean. Joscelin put him out there to forestall you. I had hoped you would evade that disgraceful cleric before— before—' He sighed and they waited for him to muster his strength. A cold draught stirred the gauze. Balian glanced beyond the canopy to where Heraclius stood in conversation with Amalric. The Patriarch seemed pleased with himself and nudged the Constable of the kingdom as if to say, 'Don't worry, I have the situation under control.' Amalric scarcely reacted, though when he saw Balian looking at him he turned away.

Then Fostus found his tongue and growled, 'King, may I speak?'

'At last that voice,' Baldwin whispered. 'Yes, hero, speak to me. God that I had as much weight in all my being as you keep in your throat. Say on.'

'If they left before you dismissed them, Guy and the others; if you want them back, I'll bring them to you. I will bring them,' he emphasised. 'I promise you, King, if you desire Guy's presence here, I'll bring him to you, if I have to search——'

'Will you drag him by the ear?'

'If you so demand it. Yes.'

'I believe you,' Baldwin murmured gently. 'You and our Lord Balian, I believe you both.'

Balian said, 'What passed between you and the Regent, Lord King? We heard something about an exchange and a plan to reseat Guy.'

'Then you heard the crux of it. I am dying, Balian. The world and I are well appraised of that fact. If I knew the day and the hour I would not mind, and there are many who would shout with joy. But the time of my death is not yet fixed, and, like any man, I would rather delay as long as possible my final appointment. There's much to be done, much that I can do better than anyone else. You know me for an intransigent. I am stubborn, but I was born king and I will be king until God gives me no more air to breathe and takes His hand from my heart. I'm a poor thing to see or be near ——'

'You are courage itself,' Fostus blurted. 'I won't hear those words. You are the king. God preserve you, you are the king!' He was close to tears and made a business of coughing. Damn' young man, he thought, heaping insults upon his own head. If he, the best in Jerusalem, called himself a poor thing, then what were Joscelin, Amalric, Guy, Heraclius and the rest? If King Baldwin was a poor thing, his supporters were insects that had scuttled in from the desert.

Baldwin smiled again, admonished. 'Very well, here, I am King Courage. However, you must admit that my body is not as fine as it might be. And here, in this clangorous, chilly city my strength diminishes faster than I would wish. It was simply concern for this ragged frame that drove me to suggest an exchange with Regent Guy. As you know, the city of Tyre is under his guardianship. It's warmer there, and the air from the sea is supposed to improve the health. So I offered him an exchange.'

'Jerusalem for Tyre?'

'Yes, Balian. A very generous offer, I think. Guy's heart would

beat with the heart of the kingdom, and he would be well-placed to
fulfil my orders.'

Dangerously generous, Balian thought. Not because of Guy, but
because his brother would have direct control over him here. Guy
was a top, and in Jerusalem Amalric would not have to reach far to
spin it.

'And yet he didn't accept?'

'He did more than refuse. He huddled together over there with
Courtenay and Toroga, then came back to accuse me of plotting his
downfall. Constable Amalric wanted him to take it, but Guy said I
was trying to trap him where he was least popular and where I had
the most spies. Ah, he made such a noise about it, you would think
I was giving him poison, not Jerusalem.'

'It's strange,' Balian said. 'He usually allows his brother to direct
him.'

'Not so much since the march from Nazareth to Tubanie. He
distrusts Amalric now. But compeers like Seneschal Joscelin still
have his ear. And Joscelin is no favourite of mine.'

'You could force the exchange.'

Baldwin rallied. 'Fear not, I'll force an exchange, though it won't
be city for city. I'll teach my selfish brother-in-law a lesson he'll
remember. If he crossed me for the sake of the kingdom I could
forgive him. He has a weak mind and a faint heart, but I could overlook all that. What I will not abide is that he ignores my wishes,
thinking me too ill to implement them. I accept that I am dying,
though the process may take months, or even years. But I am not
yet dead. I wish some of my knights and nobles would grasp that
simple truth. I am not yet ready to be interred, and therefore unwilling to be crossed.' He sighed with anger he could not release and
blinked at the dim shades of Balian and Fostus. Sweet heaven,
he mused, what would I give for this one's body and that one's
growl.

Balian gave him time to recover his breath, then said, 'What
manner of exchange, King, if not the cities?'

'Is Raymond in attendance?'

'He is.' He glanced from Baldwin to the dedicated former regent,
who responded promptly and approached the pallet. This senior
overlord was a wiry, thin-shouldered man of forty with prominent

cheek bones and a long nose that had been broken and clumsily reset. He looked haggard and tubercular, and those who did not know him thought him incapable of humour. They were wrong, but Raymond would never smile until the frowning was concluded. His scraped features and general demeanour inspired comment among his rivals. Anything he ate, they said, went straight to his nose. It was a meddlesome thing, an excellent windbreak and good for stirring soup. He had sharp eyes, and was long-sighted from continually gazing over his own bony garden wall. They mocked him in his absence because his presence was so often a douche of cold water on their flaring ambitions.

When he reached the bed, Baldwin murmured, 'Move the guard for me, Tripoli. I want none to hear this, save you and my Lord of Nablus.' He sensed Fostus move and added, 'Ah, stay, hero. You have a special place in my affections.'

With casual malice Raymond ordered the king's guard to stand in a row across the room, their backs to the canopy. Amalric and Heraclius were thus fenced off from Baldwin and kept well out of hearing.

'Now listen well,' the young leper said. 'You, Raymond, and you, Balian, are to convene as many of your fellow barons as you judge loyal to the Crown and are to assemble them here without delay. Before October is out, if you can manage it. I want to see Roger of the Hospital, the Lords of Sidon and Caesarea, Bohemond of Antioch if he can get down here in time, your brother Baldwin of Ramleh and whoever else you trust.'

Raymond asked, 'May I give them a reason?'

'I am reason enough,' Baldwin whispered. 'I am the king, eh, Fostus? God preserve me, my lords, I am the king. But that said, I will give you reasons. Come closer, I'm growing tired.' While they drew aside the curtains and hunched down beside the bed, Baldwin smile encouragement and said, 'I assure you in advance, you will be well pleased with the exchange I have in mind.'

Ernoul missed the meeting.

As Fostus had surmised, he spent most of his free hour struggling through the crowded streets in the direction of Rue de Herbes and the stall with its green awning. When he arrived the herbalist informed him that his daughter had been sent to Ramallah to nurse a sick aunt. He was understaffed and in a bad humour and said that he was very sorry but no, he did not know if Idela had left a note for Ernoul. No, he did not know how long she would be in Ramallah. No, the aunt was not his sister, and he knew only that her name was Ermengarde and that she lived in Tower Street. No, he did not know the number.

Ernoul was furious. He pushed his way sullenly along the Street of the Chain toward King Solomon Street and the Temple Enclosure, then stopped as he remembered that Ramallah was not far from the road to Nablus. Cheered, he decided to see Idela on the way home.

It was late evening before Heraclius returned home to Pashia de Riveri. When Raymond and Balian had left the Royal Palace, the Patriarch had attempted to extract information from the exhausted king. He wanted to know what Baldwin had been whispering about for so long, but he learned nothing because the king's physicians refused to let anyone near the canopy. They were adamant; the monarch needed rest, and more rest. Surely even the Patriarch could understand that.

'If you had your way,' he snapped, 'the king would spend his life asleep.'

'And if you had yours,' the physician-in-chief responded, 'he would be dead in a week.'

Furious that he could be thwarted by these wizened leeches—oh, they would not last long after Baldwin died, oh, no, they would be the first into exile—he retired and spent the better part of the day in conference with Constable Amalric and Seneschal Joscelin. The conference was unsatisfactory, since they did not know Baldwin's plans, so could not take remedial action. Joscelin felt sure that, for the sake of the kingdom—one of Baldwin's favourite phrases— he would not press the exchange.

'He won't want to make a martyr of Guy, and if he tries to force him to accept Jerusalem it'll look as though he's persecuting his own Regent. Even so, I'd like to know what went on between him and our Lords of Tiberias and Nablus.' Then, as an afterthought, 'God, the way he softens to that Fostus fellow.'

'I don't agree about the exchange,' Amalric said. 'I think Baldwin will pursue the matter. And as for the making a martyr of my brother, that's demanding the impossible. We all know that Guy's death will be a poor one, whatever it is. You're generous, Joscelin, but if the king hounds my kinsman, the people of Palestine will bay in support. The king's a nuisance, we can say that with one voice; but for every two of us who would wish him in heaven, there are twenty who would consign Guy to eternal damnation. Yes, I know he's my brother. That's the strength and the frailty of it.'

Heraclius drank wine steadily throughout the afternoon, and said little. Oh, those bow-backed savants. Just one instant after the king was interred, they would be on their way, penniless, to the emptiest island in the Mediterranean. And the physician-in-chief might be minus a few other things, beside money.

When they had talked themselves out, Amalric went to find Guy and those who had stormed out of the palace with him, while Heraclius accompanied Joscelin to a romanesque villa situated on the northern slope of the Mount of Olives. The villa was shared by the Seneschal and his sister, Agnes, though the king's mother ran the house to suit her own requirements and had taken over the entire ground floor, plus several of the upper rooms.

They drank twelve-year-old Cypriot wine and Joscelin recounted the events at the palace. While he spoke, he glanced once or twice at Heraclius, seeking confirmation of some point, some quoted comment. The Patriarch was blearily amused to see Joscelin so unsure of himself. Agnes had that effect on people. Strangers were frightened by the rumours they had heard about her. Her family and friends were frightened because they knew that most of the rumours were true. She was fifty years old, and, with four marriages behind her, there was little she had not seen or done. Even Heraclius, who was her protégé, and who prided himself on being outspoken, thought twice before voicing certain opinions. Because she had helped him in his career, he was grateful to her, though he sometimes wished for a more gullible patron. Now he held his tongue and enjoyed the dry white wine.

When Joscelin had finished, Agnes yawned in his face.

'Leave it,' she said. 'I'll visit him to-morrow.'

'I tell you, sister, he's planning something to our detriment.'

'You have already told me. But since the meeting has weakened him, he'll do nothing more before morning.'

'*He* won't, perhaps, but now that he's enlisted the aid of Tripoli and——'

'Nothing will be done that cannot be undone as quickly. Risen Christ, I know how to manage my own son.' She closed her eyes, thought about Baldwin, then opened them, smiling.

'Heraclius, my sweet one, will you stay and eat with me?'

Joscelin excused himself and left them alone. Over the years he had come to understand exactly what Agnes meant when she invited a friend to sup with her...

The Patriarch made his way home in the dark. He was blind drunk, fell twice in the road and bruised his shoulder on the corner of his own house. His head ached and his lower limbs felt heavy and unresponsive. Pashia met him at the door with rosewater, a hand towel and a glass of sweet date wine.

Foolishly, she said, 'I was worried. What happened to the messenger——'

'I didn't send one.'

'But you always——'

'Well, this time I didn't. What's all this? Do I look so dirty?'

'It's to refresh you. I thought, he must have lost his way.'

'Who? Me?'

'The messen——'

'I told you. I sent no messenger. I told you that.'

'Yes,' she murmured, 'so you did.'

She had lit three dozen candles to brighten the long room. Logs were stacked high on the fire, and the flames leapt up, warming the air.

Heraclius said, 'Are we celebrating some festival? Do you know how much candles cost these days? And look at that fire; this place is like a bread oven. You'll bake us both one day, or set the house alight.' He drank the date wine, then held the glass out to her, as though he had been kept waiting.

Pashia misconstrued the action and put the glass on an inlaid side table. She noticed the mud on his robes. He had been drinking, that was obvious, but so long as he had not been to one of the whore-houses, where he would risk contracting some dreadful—She broke the thought abruptly. Times had indeed changed, when she, herself labelled a whore by her draper husband and his hired Crusaders, now worried lest her lover fall prey to the diseases of their trade. How strange, she mused. I am no longer a whore, nor yet a lady. Nor ever will be, for a true lady would not admit to such knowledge. I suppose I am a courtesan, a mistress of the court. If so, I'll settle gladly for it.

Her reverie was interrupted by Heraclius.

'Must I keep the flask beside me?'

'Oh. I thought you may have found it too sweet. Have you eaten to-day?'

'I have, and better food than here. Come along, pour the wine.'

'At the palace? Did you eat at the palace?'

Questions, questions. Would she never stop asking her silly questions? Are you well, are you tired, are you clean, are you hungry? Where did you eat, and what, and how much, and with whom? Did this one speak of his wife, or that one of his recent travels? Is Elvira still at court, Ranulf still jaundiced, Walter still raising the ransom for his uncle? Questions, questions, and then, on the heels of the answers, more questions.

He put a jewelled hand to his aching head. Pashia filled his glass and brought it to him. He snatched at it. The glass was wet and it slipped from his grasp and shattered on the mosaic floor. He turned on her, his eyes bright with anger. It was too much. He had been insulted by Balian and his squat bodyguard, twice barred from the king's presence, first by Raymond and the men-at-arms, then by the shuffling physicians, sapped dry at the villa, and now left to the mercy of a clumsy, questioning——

'No!' he shouted. 'I did not eat at the palace. I ate with the Lady Agnes. And while I ate, I drank a flask of good wine. Grape wine, not this—this sticky fluid. But that's not all. You ask me what I did?'

'No, I——'

'I'll tell you. I enjoyed her wine, and then I enjoyed her body. The Lady Agnes. I made love with her——'

'Oh, no.'

'Yes, silly woman! And not for the first time. Nor the first hundred. Really, do you think I had so many meetings? Did it not occur to you, in all your questioning, to ask the messenger who paid him? He would have told you that he belonged to the household of Lady Agnes of Courtenay. You see? Your questions reveal so little. You are a late-comer to my love, compared with her.'

'But she's—*ugly*!'

'You say, though let me tell you this. At fifty she is better versed in the art and practice than you. Yes. Oh, yes. Oh, indeed so.'

'She's ugly!'

'Better, you hear? Much better. Now clear the mess and save some of these candles. And fetch some real wine. If there is none here, the shop in Via Dolorosa will open for you. Tell them who you are. Say, ah, say you are Madame la Patriarchesse. Yes, they'll open for you then.'

She did as she was told. When she returned, Heraclius had fallen asleep in a chair, his legs twisted under him, his face turned, bright red, toward the fire. Pashia dared not wake him. She stood the flask on the inlaid table, capped all but ten of the candles, then sat opposite him, gazing at him for a long time. He slept through her whispered thoughts and her memories and her eventual tears, warm tears that tasted of salt and much sharper bitterness . . .

# CHAPTER SEVEN

# Kerak

## October 1183

He had once seen a set of Chinese boxes; seen it first as a single cube of ivory filigree. Then inside the openwork, he had noticed another box, and inside that another, and another, and in the centre one more, so small, so intricately carved. There were no seams or hinges, no latches or sliding lids. Each box was complete, free to rattle within the confines of the next, yet completely caged by it. He had seen it years ago, and now, remembering it, he used each box as a container for his dreams.

The politically incestuous Kingdom of Jerusalem was threatened as never before by a united Islam. That was the outer box. The next held the city of Jerusalem itself and the dying king, together with rumours of an imminent clash between Baldwin and Guy. That box encompassed, but did not control the third—Oultrejourdain. Nor did the vast frontier territory do more than surround the cage that held Kerak. Reynald of Chatillon had said, 'I am Oultrejourdain!', but for the moment he had turned his back on the county, as he had ignored the rest of Palestine. He had sealed himself in the fourth box, inside the walls of his impregnable fortress.

There was one more, the smallest and most cramped of them all. This held Reynald's step-son, the seventeen-year-old Humphrey of Toron. It held him and his dreams, which were fast becoming nightmares, and it held him captive. For several weeks he had remained under guard in his chambers, awaiting Reynald's displeasure. He had been allowed to exercise on the western wall-walk, again trailed by a man-at-arms, but apart from these brief daily excursions he had stayed alone in his rooms, shunned by his family and scorned by the occupants of Kerak. Reynald had prescribed this treatment as part punishment for the young man's defeat on the slopes of Mount Gilboa; the second, harsher part was yet to come.

Now Humphrey dragged himself from the shallows of sleep. He lay exhausted by his dreams, aware that to-day was the day Reynald had chosen on which to put the second part into operation. To-day Reynald would begin 'working him into a warrior.' That was the phrase he had used, meaning that he would personally refresh his step-son in the ways of battle. Humphrey was to be taught again how to wield a sword and couch a lance; he was to learn anew how to control a frisky destrier and parry a mace stroke with a leather buckler. To use another of Reynald's terms, the young man was to be 'muddied and bloodied,' then encouraged to treat pain as though it were humour, as a reason for laughter. The lessons would be held in public, under the critical gaze of the men and women of Kerak. They would see Humphrey of Toron emerge as a man—worked into a warrior—or they would watch him beaten to the ground, bloody proof of his own ineptitude. Few had any sympathy for him; too many good men had been lost in the Saracen ambush. But for days the castle had seethed with excitement. One way or another it would be a worthwhile show.

Sweating with fear, he turned his head and glanced at the studded door of the bedchamber. If he did not leave soon and make his way to the training yard, Reynald would send men to fetch him. There was no escape and there would be no reprieve. A dozen men-at-arms, probably led by Captain Azo, would burst in, drag him from the bed and bundle him down to the yard, naked for the amusement of the waiting spectators.

He moaned and threw back the hand-worked coverlet and rabbit-skin blanket. The coverlet was a gift from his betrothed, Isabella, the girl he was supposed to marry before the year was out. He sat on the edge of the bed, holding the coverlet and murmured, 'Hurry, dear Isabella. Reynald will not rest until I am dead, or far gone from Kerak.' His voice died away and there was no sound as he mouthed, 'Hurry, little girl. I pray you, hurry.'

When he had said that he realised just how frightened he was. He was calling on a girl for help, the first time he had done such a thing. Isabella was a princess, half-sister to King Baldwin and Guy of

Lusignan's wife Sibylla, but for all her regality Humphrey felt ashamed of himself, for Isabella was not yet twelve years old.

He threw faintly scented water on his face and body, then put on a grey, wide-sleeved tunic, chased leather belt and calf-length boots. The cowhide was scuffed and dirty, but he was too preoccupied to care. Injury and death waited for him in the yard; clean boots would not keep him alive. He stared out of the window at the cool grey dawn above the Moab hills, shivered and donned a pelisson, an over-tunic lined with squirrel fur. Finally, by way of apology for having weakened and called on Isabella for help, he pinned a heavy silver brooch to the pelisson. She had sent him the brooch from Nablus, where she lived with her mother, Maria Comnena, and her step-father, Balian of Ibelin.

In an accompanying note she had written:

'This token is magicked, sweet. I have worn it to mass and in bed, and I have pricked my finger and let blood fall on it. Please do not think me pagan. It was the way I judged best to make it special for you. Wear it, sweet, handsome soon-husband. It will aid you in all things, I am sure of it.'

At the time he had been both pleased and embarrassed—sweet, handsome soon-husband!—and his emotions were still mixed as he attached it to the pelisson. Was he wearing it only for Isabella, or because, in part at least, he believed her claims? It was easy for a young man to accept that the warmth of a girl's body and a drop of her pricked-out blood combined to produce an indestructible formula for good. The world was full of such stories; had not Angelica, Princess of Cathay, possessed a ring with which to counter all evil, and had not the lady knight, Bradamante of Clermont, used the ring to overcome the Enchanter of the Pyrenees, defeating both him and his horse-eagle, called a Hippogriff? And even to-day, what knight worthy of his name did not believe in the magical properties of a *favor*, be it a lady's scarf, or sleeve, or weighty silver brooch? Of course the brooch was magicked. A princess of Isabella's standing had only to say it, to make it so. Anyway, Humphrey admitted to himself, he had need of such a talisman.

He walked round the carved, leopard's foot bed, poured himself a glass of thin red wine and swallowed it, along with some day-old lumps of black bread and a handful of dates. Then, pitching his voice down, he hammered on the door and called, 'Wake and open! I have business with Lord Reynald.'

'I was awake,' the unseen guard retorted. 'I'm goin' with you to the yard. Prince Reynald'll be waitin'——'

'Then he must breathe the morning air for awhile. I'll see him after I've said mass. Open up.'

The guard pulled the door open and wrestled with his first problem of the day. 'Prince Reynald said nothin' about mass.'

'Why should he? He rarely attends. But I'm going, so you may either hook on, or tell him of the delay.'

'Now, see 'ere, young 'Umphrey. Your step-father won't want to be kept waitin'.'

Humphrey remembered the visit of Balian and the Hospitallers, and smiled grimly. 'That's true,' he said, 'but nor does God.'

'Well,' the guard muttered, 'put like that, I s'pose it's allright. Though I'll 'ave to tell 'im.'

'Do so.' He was about to add, 'And tell him I am praying for his soul,' but thought better of it.

The guard grunted unhappily and moved away along the cold stone corridor. Humphrey followed him, then turned aside and descended a circular stairway that led down to the family chapel. Isabella's silver brooch hung heavy and reassuring on his chest.

When he reached the chapel he found his mother waiting near the door. It was closed and after he had bade her a muted good morning he reached forward to lift the latch.

'It's locked,' Stephanie said. 'The priest just came by.'

'The chapel locked? Why?'

'He was fully apologetic.'

'Mother, what are you talking about? Has he mislaid the key?'

'He had a chill in the throat. He says he's unable to conduct the service.'

Humphrey shook his head, bewildered. Stephanie shrugged delicately, as though that explained everything, then said, 'I am so proud of you, Humphrey. I know you will acquit yourself with honour.'

For the moment he had forgotten Reynald and the yard. He was still trying to make sense of the locked chapel and the priest with a sore throat. 'Tell me again,' he said. 'What difference if the priest is indisposed? We have more than one cleric. I'll fetch somebody——'

'No. You must leave it now.'

'—with a key. What?'

'Let it rest. Reynald says——'

'Aah, Reynald says. I see. It's clear now how a churchman can suffer with an inflamed throat, yet be able to apologise at length. Reynald ordered the chapel locked. I am to derive no comfort from prayer, nor ask God for His protection, is that it?'

Stephanie mewed to herself and said, 'I have a present for you. Over there, in that sack. Truly, I am proud of you.'

He glanced at the sack, then looked directly at his pretty, foolish, carefully painted mother. 'Why?' he asked.

'Well, because I—That's a silly question.'

'Is it? Have I grown in your esteem because I'm about to fight for my life with the Red Wolf of the Desert? Do you think me more akin to that swaggering bully because he forces me into mortal combat? Your husband pitted against your son? Does that fill you with pride? Does it, my lady?'

'Of course not. And don't be disrespectful. I just think——'

'Yes.'

'I think it's time you showed everybody that you're as brave as——'

'As my step-father?'

'As I know you are,' she finished weakly. 'I am proud of you. You won't alter that.'

'Oh, Mother,' he sighed, 'I devoutly wish it were so. However, you avow it, so take my arm and walk with me to the yard. Together, we will show the eager crowd——'

'No, you go ahead. I have to, ah, fetch some medicine for the priest. God bless you, Humphrey. Don't forget your present.'

He gazed at her until she turned away, then nodded, scared and empty. There was no point in reminding her that the priest was in perfectly good voice, so her excuse was a bald lie. She was proud of him, but did not want to be seen with him. Amen. Neither did anyone else.

He collected the sack, surprised at its weight, and peered into it.

It contained a crested helmet, a beautifully worked, silvered steel hauberk complete with hood and mittens, a dyed doe-skin gambeson, soft and supple, and a folded silk tabard, decorated with brilliant green leaves on the sleeves and borders. Frowning at such a practical display of generosity—the hauberk alone was worth a prince's ransom—he straightened up to thank her. She had gone, leaving him with his armour. Well, he thought, now I have been dressed by two women.

There were no banners or pennants in evidence, no fruit stalls or palmists' booths, no jugglers, acrobats, monkey men or *fabliaux* tellers. Dogs and children ran excitedly about the stamped earth bailey, aware that the day's routine had been interrupted without caring why. The children, offspring of servant girls, soldiers' wives and camp followers, were anxious to show off their speed and agility before the growing number of spectators. They ran better, they felt, if they screamed, so they opened their lungs, inspiring their friends to shriek and the dogs to snarl and worry their ankles. Around the perimeter of this noisy play-pen the adults assembled: off-duty soldiers and their women, civilians from the lower town, workmen who had managed to slip away from the armouries, or bakeries, or mason's yard. The garrison captains, Azo and his cousin Aegelric, were there—'Pray God that Saladin does not attack us now!'—plus a group of Syrian traders who had stopped off on their way to Damascus—'Is it not better that we pay the Lord of al-Kerak the toll he demands than risk losing the entire caravan?' And there were the members of Reynald's household: maids and jongleurs, clerks and troubadours, cooks and interpreters. Some had brought blankets and cushions and had settled down on the steps and in doorways. Others stood on the battlements, their backs to the sloping merlons, or sat with their feet dangling over the inner edge of the wall. They were dressed in warm working clothes, and those who had thought ahead refreshed themselves with wine and meat-in-muslin.

The combatants had not yet appeared. Reynald was being dressed in an anteroom beneath the Great Hall, while Humphrey was left alone in a storehouse, above which were the lofts that held Kerak's messenger pigeons. The young man's armour—taken from him when he was first locked in his chambers—had been dumped in the storehouse. Fortunately, no-one had inspected the contents of his sack, and he placed it beside his own stained gambeson and much-repaired hauberk. The storehouse was damp and unlit, the floor spotted with pigeon droppings and slippery with rotted straw. He stood for a moment, listening to the noise from the inner bailey, then undressed and took the doe-skin shirt from the sack. Without help it was difficult to don the silvered hauberk, but he managed it, laced the tabard at the shoulders, then reclaimed his sword and cingulum. He buckled the decorated belt, fumbled in the darkness for the polished, crested helmet and tried it on. As with the rest of Stephanie's presents, it fitted well. He suspected that the overall affect was patchwork—his boots, sword, scabbard and belt were old and worn—but he was glad that he had supplied some part of his outfit.

He searched for the door, then remembering Isabella's brooch, went over to his cast-off clothes and unpinned it from the pelisson. He fixed it to the silk tabard, changed his mind—the tabard might be ripped and the brooch lost—and pushed the pin through one strap of his sword-hanger. If the brooch was magicked—If? Of course it was magicked;—perhaps its rays would reach his horse and saddle.

He heard a roar of acclaim from the crowd and guessed that Reynald had appeared in the yard. The sound frightened him and he laid his palms together and whispered a short, uncertain prayer:

'Sweet Jesus, aid me. If I am to die, help me do so as a man. If not, give me the strength to oppose him—that's my Lord Reynald, I'm to fight him—so I don't disgrace myself or the House of Toron. I don't want this day, You know that, but he gives me no choice in the matter. Praise be to God the Father and Christ the Son. Amen.'

Then he found the storehouse door and rapped on it. A guard opened it and motioned him out.

The dogs and children had been chased from the bailey, and a solid-looking quintain erected near the west wall. This structure consisted of a tall oak post, the lower end of which was driven deep into the ground, while the upper supported a bracketed cross-bar. A captured Moslem shield had been nailed to one arm of the cross-bar, a bag of sand tied to the other. The weight of sand equated that of the wood and leather shield, so that the balanced beam would revolve laterally if the shield was struck.

Humphrey had tilted at a quintain before, but at the simpler man-on-a-pole version. He understood the purpose of the cross-beam and hoped he could duck in time. Otherwise, he risked being caught by the sand-bag and knocked forward from his horse. He shrugged and walked out into the bailey.

The crowd saw the silk tabard, the flash of silvered steel, the bright blue horsehair on the tufted crest of his helmet. They applauded wildly, convinced that Humphrey himself must have raised the money for his armour, selling and saving in preparation for this day. They welcomed such a display of confidence—God knew, Humphrey of Toron was a feeble soldier, but he was a like-able enough young man—and a few of them dared to wish him well. He did not respond to the cheers, but continued across the yard to where Reynald waited with horses, weapons and attendants. When he reached his dully armed step-father he bowed and said, 'I see you still want to work me into a warrior. Then go to it. These people have waited long enough.'

In the time it had taken for Humphrey to cross the bailey, Reynald's emotions had swung from bored disdain to blazing animosity. He was dumbfounded by his step-son's appearance. He had seen Humphrey's armour as it was being dumped in the store-house and had remarked on it at the time, making much of the theory that the rusty hauberk would probably fall apart during the first contest. He knew, too, that Humphrey had been under close guard for several weeks, and that there was no way by which he could have obtained new armour. Yet he had managed it somehow. And not merely new armour, but one of the most expensive outfits he had ever seen. Hell's fangs, how had the bony book-worm fixed that?

He cleared his throat and charged, 'Where did you get it? Your petty resources don't stretch this far. Who advanced you the money?'

'Nobody, Lord Prince.'

'Liar! You stand there, dressed like a coin, telling me——'

'I tell you that no money passed hands, either way.'

Reynald slapped the back of his mailed hand against Humphrey's chest. 'Then I ask you again. Where did you get this finery?'

'It was a present.'

'Now, now,' Reynald warned. 'The silk and silver make you uncommonly insolent. Nobody gives *you* presents these days. Not if they value their life.'

The crowd could not hear the words and muttered impatiently. Reynald rounded on them, glaring up at the walls and balconies. The noise diminished. Evidently the Lord of Kerak had not yet completed his instructions.

'Nevertheless,' Humphrey said, 'it was a present.'

'From whom?'

The young nobleman had already decided to lie. The truth would bring a welcome delay in the proceedings, but if Reynald learned that his own wife was responsible he might accuse Humphrey of more than military ineptitude. Stephanie would have to appear blameless, an unwilling pawn in some devious game. It was well within Bloodhead's compass to bring a charge of incest and black-mail against him, and once the court had valued the silvered hauberk they would find it easy to side with their prince. So he kept the name to himself and said, 'I don't know who gave it. I found it in a sack outside the chapel. Perhaps Gabriel——'

'Blasphemous pander! You found it, so you stole it!'

'It was marked out to me.' Hastily he embellished the lie. 'It was written on ribbon: "To Humphrey of Toron, that he may look the part." That's what it said.'

'Where is the ribbon?'

'What? Oh, I don't know. I didn't keep it.'

'Listen to me,' Reynald snarled. 'You know who gave you your clothes, but you think fit to swallow his identity. You're mistaken, because you'll cry out to tell me before you leave the bailey. Unless of course, you take the name with you to your grave. Now get on your horse.' He raised his voice. 'Sergeant-at-arms! Pass out the lances. Man the quintain. I want three clear strikes. Do you hear me, Toron?'

Humphrey nodded, then mounted awkwardly in the unworked mesh. He realised that it would be some time before the stiff, link-mail hauberk allowed any ease of movement. Forcing his arms this way and that, he murmured, 'God grant that it's I who make you malleable, not some new recipient.'

Reynald called again, 'Give him a lance!' and Humphrey stopped exercising as the sergeant handed it up to him.

The quintain detail stationed themselves behind the wooden cross and the spectators leaned forward, waiting for the first rider to make his run. Humphrey scanned the crowd for Stephanie, then saw her with two of her maids on the steps that led up to the Great Hall. He wanted to signal to her, to show his gratitude for the contents of the sack, but before he could think of a way Reynald called out, 'Our young Lord of Toron, grandson of the great warrior constable, will ride first. Remember Gilboa, Humphrey, as you tilt.'

'And remember to duck!' somebody shouted, bringing laughter and free advice from the crowd.

I'll remember, he thought. That's all I'll remember. I'll forget Mother and Reynald and the flies up there on the wall, and I'll concentrate on the task. Strike the shield. Duck. Pull away to the left. God help me do it. God help me—*now*!

He pressed the lance tight against his body and spurred forward. The crowd watched, suddenly impassive. Stephanie watched, her fingers twisted together. Astride his horse Reynald watched, grinning.

Humphrey neared the quintain. He swerved to correct the line of approach, raised the tip of the lance and hit the round leather target almost dead centre. It was a perfect blow, but as the blade buried itself in the shield he knew he had been tricked. *The arm did not swing away*. The ten foot pole was torn from his grasp and, already bent forward to avoid the swinging counter-weight, he crashed full-tilt into the immovable shield. His helmet hit the end of the cross-bar, while the edge of the shield caught his right shoulder. He was wrenched upright and hurled from his horse. He fell heavily, tried to rise, then fell back beneath the quintain.

The crowd stayed silent until they saw Reynald shake his head in feigned despair. Then they realised it was a practical joke and howled at the unexpectedness of it. The cross-bar had been nailed to the centre post! Of course! It was Prince Reynald's way of testing his step-son. He was simply illustrating a cardinal rule of warfare; never underestimate the guile of the enemy.

The quintain detail waited for a signal from Reynald, then came forward to assist Humphrey. He was stunned and bleeding from a long cut on his forehead. For a few moments he could neither see nor think straight, so the soldiers dragged him over to the quintain and left him sitting there, with his back against the centre post. The crowd enjoyed that and called down, 'Have you lost your way? You go right for Shield Street! Left for Sand Street!'

He heard them, but felt too sick to do more than mumble senseless imprecations. Blood ran into his left eye and he used the hem of his tabard to wipe it away. He made a clumsy, ineffectual job of it, smearing more blood over his face and the curled green leaves of the tunic. His back and right shoulder were stiff and raw, and he was unable to stop his limbs shaking. He realised how foolish he looked —no more so than he felt—and gazed down at Isabella's silver brooch. He no longer believed her claims and was tempted to unpin it when a fresh wave of comment made him look up. Reynald had crossed the bailey and now stood over him, one hand outstretched.

'Find your feet,' he said. 'You have yet to make three strikes.' In a low, hard voice, intended only for Humphrey, he added, 'It'll go easier if you name your benefactor. Who armed you?'

'I don't know.'

'You know, and you'll tell. But no hurry. You're affording too much enjoyment for it to end so soon. Now, get up and make your marks.'

Humphrey closed his eyes, ignored the proffered hand and twisted up, using the post for support. His legs threatened to buckle under him and he staggered as he went to reclaim his lance. Reynald offered no further assistance, but turned on his heel and strode back to his horse. He had expected Humphrey to reveal the name, and did not like the book-worm's stubborn attitude. He was laying a dangerous path for himself, was skinny young Toron. The next time he was thrown from his mount he'd find no hand outstretched to help him.

The quintain detail removed the nails that had immobilised the cross-bar and Reynald took his turn. He struck cleanly, ducked and pulled the horse away as the counter-weight swung round, spilling sand from a split seam in the bag.

Humphrey tried, hit the shield square on, but ducked too slowly.

The beam sliced round and he lurched, vomiting across the neck of his destrier.

'No strike!' Reynald shouted, spurring forward for the second time. Again he tilted faultlessly and again eluded the bar.

Humphrey struggled to keep his senses. The last blow would have broken his neck but for the unusually low rim of his new helmet. As it was, blood still poured from the gash in his forehead, while his nerves screamed with every movement. He was nearly finished, and knew it. If Reynald wanted the name of his benefactor he would not keep it from him. This time he had only to ask.

But Reynald was away, impatient to make his third strike. He tilted cleanly, leaving the cross-bar to spin and catch nothing. The crowd applauded what they had known all along; Reynald of Chatillon was a horse soldier *par excellence*. He rode into the centre of the bailey, pointed a mailed finger at Humphrey and called, 'Match that if you will, Toron. Three strikes, and the lance is still unbroken.'

A sycophant echoed, 'Three out of three!' The onlookers cheered anew and made bets among themselves. How many attempts before Humphrey hit the shield and escaped the sand? How many before he made three clear strikes? Before he was knocked from his horse again? Before he splintered his lance? Before Reynald took pity on him and let him go?

Many of those who wagered lost their money.

The young knight realised that he would never match Reynald blow for blow—the Red Wolf was too experienced—and that he could not successfully mimic the older man's style. Reynald held himself upright as he tilted, pushed his body down at the last instant, then rose again as he wheeled his horse. It looked splendid; the Christian warlord riding triumphantly away while the cross-bar spun in confusion, spilling sand like a man's blood. It was a magnificent display, but surely it was not the only way to beat the quintain.

Pleased with the progress of the course, Reynald removed his helmet, pushed back the hood of his hauberk and rubbed a mittened hand through his red hair. Almost as an after-thought he waved Humphrey forward. He had now given his step-son to the people of Kerak. Let the book-worm amuse them for a while.

Humphrey wiped around the slowly closing cut, manœuvred

his horse in line with the shield, then couched the lance and bent low
in the saddle. The crowd stared in amazement, then threw their
laughter into the yard. A knight riding crook-back! What next?
Foot soldiers going into battle on their knees? What on earth did
young Humphrey think he was doing?

He knew full well what he was doing and spurred his horse at the
ragged leather shield. The leaf-blade caught it to the left of the central
boss and glanced off. The beam swung round and the counter-
weight sliced harmlessly above his head. He wheeled his horse,
drew erect and circled the bailey. The quintain detail walked forward to control the cross-bar, but Humphrey would not wait. They
saw him crouch again and spur the horse and they scattered as he
galloped in to hit the target while the beam was still moving. The
lance struck home and he pulled the horse aside, clear and safe.

The spectators were on their feet, yelling, tossing caps, gloves,
even wraps and cushions. The incredible had happened. Of all the
proud, iron knights who had lodged at Kerak, none had shown such
invention as the skinny Humphrey of Toron. Now they were on his
side. Now they wanted him to make his third strike. They shouted
at the soldiers, 'Stand back! He doesn't need you! He's able.' A
dozen of the watchers stamped their feet and the rest caught the
rhythm and chorused, 'Hum-phrey! Hum-phrey! Hum-phrey!'

He brought his horse round, checked it for an instant as the shield
arm swung past the wall, then urged the destrier toward the
widening target. He almost forgot to crouch, threw himself down
in time and drove the lance as hard as he could into the target. It
held, swung back with the beam and circled the centre post, its thin
shadow sliding over the ground, along the wall, across the scattered
garments and up again on to the limestone blocks.

Reynald watched and said nothing. Humphrey straightened in
his saddle, wiped a persistent rivulet of blood from the side of his
face and patted his horse, gentling it as Kerak roared approval. In his
own time he sought out his step-father. He, too, said nothing, but
held up his right hand, three fingers protruding. He had made his
strikes, and created his own magic.

There was to be no respite. Reynald was diplomat enough to allow
the onlookers their moment of exaltation and when the cheers had

subsided he was suddenly fulsome in his praise of Humphrey. He
spoke in a voice that could be heard on the balconies and ramparts;
only his step-son and nearby attendants saw the hard, angry gaze
that belied his words.

'You did well, Toron. Even I, who claim to know as much about
these things as anybody, might learn from your, well, unusual
technique. It would have been sufficient for you to scar a stationary
target. To tilt while it moved showed a pretty courage. It's a shame
you were not so perfect at Gilboa.' He opened his hands, dismissing
the defeat. 'But that's past. Now you are a proven warrior—' He
paused, then concluded, '—with a horse, and with a lance. I wonder,
are you so nimble on foot, armed with a long-sword?'

So that's it, Humphrey groaned. I'm to be cut down by his
favourite weapon, the hundredth, or two hundredth victim of
IN NOMINE DOMINI. He knows that my wrists are too weak and my
sword too light to turn his own monster blade. I don't know anyone who could deflect it, save perhaps Lord Balian of Ibelin's constable, what does he call himself, Fostus? He might block its path,
but I doubt that I could even lift such a piece.

'Give your answer,' Reynald invited. 'If you would rather wait
in your chambers for a week or so and catch your breath——'

'No, I've had my taste of prison.'

'Your head spins, kinsman. You were no prisoner. You were
contained for your own protection, nothing more. However, do
you say you will play with me?'

'When you offer that choice you know I'll play.'

Reynald nodded. 'Good. Sergeant! Take care of the horses. Azo!
Supervise the barricades.' By way of explanation to the crowd
he said, 'We cannot chase the length and breadth of the yard, but
stay where you are. We'll play here, in the centre.'

Soldiers hurried forward with stakes and trestles which they
arranged in a rough, roped square. Reynald was not satisfied with
the size of the combat area, so the spectators turned to their meat and
wine while the soldiers tore down a small shed and appropriated its
planks. Humphrey fingered the silver brooch, glanced anxiously at
Stephanie and imagined himself lying broken beneath Reynald's
heel. Under such circumstances, what could he do but reveal her
identity?

By the time the square had been enlarged to suit Reynald's requirements the sun had scaled the eastern walls of Kerak. It hung for a moment, poised on the battlements, then poured into the bailey, rougeing the faces of the assembled complement. Those who had not already thrown their blankets into the yard discarded them now, as the coolness of dawn gave way before the growing heat of day.

Humphrey held one of the tossed scarves to his head, then brought it away dry. The bleeding had stopped, though the long crusted cut still throbbed. He thought of binding the scarf round his head for protection, but was frightened that it would slip down and blind him to an on-coming blow. At that moment Azo dismissed the soldiers and Reynald announced that all was ready, so he let the scarf fall and climbed into the fenced square.

His step-father asked, 'Do you want a shield or buckler, Toron?'

'I don't make the rules, Lord Reynald. If you will use one——'

'You know better.'

'Then I'll manage without. But before we start, tell me something. Is it your intention to fight *à outrance*?'

'What? God's elbow, you say some senseless things. I'm not out here to kill you. We will fight for the instruction, and *à plaisance*, for the fun of it. Captain Azo will edge us apart if we get too heated.'

Azo nodded and the combatants moved to opposite sides of the square and drew their swords. As the metal caught the light a murmur rose from the crowd; Humphrey's weapon was three feet long, long enough to be set against any normal opponent, but a mere needle compared with IN NOMINE DOMINI. The slender blade bore no inlaid inscription, though the sword boasted a crystal pommel and terminals carved into leopards' heads. The wooden grip was bound with once-scarlet leather, but the colour had long since worn off. Unlike most knights, Humphrey attached no particular value to the sword. He had slain no monsters with it, nor dispatched any heroes of Islam. He used it when he had to, then hung it with the rest of his armour and forgot about it. It was an invaluable instrument in battle, but a weighty impediment in peace-time. He knew that his attitude was the complete antithesis of Reynald's. It could be nothing else.

Azo called, 'Begin!' and the Lords of Chatillon and Toron moved toward each other.

From the start, Reynald held his sword in both hands. The massive weapon measured four and three quarter feet from point to pommel, while the blade at the hilt was more than five inches wide. It was one of the longest, broadest and heaviest swords in the Christian kingdom at that time and it suited Reynald admirably. It was old—he had carried it at the battle of Montgisard in November of 1177, when the Crusaders had defeated and almost captured Saladin—and he revered it as he could revere no religious object, holding it above even the True Cross. IN NOMINE DOMINI was a part of him. With it he was invincible. Without it—well, it had never yet been taken from him. He could account for every notch and scar, remembered the one time it had been knocked from his grasp—in the mud at Jacob's Ford, two years after Montgisard—but had lost count of the number who had been cut down IN THE NAME OF GOD.

They stepped closer, Humphrey holding his sword low, Reynald resting his with the flat of the blade on his right shoulder. The spectators followed each deliberate, cumbersome movement with interest. They had seen many sword-fights, affairs of honour, drunken brawls, punishments and military conflicts, and they had become expert, if not as participants, then as arbiters. They knew a good swordsman when they saw one, and in Reynald of Chatillon they saw one of the finest. Having set himself against young Humphrey, he guaranteed the outcome. The rest was a matter of time.

Humphrey moved sideways, saw an opening and lunged. The crowd remained mute; it was an obvious trap. As he pushed the narrow sword forward, Reynald swung his left foot back and behind his body, then let IN NOMINE DOMINI scythe down and across. The massive blade caught Humphrey's sword near the tip, lifted it and sent it spinning toward the fence.

'Pray to God,' Reynald said calmly. 'You are a dead man.'

He grinned at Azo and waited for Humphrey to reclaim his sword. In the next few moments he knocked it twice more from his grasp, twice hit him with the flat of the blade, felling him, and finally stabbed at his thigh with the sword point. This last tore the links of the silvered hauberk and sent blood coursing down Humphrey's leg. As he gasped and stumbled against the fence Reynald commented for the sixth time, 'You are a dead man.'

The spectators did nothing to help. Inured to death and the extinction of the weak, they sat on the walls or stood in the doorways, waiting for their overlord to make an end of his step-son. Leaning heavily on the barricade, which threatened to give way, Humphrey watched them and felt the blood run down into his boot. Suddenly, his eyes filled with tears and he raged soundlessly at the rows of attentive faces.

'You devils! You stupid, do-nothing, bastard devils! In the name of God, what do you want? Must the brutal always seize the day? Will you always sit by while they stamp their path? Oh, Christ, it hurts. Isabella, it hurts me so . . .'

While he cursed, a group of servant girls, bored by the proceedings, giggled at something one of them had said. Humphrey believed that they were giggling at him. Normally he would not have cared what such young women thought or said, but now he could no longer separate them from the callous mass of onlookers. Soon more would join in, until Kerak shook with their murderous cackles . . .

Humphrey did then what Reynald was prone to do; he threw over all self-control and lurched, howling, to his feet. Reynald was taken by surprise and stood flat-footed as Humphrey stumbled against him. He made a grab at the young man's swirling tabard, missed and fell backward. IN NOMINE DOMINI slipped from his grasp and, more by accident than intent, Humphrey stamped on the blade.

Later, he could remember none of what followed, but they told him that he stood over the Red Wolf, shouting down at him something about a present from Isabella, a present from the Princess of Jerusalem, and what could Reynald do about that? Then he let his own sword fall, narrowly missing Reynald's open hand, and staggered to the far corner of the square, where Azo had already torn an exit in the fence. They told him that Reynald came to his feet roaring, 'Six to one! Six to one!' but that Azo, supported by the crowd, announced that the contest was over. He thought he remembered bowing low to Stephanie, his mother, though the onlookers said he simply doubled over and collapsed in a cold faint. After that, Azo's men-at-arms collected him and carried him gently to his own chambers, where he was left in the care of his mother and the family physicians. He heard later, from some of his more courageous friends that Reynald of Chatillon remained in his study for three days and could be heard crying and smashing things, probably with IN NOMINE DOMINI. During that time he neither ate, nor drank, and when he eventually emerged he was still wearing his armour.

Three days and nights without water seemed too long, but Humphrey wanted to believe the story. It had the ring of truth about it, because Reynald was known as one who could not abide defeat. It was as well that he did not know about the brooch, or he would insist on fresh instruction, naked and away from the aura of the magic Isabella . . .

# CHAPTER EIGHT

# Ramallah, Nablus, Jerusalem

## *October, November 1183*

Balian of Ibelin's serious minded young squire was day-dreaming. More exactly, he was indulging in an erotic fantasy of limited proportions. He was on his way to Ramallah to wrest Idela from her sick aunt Ermengarde, but in his mind he had already climbed the winding road, entered the walled hill town, located Tower Street and Ermengarde's house and was now wrapped in Idela's welcoming embrace. He had left Lord Balian and Fostus to continue along the rift valley road of Sahl Mukhna toward Nablus, having promised to rejoin them the next morning, with or without Idela.

There was no question of her refusing to leave with him. He had told both men as much and they had grunted and remarked, 'Good news, indeed. Then we'll expect you before nightfall.' Ernoul was not convinced that they shared his optimism, but *he* knew the girl would come with him, and that was all that mattered. The only problem was that, if Ermengarde was really ill, perhaps even on the point of death, he would have to wait around until, she—well, until Idela's ministrations were no longer needed. It was his impartial and heartfelt desire that the old woman would either sustain a miraculous recovery, or die without further delay.

However, in his fantasy she was not only dead, but buried and forgotten, leaving Idela in need of comfort and a friendly face. The herbalist's daughter was standing in the window, gazing wistfully over the terrace hillside toward the Jerusalem road when who should appear, in answer to her unspoken prayers, but the handsome, courteous, magnetic, amusing and virile . . .

She was out in the street before he had time to dismount. Careless of what the passing townsfolk might think she ran to him and embraced him, then took his hand in hers and led him into the cool, shuttered house . . .

'Ah, my love, is it really you? Let me hold you. Let me touch you. I must know that I did not invent you, that you're, aah, yes, my strong, wonderful . . .'

They climbed rickety wooden steps, passed the room in which Ermengarde had died peacefully—'She must have been a fine, brave woman. Oh, she was, she was. But I don't want to think of her. I want you. This is my room. I want you. I want your love, all you can give me, everything, everything . . .'

He reached Ramallah and had to be re-directed twice before he found Tower Street. He rode the length of the street, then back, then along it again, looking for the open window and Idela. The sun was hot and the shutters were closed over every window in the street. He asked two black shawled women if they knew where Ermengarde lived. 'She is ill. A young woman called Idela is nursing her.'

'Ermengarde,' muttered one of the women. 'Ermengarde, Ermengarde. Ill, you say.'

'So I understand.'

The other woman said, 'A young woman called Idela, eh? Nursing her, this Ermengarde.'

'So I—Yes.'

'Idela. How do you spell that?'

He spelt it, and they said, 'Ah, yes, that's the way.'

'Do you know where she—where they—do you know the house?'

'No. In truth, I cannot say I do.'

'Nor I. Ermengarde, was it?'

'Idela, hmm?'

They shook their heads and shuffled away, passing the names between them. He watched them go, grumbled under his breath, then dismounted and banged on the nearest door. There were sixty or so doors in the street, and he wondered how many——

Idela answered it.

'Oh,' she said. 'It's you, Ernoul.'

'Er, yes. Yes, it is. I came by—Are you well?'

'I was never otherwise. It's my aunt who's ill. She was asleep, but I expect you've woken her with your hammering. How did you know I was here?'

'It was simple luck. Of all the doors——'

'I mean in Ramallah.'

'Oh, your father—Look, may I come in? And find some shelter for my horse?'

'In the house?'

'Yes.'

'Your horse?'

'What? No! Me!'

'Go round the back, round that way. There's a stable. Only please keep quiet.'

He nodded, bemused, and led his mount along an alley and under a vine covered bamboo arch to the rear of the house. He found water and grain, unsaddled the animal and left it with three others in the shade of a sagging rush canopy. Then he returned to the street to find the front door shut.

He was hot and dusty and the fantasy had turned to vinegar in his veins; was this tart, efficient nurse the same girl he had met in Rue des Herbes? Was the sum of her welcome to be 'Oh, it's you?' And now she had shut him out in the street, like an unwanted trinket seller. A woman, the daughter of a paste and powder herbalist, denying entry to Lord Balian of Ibelin's squire and chronicler! Jambes de De! It was too much. He rapped angrily on the door, then stood back, his hands on his hips.

This time when she opened the door she was not so restrained.

'What *are* you doing?'

'Trying to gain entry, what else?'

'You're crazy! I told you to go round the back!'

'Don't shout at me! I thought——'

'No you didn't. You didn't think at all. My aunt's room is right above—' She broke off as a querulous voice implored, 'What is it, Idela? Is there a fight in the street? I can't sleep.'

Idela glared at Ernoul, hissed, 'Round the back!' then closed the door quietly but firmly in his face. He heard her answer Ermengarde; 'All is well, Aunt. It was just some poor lunatic,' and he kicked irritably at a half-buried pebble before making a second journey along the alley and under the arch.

He let himself into a cool, grey-tiled kitchen and sat hunched over on a heavy oak bench. Then he stood up again, in case Idela thought he was making himself too quickly at home. As for that, he thought, I've no intention of making my home here. In fact, I'm sorry I ever left the Sahl Mukhna road. I should have stayed with Lord Balian and Constable Fostus instead of wasting my time in the pursuit of some officious little stall girl. So I'm a poor lunatic, am I! Well, I can still catch up with them. I'll stay and tell her what I think of her, then be on my way again. Now where's she gone?

He gazed critically round the kitchen, trying hard to find fault with the spotless pans and cauldrons, the wood-handled knives and spoons, the scrubbed boards, the jars of beans and onions, olives and rough-milled wheat. He noticed a row of herb jars, peppers and marjoram, cloves, nutmeg and almond powder, and thought, I'll wager she doesn't allow Aunt Ermengarde near those. He walked over to a line of casks, lifted the lid of one and sniffed a stew of apricots, known as plums of Damascus. It smelled good—who was the cook, Ermengarde or Idela?—and he was tempted to fetch a spoon and——

'She's asleep again, though I don't thank you for it.' She stood in the inner doorway. Beyond, Ernoul could see a short corridor and a flight of painted stone steps. He frowned, acknowledging that his fantasy had been inaccurate, even to the type of stairs.

Without sincerity he said, 'I'm sorry if I disturbed her.'

'If? You did disturb her.'

'Yes. Well, I'm sorry.'

They stood, each watching the other, the slim young squire, his tanned face whitened with dust, and the dark-eyed, black-haired herbalist's daughter. He thought, however you behave, you're beautiful, and he smiled hesitantly.

She said, 'I don't see what you have to smile—' then shrugged and returned the greeting. 'You should have warned me.' She plucked at her simple linen kirtle. 'I work all day. I don't dress for ——'

'There's no need. You look——'

'—visitors.'

'—most fetching.'

'Were you about to help yourself?'

K.D.R.          H

'Mmm? Oh.' Replacing the lid; 'The fruit. No, I was merely, ah, looking.'

'Sit down. Unless you are in such a hurry——'

'No, I'm not. But won't Ermen—your aunt——'

'I told you, she's asleep. If you keep your voice down she will sleep most of the day. Here, they are quite refreshing.' She placed a bowl of plums on the sanded table, then drew up another bench and sat opposite him. While he ate, she said. 'I am sorry, too. I didn't mean to snap at you, but you startled me.'

Ernoul nodded magnanimously, then asked, 'Why did you not leave a note with your father?'

'Why did you not send one to say you were passing this way?'

'I didn't know I would be.'

'Then this is not a special journey.'

'Oh, yes it is. But I was not sure my Lord Balian would be returning to Nablus. I travel with him. We might have gone south to Kerak again, or across to the coast. Fortunately——'

'I left no note because I, too, was unsure. We've only met each other twice.'

'You thought I would not come?'

'I wasn't sure. You and I——'

'You and I what? Does your father disapprove?'

'Of course not. He allows me great freedom.'

'Then is it—?' pointing at the ceiling.

'No. It's as I said. It's you and I. We're, well, unlikely. I have never been in a castle.'

'And I had never visited Rue des Herbes before I met you. These plums are good. Did you——'

'Aunt Ermengarde. She stews a lot of fruit.'

He nodded again, slid the spoon round the bowl, then pushed it aside.

'Listen to me, Idela. I want you to—I want to ask you something.'

'I cannot.'

'What?'

'I know what you want to say. You want me to leave with you.'

'Yes.'

'I cannot.'

'Oh.'

'Not yet.'

'Oh.'

'When she's well again——'

'Yes?'

'Yes, then perhaps.' She put her hands on the table, so that he could hold them if he cared to and murmured, 'I like you, Ernoul. I respect you and admire you. You're——'

'Yes?'

'You're amusing, usually. I am flattered by your attention. Looking for me at the stall. Riding up here. Asking me to go with you ——'

'Yes, that's right.'

'But you must see, I cannot leave her alone, not yet.'

'No,' he said, 'I suppose not.' He glanced at his spoon, then at her surprisingly elegant hands. He chose the spoon and tapped it unrhythmically against the wooden bowl. It made a hollow clock-clock, so he put it down again.

'How long——'

'—will the illness last? Some weeks, I fear.'

'Dog's vomit!'

'That's not——'

'Oh, I'm sorry. But I could be at the farthest reach of the world by that time.'

'Not quite.'

'You know what I mean. Few men are as busy as Lord Balian.'

'It's not my fault, Ernoul,' she sighed. 'I'd go with—I might think of accompanying you, if it were possible.'

'What's the matter with her?'

'She has stomach pains, and she finds it difficult to move her head. The doctors say——'

'So you'll stay with her until she recovers.'

'I must.'

'Won't your father miss you?'

'He will hire an assistant. Do you want some more fruit?'

'No.' Then, realising that it would prolong his visit, 'Well, yes, a little.'

She refilled the bowl and brought it back to the table. In truth, you're attractive, she thought. I would go with you now, if I could. What a shame you are not a chemist. If you were of my class we might marry and save our money for a shop and I would have your children and they would all be as handsome as you. But you have stepped down from the courts and castles, and when you've taken me away and loved me and lost interest in me there will be no marriage. But I don't mind. If you will wait until my aunt is in good health again, I'll go with you. Which girl would not? I have never been loved and I would like to see Lord Balian's castle, or wherever you take me.

'Here,' she said. 'Will you have some wine?'

'Thank you. Will you?'

'I don't—very well, a little.' She found two pewter mugs, poured the wine and sat opposite him again, her hands on the table, waiting to be touched.

'Good,' Ernoul commented, his mouth full. 'Tell your aunt, that is, if you tell her I was here——'

'I won't.'

'Well, that's for the best, perhaps.'

'Where will you go now, I mean, when you leave?'

'On to Nablus. The king has convened a council of barons, but first they have to be found and alerted. Letters must be written——'

'I can write,' she volunteered.

Ernoul coughed into his mug. 'Can you? That's excellent.' He reached forward and patted her hands. 'Well done! There are not so many.'

Idela blushed from his praise and because at last he had touched her. Pressing her good fortune she added, 'And, of course, I read. I enjoy fables and songs; the stories of Charlemagne.'

'Yes, yes! Wonderful. I allow, I did not think you could—would——'

'I understand. Oh, yes, I have the appetite for it.' With inspired insight she mourned, 'But I lack the opportunity. As you say, there are not so many of us. If I could find the books——'

'I'll bring you some. Do you like poems?'

'Did I not say so? Poems best of all.'

'How strange. I, uh, sometimes, when I'm not too busy——'

'*You* write poems?'

'Mmm.'

'Please, you must show me some. I've never met a poet.'

'Well, I'm not a, not what you might term——'

'But if you write poems, you are a poet.'

'Put so,' he shrugged modestly, 'I suppose I am, in a way.'

'I'm sure you are a fine poet. When will you——'

'That depends on Lord Balian. If I am not required to assist him with the king's convention, I could return in four or five days.'

'Four?'

'So be it. Four. But will your aunt——'

'I'll give her something.' She smiled. 'I know a herb that induces sleep. It's harmless, of course.'

'Naturally. Idela?'

'Yes?'

'Thank you for—' He gestured aimlessly, then concluded '—the plums and wine.'

'It gives me pleasure, dear Ernoul.'

He coughed again, inspected her hands and said, 'You keep them well. They're—well-kept hands.'

'Thank you. Yours seem very strong.'

'It's the riding. It toughens them.'

'Yes, I expect it does.'

They sat in silence for a moment, each awkwardly studying the other's hands. Then Ernoul nodded, as though Idela had told him something, and stood up. He drained his mug, said, 'I must hurry if I am to catch my Lord Balian,' and put the mug down over-hard on the table. 'I will do my best to return in three, I mean four days.'

'I will look for you, my dear Ernoul. And don't forget your poems.'

She went with him to the back door, moving close behind him. He turned abruptly—what is the matter with me, he thought, I'm moving like a pole-axed ox—and accidently swept his arm against her breasts.

'I'm sorr——'

'It's noth——'

He caught her by the shoulders and she rested her hands on his hips. Then they sought no more excuses and embraced with clumsy exhilaration.

*He is strong. He, aah . . . Well, now, Fostus, this'll stop your taunts . . .*
*Four days . . . Die, you feeble old woman, let her free . . . I'll memorise*
*every word he writes . . . Idela, Idela . . . which castles will we see? I'll*
*be terrified, no, not with you beside me . . . Idela . . .*

They moved apart, smiled and bade each other a demure good-
bye. She waited in the doorway until he had saddled his horse, then
indicated that he should lead the horse round, while she crept to the
front of the house. When she opened the street door he was mounted
and waiting. They whispered good-bye again and he rode away
through the hot, dead town. She waited until he had turned east,
toward the town gates, then closed the door quietly. Humming to
herself, she walked back to the kitchen to wash the bowl and mugs
and to gaze at where he had sat and stood. Then she hunted for the
sleeping draught that Aunt Ermengarde would take in soup in four
days time.

Ernoul's fantasy had not come true, yet could not compare,
would never compare with the reality. He rode at reckless speed
along the Sahl Mukhna road, mumbling, not caring that the dust
blew into his mouth. Could dust ever prevent a poet from com-
posing lines dedicated to a beautiful, dark-eyed girl?

Ernoul failed to overtake the Lord and Constable of Nablus and
learned, not for the first time, that Balian of Ibelin could behave
with as much severity as any feudal castellan. Fostus was in no way
involved, yet found to his disgust that his sympathies were aroused
and divided evenly between his irate master and the protesting
squire. Ernoul's stupidity might have been overlooked at another
time, but now time and tempers were running short.

What had happened, on the young man's own admission, was
that he had driven his horse so hard in his efforts to catch up with the
riders that the animal had eventually stumbled and gone lame. This
necessitated his making a five mile journey on foot in the furnace
heat of the valley, heading northward along the road to the nearest
village. When he had reached it he had purchased a fresh horse and
saddle and arranged for a cart to be sent back to reclaim the injured
palfrey. As though that was not trouble enough, he had then ridden
a hundred yards out of the village on the fresh horse, shaken his
head and collapsed in a heat faint. The villagers had carried him

back and put him to bed, stabled the horse—who may have wondered at the brevity of his outing—then sent the local veterinarian off in the cart to bring back the lame animal. The veterinarian was actually a blacksmith and only treated animals to supplement his earnings, so he decided to charge for the heat as well as the distance and spent the ten miles there and back counting on his fingers.

It was not until two mornings later that Ernoul rode into Nablus, the city called 'little Damascus,' and made his way up the hill road to the castle. He had stretched his leave of absence by a night and a day, and Balian was in no mood for pleasantries.

When Ernoul presented himself in the library, Balian snapped, 'I was on the point of dispatching a search party. I hoped they would not find you still in Ramallah.'

'They would not, my lord.' He recounted his story, while Balian listened without expression. When he had finished he was told, 'You may expect no refund for either animal. If, in truth, you left your lady when you say you did——'

'Yes, I swear——'

'—then you had no need to travel so fast. You were told to report here, in the castle, yesterday morning. Now you are late, overspent and a victim of the heat. What value are you to me at this time should I need some urgent service of you?'

Ernoul hung his head and thought, how do I tell you that I was wearing the wings of love?

Angry though he was, Balian had already guessed the reason for the accident. He said, 'I imagine your visit was a success——'

'Well——'

'—and that you were hurrying after us to crow about it. You're loyal and industrious, but I cannot believe that it was merely your anxiety to return to duty. No doubt you will want to visit her again.'

Ernoul shrugged. 'If I happen to be passing that way.'

'Yes, I'm sure,' Balian smiled wryly. 'However, I hope you have not arranged to pass that way on a set date and day.'

*In two days' time.*

'Oh, no. I would not think of——'

'That's as well, because I have several commissions for you. Word

of the king's council is on the lips of the people: God knows how
they learn of these things so quickly. So our friends and allies
must be brought to King Baldwin before others move to delay the
meeting. I am sending you with a letter for Walter Garnier, Lord of
Caesarea . . .'

*On the coast, some thirty miles north-west of Nablus. Time enough to
return here, then ride south*——

'When you have delivered it to him in person, you will go down
to my brother Baldwin's domain of Ramleh. I'm told that Reginald
of Sidon is staying with him, so we can catch two loyal fish with
one net.'

*Forty miles south of Caesarea. Twenty or more from Ramallah. I
cannot keep the tryst. Aah, Idela*——

'From there you will go directly to my house in Jerusalem. When
were you supposed to see her?'

'Two days from now,' Ernoul blurted. 'I mean——'

'I know full well what you mean. You mean that you hate me
and our Lords of Caesarea and Ramleh and Sidon, and the king and
his politics, and all councils and letters and anything that keeps you
from that dusty hill town. I advise you not to make a habit of lying
to me, but I know what you mean and I understand it.' He paused
and looked down at the quills and parchment rolls on the table in
front of him. Then, facing Ernoul again, he said, 'You've taken my
anger fairly; will you now accept my apology? Not for the anger,
that was correctly placed, but for driving a wedge between you and
Mistress, ah——'

'Idela.'

'Yes, of course.' He turned to the single library window. It was
a rarity—small, uneven diamond panes of coloured glass set in a
heavy lead frame. There were no latches or hinges and the window
was sealed in place. The glass had been brought from Constantinople
in 1178, and the window fitted while Balian was absent from
Nablus. On his return Queen Maria Comnena had taken him to the
library and shown him the window—her present to him. Like
most men, he had asked, 'Why?'

'Because you light my life,' she had told him. Then, like most
women, she asked, 'It pleases you, doesn't it?'

Balian treasured the window and, when no-one was looking, he would sometimes stand on a bench and wipe the glass with a rag. Now the crimson and violet diamonds made a player's mask of his face. He blinked orange eyes and moved dark green lips as he mused, 'This meeting. I am of the opinion that it will tear the kingdom like rotten cloth.'

'Do you know what the king will do to Regent Guy, sire?'

'No, but he is no longer interested in the exchange of cities. It will go beyond that. Danger builds up ahead of us, my friend.'

Ernoul said, 'Danger for Guy, I hope.'

'I hope for nothing of the kind,' Balian corrected. 'Guy is weak, but so is the kingdom. None of us will gain from bleeding each other.' He moved and his lips turned blue as he added, 'Christ, if only he had accepted Baldwin's offer!'

'Perhaps he would have done so, if Amalric had not forbade it.'

'Amalric? He has a simple creed concerning Guy. He wants his brother to do everything he says, and refuse everything others tell him. What with the Lusignans and the Courtenays—' He sighed and ran the tips of his fingers over the lower panes. 'We're like this window. All of the same shape, yet each of a different thickness and colour. The lead binds us, but lead can be so easily melted . . .'

Ernoul nodded, though could think of nothing to say.

Balian stood for a moment, scouting the uncertain future. Then he brought his hand down and turned from the window. 'Enough of this; I'm no seer. If you're ready, let's make some progress with these letters.'

That evening, Ernoul found Fostus in the main armoury.

Although he had noticed the squire ride in during the morning and had subsequently learned of the lame horse and the heat stroke, he could not resist taunting him about Idela. He let Ernoul wait awhile, then looked up from a pile of carefully selected cross-bow bolts and grunted, 'Oh, it's you. Just arrived?'

Ernoul had come with the express purpose of asking a favour of the constable, so he stifled a retort and said, 'I know I was late back. Lord Balian made me smart for it. I thought you'd have heard about it by now.'

'I never listen to petty gossip. Your late-coming is not so remarkable, is it?'

'I don't mean—Listen, Fostus, will you help me? I have to leave for Caesarea at dawn. I want to send word to Ramallah——'

'To your lover?'

'She isn't yet, but believe what you will. Anyway, I said I would visit her there in two days' time——'

'That was foolish.'

'Perhaps it was. Anyway——'

'You're tongue-tied. Anyway this, anyway that.'

'Anyway,' Ernoul insisted, 'by then I'll be on the road to Ramleh. If you could find some excuse to——'

'You want one of my men to waste their time running errands for you, is that it?'

Ernoul wanted to point out that they were Lord Balian's men. Instead, he said, 'Please. It's important to me.'

'What do you want sent, a letter?'

'Yes, and some—just a letter.'

Fostus selected more vicious looking bolts. 'I don't know. I'll have to see who's free.'

Ernoul nodded and remembered not to thank him. But he knew Fostus would do it. He had not said yes straight out, nor had he said no. But he would arrange it, and he knew that Ernoul knew it.

They continued with the pretence, the squire saying, 'Yes, see who's free,' and the constable growling, 'Write your silly letter. It may get sent; it may not. And don't fall off your horse again.'

'Then you did hear about it.'

'It was not to be avoided. Everybody laughing...'

Ernoul wrote his silly letter by candlelight. He also wrote a poem —TO IDELA—a flowery, ill-disciplined affair that was intended to make her smile at his wit and weep at his absence. The poem made a nice balance with the business-like letter of apology, but in order to give her a better impression of his range, he also included two other poems and his account of the confrontation between Lord Balian of Ibelin and Lord Reynald of Chatillon at Kerak, last June. He sent no books, because he had written none, and did not want her to be confused by conflicting styles.

When he took the package to Fostus, the hirsute warrior weighed it in one hand and asked, 'Am I supposed to find you a horseman, or a camel train? What more can you find to say to her, after she has leafed through this?'

'Quite a lot.'

Misunderstanding him, Fostus said, 'Indeed it is.'

They came from Nablus and Caesarea, Ramleh and Antioch, Tiberias and the great Hospitaller fortress of Belvoir. They came, the loyal barons, together with the Grand Master of the Hospital, because Baldwin the Leper had summoned them. This alone proved that his strength was not yet gone.

Other leaders were not invited and did not make the journey to Jerusalem. Guy of Lusignan remained in Ascalon, Reynald of Chatillon in Kerak. The Grand Master of the Temple, Arnold of Toroga, stayed in the Templar stronghold of Safed.

Still more were in Jerusalem itself, but were barred from the council. The Seneschal of the Kingdom, Joscelin of Courtenay, along with his sister Agnes, Patriarch Heraclius and the Constable of the Kingdom, Amalric of Lusignan, were all refused entry to the Royal Palace. They knew the nature of the meeting—it might be King Baldwin's last chance to exert pressure on his recalcitrant Regent—but they did not know, none knew, exactly what fate he had planned for corn-haired Guy.

Little had changed in the throne room. The young monarch still lay inside the gauze tent and was still propped up with scented pillows and silk cushions. He was still guarded, but now by a special detachment composed of men-at-arms from his own household, plus two Hospitallers and two donated by Raymond of Tripoli. This was no time for equality; however fast the vile disease corroded his body, however much he might welcome death, he had to be safeguarded from sword thrust and arrow shot. When the king died it would be at God's decree, not a Frank's.

The palace had been scoured for chairs and six of them were now arranged in a half-circle, facing the curtained pallet. The members of the council had gathered at Balian's house and come on with him; the king's secretary fetched them from the ante-chamber and they entered, two by two, knelt before the bed, then took their seats. The royal guard manned the doors and windows, while the squires and stewards took their places behind their respective warlords.

Baldwin's secretary, with two clerical assistants, settled himself at a small desk, ready to record the meeting.

Ernoul's first thought—pure vanity—was that the secretary looked frail and tired, and would probably never write a history of the kingdom. It was a pity, because the old man held a unique position; he was witness to all the decisive moments in the affairs of Palestine, and had access to every document and record in the royal coffers. Against which Ernoul had half a letter from King Baldwin to Reynald of Chatillon, the half that had rolled from the *table dormant* when Bloodhead had hacked out his answer to the king's demands. He eyed the secretary until the old man caught him looking, then dropped his gaze and waited for Baldwin to speak.

'My gentle lords. You have all travelled from other cities to be with me here. Some of you have covered a great distance. You, Raymond, who with Balian helped bring about this council, and you, Grand Master Roger. To all of you I would show my gratitude, and wish only that your numbers were doubled.'

Some of the barons leaned forward in their chairs. Baldwin's voice was failing, there was no doubt of it. They made an effort to keep silent, knowing he would be unable to repeat his words.

'You are here, as you know, because I need your advice in the matter concerning my present Regent, Guy of Lusignan, and the offer I made to him to exchange jurisdiction of Tyre for that of Jerusalem. It was my intention to move the palace up to Tyre and to give Guy some measure of control of this windy city.'

The barons had already seized on two points. Baldwin had spoken of Guy as 'my present Regent'. Did this mean that the Poitevin was to be deposed? Secondly, he had said that it *was* his intention to move. Was he no longer pursuing his offer? Now it required no effort for them to stay silent. The Leper King had already planned his stratagem. It was not their advice he sought, but their nod.

'However, as you also know, that offer was flatly rejected. He claimed I was laying a trap for him, putting him among his enemies, so on and so forth. There was no trap, and his enemies are his own affair. But I will not be gainsaid over some reasonable request. My Seneschal is against me. So is my Constable. And now my Regent. I swear to you, if I could rise from this mattress, if I could shed this filthy skin, if I could only do that—' He coughed feebly and a physician appeared from nowhere, pushed aside the curtain and poured a few drops of dull liquid into his gaping mouth. After a moment Baldwin moved his head and the phsycian withdrew.

'I am sorry. I am too ill to pretend otherwise. Anger turns pathetic on my tongue. Yet—I am coldly angry, don't think me incapable of the emotion. It comes with the knowledge that I have hatched a nest of vipers. I have, it seems, made an error in all my most influential appointments. It's past time I did something to rectify them. In Guy's case I am about to do so.' He paused to catch his breath, then said, 'With your unanimous approval I shall depose Count Guy of Lusignan from the post of Regent of the Kingdom of Jerusalem, confiscate the lands he holds at Ascalon and Jaffa, seize control of those several other cities and fiefs I allotted him and, in his stead, appoint my former Regent, Count Raymond of Tripoli, Lord of Tiberias. Do you so approve?'

There was a gasp and a shout. Yes!

Baldwin let his eyes roll sideways. His secretary signalled for silence.

'Furthermore,' he whispered, 'I intend to seal the door on Guy and all his faction, by proclaiming my baby nephew and namesake heir to the throne of Jerusalem.'

There was another gasp and Reginald of Sidon exclaimed, 'But he's Guy's step-son!'

'He is,' Baldwin agreed, 'and he is also the son of my fool's-mate sister, Sibylla. A nicety, don't you think? Now the Lusignans will have the thankless task of raising young Baldwin as a constant reminder that he will one day reign and they won't. Guy's buttocks will itch like the devil, but he'll never scratch them with the throne.' He stretched his eaten lips in a grotesque smile and boasted happily, 'I find the idea not far short of brilliant. Raymond will govern during the child's minority; you will all give him such assistance as is necessary. And I—I will gain some quiet satisfaction, knowing that I have cut off the heads of a few Frankish vipers. I would that they were Moslems, but a snake is always dangerous, whether in the hills or the house. In the matter of the child then, do you approve?'

They nodded. They had reservations, but these they kept to themselves. Guy was unlikely to accept the loss of his title and his lands without a fight. The question was, could he be broken before the kingdom was thrown into the turmoil of civil war? What help would Amalric give him? Or Joscelin? Or Reynald? If they added their weight to his, the kingdom would hang in a precarious balance...

As for placing Sibylla's son on the throne of Jerusalem, that presented even graver problems. The child was sick, had always been sick, and showed no signs of improvement. If he was to be proclaimed heir, he must be brought into safe-keeping before the feather-brained princess starved or smothered him. Then he must be guarded night and day for as long as was necessary. And what if the soldiers and physicians failed to keep him alive? How long would the Lusignans and Courtenays and Chatillons acknowledge Raymond of Tripoli as their ruler? Would they even accept him now as Regent?

Yet, with all these reservations, the barons were convinced that King Baldwin had acted correctly. The present situation could not be allowed to continue. He had chosen to tear open the vipers' nest. It now remained to be seen which among them would be first bitten.

# CHAPTER NINE

# Kerak

## *November 1183*

The Lusignan-Courtenay alliance reacted predictably to Baldwin's demands. Joscelin, the Patriarch Heraclius and Arnold of Toroga came to plead with the king, stayed to argue and were ejected from the palace by the royal guard. The sick child was snatched from Sibylla and given into the care of the court at Jerusalem. Sibylla had never cared much for her son, but now she made a show of protest, claiming that her brother monarch was no better than a thief. When this tactic failed she retired with Guy to Ascalon, where they closed the city gates against the king's agents. Joscelin of Courtenay made the mistake of insisting that, as the child's uncle, he should take care of young Baldwin. The king consented with alacrity; it gave him the opportunity to have his Seneschal watched, his every movement noted.

With Guy barricaded in Ascalon, Raymond of Tripoli caught up the reins of the regency. He was ably assisted by his fellow peers, though Balian of Ibelin was excused so that he might return to Nablus and help his wife in preparation for an event of some importance to the family. This was the forthcoming marriage of his step-daughter, Princess Isabella of Jerusalem, and Reynald of Chatillon's step-son, Humphrey of Toron. The ceremony was set for November 19th, at Kerak, and was, by any judgement, an extraordinary mixture of sugar and salt.

Queen Maria Comnena had little time for Stephanie of Milly and less for Reynald and his friends. Balian, himself, was a sworn opponent of all that the Lord of Kerak held dear and, like Maria, he had nothing in common with the Red Wolf's pack. Joscelin and Agnes of Courtenay might be there, as might Amalric of Lusignan and the Grand Master of the Temple. The knights of Shaubak would be invited, plus an upstart Templar named Gerard of Ride-fort, who was fast becoming a protégé of Reynald's. There would be the usual motley collection of minor barons and, if he knew anything about Reynald, several representatives of Italian commerce and Bedouin brigandage.

For their part, Balian and Maria would go with a small group from Nablus and whoever else among their friends was free. Unfortunately, Raymond of Tripoli was still trying to get Guy out of Ascalon without laying siege to the city, and had taken Reginald of Sidon as his aide. Balian's brother, Baldwin of Ramleh, would come and hopefully so would Walter of Caesarea and Roger of Les Moulins. The king's physicians had been approached as to the state of his health, but they had insisted that he was too ill to make the journey.

So Balian went home to his wife and step-daughter and allowed them, this once, to inveigle him into sharing the problems that confronted a worried mother and an eleven-year-old bride-to-be.

In Kerak, both Reynald and Humphrey were out in public again. The citadel was large enough for them to avoid contact, save at mealtimes, or when the court was in session. Humphrey still carried the scars of the month old 'martial instruction,' but he had risen in the esteem of civilian and soldier alike. He had proved himself inventive at the quintain, lucky in the sword-fight, and courageous in both. They had not thought he had it in him. So far as they were concerned he now had every right to return to his books; he had earned their respect and they were satisfied.

Reynald, of course, was far from satisfied. He still did not know in the heart of his heart if he had really intended to kill his step-son. He professed innocence to Azo and those others who dared discuss it with him, but it annoyed him to see Humphrey up and about, the hero of the crowd, one of the very few to escape IN NOMINE DOMINI and only the second man ever to knock the sword from his hand. For a short while he made a sincere attempt to turn the incident to profit—'Humphrey is a product of Kerak, and he is my step-son. He has drawn his skills from me. He has become a warrior because he lives with a warrior. It is as though I fought against myself.'—

but he did not believe it. It had been a fortuitous accident. If they were to fight again to-day, Humphrey would fall quickly and stay down.

Also, the business of the silver armour still rankled. Humphrey was right when he had shouted, 'What can you do about that?' Reynald knew there was nothing he could do. Humphrey had claimed that he had received a present from Isabella, Princess of Jerusalem and his future wife, leaving Reynald with no choice but to call off the wedding, or swallow his anger.

If he had known that Humphrey was referring to the silver brooch and not the armour he would have extracted the truth from him, by strappado or thumb-screw.

Looking back, Humphrey realised that this misapprehension was the luckiest part of the whole dreadful day. Well, no, it wasn't luck. It was pure, sweet magic.

A few hours after the fight he had mentioned to his mother that it would be better for everybody if she kept silent about her present to him. She gave one of her delicate, if-you-say-so shrugs and asked him if he had made a list yet of the people he wanted at his wedding. He named three or four, commented on his paucity of friends—thanks to Lord Reynald's anti-social ways—then said, 'Doesn't it concern you that no honourable man will come here without protest? You, yourself, have hardly any friends. You are the châtelaine of the second greatest fortress in the kingdom——'

'I have Reynald,' she said simply.

'Yes,' Humphrey sighed, 'and I grant you he is not from the usual mould. But is any one man really enough?'

'Enough for what? He is my husband. I ask little or nothing of him, only that he be——'

'You don't talk together. In all my life I cannot remember a time when you did.'

'What nonsense. We speak at length. Not all our words have to fall on your ears.'

'I didn't suggest——'

'And as for the other aspects, I have troubadours and jongleurs, maids, nurses, children and travellers. There are always travellers passing through.'

'That may be,' he said, 'but I mean intimates, confidantes, the

wives of other nobles. Look, you do not enjoy the company of
Queen Maria, nor that of Raymond's wife, Eschiva. Nor, on the
other side, Agnes of Courtenay, or Princess Sibylla——'

'I quite like Agnes.'

'You loathe her, as we all do. It's politic to say otherwise, that's
all. Tell me what you have in common with Agnes.'

'Well—We both enjoy Kerak.'

Humphrey exploded. 'Enjoy it? She doesn't enjoy it, she covets
it!'

'And flowers.'

'Oh, and flowers. Your cooks probably like flowers, but I don't
see you in conversation with them.'

'Say what you will, I'm content.'

'Yes,' he murmured, 'I believe you. That's the sadness of it. Or
perhaps it's a mercy.'

'I don't know what you mean by sadness and mercy, but then
sometimes I don't understand you at all. Are these four young men
the only ones you wish to invite?'

'No, Mother, they are not. But they are the only four I know who
will dare to come. Still, with luck I will have Lord Balian's squire to
converse with. Perhaps Reynald will challenge *him* to single combat; he's about as strong as I.' He rubbed his eyes wearily, then
gazed at Stephanie and said, 'Do you know something terrible,
Mother? When the wedding is over I will go and take my place in
the family castle, *my* family castle at Toron, and I will then be just
like the others. It would take a very special compulsion to bring me
back here again, even for a day. I don't share your love of this place,
nor its master. What do you think of that?'

'I think it's stupid, hurtful talk. You'll visit us, and we will visit
you——'

'Oh, no. You may come as often as you please. I encourage it;
it's time you stepped beyond these walls. But not Reynald. His lair
is here. I'll not have him soiling mine.'

'You should not speak——'

'I give you my word. My step-father will not set foot in Toron
And if he tries to——'

'You should not speak so about your——'

'If he tries to, Mother, I will stand in the gateway with a cross-bow and shoot him before he reaches the drawbridge. God be my witness.'

Stephanie chewed her lip and went away, leaving her son to his books and his dreams . . .

Isabella spent the week prior to her departure for Kerak listening to a variety of stories, some pleasant, some horrific. Directly, or indirectly, they all had to do with the wedding night. She was amazed at the number of women who insisted that she be the receptacle for their experience and ignorance. The older ones, who had been married perhaps three or four times and had had a dormitory of lovers, told her that one man had done this to them, another had done that. The first husband was a risible lover, the third magnificent. She heard how some men concealed their shyness with violence, how others would only make love in total darkness, or with their clothes on, or their eyes tight shut. The women recited tales of brutality, bestiality, or, with a blush or a laugh, told how some were unable to—how should they put it?—enter the temple of love. The eleven-year-old princess listened solemnly to the flow of memory and opinion, then relayed what she had heard to her mother. Queen Maria Comnena was horrified, though sensibly did not betray her feelings. Instead, she told Isabella how it was with her and Balian, how she hoped it would be for Isabella, once Humphrey shared her bed.

The girl asked, 'But suppose he cannot, what they said, suppose he's unable?'

'Sadly, it's a common enough failing among men out here. But it can be cured. If it should be so with him, send him to speak with Lord Balian.'

'Was he ever like that, unable?'

Maria smiled. 'No, but he would not think poorly of one who was. Though I feel we are putting the most dreadful slight on the handsome Humphrey.'

'No matter,' Isabella said promptly. 'If I'm to help him, if he needs such help, I must know how.'

'Then, as I say, if he should be too nervous, and so for a while incapable, send him to our Lord Balian.'

'What if he beats me? I've heard that many men take a stick to their wives. Does my step-father——'

'He has no need.'

'I don't think I would mind,' the girl said. 'If it was done with love, I mean. Or if I deserved it.'

Maria raised her eyebrows. 'But no-one has ever laid a hand on you.'

'No, but it would be different with Humphrey. I wouldn't mind what he did. Don't you think he's the most wonderful man who was ever in the kingdom?' Her eyes shone and she bubbled with laughter.

'I've heard,' she said, 'of course, I don't know how true it is, but I have heard that there are men who—' She dropped her voice to a whisper and continued, 'who ask their women to beat *them*! With sticks and branches and such! Is that possible? I hope Humphrey is not so inclined. He has beautiful skin. I couldn't bear to hurt him.' She regained her matter-of-fact tone. 'But don't worry. If I find he has trouble of that sort, I'll send him to Lord Balian. Now, what else should I know?'

Well, Maria thought, at least you will not hide your body, or hang your head as I was taught to do. Poor Balian, he had a miserable month when we were first married. Humphrey is luckier than he can know. His young bride will be more woman to him than most who are twice or three times her age. A man needs that, but I gave Balian a chilly month before I learned it.

'What else?' she replied. 'Very little, I would say. You seem as well appraised of the facts as anyone.'

'I think I am,' the girl nodded. 'I only hope he is.'


November 16th . . . 17th . . . 18th . . .

The chaos of preparation took on a more ordered shape. The guests arrived in groups of ten and twenty, each with a heavily-armed escort. It was rumoured—when was it not?—that a Saracen raiding party had been seen in Moab, so the guests wasted no time in reaching the walls of Kerak. Reynald enjoyed his new role of host, protector and paterfamilias. He welcomed his friends, acted as guide for those who had not visited the fortress before and behaved with rare indulgence toward the lower order. He shook hands with smiths and carpenters, commended lonely wall guards, and several times went out of his way to exchange a joke with the sentinels who manned the watchtowers.

Stephanie glowed with pride. Here was her answer to all those who thought him gross and brutal.

'Look at him now, and listen to him, then tell me if he is anything but a courteous man, a gentleman.'

Reynald's urban friends reached Kerak within a few hours of each other. Joscelin of Courtenay came with his fifty-year-old sister, Agnes, and there was speculation in the kitchens as to whether or not she would seek a fifth husband among the noble gathering. The weight of opinion was in favour of her finding somebody, if only because, as they put it, 'The pinch-faced hellcat has already bedded every easy man in the land.' The cooks and serving girls were unashamedly spiteful toward Agnes. After all, free men were scarce—unless one wanted to marry a dirty-fingered farmer, or a drunken soldier—yet at fifty she was able to fill her bed like a basket in an apple orchard.

Amalric of Lusignan arrived, accompanied by the Grand Master of the Temple and the young Templar knight, Gerard of Ridefort. It was as well that Raymond of Tripoli was immersed in his work as regent, for Gerard of Ridefort nurtured a deep and abiding grudge against him. The young Flemand had reached the Holy Land ten years earlier and had joined the Count of Tripoli's household. Gerard was a penniless adventurer, seeking, like so many, 'hand and land.' Raymond told him what he told every other new recruit. 'Serve me loyally and do your work well and in time I will give you a place and a woman of your own.' He did not like Gerard— he found the knight sullen and churlish—but he was prepared to admit that he fought well, though with a complete disregard for his own safety or that of his companions. Gerard was a weighty young man, with a round face and cheeks that gave him the appearance of one who lived with his mouth full of food. He was not Raymond's kind, physically or mentally; nevertheless, the dour warlord favoured him in an attempt to smother his dislike.

Then, within a year of Gerard's arrival, the vassal Lord of Botrun died, bequeathing his territories to his daughter Lucia, now Raymond's ward. Gerard asked for her hand in marriage. Without hesitation, Raymond refused. He could no more imagine Gerard and Lucia sharing bed and board than—well, than a pig and a pelican.

If the Count of Tripoli had allowed some other knight, better suited, to marry his ward, he might have contained Gerard's anger. But he did not. In a display of uncharacteristic cupidity he gave the girl to a Pisan merchant named Plivano, and took in exchange the bride's weight in gold coin. In this way he made himself ten thousand besants and an implacable enemy. Gerard left his employ and joined the Knights of the Temple.

By 1183 he was regarded as the logical successor to Grand Master Arnold of Toroga . . .

Reynald treated the young Templar to a noisy and effusive welcome, then took him on a conducted tour of the castle. They had met before in Jerusalem, but this was Gerard's introduction to Kerak. He was suitably impressed.

'There are others,' Reynald told him. 'Not so large, but adequate for your needs. 'We'll have to secure one for you. Though, if my friend Toroga were to waste away——'

'Say it not, Prince,' Gerard murmured piously. 'The Grand Master is a great man. I have never served better.'

'Then we won't say it,' Reynald winked. 'But if it were to happen, you would have your pick of strongholds. The Temple controls a good many of them, and you're sure to be elected. Just be patient, my friend.'

'I am, Prince. Naturally in time I would wish for a domain of my own, but for the present I am content to serve men like yourself and my Grand Master.'

Reynald clapped him on the shoulder and sniffed the air. 'Wine,' he said. 'Let's hunt it down.'

The light was fading as Isabella arrived with her mother and step-father and the entourage from Nablus. They crossed the deep north fosse, rode under the wall that separated the castle from the town, then turned south again, wending their way through the inner fortifications. They dismounted in a flower-strewn yard, and Balian led Isabella forward to be presented to the châtelaine of Kerak.

'My,' Stephanie essayed, 'you are a beautiful young lady. It's so long since I last saw you——'

'And since I saw Humphrey. Where is he, Lady Stephanie?'

'You'll see him soon enough, child.'

'I'll have to, if I'm to marry him,' the girl retorted. 'But I want to know where he is now. Then I can hold a picture of him in my mind.'

'Yes, well, I expect he's being rehearsed by the priests.'

'Don't you know?' Isabella pressed her. 'I would know where he was every moment of the day.'

Balian grinned to himself, but made no attempt to extricate Stephanie. He decided it would do her good to match wits with an eleven-year-old. She might learn something from her future daughter-in-law.

'He is,' Stephanie said, 'he is with the priests.' Then, changing direction, 'Dear Balian, do we find you well? And Maria. You show no ill effects from your journey, but then I remember you never do.'

Maria smiled and inclined her head. She thought Stephanie over-painted, but was happy to concede that her hostess had a charming simplicity about her. They were not friends and would never be close, though Maria hoped that this time the reason for their meeting would be sufficient to draw them together. It would be a pity if the mother of the bride could not hold hands with the mother of the groom.

She said, 'I am sure the journey is as nothing compared with the effort you have engaged in here. I know this will be a fine marriage——'

'If I could only see Humphrey,' Isabella piped. 'Not speak to him, just see him.'

'You will do both,' Maria said sternly, 'but in good time. Now, come with me.' She glanced at Stephanie, who hastened, 'Ah, yes, of course. We have given over to you the entire north tower. The round tower. The, ah, wedding chambers are on the upper floor. The rest is as you wish to arrange it. Shall I lead the way?'

Isabella sniffed and trailed after her parents. It seemed rather pointless to be going to the wedding chamber without Humphrey, and she dragged her feet to register disenchantment.

In fact, Stephanie was wrong. Humphrey had eluded the clergy minutes earlier, when he had seen Balian's party enter the castle. On the pretext that he was searching for some reference to a disputed phrase in the marriage ceremony, he had leapt two at a time down the stairway from the chapel and crouched in the shadow of the wheelwright's shed until the group rode by. He let Isabella and her parents go without a sign—'God, she's a fine-looking girl!'—then stepped out quickly and gestured to Ernoul.

'Dismount! Dismount!' he hissed. 'I want to talk to you.'

Fostus, who was riding alongside the squire, thought, Hellfire! Young Toron doesn't want to go through with it. He wants a horse. He's bound to ride out of here.

He put a heavy hand on Ernoul's arm, then thought, nonsense, and released him. Ernoul slid from his horse, let Fostus grab the reins and edged over to where Humphrey waited. They greeted each other warmly, something they had been unable to do during Ernoul's last visit to Kerak in June.

'You seem well, my lord.'

'Do I! In truth I'm bruised from head to foot. Did you hear of the fight I had with Reynald?'

'I heard that you gave a magnificent account of yourself.'

'Luck and magic, I swear it. I thought he was out there to kill me. I still believe he would have if I had not——'

'Thank God it was not so.'

'—mastered the quintain. I evolved a completely different approach. You see, instead of riding upright——'

'I'm sorry, but I should rejoin Lord Balian in a moment. If you will tell me later. All the details; I may write about it——'

'Ah, now, that's what I wanted to ask you. Have you written songs?'

'One or two. They're played at Nablus, and I believe Lord Balian's brother took one to Ramleh. But they are not generally known.'

'No matter. I'm sure they have wit and grace. What I must know is this. Will you write one for me?'

'You want one dedicated to you? Because you bested Lord Reynald? Isn't that rather prideful?'

'Idiot! You don't understand. I did not say *to* me. I said *for* me. So that I can give it to the Princess Isabella.'

'But you are better schooled than I, sire.'

'Humphrey. My name is Humphrey.'

'So be it, Humphrey. It doesn't alter the fact that——'

'Oh, you are so wooden. I cannot write songs. I never could. Letters, articles, criticisms, such things, yes, but not songs. It takes a special talent. Will you try? I'll pay you——'

'Not if you value my friendship. I don't want payment from you. I'll do it, or I won't——'

'Well, which is it?'

'I'm thinking.'

'Oh, you artistic men! Can you never stop thinking long enough to decide? I'm supposed to be nodding with the priests at this moment. All I need is a song to be performed for Isabella. To-morrow.'

'To-morrow! No, I'm sorry——'

'Tell me. Have you ever been to Toron? The castle, I mean.'

'What? No, never. What has that to do with——'

'When we are married, Isabella and I, we will go to live in Toron. I would like you to stay with us there. For as long as you wish.'

'I have a girl now.'

'Excellent! Bring her with you. The four of us, we'll have a wonderful time!'

'To-morrow, hmm?'

'Yes.'

'Very well. I'll do what I can. I cannot promise that it will be——'

'Wit and grace, I know it.'

'I don't promise.'

'What a time, the four of us. I thank you, Ernoul. You're a good friend.'

'I'll give it to you after the service, my lo—Humphrey. Now I must go and find——'

'They'll be in the round tower. After the service, then. God speed you. Wit and grace.'

'Wit and grace,' Ernoul mumbled, worried that he had spent all his wit and grace on Idela . . .


November 19th . . .

They dressed her in a plain white chemise, a brown and grey

kirtle that clung to her child's hips and was laced tight below her small, underdeveloped breasts, a fur-trimmed cloak threaded in gold and black, and small pointed leather shoes, embroidered to match the cloak. Her pale, sun-lightened hair was plaited and cross-laced with green ribbon, while the kirtle was further decorated with a heavy silk girdle, again in green. The girdle was tied low in the front and ended in two huge tassels that hung to within a few inches of her shoes. She wore several brooches, agates and rubies set in silver, a cluster of emeralds held together with claws of gold wire, while her thin fingers were hidden by huge, chunky rings, each an an iridescent reminder that the Comnenas and the Ibelins boasted as much history as any at Kerak.

They dressed him in a simple linen shirt, a purple and grey tunic with tight sleeves and wide, pendulous cuffs, and a ginger pelisson, also trimmed with fur. Over the pelisson he wore a mantle, its borders crusted with jewels. His feet were encased in stiff leather shoes and they pinched like the devil. His hair had been curled and larded and now felt as stiff as the unwelcome footwear. Like her, he wore rings, and to reassure her of his love, the magicked silver brooch. They told him he looked resplendent, but all he cared about was that his feet hurt and his head ached. Why wouldn't they let him wear his old boots, and in God's name why did they have to smear that perfumed grease on his hair? If this was what it took to be resplendent, he would rather towel his head and change his shoes and appear ordinary.

When the young couple were ready they were led from their respective chambers to where the families and guests waited in the bailey. The family chapel was too small to hold all those with a right to witness the ceremony, so a group of troubadours and jongleurs headed the procession as it moved slowly across the yard toward the main chapel.

She walked with Balian and Maria. She did not turn her head, though the temptation to do so was becoming unbearable. Here she was, a matter of yards from the church, and they had not yet let her see him. Did they expect her to go through the ceremony without looking to see if it was indeed Humphrey at her side? The idea of it made her giggle, and Maria put a hand on her arm to calm her. Balian, splendid in laced hose, scarlet and grey pelisson and fur-lined mantle, frowned down at her. Then, when she had stopped giggling, he murmured, 'Have you ever heard such an unmusical mob?'

She erupted with mirth and shook her head in agreement. Maria glanced sharply at her husband, then smiled with him. It was true. The musicians of Kerak were making a dreadful racket.

He followed some way behind, separated from her by a crowd of guests, with an escort of dogs and children. He was accompanied by Reynald and Stephanie, and he took good care not to brush against his step-father. He was now so suspicious of Bloodhead that he looked him over quickly to see if he wore a knife. Reynald had never wanted the marriage. It had been forced upon Kerak, as upon Nablus, by King Baldwin. However, in a few moments the children of the rival houses would be joined in wedlock. Unless the groom fell dying from a knife thrust . . .

Reynald was deft enough to do his work unseen, and when it was done he could shout, 'Assassin! Nablus!' or even, 'Jealous suitor!' There were many in the procession at whom he could point an accusing finger; his step-son knew this, so kept his distance.

The reached the chapel and filed inside. Stewards guided the guests to their pews. There was no mingling; Kerak sat with Kerak, Nablus with Nablus. It was cool and quiet in there, and Balian stilled a pang of envy as he looked up at the four, glassed windows. They were not as pretty as the window in his library, but they were much taller, and the top quarter of each window could be pivoted open.

When the guests were settled, the young pair walked forward to take their place at the foot of the choir stalls. Now able to look at each other, but not daring to, they knelt side by side and waited for the churchmen to enter.

They nearly cried out with shock when Heraclius, Patriarch of Jerusalem, took his place at the altar.

Reynald revelled in the murmur that ran round the chapel, then grinned at Stephanie. It had been a well-kept secret.

Mass was said.

Heraclius embellished the celebration with his own brand of sophistry. The man, he said, must remain faithful to his wife, what-soever the temptations of the world. He must be pure of mind and body, scrupulously honest, generous and forbearing. He would have learned much of value from his guardian and step-father, Prince Reynald of Chatillon, Lord of Oultrejourdain, and he must carry those teachings with him, wherever he went. Gratitude was a virtue, and the young man had ample opportunity to show it now.

'He means,' Balian hissed, 'that Reynald would take it well were he to be given a large portion of land in Toron.'

The woman, for her part, should control her own unnatural yearnings until it came time for her to conceive. Men had the demon in them, howling for release, and it was a woman's duty to see that it remained encaged. God had seen fit to bring man and woman together in bed for the sole purpose of procreation, but once the seed was sewn in the woman's belly there was no spiritual advantage to be gained from further love-play.

Answering Balian, Maria whispered, 'In other words, young Humphrey is to give his lands, while Isabella is forbidden to give herself. That paunchy cleric is a brazen liar, and a hypocrite withal. However, I cannot see his advice sitting well with my daughter.'

Balian grunted. 'I doubt if he's so damned pious when he's abed with Agnes of Courtenay or Pashia de Riveri.'

'He makes me sick. If I'd known that Reynald had recruited him for this—' She sighed and held Balian's hand. Heraclius droned on, flattering, condemning, passing out suggestion and monition. To hear him say it, a stranger would think Reynald nothing less than a disciple of Christ and a paragon of virtue. And he took his time saying it, so that, when he had concluded the celebration, the chapel was filled with an audible sigh of relief.

He motioned the couple forward, kissed the groom, then indicated that the young nobleman was free to embrace his wife.

So the seventeen-year-old Humphrey of Toron was married to the eleven-year-old Princess Isabella of Jerusalem, while, in theory, the fiefs and families of Nablus and Oultrejourdain were united, henceforth to act as one in the common cause.

In practice, Reynald strode up the aisle to speak with the Patriarch, and Stephanie hurried over to hug the bride and groom. Balian and Maria were left to make their own way from the chapel. They did so with good humour, though Maria hesitated at the door, loath to leave her daughter so soon in strange hands. It was not

Humphrey who worried her; she judged him an attractive and intelligent young man, and Isabella was clearly dizzy with love for him. But it would unsettle the girl if Heraclius or Lady Stephanie attempted to implement any part of the Patriarch's sermon. The couple should be allowed to stroll together among the guests, showing themselves in their finery and acknowledging the well-wishers. It was no time for discipline or morbid warning. The day now belonged to the children of Toron and Jerusalem.

Fortunately, Reynald and Heraclius disappeared into the vestry, while Stephanie contented herself with an embrace for each of the pair and a fussy, 'Now, come along, you two. Everybody is agog to greet you.'

He is mine, Isabella beamed. I will always love him. I will never let him go. He is mine for ever.

It took Humphrey longer to realise his good fortune, but when he did he summed it up in the thought, from this day forth, I am a free man. Do what they will, they will never bring me back.

Then, with his right arm held forward and slightly raised, and with his little finger crooked round Isabella's, he escorted her out of the chapel and down the washed steps to where their peers attended.

# CHAPTER TEN

# Kerak

## *November 1183*

It was said that when God closed His eyes that night, He found a burning spark lodged under His eyelid. The spark was Kerak, and the lights of the castle blazed too brightly for night to fall . . .

By late evening, most of the female guests were drunk or asleep. Two tradesmen from the town had been killed in brawls, and in both cases their murderers had been absolved by the crowd.

Ernoul had written the song that Humphrey had requested, and it had been passed to Humphrey's favourite troubadour, who had performed it for Isabella. The song—TO ISABELLA—was almost identical with the one he had written—TO IDELA. He assumed that Humphrey would never learn the truth, but scowled nevertheless when he heard his newly-married friend taking the credit for it.

'I didn't know you could do it,' Isabella exclaimed. 'Such style! Such a feeling for——'

'I could not have done it but for you,' Humphrey replied. 'You inspire me. For you I could do anything.' He avoided Ernoul's angry glare and dismissed the troubadour as soon as possible.

The Patriarch Heraclius was seen about the castle with several different women, then was not seen at all for some time. Nor were two of the women.

Stephanie and Maria tried to converse, gave up and drifted apart, only to try again later. They searched doggedly for some common topic of interest, and finally settled on maternal anecdotes and whatever side paths might lead from them. Children could be very useful as the straws with which to kindle conversation.

Balian managed to exchange a few words with his son-in-law and, as he had supposed, found Humphrey an easy companion.

When they had discussed the wedding and the guests, Balian said, 'Will you take it amiss if I proffer advice so soon after your marriage?'

'I would take it amiss if you did not, sire. We have met infrequently, though I learned early to heed what you say. Apart from Lord Reynald's rages and the pious droppings of the Patriarch, advice is in short supply at Kerak and always was. And if I don't like what you say, I'll find the courage to tell you. You wouldn't want it otherwise, I know, my lord.'

'Nicely put,' Balian acknowledged. 'You will have no trouble from me.'

'Nor will I give you any, my word on it. But hand on the advice before Lady Stephanie sends me round again.'

'Just this. Remove yourself and your wife from Kerak without delay. I have an ominous feeling about this place.'

Humphrey grinned. 'Your words tread the heels of my own desires. We'll be gone from here in a week. North to Toron. Gone and for good, be assured of that. I tell you, sire, if I had nothing more to offer Isabella than some forest hovel I would still take her from here without a second thought. It wouldn't look so well, a Princess of Jerusalem in a woodsman's hut, but I'd rather she had a few leaves in her hair than be prey to the vapours of Kerak. Does my attitude anger you, Lord Balian?'

'Far from it. Though, as man to man, let me say this. Respect her because she is a princess, but do not live in awe of it. My wife is a queen. One day Isabella may also be queen. But first they are women, and second our wives. If she will sit with leaves in her hair, it's no concern of mine.' He smiled at the thought, knowing Isabella would enjoy every moment of it. The sweet, grubby little creature. Then he added, 'You will pass through Nablus on your way to Toron. Will you stop a few days? I appreciate that you'll want to reach your own lands——'

'I've waited seventeen years, sire. But once I'm—I mean, once *we* are out of here we'll not be pressed for time. We'll be pleased to stay with you.' Not sure of the response, he said, 'Anyway, you will want to see that Isabella is still happy.'

Balian laughed easily. 'You see clear through me, Toron. And you're right, both Queen Maria and I will look her over with a critical eye. It's expected of us, as her parents. So make sure her bruises are healed by the time you reach Nablus.'

'I promise you,' Humphrey smiled, 'you won't find a mark on her.'

'You know, of course, that the young woman makes a fool of herself over you. At the risk of swelling your head, I can tell you there were times when I grew tired of the sound of your name. Humphrey this, Humphrey that, Humphrey stood, Humphrey sat. Again, as a parent I'm bound to tell you that you're well blessed with her, but I can also say it as a man. And, to be fair, she seems well off with you.' Saving Humphrey from a dutiful reply, he concluded, 'Now go and join her. She probably pines for you; you've been parted too many minutes already.'

Humphrey bowed to his father-in-law and vanished into the gaudy, swirling crowd. Balian stayed where he was until Baldwin of Ramleh tapped him on the shoulder and greeted him with a slurred, 'Hallo, brother. Why aren't you drinking? I'm out to drain this wine shop dry.'

'Indeed? Then success appears to be within your reach.'

'Hmm? Oh, I see. Within my reach. That's very good.' He raised his mug, found it was empty and lurched away again, in search of success.

Isabella was passed from well-wisher to well-wisher. She thanked them for their congratulations, agreed with their advice and laughed politely at their jokes, most of which she had heard before. They drank to her happiness and the children she would bear, to her husband and her new home at Toron, to her wedding dress, and, if they knew her well, to her wedding night. She smiled and nodded and wondered if the night would ever start. How shameful it would be if Humphrey became drunk and, as they said, unable. Or if she fell asleep and had to be awakened so that he might love her. The thought shocked her and she looked round for him. She vowed, the next time he appears I shall untie this girdle and rope him to me. Then the guests might take the hint and leave us in peace.

Amalric of Lusignan and Captain Aegelric of the north garrison moved flat-footed through the castle grounds. They had been drinking heavily and Aegelric had promised to take the Constable of the Kingdom to a place he knew in the lower town where the

women were more compliant than those in Kerak. As they made
their way toward the north gate Aegelric said, 'Prince Reynald is
sure to be there ahead of us.'

Amalric belched a reply. 'What better recommendation could
we have than the presence of our own host at the festivities? You
say these girls are prepared to——'

'Anything,' Aegelric snapped. 'You'll see. I've told you what it's
like there. If you choose not to believe me——'

'I didn't say I didn't believe you, Captain. I just wanted to be sure
I'd heard correctly.'

'You did, Lord Constable. You heard me right. This way, it's
quicker.'

What a sour-tempered bastard he is, Amalric grumbled. If I knew
where the place was, I'd leave this one in the nearest ditch. With a
knife blade to chew on.

Aegelric's ill-humour rose from a mixture of mead and wine,
now churning in an empty stomach. Though he would not admit
it, even to himself, he was no drinker. Nor was he the type to ram
a thumb down his throat, thus making himself sick and free of the
fomentation. So the grain and the grape fumed inside him, while
his head throbbed and his eyes refused to focus. Personally, he
wished only for a bed—without a woman in it—but after Amalric's
haughty, 'Does Prince Reynald offer nothing more than music and
dance?' he had felt constrained to show him that whatever happened in Jerusalem happened more permissively in Moab. And at
far less expense. A Moabite woman, particularly one who lived
under the shadow of Kerak, would perforce be less choosy than her
counterpart in the capital; it paid to please the Frankish knights,
and it paid well enough by frontier standard.

They disappeared through the great gate arch, emerging on the
lowered drawbridge, then continuing on to the stone bridge that
spanned the fosse. Ahead was the town, rising steeply in a tangle of
stepped streets and close-built houses. Amalric was glad that he had
not ditched his guide. Without him he would never find the
brothel.

As Aegelric had promised, Reynald of Chatillon was already
there, keeping company with Gerard of Ridefort and several Arab
women. When the captain and Constable entered the crudely

furnished anteroom—the whore market, where requirements and prices were discussed—Reynald staggered to his feet and began herding the women forward.

'Here they are, Lord Amalric. Take your pick. This one's new to the game, but if you've the mind to teach her—If not, I suggest one of these two, they're well versed. Or both, if you're feeling strong.' He laughed noisily and turned to Aegelric. 'You look poorly, Captain. You had better choose next, then you can find solace in one of the back cubicles.'

Amalric inspected the women and beckoned to one. Aegelric shook his head. 'Forgive me, Prince. I am not in the mood. In another hour, perhaps.' He lowered himself on to a bench and pressed his head against the cold stone wall. Christ, it throbbed. He heard Gerard ask, 'Do we stay together, or take them to separate beds?' Then a wave of pain broke inside his skull and he was hurled across the room. He glimpsed the others, thrown in a heap on the ground, and saw that one wall of the house had subsided in a welter of stone and dust.

Reynald yelled, 'What happened? What in hell is it?' The women screamed and dragged themselves toward the back of the house. The men gazed stupidly after them, and thus saw two of them crushed by the massive rock that smashed down through the roof. The rock fell, bounced high and tore out a ten foot section of street wall. The entire roof threatened to collapse. The women who had survived lay in the rubble, shrieking insanely. The Crusaders crawled like beetles into the street. Another rock flattened a nearby building and spun off toward a crowded night market. Two more fell, then ten more, then it was raining sixty-pound missiles . . .

The men clambered to their feet and instinctively drew their swords. They were powerless against the terrible crushing stones, but they knew now that Kerak was under attack. They held their swords ready and stood together, sick with fear and drink and unspent sex.

Rocks fell around them. Some entered a house by its roof, then burst out through a wall. Some splintered on impact, throwing off a thousand fragments at random. Men and women lay in the streets and ruined buildings, crushed, or pierced by the flying shards, or staggered about, stabbed by the stone. One of the prostitutes stood in the doorway of the brothel, her clothes torn, her face bleeding from splinter cuts. For reasons of his own, Gerard of Ridefort shouted, 'Over here, girl!' but his words were swamped by Reynald's louder roar. 'Look! Christ help us! Look!'

They saw ten or twelve Saracens running toward them along the street. When the Moslems had halved the distance, five of them leapt aside and stopped, and an instant later five arrows flew at the astonished Crusaders. Reynald threw himself against the wall, while Gerard and Aegelric crouched in the dust. Amalric stood, still unwilling to believe his eyes. The arrows missed, but the archers were already reloading. He felt Aegelric snatch at his sleeve, and the four men ran for their lives. Casually, as though keeping an appointment, one of the archers trotted toward the dazed prostitute and shot her through the heart. She may have been too stunned to notice him, for she did not turn her head until the arrow hit her. Then she blinked and fell back into the house, while the Saracen chased after his companions.

Reynald led the way down a flight of steps and along a street that ran parallel with the first. He snarled, 'Back to the castle! We can't hold this.' As he spoke, another group of Saracens ran out from an alleyway. They did not yet know that they had found Bloodhead himself, along with the Constable of the Kingdom. They were just Frankish vermin, to be exterminated without delay. The Saracens advanced, six of them, swinging their curved scimitars, or poking forward with reed spears. Reynald raised IN NOMINE DOMINI and shuffled toward them. With Gerard at his side and Amalric and Aegelric blocking the other side of the street the fight was short and bloody. The Lord of Kerak was cut on the left arm. Gerard lost a finger from his right hand. Amalric sustained two shallow wounds, Aegelric a deep gash in the neck. Four of the six Saracens were killed there in the street. The fifth stumbled away to die, while the last ran back unhurt to report that the Red Wolf was caught outside his lair.

Shocked and bleeding, the four men retreated to the edge of the fosse. They were some way from the stone bridge, but it was already too late to cross there. The wooden section would be raised, the portcullis lowered, the gates shut, the arrow-loops manned. There was only one place through which a stranded Crusader might still enter the north face of the fortress. This was a tiny postern gate set in the base of the wall below the bridge. It was narrow and angled so that only one man at a time might use it, but unless some over-zealous soldier had shut the inner door, this was where they would enter. But before they reached the postern, they had to descend the incredible north ravine. This varied in depth from eight hundred to twelve hundred feet, a dizzy wall of shale and scrub, and as a reward for a careless foot-step, nothing . . .

They ran to the lip of the fosse, turned to see if their point of descent had been marked, then started down. Aegelric was bleeding copiously and kept a hand clapped to his neck. Although Gerard had lost a finger, he still carried his sword in his right hand, but before long they were all forced to sheath their weapons. The children of the town had explored the upper reaches of the ravine, but all vestige of a path was soon concealed by jutting rocks and thorn bushes. The Crusaders took it in turn to look back at the lip; they expected to be followed and perhaps overtaken by the more nimble-footed Saracens. They were not disappointed.

They had completed a quarter of the descent when the first fire-arrows swooped down toward them. They leaned in against the rock face, not so much for fear of the arrows, but because the flames would reveal their position. As it was, the arrows landed too far down the slope and failed to ignite the dry bushes. They took heart and continued clawing their way down toward the wadi. The lights of Kerak burned dangerously bright above them, but so long as none of the north garrison feared a Saracen attack from the floor of the ravine, the locked-out Crusaders remained in shadow.

But because they could not see well and were encumbered with swords and mantles they climbed slowly. The rattle of loose chips told them the descent had been too slow. Once again they shrank back against the rock, but this time they eased their swords from their scabbards. Aegelric was the last and so the highest in line. He held his sword in his right hand and kept his left pressed against his neck. He felt weak and dizzy, and blinked into the darkness above him.

They must have seen the flash of metal, or heard laboured breath-ing, for they came down in a rush, ten or more of them, their scimitars striking sparks from the rocks. There was little skill in the fight; the air was too dark, the ground uneven. They cut Aegelric again, but again failed to kill him. While some engaged him in the slash and probe of sword play, others moved below, then sprang across to attack Amalric. The Constable used his sword and feet and sent two screaming into the wadi. A third came in close and they wrestled and the heavily-built Frank won. When the Saracen was dead Amalric knelt among the rocks and nursed a fresh stab wound in his leg. Gerard roared a Templar oath and went straight at his own attackers. In their flight one lost his footing and fell like a split sack to join his companions on the wadi floor. None of the Saracens had reached Reynald. The shale stopped moving.

'Follow on,' Reynald hissed. 'Next time they'll bury us with stones.' He did not ask who was hurt. There was no point to it, since he could do nothing for them. They went on, kicking footholds, snatching at thorns and bush roots, slithering down the escarpment like lizards with bloodstained claws.

More fire arrows followed. The Christian archers on the north wall fired at the Moslems, but with little result. The guards guessed what was happening, so dared not illuminate the scene. Prince Reynald and his comrades would have to save themselves. All that Kerak could do was pray.

The Saracens made no attempt at secrecy. They hurled spears and stones, leaning far out to do so. The four fugitives had to be stopped and killed, that was the sum of it now.

Then Gerard of Ridefort showed why so many thought him the natural successor to Grand Master Arnold of Toroga. Calling Reynald back, he pointed to a narrow, God-made path that angled down in the opposite direction to the postern, but away from their pursuers. Reynald said, 'Yes, take it,' and followed him, crouched low. They made good time—as good as their wounds would allow —and reached the wadi floor unhindered. Gerard wiped a hand across his rotund face, then gasped as he jarred the stump of his severed finger. He intended to joke about it later—'Better the finger than the phallus!'—but for the moment he sweated with pain. Amalric was limping, ignoring his previous flesh wounds in favour of the stabbed leg. Aegelric came off the path and sank down, then turned away so that they would not see the extent of his injuries. A knight might be proud of his wounds. if he expected them to heal, but Aegelric knew he was dying and was ashamed of it.

Reynald snapped, 'Get to your feet, we are not home yet. If we run for the postern, we may reach it before they do. With luck our men will sortie and hold it open for us. Are you ready? Captain, are you ready?'

Before Aegelric could reply, they heard feet pounding on the path above them. Moslems, too, it seemed, used the God-made routes. Amalric limped off without a word. Gerard said, 'Get on, Prince! I'll see to the Captain.' He turned to rouse Aegelric, but the garrison commander was already moving up the path. It cost him too much blood to speak, so he waved down to his companions, sweeping his sword hand toward the bridge and the postern. Gerard started after him, but Reynald snarled, 'No! Let him be! Look at him, he's too far gone.'

The Templar hesitated, then whispered, 'God save you, Captain,' and ran with Reynald.

The Saracens were surprised to find the Crusader in their path. He fought like a trapped boar, giving ground a foot at a time. He accounted for two of them, and looked set fair to block the path indefinitely, when the swordsmen retreated a few steps, making way for the archers. They fired seven arrows at him, and all save one found their mark. The swordsmen moved forward again, slashed at his body as they passed and ran on in pursuit of their prey.

Reynald and Gerard helped Amalric along the wadi, then pushed him aside as several figures loomed out of the darkness. The Crusaders' swords were cutting circles in the air when a voice hissed, 'Lord Prince, is it you?' Members of the north garrison hurried to assist Amalric, while Arnold of Toroga shook hands briefly with Reynald and the Templar. The Grand Master asked, 'Are they close?'

Reynald nodded and pushed Gerard toward the postern. Then he looked back along the wadi and spat contemptuously. 'Another time, you pigs! Try for me another time.'

'Come.' Arnold told him. 'You are vulnerable here.'

'Pigs.'

'Yes. Go through, Prince.'

'They'll not bring me down. Nor will they ever take Kerak.'

'I pray you, get on. *Sauve qui peut!* They are coming!' He sheathed his sword and scrambled up the bank to the postern. Reynald followed, almost reluctantly. Four of the garrison stayed to hold the Saracens at bay until the inner door was closed. They died there, while the Red Wolf re-entered his lair.

Inside the walls, the natural leaders had assumed command. Women and civilians had been herded into the nearest cellars and passageways. The south garrison remained under the control of Aegelric's cousin, Captain Azo. Joscelin of Courtenay put himself in charge of the north garrison, while Balian organised the defence of the eastern fortifications. The west wall had not yet come under attack, but when Arnold and Gerard returned through the postern they sent men pouring up the narrow stairways to the western ramparts. Amalric retired to have his leg wound dressed. Reynald joined Joscelin in one of the north towers.

The buildings had taken a terrible battering. The roof of the Great Hall was holed in five places. Two of the windows in the main chapel had sustained a direct hit. Many of the pews were crushed to kindling. The altar rail was bent, the solid silver crucifix scarred by fragments. Half the buildings around the inner and outer baileys had been damaged, and huge stones littered both yards. No count had been taken of the dead and wounded, but thirty or forty bodies lay on the steps and ramparts, most of them victims of the whirling missiles. Bales of burning straw had also been sent over, and small fires raged among the demolished wooden out-houses. The leaders detailed men to draw water from the central reservoir and dampen all the inflammable structures.

Isabella, Maria, Stephanie and Agnes were all safe in the round tower. Humphrey stood with Balian on the curtain wall. Both men were armed with swords and Norman shields, though neither had found time to don a helmet or hauberk.

Humphrey asked, 'Is it Saladin?'

'It's his work, I'd say, and he's probably down there directing it. That raiding party we heard of——'

'It must have been a scouting party.'

'Yes. We jumped too quickly to conclusions. We should have sent the women on with the escort, and stayed to investigate.'

'But we were not to suspect,' Humphrey retorted. 'We have had no trouble from him since Tubanie.'

'Nevertheless, that's exactly what we should have done, sus—— For your life!' They threw themselves flat as a wad of flaming tar flew between them, scraping the inner lip of the wall. The tar stuck for an instant, then fell into the bailey. Men ran out to hurl sand on it. Balian grabbed a cross-bow, wound it and fired a bolt into the darkness.

'This is not good,' he snapped. 'All the light is on us. Humphrey, collect some men and set them to extinguishing the torches. The enemy can see us clearly, while we remain blind. Get to it, kinsman.'

Humphrey crawled away, pleased that Balian had called him kin.

In another part of the castle, Fostus and Ernoul helped prepare one of Kerak's own mangonels. In this way, most of what was catapulted into the castle could be retrieved and thrown back. Little damage could be inflicted until the Crusaders learned where the enemy machines were placed, but it cheered the garrison to see that a reply was being drafted for the Saracens. In fact, Ernoul was not much help. He was wiry, but lacked the bullish strength that was needed if the rocks were to be collected and stacked for loading. Recognising this, Fostus indicated a darkened part of the wall, from where a watcher could estimate the enemy positions.

'Climb up there,' he said. 'When you see them, we'll fire a shot. Mark where it lands, then guide the next flights. But stay low, or I'll have that girl of yours after me.'

Ernoul nodded and was about to run for the steps when Fostus grabbed his shoulder, jerking him back beside the mangonel. A rock landed twenty feet away, sprang up and flew within inches of the machine. It smashed through a row of horse troughs, then spun away in the direction of a wrecked guard-house. Fostus hauled the young squire to his feet, growled, 'Scale that wall!' and pushed him forward. Ernoul ran.

He reached the steps unhurt and started to climb. Midway up he came across the corpse of a soldier, the body and head cruelly broken. Stifling his revulsion, he rolled the corpse from the steps, trying not to hear as it landed with a dull sound in the yard. He went on, his hands wet with blood.

The lights were going out all over the castle. It made movement difficult—one false step could send a man over the wall, or off the edge of a stairway—but they no longer felt exposed to the enemy's gaze. The archers fired tar-tipped arrows and the men-at-arms hurled barrels of Greek Fire in an attempt to locate their attackers. The Greek Fire smeared the slopes of the wadis with liquid flame, and they could see men running or on horseback. It was the consensus of opinion that Kerak was ringed by a major Saracen force and that Emir Saladin was in command.

In the round tower, Stephanie of Milly posed an ingenious scheme whereby the attack might be delayed.

She said, 'Perhaps he does not know of the wedding. If we were to send out meat and drink, if we were to appeal to him as an honourable man . . . He's a strange one. It might work with him.'

Had she suggested that, at the height of the battle, they exchange courtesies with anyone but Saladin, she would have been scorned, or ignored. But, as she had said, Salah ed-Din Yusuf was a strange one. He forgave penitent murderers and then, having pardoned them, gave them money from his own coffers. He made treaties and held to them. He released high-born prisoners so that they might return to their lands and raise their own ransom, and he was genuinely shocked when they failed to do so. He gave his word and kept it more often than any Frankish leader, and the Crusaders made much of this self-restricting weakness. He prayed regularly, studied foreign languages and wrote poetry. He was indeed a strange one to Christian eyes.

The attack continued for the next hour, but in that time the Emir's headquarters were located and Saladin himself was contacted by a deputation from the castle. He listened patiently to what they told him, then accepted the token food and asked, 'Which part of al-Kerak do the young couple occupy?'

They said, the north tower.

'Then that shall be sacrosanct. And when I have taken this dreadful place I will give them safe-passage from Moab. I have heard of them. Allah grant that there were more of their kind. Tell the Ladies Stephanie and Maria and Agnes that they, too, are safe, and that I will deal with their husbands fairly in due time. Now leave me and make your defence.'

The deputation retired, awed and frightened.

Reynald left his watchtower and went among his men. He carried no shield and moved openly along the ramparts, roaring, bellowing proof that a Christian hide was impervious to Moslem darts. Men died around him, but their deaths changed nothing; they expected to die, for they were not touched with immortality. Two arrows flew close to him, and by word of mouth became twenty that bounced harmlessly from his chest. Nothing, they knew, could hurt their Prince, the master of Oultrejourdain . . .

While Ernoul directed the aim, Fostus and others loaded and fired the mangonel. The first six missiles hit nothing they could see. The seventh scored a glancing blow on one of the Saracen machines. After that, they smashed the machine to splinters.

Azo and the south garrison repulsed two attacks on the wall. On the eastern ramparts Humphrey returned to help Balian reposition the thinning line of soldiers. He was some twenty feet from the Lord of Nablus when he stumbled and knocked himself cold. Balian was glad—now, in all honesty, he could have his son-in-law carried to the round tower and given over to Isabella. He had already decided to engineer something of the kind, but this way, with the accident witnessed by several men-at-arms, he could not be accused of favouritism.

Then, to make this night one of the most incredible in the history of the forty-year-old fortress, the surprise Saracen attack was balanced by an equally unlooked for interruption.

The soldiers on the west wall and in the high towers there saw a distant smudge of light between the castle and the Dead Sea. Gerard of Ridefort shouted for his Grand Master, who in turn shouted for Reynald. By the time he reached them, the lights had spread into a wide, snaking column.

'Sweet Christ,' he breathed. 'This cannot be. It's some devious trick.'

Suddenly men on the north wall were also shouting. 'Prince! Leaders! They withdraw! They withdraw!'

'No,' Reynald muttered. 'They fool you. Don't be hood-winked. It's an easy trick.'

But it was no trick. Within less than an hour the Saracen force had disappeared into the hills, leaving behind them broken equipment and a scattering of dead. And before another hour had passed the Christian army was under the walls, flares showing where Raymond of Tripoli stood beside the litter that bore King Baldwin IV.

Leaving Kerak to his commanders, Reynald went down to meet them.

Addressing Raymond, he demanded, 'In God's name, how did you know of this?'

The Regent merely nodded at the king, redirecting the question.

'How did we know?' Baldwin whispered, in no hurry to satisfy Reynald's curiosity. 'You ask us how?'

'I do, yes.'

'We heard that a raiding party——'

'So did we all! Yet it aroused no suspicions.'

Baldwin smiled. 'So I see. For myself, I am not so trusting.'

'But why you? You heard something we did not——'

'No. They reported sighting, that's all.'

'*Then why you?*'

'I will tell you why, Chatillon. Because I am the king, and because it is the king's part to sense these things. In my place your suspicions would not have been aroused, and all this would be razed to rubble. But you are not in my place, thank God, and so you and yours have been saved.' In the silence that followed, the young leper's heart burned with the knowledge that he had magnificently justified his crown.

# CHAPTER ELEVEN

# Toron

## *May, June 1184*

They were six months older. Humphrey was now eighteen years and a few days; Isabella had turned twelve, claiming, 'I am in my thirteenth year.' Now, too, they were almost one hundred miles by road from Nablus, and more than twice that distance from Kerak. They had left the old world and embraced the new.

Both revelled in their new-found freedom. Humphrey proved himself a judicious overlord and a capable administrator, while, at home, Isabella wrote in her diary, 'There can be no more attentive a husband,' then, in a code she had devised, 'nor inventive a lover.' He was not unable. He did not maltreat her, nor did he wish her to hit him with sticks. There was no reason whatsoever to send him to Lord Balian, unless it was to parade him as a perfect knight. She remarked openly to her handmaids that she sometimes wished she were a dog. Then, like a dog, she could follow him around all day. As a princess, she was content to fill her diary in clear and in code and write long letters to Balian and Maria, a sheet of general information for her step-father, another of more intimate comment for her mother. She felt sure that they both read each sheet, but she continued to divide the letters in case Balian admonished her for her unladylike disclosures.

One morning, for the sake of amusement, she showed part of a coded entry to Humphrey. He broke the code within five minutes and blushed at what he read.

'Did I really say that?'

'You did. The other night. Do you remember, I was on this side of the bed, and you were over there, and you took off your tunic and said——'

'Yes, well, I don't think you should record such remarks.'

'But nobody can read them.'

'I can, now.'

'Ah, but you have a brilliant mind, sweet. Who else could make sense of it?'

'I don't know, but if it was to fall into the wrong hands——'

'Then it could only enhance your reputation. Here, read this passage.' She smiled and pulled the covers around them. They both realised that the day would start late for Lord Humphrey of Toron and Princess Isabella of Jerusalem . . .

One week later, Ernoul sent word that he and Idela would soon reach the castle. Balian's squire was now a month short of his nineteenth birthday, Idela some three years younger. This time there had been nothing to prevent her coming with him. Aunt Ermengarde had recovered from her stomach pains and was busy gardening and bottling fruit. Idela's father had employed another assistant and did not disguise the fact that he found the new girl quicker and more hard-working than his daughter. He wanted to ask Ernoul if he intended to marry Idela, or merely take pleasure in her, but commented instead on the dilapidated state of the awning above the stall. He feigned surprise when the young man purchased a replacement, then gave the pair his paternal blessing and went back to work.

On their way to Toron they spent two nights beside the road, but because it was necessary to keep watch for wild animals and brigands, they did not take pleasure in each other. As a result they arrived in the seigneurie tired and tense and Ernoul refused to go on to the castle.

Idela said, 'But we are expected. Didn't you say we would arrive to-night?'

'I didn't say to-night for certain. To-morrow will be soon enough.'

'Then where will we stay?'

'In a hostel, or a tavern. I'll find somewhere. We'll feel better when we've eaten.'

'And slept,' she said. 'I could sleep the sun round.'

He did not pay particular attention to the remark until he had found a travellers' hostel, ordered food and a room for two. Then Idela said, 'No, I would prefer a room of my own.'

'What? But you can't! I mean, you didn't think that after all this time——'

'Listen,' she sighed. 'Sit down here by the fire and listen to me.

'I don't understand you. I thought——'

'I know what you thought, and you are right to think it. But now think of this. If we are together we will want to have love——'

'Of course. I do want it.'

'And I, dear Ernoul. So together we will try, hollow-eyed and snappish.'

'Who's hollow-eyed? I feel as well as, as——' He clasped a hand to his mouth, but was too late to stifle the yawn.

'Just so,' Idela said, 'and it will be unsatisfactory, and we will remember it with shame.'

'Shame?' he gaped. 'I'm not ash-ashamed.'

'With sorrow then. But when we have slept and recovered——' She smiled at him, and after a moment he nodded wearily.

'You are probably right.'

'It will be better, I promise you. And in a castle! The very thought of it excites me.'

He wondered what difference a castle would make, but saw the light in her eyes and said nothing. He, himself, had always wanted to have love with a girl beside a river, so supposed it was much the same thing.

The hostel keeper came to tell them that the food was ready and to make sure that they did, in fact, want separate rooms. Ernoul nodded, and they left the fire and ate in silence, the only couple in the wood-walled dining-room. Then, still silent, they mounted the stairs to their rooms. The hostel keeper watched them and shook his head in disgust. Two rooms. In his day he would never have allowed a pretty girl to escape so easily. If necessary he'd have broken down the door to reach her. Then he remembered that the door was hostel property and reminded himself to check for damage in the morning. Young people to-day were all the same. They had no respect for persons or property . . .

In December, 1183, when Humphrey and Isabella had arrived at

Toron, they had decided to put into practice much of what Humphrey had learned from Reynald of Chatillon. The young nobleman was so terrified of what his step-father might do once he realised that he was to receive no lands or income from the seigneurie, that he planned to increase the garrison of the castle two-fold and, at whatever the cost, to extend the fortifications in the form of a vast outer wall.

But by the end of January, 1184, they were less frightened. The inhabitants of the county were a friendly lot; they had lived too long without a father in the family, and they welcomed the grand-son of the great warrior Constable Humphrey II. They found Humphrey IV different in many ways, yet bearing the same ideals and aspirations. And, glory of glory, after a lifetime spent in Kerak, he was still loyal to the crown.

Humphrey was profoundly glad that they did not continue to draw comparisons between his grandfather and himself. Humphrey the Constable had been a man of stature, God knew it, but Isabella's husband had no wish to step from the shadow of Chatillon into that cast by an earlier Toron. He encouraged the populace to assess him on his own merits, and before many weeks they were telling their friends, 'We are of Toron, Lord Humphrey's seigneurie. He has forsaken Moab, he and his little princess, to be with us.'

So the policy was changed, and the outer wall remained in the quarries. He increased the size of the garrison, not so much to strengthen his military standing, as to give employment to the young men of the area. Fifteen of the most intelligent received the buffet of knighthood and were sent as the knight's fee to the capital. With them went sixty men-at-arms, being the quota demanded by the Assizes of Jerusalem. They joined the royal army and drew their pay from the king.

In the castle court—held in the Hall of the Constable—Humphrey had judged his first cases of theft, arson and murder. Although his people were friendly they were also human, poor and fallible. In the first murder trial, Humphrey found the allegations proven, but could not bring himself to pass sentence of death. He announced that he would give his verdict later in the day and adjourned the court. The friendly townsfolk, anxious to ease their young lord's conscience, took the murderer away from his guards, carried him a decent distance from the castle, then tore him to pieces.

They were stunned and impressed when Humphrey ordered four of them to be flogged, back and chest, sentenced the guard sergeant to a lifetime's servitude in the fly-blown outpost of Raheb and fined every member of the guard detail six months pay . . .

Now it was May and he stood on the battlements above the barbican gate, waiting for his friend to arrive from Nablus. He had begun his vigil soon after dawn, armed with a volume of William of Tyre's *Historia Rerum in Partibus Transmarinis Gestarum*. William of Tyre, one-time Chancellor of the Kingdom and later Archbishop of Tyre, was the man who had unsuccessfully challenged Heraclius for the post of Patriarch. Having gained the position with the help of Agnes of Courtenay, Reynald of Chatillon and the Lusignan brothers, Heraclius had promptly excommunicated his popular rival. William left Palestine for Rome to plead his case before the Pope. Time and again a decision was deferred and, so far as Humphrey knew, William was still there, writing his history and awaiting the papal decree. He had already completed some twenty volumes of the *Historia*, and various copies found their way back into the kingdom. Humphrey wondered if Ernoul had read them; they were the sort of thing he would enjoy.

He glanced along the road that twisted up from the town, saw no one and continued reading. He learned that the castle of Toron had been built between 1103 and 1105 by the French knight, Hugh Falconberg of Saint-Omer, but that the Prince of Galilee did not live to enjoy it. Within a few months of the completion of the fortress he was killed by a force from Damascus, and the fief passed to another Frenchman, Gervase of Basoches. According to William, Gervase fared no better, for three years later he was captured by Toghetin of Homs, atabeg of Damascus. With such an important Frankish prisoner in his cells, Toghetin demanded that the king, Baldwin I, surrender the citadels of Acre, Haifa and Tiberias. Not unnaturally, the king refused and, not unnaturally, Toghetin directed his wrath at his captives. Gervase of Basoches was killed and scalped, and his pale hair woven into a Moslem banner.

Humphrey touched a hand to his head and looked up from the

book. Two figures on horseback were rounding the final bend in the road. It was difficult to tell, but—yes, surely it was them. He waved, and the taller of the two waved back. Ha! It was! He called to one of the men-at-arms, gave him the book and told him to return it to the library. Descending the steps inside the gate he yelled, 'Sergeant of the guard! Turn out your men! Good friends arrive!' and started out to meet them. Then he remembered that his wife had intended to take a bath, ran back and said, 'Tell Princess Isabella that the scribbler is here.'

The sergeant frowned and repeated, 'The scribbler.'

'Yes! The writer, the poet, the chronicler. He's my friend, it's a term of affection.'

Measuring his words the sergeant intoned, 'Oh, very well, my lord. I'll tell our Lady Isabella that the scribbler is here.' Both men turned away and both raised their eyes to heaven. Then Humphrey plunged through the gate again and hurried along the road. He did not mind if the soldiers thought him a little mad to-day, for though he had settled well at Toron, he missed his few old friends, and in particular Ernoul. He hoped that the girl Idela would enjoy herself and get along with Isabella. He acknowledged that she must have something, to be Ernoul's companion, but prayed that she was not prone to fits of giggling. He had eradicated that nervous vice in Isabella; with luck Ernoul had done the same for Idela.

They trotted nearer. Humphrey stood beside the road, one hand raised in welcome. He recognised the slim young squire and hummed approval at Idela's appearance. She did indeed have something, and would still have it even if she was deaf or dumb. A wave of black hair under her travelling hood, dark eyes and a clear, pale complexion. He glanced unashamedly at her legs, what he could see of them between boots and kirtle, and at her breasts, laced within a lemon coloured bodice. Hmmm, he thought.

Ernoul called, 'Good day, my Lord Humphrey. We seek permission to enter your castle.'

Humphrey thought he was making fun of him, then saw he was not. He was confused by the courtesy, waited a moment, then replied in kind.

'You are welcome here, dear Ernoul. You and your fine Idela. Give me your bridles.' He went forward between the horses and treated the gate guards to a sight they had never seen; the Lord of Toron leading animals like a common ostler. The men-at-arms exchanged glances. This Ernoul fellow, and his lady Idela, they'd need special treatment. Lord Humphrey was making that quite clear.

The guard of honour was drawn up for inspection. Humphrey stopped the horses short of the double line and, while Ernoul dismounted, he helped Idela to the ground. The girl was tongue-tied. Ernoul had told her that Toron did not compare in size with Kerak yet the castle seemed to stretch away to infinity, tower after tower, wall beyond wall.

Humphrey grinned at her, enjoying his work, then set her lightly on her feet. She stammered, 'I thank you, sire, my lord,' and glanced round desperately for Ernoul. Humphrey clapped his hands together and laughed up at the gate arch. All would be well. His friend was here and the girl was a delight. Now all he wanted was Isabella, to make his happiness complete.

The horses were led away. With Ernoul at one side and Humphrey at the other, Idela walked between the double line.

Humphrey asked, 'Do you approve of them?'

'I don't know,' she admitted, 'they look so stern. But as soldiers they seem well set.'

'That's a fair view. Ernoul?'

'You could teach your step-father a thing or two about discipline.'

'Well said. Mine are a deal better than his slovens, aren't they? And I pay them more, with less in the coffers.'

'It shows, though you wouldn't get them to stand so just for the money.'

'You're right again. They have pride in themselves and, I like to think, in Toron.' He glanced at Idela. She was clearly over-awed and he chatted to her, to put her at her ease. They reached the end of the lines and entered the main bailey. 'There,' Humphrey said, 'that terminates all ceremony. Now, if you will excuse me for a moment——'

He strode back toward the gate, then turned out of sight behind a high, wooden hawk house. Ernoul and Idela held hands and moved to one side of the bailey.

He asked, 'Is this how you imagined a castle to be?'

'Not so large.' She gripped his hand more tightly. 'Ernoul, what am I to do when I meet Princess Isabella? Lord Humphrey makes it easy for me, but his wife——'

'His wife, as you know full well, is twelve years old. You will curtsy to her and I will bow, and then she will probably want to know if you play *jeu des dames* or knuckle bones. Don't worry, sweet, she will be as easy as Humphrey. She—now what?' They stood watching as the young Lord of Toron reappeared, this time leading a sleek Arab stallion. The proud, high-stepping horse wore a decorated saddle and bridle. Its mane and tail shone like Sicilian silk; its hooves had been stained and polished.

Humphrey brought the horse across to them and said, 'Ernoul, with your permission.'

Not quite knowing what he was supposed to permit, the squire responded, 'Well, yes, of course.'

'Thank you. Then, Idela, I offer you this token of welcome.' He paused, saw the pleasure and confusion in her face, and spoke on to save her stammering a reply. 'I knew that Ernoul would one day find a young lady with both wit and beauty, and when I heard that you would visit us here I sensed—no, I *knew* that his day had come. He is undeserving, though I don't expect you to agree.'

'No,' she smiled, 'I don't.'

'Quite. Then I will say that his patience has been fully rewarded. Now, will you reward me and accept this animal?'

Idela turned to Ernoul, and Humphrey gave the reins an imperceptible tug so that the horse moved, pulling him round. Ernoul nodded, yes, accept the gift.

'My Lord Humphrey——'

He stilled the horse and turned back to her. 'Dear Idela, don't think of a speech for me. Just say "I will take it".'

'Oh, yes, my lord, yes, I will take it!'

'Good. His name is Zerbino. He was the gallant son of——'

'—the King of Scotland,' she concluded excitably. 'Yes, I know. He married Isabella, daughter of——'

'—the King of Galicia,' Humphrey grinned. 'So you are conversant with the legends of Charlemagne?'

'Tolerably, though I admit I have now thrown them over for the writings of one Ernoul.'

While Ernoul indulged in a coughing bout, Humphrey re-appraised the herbalist's daughter. If she read, then she probably wrote. These attributes, together with her undeniable good looks, made her a catch to be prized. He bowed with admiration, then called his horsemaster.

'Zerbino now belongs to our lady Idela. I return him to your charge, master, until our lady requires him.'

'Does she ride?' the horsemaster inquired rudely, 'or am I to give her lessons?'

'She rides as prettily as you'll ever see,' Humphrey said. 'As for lessons, you could do with a few in common politeness. Take the animal.'

Idela asked, 'Are you responsible for his appearance, master?'

'Yes, lady, that's so. What's wrong with it?'

'Nothing whatsoever. He's been kept with some great care, I'd say. You must be well thought of in your work.'

'I am,' he said. 'I am the best in Toron.' He sucked his teeth and went off without waiting to be dismissed.

Ernoul remarked, 'The man is an artist, eh, Humphrey?'

'I'm surrounded by them. By artistic men and clever women. I feel like a clod.' With malicious innocence he said, 'By the way, have you ever chanced to read William of Tyre's *Historia Rerum in Partibus*——'

'——*Transmarinis Gestarum*? Some eight or nine volumes, yes. Have you read them all?'

'Am I not allowed to finish a phrase these days? No, I haven't read them all, damn your spinning brain. But I should have known better than to try and trick you.' He sighed melodramatically and gestured toward the walls. 'I'll catch you out yet. Do you know when this place was built, and at whose command?'

'Wasn't it by Hugh Falconer of Saint-Omer?'

'Ha, no, it wasn't. It was Falconberg. The year?' He had already decided to dodge one way or the other within the three year span, forcing Ernoul to be wrong, whatever he said. He was so keen to spring his trap that when Ernoul admitted, 'I'm ignorant of the year,' he retorted, 'No, wrong.'

'What?'

'You're—didn't you give a date?'

'No, I told you, I don't know.'

Humphrey sighed again. 'Oh, no matter. Come on. Isabella will be waiting for us.' They walked toward the octagonal tower that soared up behind the Hall of the Constable, their voices fading into muted question and answer.

'In what year did we fight the battle of Dorylaeum? . . . In July, 1097 . . . What is so memorable about it? . . . It was the first time we engaged the Saracens in pitched battle . . . Good. When was the year of the great Syrian earthquake? . . . Easy. 1170. And the month was June . . . Yes, that'll do . . . And the date was the 28th or 29th . . . Yes, yes. What do you need to make Greek Fire? . . . I have no idea . . . So! I've found a chink at last. I'll tell you. You take sulphur, wine dregs, oil, pitch, gum of Persia, salt that has been baked hard . . .'

Isabella was terrified of meeting Idela. She knew how dearly Humphrey valued his friendship with Ernoul, and she was determined to make the girl welcome, whatever her private feelings toward her. In fact, there were very few people, men or women, whom Isabella disliked outright. Her half-sister Sibylla was one, and, of course, Sibylla's mother, Agnes of Courtenay. She hated Reynald of Chatillon for what he had done to Humphrey, and she despised Patriarch Heraclius for himself. Otherwise, apart from the odd childhood pique, she had mixed naturally with both the high and low orders, and was thought of as a spirited young woman, whom only a fool would take for a fool.

When she saw Idela for the first time she sensed instinctively that things would go well between them. For one thing, they each owned the same type of travelling cloak. For another, Idela seemed, if anything, even more apprehensive. Isabella thought, she's uncommonly pretty, withal. That's good, she can show me how to use cosmetics.

She stayed where she was in the doorway of the octagonal tower until Humphrey and his guests were a few feet from the steps, then ran down to them.

Ernoul coughed quietly and bowed. 'Princess Isabella.'

Idela dropped a curtsy and murmured, 'Princess.'

Isabella glanced at Humphrey. 'There's no need for this. Didn't you tell them?'

'God's truth, I forgot,' he said. 'Anyway, it's done now; be honoured.'

In some confusion the young guests drew erect, while Humphrey came between them. 'It's my fault,' he said. 'I should have learned from your courtesies at the gate. Idela, take my wife's hand. Go with her. We'll follow in a moment.' He nodded encouragement and Isabella extended a hand. 'Yes, keep me company. Are you hungry, or shall I first show you around?'

'As you wish, Princess.'

'Oh, less formal, I beg you. You must have seen four or five more years of life than I. Let it be Isabella, or any other name you can make up. I'm sure I'll find an eke-name for you within a few days.' She smiled and led Idela into the tower. The men remained below, watching their women.

They ate before the sun was too high, and then the women retired to Isabella's solarium to discuss the merits of paint and powder, song and superstition, Humphrey and Ernoul.

The men left the tower to play hand-ball in the yard, hurling the tough, sewn skin at each other and grinning as the dust covered them. After a while Humphrey said, 'Enough. You'll never out-point me now. The cooks keep water boiling, so we can bathe at any time.'

Ernoul choked with indignation. 'Out-pointed? I'm not! You're the one. How many times did you drop it, or miss it?'

'Five by my count. And eight for you.'

'Dog's vomit! Power has turned your head. *I* made five errors, whereas you—you spent more time prostrate than on your feet. I win, it's beyond dispute.'

'Your eyes must be blocked with dust. Still, as you're the guest——' He shrugged, then slapped his clothes.

Ernoul did not realise that he was being teased. 'No charity!' he fumed. 'I won, fair and clean. Start again, and I'll win again. I'l even give you two points, because I'm better.'

'No, no, it's done with now.' He picked up the skin and, as Ernoul made ready to catch it, kicked it out of the yard.

'But that's not fair!'

'Come and bathe.'

Ernoul tetched and glared balefully at his friend. Then Humphrey laughed and said, 'You did win, five against eleven, but you're not very humble, are you?'

'No, not when I'm good at something. Fostus told me that——'

'Ah, that iron man. I could do with a Fostus here.'

'He's pledged to Lord Balian. I don't think he would go with any man on earth, save Balian.'

'Don't worry, dear friend, I wouldn't try to take him. God made them to ride together, anyone can see that. Now, if you've regained your composure, I'd like to wash away the dust of my defeat.' On the way back to the tower he asked, 'How do you find Isabella?'

'Well, Humphrey, since I first met the princess I have thought her——'

'Ernoul, Ernoul. We will have a stiff time if you are so formal. I liked you better when you were disputing the score. We stand on few ceremonies here, that's the marvel of it. I am free to say what I want, to be what I want. To be—Humphrey IV of Toron, and now not only in name. I've already extended you the same freedom. So, how do you find her?'

'She's more than you deserve.'

'Ha! You're right, and I am aware of it every day. She and Idela seem well suited. She's a beauty, your Idela.'

'She was much in awe——'

'And Isabella. It's wonderful, you know. The four of us. As I promised at Kerak, we'll have a fine time. It was good of Lord Balian to release you. When are you due to return?'

'At your pleasure.'

'Then never! I'll give you half the tower, or anywhere you like. And I'll knight you—I can do that now—and your girl will be our lady Idela. That has a ring, doesn't it? Say yes.'

'It would be a way, though Lord Balian still finds things for me to do.'

'So you do have some humility, after all. Things to do. He relies heavily on you, and trusts you more than most. You'll go back there, because, like Fostus, you belong with him. But promise me this. Stay as long as you can, this time. I——' He opened his hands and Ernoul encouraged, 'Say on, lord.'

'I can't find the words. But I have this strange feeling, even here, so far in the north. I fear that this year may be the last in which we retain such an easy grip on the Kingdom. Does that make sense to you?'

'Some, but things are always stirring at court and on the frontiers. What makes this year so final?'

'I don't know. So much may happen, or so little. The king may die, and, when he does, you'll see them scramble for the throne.'

'But he has made provision for that. His nephew, the child Baldwin, will reign, with Raymond of Tripoli as Regent.'

'If the child remains alive, yes. But suppose he were to die before our present king, what then?'

'You and the other barons would be called upon to vote. The Lord of Tiberias——'

'Oh, yes, Raymond is the man, and I would cast in his favour. But all that is too simple. There will be massive opposition from the Courtenays and the Lusignans and my step-father and God in His wisdom knows who else. And though I say we will hold our flaccid grip this year, I could be proved wrong to-morrow.' He gazed at his friend, then rested his hands on Ernoul's shoulders. 'So stay for as long as you want. We may not sit together again for some time.'

'We'll stay,' Ernoul nodded. 'You would be hard put to drive us away. On another subject, my Lord Humphrey——'

'Yes?'

'You're filthy.'

'And so are you, scribbler. Come on, let's steal the cooking water.'


Ernoul moved the massive pewter war-horse one space forward and one diagonally. He enjoyed *escas* and could hold his own with Balian and most of the knights who visited Nablus. But he had not played the Eastern variation—Shatranj—and was being hard pressed by Humphrey.

In reply, the young Lord of Toron moved his Elephant two spaces diagonally, jumping the Charger. Ernoul smiled weakly at the women, and Idela said, 'Save your Warder.'

'Please,' he snapped, 'no advice.' He studied the gold and silver board, then saved a five-inch-high scarlet Warder.

Idela started to protest, 'Not that——' but Humphrey had already lifted his silver Shah and carried it toward Ernoul's second Warder.

With great tact Isabella pretended not to see Ernoul's latest loss and moved to the far side of the solarium to fetch a fresh wine jar from the cooling bin. By the time she returned Ernoul had moved his own Minister—the *Phrez*—and lost a *Baidaq*, carved to resemble an Arab physician.

'This is hopeless,' he grumbled. 'If this continues I shall lose everything.'

'Have you lost bare Shah before?' Humphrey asked. 'I have.' With a smile of pride he elaborated, 'I lost bare Shah two weeks ago.'

'He must have been a cunning opponent.'

'He was a pretty one, I'll grant you that. *He* was Isabella!'

'I don't know whether that makes me joyful or despondent. Wait, I have a plan.'

The plan did not work and in a dozen moves he lost another Baidaq—this one a butcher—the Warder he had previously saved, and his last Minister. Humphrey let him take a Charger, then trapped his Shah between two Elephants and a Baidaq philosopher.

'Check and mate!'

'Well, at least it isn't bare Shah. I have a few pieces left.'

'It would have been,' Humphrey trumpeted, 'but I chose to be merciful.'

'Then also be more gracious,' Isabella said. 'There were times when Ernoul made you think hard.'

'I suppose so. But when I took your first Minister so early . . .' They analysed the game, each correction countered with a wordy justification. Idela and Isabella looked at each other, then yawned conspicuously.

Humphrey said, 'We must play again to-morrow. I have

a Christian set. You will be more at home with it. And, if you like,we will ride in the morning. Now that you have Zerbino, Idela——'

'Thank you again.'

'No, no.' He finished his wine, read Isabella's expression and bade his guests good night. Idela had told the princess that she and Ernoul had not yet shared love, so Isabella was anxious that they should reach the bed in their own time.

She said, 'I am glad you are with us. As for the morrow, we'll not ride too early, so take your rest.' She smiled at them and went out. Humphrey followed, closing the door behind him.

Ernoul picked up his trapped Shah and turned it round, studying it from this angle and that. Idela watched him, then pushed the cork stopper into the wine jar and ranged the four mugs side by side on the table. The silence lengthened and grew louder. Ernoul replaced the Shah, tugged at his ear, examined his iron belt buckle. Idela took the wine jar back to the bin, then stood near the door, yawning. In a strangled voice she said, 'It has been an eventful day.'

'Yes, hasn't it? You seem tired.'

'No, not so tired. A little chilly.'

'Shall I fetch a mantle?'

'Oh, I'll be warm enough. In bed.'

'Yes,' he agreed, 'you should be. They've put on some fine covers.'

She asked, 'Aren't you at all cold?'

'I don't feel the— Well, now that you say it, it does grow cool.' He sat for a moment, then stretched his arms and opened his mouth wide. She almost laughed, his pretence was so poor.

'You see,' she abetted, 'the day does take its toll.'

'So it does. I'm more weary than I thought. If there is nothing you wish to do——'

'No, nothing.'

'Then we may as well——'

'Yes.' She put a hand on the door latch and made sure she could not work it. Ernoul sprang up and raised it for her. 'It's stiff,' he explained. 'They are probably all newly fitted.'

Idela nodded and moved into the corridor. Fortunately, most of the torches had been extinguished, so she said, 'I don't trust the dark,' and put her hand in his. In this way, moving slowly, close together, they reached the bedchamber.

They undressed on opposite sides of the bed, their backs to each other. Moonlight striped the room and a dog barked far below in the bailey. They felt their way under the covers and lay still, not touching.

They were silent for so long that Idela feared she would fall asleep. Ernoul did fall asleep, but came awake instantly. Shocked and ashamed, he turned on his side and murmured, 'I have to tell you something.'

'I know.'

'There have not been so many women in my life——'

'It doesn't matter, I don't want——'

'Not many at all——'

'I'm glad.'

'In truth, none.'

'I know. Here. Yes. Here.' She moved against him. 'Ssh. Yes. Ah, dear Ernoul. Ernoul. Ernoul.'

'I'm glad, too.'

'Ssh.'

'I am.'

'Yes. I will be your woman. Sweet, be gen——'

He hurt her and she tried to move away. He held her and hurt her for an instant more, and then the pain diminished and they shared love, caught and carried by the waves that grew stronger and more intense until their ears dinned and they were buried alive, moaning low, each with the other.


They all knew that there would never be another period like it in their lives. They would never be so happy, nor so free. They seized their opportunity, knowing it to be unique, and stitched the days and nights together into an unbroken tapestry of love and fulfil-ment. As God had made Constable Fostus to ride with Lord Balian, so He had made these four to enjoy each other. Nothing was too complex for them, nor too simple. They shrieked and ran through the mornings, rode the hills flat, and talked early or late of every subject that touched their lips. The men fought twice in earnest, wrestling to the ground, and the women fell out once and complained like spoilt children to their husbands. Each quarrel was ended on the day it started, leaving no trace of bitterness or undigested spite. Isabella and Idela loved the other's husband almost as much as their own. Almost, but not quite. It was that that made it perfect.

They knew there would never be another period like it. They did not need another. The memory of this would last them beyond heaven.

# CHAPTER TWELVE

# Palestine

## *March 1185, September 1186*

The Leper King began to die. It could be said that the inexorable march toward death had started with the first blemishes of his dreadful disease, but during the last few months of 1184 the speed of deterioration had increased. He was completely blind and had lost most of his fingers and toes. An embroidered blanket was pulled up to his chin, though there was no way of disguising his visage. He was twenty-four years old and caused revulsion in almost all who approached and laid eyes on him.

His six-year-old nephew, taken from Sibylla when Guy of Lusignan had been deposed from the Regency, had been crowned Baldwin V in the Church of the Holy Sepulchre in Jerusalem. The child had been carried into the church by Balian of Ibelin, and had later sat with his nurses whilst the loyal barons swore fealty to him. He cried in church and in the palace, an unhappy little boy who choked on solid foods and grew thin on soups.

Raymond of Tripoli, now Regent in place of Guy, drew up a list of prudent conditions under which he was prepared to govern the Kingdom for the Child King. If Baldwin IV suffered further pain from being present at a discussion in which he was already regarded as dead, he did not show it. The age and condition of his nephew presented certain unique problems, and the leper accepted that Raymond would have been a fool to ignore them.

The Lord of Tiberias stipulated that he would continue as Regent for ten years, provided that Joscelin of Courtenay retained responsibility for the child's physical well-being. The king saw this as an attempt by Raymond to rekindle Joscelin's failing loyalty to the crown, but Raymond had included that particular condition in order that the child would not die too directly under his own guardianship. The last thing the Lord of Tiberias wanted was to be accused of regicide.

However, it was likely that the enfeebled Baldwin V would die before Raymond's ten year Regency was concluded. When this happened, all claims to the throne were to be presented to the King of France, the King of England, the Pope and the Emperor of Germany. These four would arbitrate between, most probably, Guy of Lusignan's wife, Princess Sibylla, and Humphrey of Toron's wife, Princess Isabella. Both were the daughters of Amalric I and, because Agnes of Courtenay had been Amalric's first wife, whereas Maria Comnena had been his second, Sibylla had the marginally better claim. But they were women, and it had not yet come to that.

The young leper had readily accepted Raymond's conditions, and his position as Regent had been made official. This left the dying king free to settle one last outstanding score—he would deal with his vassal brother-in-law, still ensconced in Ascalon.

But Guy of Lusignan was not so easily evicted. He had turned the town into a fortress and, short of sending a punitive expedition against him, there was little that Baldwin could do. Such an expedition would be tantamount to a declaration of civil war, and might bring about the subsequent ruin of the Kingdom. So the leper raged behind his grotesque mask, while Guy held fast, daring him to attack.

Three well-known figures were missing from the streets of Jerusalem.

Some months earlier, the Patriarch Heraclius and the Grand Masters of the Temple and the Hospital had left Palestine for Europe, intent on gaining an audience with the rulers of the Christian West. The Grand Master of the Temple, Arnold of Toroga, had fallen ill *en route* and died at Verona in Italy, but Heraclius and Roger of Les Moulins had continued their journey; almost, as the Patriarch put it, 'A pilgrimage in reverse.' He had prepared three speeches, one for Frederick Barbarossa, Emperor of Germany, one for the chilly King Philip of France, one for the quick-tempered Plantagenet, Henry II of England. In these speeches

Heraclius pleaded with the rulers to take up the True Cross and lead an invincible Christian army on a fresh Crusade. Along with the parchment rolls, his staff of clerics carried the Royal Standard of Jerusalem, the keys of the city and of the Holy Sepulchre and the Tower of David.

By March, 1185, he and Grand Master Roger had been received by Frederick in Mainz, by Philip in Paris, and by Henry at Reading and London. The Emperor and the Kings had listened to his pleas, made suitably pious comments about the relics he laid before them, then told him why they, personally, could not leave at this time for Palestine. With unprecedented courage Heraclius challenged their motives and railled at them as though they were merchants or men-at-arms.

On March 18th, Henry II convened his Great Council at Clerken-well, a northern suburb of London and a little over a mile beyond the city wall. There, in the presence of the Patriarch, he put to the Council a blatantly slanted question.

'Tell me,' he said, 'in your opinion do I go now to sustain Jerusalem, or, as I swore to you some time past, do I remain here and on no account cease to rule over the English Realm and to govern it in the eyes of Mother Church? Speak freely, and let our beloved Churchman know your mind.'

They deliberated at length, then said what they had been told to say.

'It seems better to us, King, and more healthful to your soul, that you should remain to govern your realm and protect it from the onslaughts of the barbarians, than that you should leave us in favour of the East.'

Henry assented without demur, then made a business of extracting from the Council the promise of 50,000 marks with which King Baldwin might help finance his war against Islam.

Heraclius left the Council and their bow-legged monarch in no doubt as to his feelings on the subject.

'Heed this, King,' he stormed. 'You will not save your soul or guard Christ's property in such a manner. We came here to seek a leader, not wealth. Almost all the Christian world sends us money; the less their interest in our Holy Cause, the more money they send. But never do we get a prince whom we can follow, God knows, we need the man without money, not money without the man!'

So far, that was the last the Court at Jerusalem had heard of their Patriarch, though it was rumoured that he had vowed to stay in England until Henry either agreed to lead a Crusade, or did to him what he had done to the Archbishop of Canterbury, Thomas Becket. Evidently, Heraclius was drawing more strength from the damp airs of Europe than from the dry winds of Palestine.

Balian of Ibelin was at home, dozing on the padded seat beneath his coloured library window when Maria Comnena knocked and entered and shook him gently awake. The library was Balian's sanctum, and Maria could not remember a time when she had need-ed to interrupt him in this way. He frowned up at her and she raised a hand, forestalling him.

'I would not disturb you,' she said, 'you know that. But the news warrants it. Prepare yourself, husband.'

'Is it Isabella? Have you heard grave news from Toron? If she's ill, we'll go——'

'It is not Isabella. It's far wider in its implications. They say in the town that King Baldwin is dead. God has released him, it seems, and in my view none too soon.'

'Dear Christ,' Balian murmured, 'now we'll see some hungry eyes.'

Raymond of Tripoli had been with the young leper *in extremis*. After all the pain and anguish, his death was a gentle one. He had been heavily drugged by his physicians, yet whispered a few in-consequential phrases, all of which his secretary insisted on record-ing. He spoke of his sister Sibylla and his half-sister Isabella, of the trading ships that slid in and out of the harbour at Tyre, and of the friends he could count on the fingers of one hand, if he had any fingers left on which to mark them.

Then he hissed, 'God protect you, Regent. God save you, so you may save us all. Ah, Fostus, you iron man. Raymond, I cannot see you. Are you still with me? I would have enjoyed a life at sea. Are you still there?'

Even the dour Regent was moved to tears. 'Yes,' he said, 'I am ever with you, King.'

'And Fostus? And Balian?'

'Yes,' Raymond lied. 'They are with me. God will witness our presence.'

Baldwin lay quiet for a while, then said, 'Hmm? What? Fostus, do you speak?'

Raymond pushed his chin against his chest and gave an imitation of the gruff Constable. 'I'm at your side, Lord King.'

'That'll do quite well,' Baldwin mouthed. 'It's poor mimicry, Raymond, but it eases me.' Then he sighed and sank into a drugged sleep and, as the priests performed the rites of extreme unction, the physicians pronounced him dead. Raymond turned away, still on his knees, and crawled to a corner of the throne room. He buried his face in his hands and wept prayers for a Kingdom that had never deserved and had now lost its finest King.

Later, in a fit of tortured anger, he snatched the recorded words from the startled secretary and tore the parchment across and across . . .

Agnes of Courtenay was with her brother when she heard the news.

'Set a double guard around the child,' she ordered. 'He's the king now, and he's your responsibility, Joscelin. Raymond will be here before long to collect him.' She dismissed the messenger, then asked the Seneschal, 'By the way, have you put my advice into practice in any measure?'

'What advice, sister? You've issued more than one cautionary note in your time.'

She warned him, 'Beware, fair Joscelin. Don't dare to savage me. I have more years and experience than you, and my mind is quicker. You would arrange things much better if you were to listen more closely and swallow your sneers. In all my fifty years——'

'Fifty-two by any calendar.'

'As you will—Gentleman. Whatever, in all that time I never saw two brothers scratch each other and draw back with anything but blood in their hands.'

'Put it shorter, I pray you.'

'Just this then. You will not grow rich by opposing our all-powerful Regent. Reynald of Chatillon can afford to do it; he already possesses one sixth of the entire Kingdom. But you— You lost your lands in Edessa long ago and now have nothing more than a building in Acre and a shared house here.'

'I am well aware of——'

'It bears repeating. And so does this. My advice the other day is my advice now. Make a brother of the grey-hearted Lord of Tiberias. Assist him, be with him, befriend him.'

'I remember you said something of the kind.'

'So I did and so I do. Then get about it. Be taken to Galilee. Lay your path now, for in a few months' time——' She stretched her thin fingers and let her shoulders rise and drop.

Joscelin gazed at his pinched sister, hypnotised by her. Dully, he echoed, 'In a few months time——'

'The Child King, fool. Will it live? Look at it, it's in your care. You've seen it. Can you say that it will survive more than one winter? It's sick unto death! It'll die, and, if fortune smiles, it will die beside your path. Ah, you tax my patience too high. Get on and be the Regent's man for a while. From to-day he will welcome any friend who calls.'

Joscelin pressed his lips tight together. Not for the first time he dreamed of drawing his knife and plunging it into his sister's skinny frame. God in heaven, she was the leper's mother, yet she made no move to see his corpse! She was so cruel, so cold. Yet he knew he would not touch her, for if she were dead, who would guide him then? So he nodded and left the house on the Mount of Olives and went into Jerusalem in search of his friend the Regent.

Ernoul retired to his chambers in Nablus and lay distraught on his bed. Idela, who now lived with him at the castle, came to comfort him, but achieved nothing. She had never seen King Baldwin IV and could not understand what there was about the young monarch that made his loss so deeply felt. But it was enough for her that Ernoul was miserable. She sat with him for an hour, and then he climbed from the bed and showed her his half of the letter that Reynald of Chatillon had hacked in two at Kerak. She thought the royal seal was magnificent, but beyond that she could not share his pride, nor his grief. She had grown used to castle life; courts and Kings were another matter.

Fostus went alone into town and drank himself into a stupor. The innkeeper recognised the Constable of Nablus and sent him back to the castle in a hay cart. The innkeeper's son drove the cart and made the horse walk round all the pot-holes in the road. He was terrified that the squat figure slumped in the back would awake and make trouble. He decided that if Fostus did wake, he would jump from the cart and run home and tell his father that the horse had bolted, throwing him into the road.

The Lord of Kerak received the news by carrier pigeon. He was not moved, one way or the other. Baldwin had been a nuisance to him in the past, though, set against that, the king had come to the rescue of Kerak. He was a leper, and lepers were bound to die sooner than most. And it was not yet time to move against Regent Raymond. For one thing, the Kingdom, and Moab in particular, was suffering from the worst drought in fifty years. There was plenty to do in Oultrejourdain, without becoming involved in the politics of Jerusalem. And for another, the child Baldwin had to live out its puny life and die, leaving the succession in dispute. Then, and not before, would he make his move, and do so with all the power at his command. He was an impatient man, but he was always prepared to wait, if he knew that the waiting would not last long.

So the twenty-four-year-old king was buried, and his seven-year-old nephew was lifted on to the throne of Jerusalem.

Raymond gained an early success when Saladin accepted his proposals for a four-year truce. Whatever hotheads like Reynald might have thought about it, the people of Palestine heaved a sigh of relief. Food was scarce and becoming scarcer; they could well do without the Saracen raiding parties, the burned crops and rustled livestock. The truce had come at the right time. Now all they needed was rain.

Heraclius and Roger returned from Europe, angry and despondent. None of the three Western rulers had answered the call to arms.

The Grand Master sought solace within the Hospital, the Patriarch with his mistress, Pashia de Riveri.

The death of Arnold of Toroga left a vacancy at the head of the Temple. Reynald heard of it and came from Kerak. With the help of Heraclius and Constable Amalric of Lusignan, he secured the post of Grand Master for Raymond of Tripoli's old enemy, Gerard of Ridefort. Joscelin of Courtenay apprised Reynald and Gerard of his intended temporary friendship with the Regent, and with their connivance voted against Gerard's election. Raymond, naturally, was surprised and pleased by this *volte face* on the part of the Seneschal. He did not yet welcome him with open arms, but he was prepared to give Joscelin a try.

Amalric's brother continued to hold Ascalon, and many of the Frankish leaders came to accept that Guy and Sibylla had all but vanished from the political scene. They could not have reached a more dangerous conclusion. Until now a weakling and a vacillator, Guy of Lusignan believed that by having resisted the king's demands to open the gates of the town he had shown a new and durable side of his nature. Guy irresolute was bad enough; Guy inflexible for the wrong reasons presaged a disaster.

Time passed.

The inhabitants of Palestine died, or lived at starvation level, or were hardly aware that the earth had turned to stone. Food was sent from Sicily and Cyprus, Italy and France. The winter came, and the rains, and then the gentle spring of 1186. The worst was now over for the farmers; little by little the foodstocks were replenished and the animals grew fat. None on either side had broken the truce and, as Head of the Kingdom, the child Baldwin seemed less pallid than before. In the autumn of 1186 he was moved to the Seneschal's palace at Acre.

In the first week of September he coughed blood, whimpered and died.

The doors of hell banged open and the demons sprang free.

# CHAPTER THIRTEEN

# Acre, Jerusalem

## *September 1186*

For the first time since he had become embroiled in his sister's plans Joscelin of Courtenay realised why Agnes had sent him to be Raymond's man. He knew what he had to do—what she would have done in his place—and within an hour of the child king's death the Seneschal was in conference with the Regent.

'It's time to move,' Joscelin said. 'When Saladin gets word of it——'

'He will do nothing,' Raymond asserted. 'He will honour this truce as he has honoured those in the past. We have nothing to fear from Sultan Saladin.' He glanced down sharply as Joscelin gripped his arm. He did not care to be touched by another man and started to pull away. But the Seneschal would not let him go. His words took on a greater urgency and, holding Raymond, he all but convinced himself that his motives were honourable.

'Your sincerity is without equal, Regent, but think on this. We are a dispersed force at the best of times. True, you have held us together, off and on, for many years. But we have always had a figurehead, be it a leper or a child. Now we have none, and, with respect, how long can we cohere without a king?'

'Release my arm.'

'What? Oh, I was hardly aware——' He withdrew his hand. raised it as though to touch the Regent on the shoulder, then said, 'Look, Raymond, see it for what it is. You are not given to false modesty, and you know full well that the people look to you to lead them.'

'As Regent I do what is expected——'

'Yes, and it's exemplary. But as king——'

'You would have me crowned? Are you saying——'

'Ah, such piety. You've thought of it more than once.'

Angrily Raymond snapped, 'I am not after the throne for its own sake. If you think that, you don't know me.'

'I think only that you are the man.'

'I lay no claim to the throne.'

'No, and you have none, by blood or title. But you have earned it. Or put another way, if not you, then whom? Princess Sibylla, with a head full of feathers? Princess Isabella, for all her awareness still little more than a child? Constable Amalric? Myself? Or would you rather see it seized by Reynald of Chatillon, or some other firebrand? No, Lord Regent, it must be you. And you know it, I would say.'

Raymond frowned. 'You would support me in this? Until recently, you and I had a poor record of agreement.'

'I voted against Gerard of Ridefort, don't forget that.'

'Yes, and since then I've placed some trust in you. But——'

'For the Kingdom,' Joscelin mouthed, 'I would support a troubadour, if he were the right man.'

'I don't know. There are so few for it, and so many against.'

'God in heaven, Raymond, how can you say that? The people themselves are for it. And among the barons you have the Lords of Ibelin and Ramleh. Antioch is with us, and Sidon, and Roger of the Hospital, and others who can be talked round. Delegate your duties here, then return to Tiberias and alert your wife. By that time I will have—' remembering his sister's phrase '—laid a path in Jerusalem. I'll send word to you in three days, four at most. You *are* the man, Raymond. Can you say otherwise?'

'I'll think on it.'

'Then for God's sake think fast. I'll be in the palace. Send your aye or nay to me there.'

They parted, and Joscelin dictated a hurried report which he sent in secret, by relay, to Agnes. Raymond discussed the situation with no one, then told Joscelin what the Seneschal already knew; if it was truly the will of God and the people, the Count of Tripoli would wear the Crown of Jerusalem.

That evening Raymond left Acre for Tiberias and, an hour later, Joscelin rode south toward the capital.

Agnes of Courtenay read the report once quickly, then a second time, memorising it. She was alone in her house that night—alone save for the servants who were in their own quarters—but even so she took a taper from a jar, lit the wax stick from a pitch torch held by a bracket to the wall, then burned the report and scattered the ashes. 'Good brother,' she murmured, 'for once you have followed your orders.'

The report stimulated the woman into action; she had anticipated the child's death and planned accordingly. Now she had confirmation of what she had long suspected. Raymond of Tripoli was after the throne, and the precautions she had taken were shown to have been both timely and needful.

Without waiting for Joscelin to arrive she dispatched two letters, each bearing the Seneschal's seal. Then, when her runner had left to raise the relay riders, she wrapped a mantle round her thin shoulders and hurried down the Mount of Olives. She took no guard with her—it would be a foolhardy brigand who dared waylay Agnes of Courtenay—but she kept a needle-sharp knife under her cloak in case she was attacked before she was recognised.

She paid her first call on a white, Moorish style building at the western end of the Street of the Furriers. The house had a small street door and exterior steps that led up to the main sleeping chambers. The steps were closed off at night by an iron gate. A bell pull hung beside the gate, and Agnes jerked the handle continuously until a servant emerged from the street door. In the darkness he mistook Agnes for a man, and an unimportant one at that.

'Yes, what is it? The household is asleep.'

'Is the Constable within?'

'Who wants to know?'

Agnes threw back her hood and the servant gasped and said, 'Forgive me, my lady. I didn't see——'

'Well, is he in?'

'Yes, my lady, he's upstairs.' He fumbled with a heavy key and pulled back the gate.

Agnes started to climb, then turned and looked down at him. 'Your name is?'

'Bernard, my lady. My father was in the service of the Constable, and now I, I have the honour.'

The way she repeated his name made him shiver.

Inside, she found Amalric of Lusignan alerted and up from his bed. He wore a new-fashioned bed robe, a scarlet and lemon affair that curled his visitor's lips.

'Pretty Amalric,' she remarked, 'you are over-dressed for the news I bring.'

Tall and sallow, a match in height for her brother and Regent Raymond, he had once lusted with her and now loathed her. He had not shared her bed in more than two years, yet remembered her carnality as though the years were a handful of days. He had come under her spell, used her and been used by her, then regained his senses and drawn away from her. She had never forgiven him for having rejected her blandishments, while he, in turn, could not forget that this hideous woman had held him so long in thrall.

Spitefully he retorted, 'And you are usually engaged in other pursuits at this hour of the night.'

'I find no shortage of companionship, sweet Constable. Nor do I need the assistance of such finery in the bedchamber. However, I did not come out this way to admire the hang of your cloth. The child Baldwin is dead. I've sent word where it should be soonest heard. You know your part in this, or must I refresh you?'

'I know what I'm to do, though prolonging our discussion won't get it done.' He glanced pointedly at the door. Agnes had no choice but to leave.

She said, 'If you are ever lonely here after dark, let me know and I'll free one of my kitchen girls.' Then she smiled and left the ante-chamber. Amalric made an obscene gesture, winced as the door was slammed shut, stripped off his bed robe and stalked naked to his clothes.

She paid her second call on the Pale of the Patriarch. She had some trouble in finding the house, for she had not visited Heraclius at home for many months. Usually, if she wanted anything from him, he came to her. After all, he was her occasional lover, and she had no particular desire to meet Pashia de Riveri, mistress to mistress. But now time was too short; such niceties would have to be overlooked. She rang the crude spring bell over the entrance, stood back to see if a candle was burning in any of the upper rooms, then rang the bell again, repeatedly.

Heraclius himself opened the door. He blanched when he saw her, but before he could speak she stepped past him into the long, tiled reception room. A fire burned at the far end, and six candles added to the mean, wavering glow. As ever, she thought, at sundown he turns miserly. Heraclius followed her in, closed the door quietly and in an agonised whisper said, 'What are you doing here? She is in the next room!'

'Does she know about us, my dear Patriarch?'

'Yes!'

'Then my presence will not shock her. Bid me be seated, won't you? I believe you are growing more weighty in the belly. Tut, tut, you will injure me—or her—one of these nights.'

'Please, Agnes, I beseech you. Tell me why you are here. Oh, yes, yes, be seated if you must.'

'I have been with our Constable.'

'You are not——'

'Ha! I wouldn't bite a nail for that prancing creature. Can you see us together?'

'No, but——' He rubbed his round, fire-reddened face. 'Please, say what you came for.'

Agnes opened her mouth, then closed it again as Pashia de Riveri entered the room. The two women looked at each other, while Heraclius wondered whether or not to introduce them. Beneath his acute embarrassment he was intrigued to see them together. Pashia, so faithful to him for so long, the draper's wife who had been called a whore and had now become Madame la Patriarchesse, and Agnes, mother of Princess Sibylla and the dead leper Baldwin IV, a fifty-two-year-old wizen who had experienced four husbands and as many lovers as could find their way to the Mount of Olives. Though each had seen the other at a distance, they were face to face in his house for the first time, and they turned his interest inward, acidulating it until he was choked with self-disgust. He didn't want either of them, not the voluptuous one who was so easy to wound, nor the skinny one who was never called Queen. He wanted to be left alone.

'I want to be——'

'Yes?' Agnes probed, 'what do you want to be, Patriarch?'

'Nothing,' he said, 'Pashia, go to bed. I have business with our Lady Agnes.' He hesitated, then risked, 'It will not take long.'

Pashia asked, 'Do you have enough light? Some wine, perhaps? Fruit, or bread, though it's grown rather stale?'

'We require nothing. Go to bed.'

'As you wish. Then I bid you welcome and good night, Lady Agnes.'

'Pashia, my sweet. Sleep sound.'

For an instant nobody moved. Then Pashia nodded at Heraclius and went out, walking with exaggerated care.

Agnes smiled. 'She sways well for you, Churchman. I was never able to carry so much flesh on my hips.'

'Please, it's late.'

'Ah, yes. Some news to help you stay awake.' She settled herself in a chair and recited Joscelin's report. 'To-morrow you will handle the people. Your task will be easy, because the claim is sufficiently strong. Give your speech as we rehearsed it. By midday the others will be here.'

'Reynald? He cannot arrive so quickly from Kerak.'

'He is not in Kerak. For the past two weeks he has been waiting in Jericho.'

'But how did you know the child would die? We heard that it's health was improving. Reynald might have waited——' He stopped short and gasped, 'Did you *know*? Did you have aught to do with its death?'

Agnes patted his arm. 'Concern yourself with events here, my dearest. Give your speech, and do what must naturally follow and I shall be well pleased with you. Well pleased, Patriarch. You'll see.'

He thought, only Agnes could promise the best of the world and make it sound like a threat from the bowels of hell. He nodded, and she said, 'Move your chair opposite mine. Closer. Yes, like that. Now, does this amuse you?'

It was a miserable morning, with rain clouds piling up in the west and a damp breeze scudding into the city above Tancred's Tower and the Tower of David. Heraclius positioned himself on a mounting-block in the square in front of the Church of the Holy Sepulchre and waited for late-comers to join the large crowd that had already gathered. His clerics had gone through Jerusalem at dawn, proclaiming that the Patriarch would address them at mid-morning on a matter of grave importance. Rumours had circulated widely, but the people wanted to hear from the Patriarch's own lips that the Lord Jesus Christ had been seen again in the Garden of Gethsemane, that Raymond of Tripoli was to be excommunicated, that Baldwin V had died, that Heraclius was resigning his post and intended to enter a monastery in Antioch. Comment and observation passed like coins among the assembled crowd, stilling when the Patriarch raised his hands in the damp air and called for silence.

'Good people of Jerusalem! May God bless you this morning and give me the words with which to make His message clear to you. As some of you must know by now, the beloved and pitiful infant who was to have grown to govern us has been taken to Christ's bosom and now rests in peace for all eternity.'

He frowned, angry that his resonant voice should be eddied this way and that by the breeze. He liked to speak in the square on dry days. His words rolled against the far walls and along the narrow entrance streets, and the audience became malleable, indulgent when he was pleased, incensed when he ranted. However, on a gusty day it was uphill work; they just stood there like posts while the dampness settled on them. Drawing more breath into his lungs, he continued:

'His death robs us not only of a hapless, untried king, but also throws upon our shoulders the problem of a disputed succession. Claims have been laid; some so outrageous as to be an insult to all who would see fair government in this land. You!' He pointed at a nearby artisan. 'Would you lay claim to the throne?'

The man grinned good-naturedly and shook his head. He would have to tell his friends that one.

'No,' Heraclius boomed, 'and nor would I. Yet there are some.' Slandering liberally, he enumerated, 'Baldwin of Ramleh puts himself forward. More, I assume, because the name fits than for any lasting reason.' The crowd laughed at the simple joke, encouraging him to name others. 'His brother Balian would love to be king, but then he has always been a king-lover! Oh, yes, and foremost among these pretenders comes our Regent, Raymond of Tripoli. His claim? Perhaps that his father's wife was the daughter of Baldwin II. A long way to reach for a drop of royal blood!' They sensed the wit in that and laughed in the damp air.

'Unfortunately,' Heraclius pursued, 'Tiberias is of a more serious turn of mind than either Nablus or Ramleh. He will not be content to wish the crown upon his head, but will make some real attempt to have it placed there. This, as the sapient ones amongst you must have long since realised, would be a gross violation of the laws that govern succession here, in the Kingdom. Raymond has no rights beyond those that appertain to his position as Regent. You know to whom the throne belongs. You know it goes to Princess Sibylla, daughter of our Lady Agnes of Courtenay and King Amalric, who was king before the leper Baldwin. You know the rights of the case! Tell me you know!'

'Sibylla!' they shouted. 'We'll have none but Sibylla!'

Earlier that morning, Agnes had paid out a fair sum of money for the services of a dozen leather-lunged idlers. These were now planted in the crowd, and they began to earn their fee.

'Where is the Regent? Bring him before us! Patriarch, do you know his whereabouts?'

'He is at Tiberias, gathering strength, I hear. We expect him to move on Jerusalem at any——'

'No! We want Sibylla, not him. Close the gates! Keep him out of the city! Patriarch, help us!'

'Is this what you want, all of you?'

'It is!' they roared. 'Sybilla must be crowned!'

'I think as you do,' Heraclius smiled. 'Princess Sibylla left Ascalon last night. She will be in Jerusalem within a few hours. I promise you, good people, you shall have a queen by nightfall!'

Led by the noisy dozen, the crowd chorused their approval. The piled clouds broke into an avalanche of rain, and the Patriarch blessed the assembly in haste, then hurried under cover. He knew that Agnes would hear a full report of the proceedings, but as he shook his wet robes he felt confident that she would find his performance satisfactory. He was not to know that his inflammatory speech had been heard by Sir Conrad, Commander of the Knights of the Hospital, nor that Sir Conrad and three Hospitallers, Edouard de Cavanne, Cesarini the Italian and Matthew of Dorset would soon be on their way to Tiberias to warn Raymond that he had been duped.

Reynald of Chatillon arrived from Jericho. He was welcomed by his friend, Grand Master Gerard of Ridefort and by Joscelin of Courtenay and Amalric of Lusignan. Agnes, determined that the action she had planned and instigated should not pass her by, persuaded the Lord of Kerak to make his headquarters in her house. Once he had agreed, the others followed suit.

During the morning, Gerard of Ridefort and Constable Amalric left to organise the defence of the city. As the prompters had demanded, the city gates were closed—the Jaffa Gate in the west wall, St Stephen's Gate and Herod's Gate and the Postern of St Lazarus in the multi-towered north wall, Zion Gate and Dung Gate in the south, and in the east, near the Temple Enclosure, the Gate of Flowers, and of Jehoshaphat, and of Paradise. Templars manned the walls, while patrols roamed the countryside to the north, watching for signs of Raymond's advance.

At Joscelin's command, the cities of Acre, Tyre and Beirut were occupied by troops loyal to his faction. In the capital, the barons and citizens waited for Sibylla to reach them.

The Crown of Jerusalem was kept in a closely-guarded vault in the Church of the Holy Sepulchre. There were three locks in the vault door, each responding to a separate key. Heraclius kept one key, Gerard of Ridefort another. The third was held by the Grand Master of the Hospital, Roger of Les Moulins, and it was this gruff Crusader who presented the Patriarch with his first real problem of the day. Having sworn fealty to Baldwin V and having shown unswerving loyalty to his friend and ally, Regent Raymond, Roger refused to hand over his key.

Heraclius, Gerard and Reynald went to the Hospital to collect it from him.

'This is madness,' Reynald snarled, his red hair matted with rain. 'You are out-voted and out-numbered here. Sibylla will be crowned, so give your key with a good grace.' He sensed that he was bullying the wrong man; Roger was a heavy-set knight, with an untarnished reputation for courage and fidelity. But somehow the key had to be extracted from him.

'It is not madness,' Roger countered. 'It is the only shaft of sanity to pierce this gloomy scene. I and my men owe no allegiance to Princess Sibylla and you shall not have the key. You call me out-voted and out-numbered. I say I am out-witted and all but a prisoner in this city.'

His fellow Grand Master could not resist a gibe. 'Then leave your key and quit Jerusalem. We'll not detain you.'

'No, brother Gerard, that you won't. But I'll detain you.'

'We must have the key,' Heraclius snapped. 'There's no merit in your gesture.' He brushed rainwater from his face and wished they had chosen a drier venue for their argument.

Roger said, 'There's as much merit in it as in your entire action, Patriarch. The gates barred, the walls manned. Is this the way to prepare for a coronation?'

'It's the will of the people.'

'On my bare arse, it is. You juggle with them, cleric, and when your act is over you'll drop them like so many wooden balls. Don't prattle to me about the will of the people. You *are* their will, and that in itself insults them.'

'We want the key,' Gerard threatened. 'Do you give it to us, or do we take it from you?'

'One step, newcomer, and I'll use a key that'll open you You feckless man! You still have one foot wet from crossing the sea. How dare you blow your words at me!' He clasped a hand to his sword, and his eyes widened with anger. By God, if these three tried to take what was his——

Heraclius dearly wanted to retreat out of sword's length, but could not make the move.

'Listen,' he pleaded, 'Grand Master, we don't mean to ride against you——'

Reynald and Gerard both glanced disgustedly at him. What a fish he was.

'—but we must have your key.'

'Break down the door. One lock won't hold you for long.'

'That would be sacrilege!'

'To my mind it is already that, Patriarch. The Kingdom will exist a long time before it witnesses such a devious display, though I doubt that with men like you in charge it will exist beyond the year.' He glared at them for a moment, then cursed them and strode into the Hospital. Gerard started after him, but Reynald said, 'Stay put. We will get our key.'

They waited for several minutes, looking up sharply as Roger growled, 'Grovel for it then. It befits you to use a dirty key for your work.' He leaned out of a second floor window and hurled the object over their heads. Heraclius ran to retrieve it from the mud, while Reynald and Gerard stood rigid with anger. The Patriarch shouted, 'I have it! Keep me company,' and hurried away, head bowed, through the rain. They followed him like hunting dogs that had been called off at the kill.

Sibylla arrived at the headquarters on the Mount of Olives, accompanied by Guy and members of their household. Her mother greeted her as though she were already queen, then led her upstairs to speak with her in private. Guy smiled nervously at his brother, and Amalric said, 'Do you remember Sepphoria?'

'I do.'

'As we rode out of camp, do you recollect that I told you that your handsome features had purchased you a piece of the world?'

'Something like that.'

'They've done more. They've bought you an entire kingdom.'

'I don't comprehend. If you mean because Sibylla is to be crowned——'

'Did you bring your best clothes with you?'

'Yes, they are being unpacked.'

'Change into them, and be quick about it. We want the princess made queen without delay.' He watched Guy depart, then shook his head. Gerard of Ridefort came beside him. 'What is it, Lord Constable?'

'A dice roll,' Amalric said. 'One face makes a man rich, another makes him—Oh, I don't know. It's a dice roll, no more or less.'

Gerard's normal sullen expression was replaced by bewilderment. Was Amalric asking for a game of dice to pass the time? He shrugged and rejoined Reynald of Chatillon and they discussed Grand Master Roger and what they would have done to him if the quaking Churchman had not been there.

Sibylla and her mother descended the stairs. The princess was dressed in white silk, with a woven gold cord at her waist. Her hair had been brushed, her face whitened, her fingers weighted with rings. Amalric, Joscelin, Reynald and Gerard bowed low to her. She looked tired after her long ride east and pinched by the sorrow that even she must have felt for her dead child. She had neglected it during its short life, but its death had left a guilty taste in her mouth. Throughout the journey from Ascalon she had struggled to convince herself that it would have died anyway, in its mother's care or not. Beside which, it was not her fault that it had been taken from her. That was her brother's doing. Baldwin IV had snatched the child, and no mother could have prevented that.

She stood at the foot of the stairs, talking quietly with Agnes and Joscelin, then edged aside as Guy came down, apprehensively smoothing his yellow hair.

Agnes said, 'Make ready, my lords. I want my daughter protected each step of the way.' She nodded at Joscelin, who opened the front door and led the group down the hill. The rain had ceased, but the ground was still wet, and they were careful not to brush the trees and bushes as they passed.

The crowds were waiting for them inside the city walls. The group made slow progress along Via Dolorosa, and Guy noticed that the cheers and shouts of good-will were directed at Sibylla, not at him. He remembered how the Leper King had tried to make him exchange Tyre for Jerusalem and muttered with relief, 'That would have been a pretty pass. It's as I thought, they don't like me here. Well, I spit on them. When Sibylla's crowned I'll ask her to settle the court at Ascalon.'

They reached the square of the Church of the Holy Sepulchre and Heraclius came forward to greet them. Gerard murmured, 'There's no sign of the Regent, but he may circle to the south. We want no slowness about the ceremony.' The Patriarch blinked acknowledgment, signalled to the Templars to herd the crowd back a few feet, then presented Sibylla to her people. As was the tradition, he called, 'Good people of Jerusalem! Do you accept

Princess Sibylla, daughter of King Amalric of Jerusalem, as your monarch?'

'Yes!'

'Do you accept Princess Sibylla of Jerusalem as your monarch?'

'Yes!'

'Do you accept Princess Sibylla of Jerusalem as your monarch?'

'Yes! Yes! Yes!'

'So be it, in the sight of God and you all.' He turned and led Sibylla and the nobles into the church.

There was some pushing and jostling, and then Sibylla knelt before the Patriarch while he intoned, 'Do you, Sibylla, swear to uphold the laws of the Kingdom of Jerusalem——'

'I so swear,' she whispered.

'—and do you swear to respect the rights of those who hold land by grant or gift——'

'I so swear.'

'—and do you swear to give succour and protection to those in need, above all to devout widows and the orphans of Christ——'

'I so——'

'—and to mete out justice to all men——'

'—swear.'

'—and to safeguard those historic privileges bestowed by former monarchs on the Church——'

'Yes.'

'—and to hold faith in the same?'

'Yes.'

'Say, "I so swear".'

'I so swear.'

'Then, by the power invested in me I consecrate you queen, henceforth to be known to the world as Queen Sibylla of Jerusalem.' He placed the crown on her head. She started to rise, but he waved her down again.

'Wait,' he murmured, exchanging a glance with Agnes of Courtenay. Her expression told him what he wanted to know, and he continued, 'You are Queen, but in all you are still a woman. Look beside you, on that cushion, and see the crown that is there. Any woman who is Queen must have a man to assist and support her in her rule. It is for you as for any other. Therefore, take that crown and place it on the head of he who is best fitted to help you govern the realm.' Under his breath he hissed, 'Go on! Yes, who else but he!'

Sibylla took the second crown, stood up and beckoned her husband. Guy moved forward, the soles of his shoes held flat to the ground. He looked dazed and drew breath quickly through his mouth. While Heraclius whispered directions in her ear, Sibylla bade Guy kneel. She leaned down, kissed him on the cheek and said, 'Sire, wear this crown, for I know no better man on whom I could bestow it.' She placed the heavy gold crown on his head and repeated after Heraclius, 'You are the King, henceforth to be known to the world as King Guy of Jerusalem.'

Unable to contain himself, Gerard of Ridefort gave a roar of triumph and stabbed a finger north, toward Tiberias . . .

# CHAPTER FOURTEEN

# Nablus, Jerusalem, Moab

## *October, December 1186*

They moved stiffly about the Council Chamber, massaged tired eyes with clenched fists, reached up to stretch and stay awake. The Council had been in session since sunset; now dawn was not far off and the barons were no nearer a solution to their problem.

Although the castle belonged to Balian of Ibelin, it was Raymond of Tripoli who had convened the meeting. It had taken the better part of a week for the few loyal peers to reach Nablus, but all who would come were now together in the chamber.

Balian lowered himself into a wide leather chair and curled his hands over the carved chair arms. His thin, sandy hair had been worried and fingered until it hung unkempt over his forehead. He wanted to yawn, but dared not in case it became contagious. Instead, he shifted his legs, stretching them out, then gazed despondently at the smoking fire pit in the centre of the room. It's time for a drink, he thought. We've stayed away from the wine long enough. But he was too tired to rise immediately and was still slumped in the chair when Reginald of Sidon moved between him and the fire. Reginald did not see the outstretched legs, tripped and stumbled against the edge of the fire pit. Balian raised a hand in mute apology, but Reginald's patience had long since evaporated.

Straightening, he snapped, 'Is this your game, setting trip-wires for us?'

'Hold your tongue,' Balian retorted. 'If you watched where you put your feet——'

'Do you imply that I'm not alert? I'm more awake than you, host, lying there devoid of ideas!'

'Devoid of—Mind what you say, Sidon! I've put forward more

suggestions this night than you will in a winter week!' He came out
of his chair and they stood, ready to trade blows.

From the other side of the fire Raymond of Tripoli bawled,
'Does it come to this? Two friends laying on while the Kingdom
rots? Shame on you, Balian! And you, Reginald, do you travel
from the coast for a tavern fight? Make your peace and leave your
energy in your head.'

Balian had already dropped his guard. He essayed a smile and
Reginald gripped his hand for an instant. 'We're fools,' the Lord
of Sidon said. 'It's true, I wasn't watching——'

'Shush, we're all frayed to-night.' Peering through the smoke he
asked, 'Lord Regent? What if I were to fetch some wine?'

'Well said,' Raymond assented, 'I'm dried out. Do so, then we'll
talk on.'

While Balian left to rouse the servants, Reginald joined Walter of
Caesarea and Baldwin of Ramleh, and Raymond walked over to
where Humphrey of Toron was seated on the floor beside Ernoul.
Whenever the general discussion lapsed, the two young men talked
of the weeks they had spent together at Toron, reminding each
other of things they had said or done, seeing again in their mind's
eye the castle and countryside, the chess-board and dusty ball yard
and the proud, high-stepping Zerbino. Raymond stood in front of
them, waiting for them to return to the present, then asked, 'Are
you bearing with this endless discussion, Lord Humphrey?'

Thinking that Raymond had chosen to check his fitness because
he was the youngest and least hardy of the assembled barons,
Humphrey claimed, 'I'm bearing with it as well as anyone here,
Lord Regent. Like you, I'm dried out and, like the rest, I'm
fatigued, but——'

'I am not nursing you, Toron, so don't parade your irritation. I
ask your condition because I intend to propose a scheme in which
you will figure most prominently.' He rubbed his long, ugly nose
and attempted to lighten the atmosphere. As ever, he was faced with
the seeming inability of others to comprehend his sense of humour.
They maintained he had none, but he was sure that it was merely
because they did not see events from his view-point.

Now he said, 'In my scheme you will at least have cushions for
your buttocks.'

Humphrey and Ernoul frowned up at him, and he hurried, 'Yes, well, so long as you are wide awake,' and moved away through the fire smoke.

Ernoul dared to feel pity for the Regent of the Kingdom. Raymond was such a good man, so sincere, so worthy of the crown that had been held out, then snatched back again, yet withal so unrelievedly dull. Cushions for Humphrey's buttocks? The young squire shook his head and heard Humphrey mutter, 'Nor I. His wit is cast in lead.'

A few moments later Balian returned. He was followed by two servants who dispensed the wine and left three full jars to cool in the window. The barons drank greedily and waited for Raymond to reopen the discussion.

Standing near the fire where they could all see him, he said, 'This long session has confirmed the magnitude of our task. The myriad suggestions you have put forth have helped clarify the situation, though, thus far, we are faced with only two choices. For myself, I find each of these as unworkable or unpalatable as the other. Nevertheless, they are all we have, and I'll remind you of them.'

Balian surrendered and yawned behind his hand. He felt that Raymond was being too dogged. In the Regent's place he would have sent everybody to bed and resumed the discussion in the morning. Though, gazing red-eyed at the uncovered window, he realised that it was already morning. He yawned again and settled down in the chair, trying hard to concentrate on Raymond's words.

'First then, we can accept the situation as it is. Whatever the circumstances of the coronation, Guy and Sibylla are king and queen. So, if you ask me to free you from the oath of allegiance you made to the child Baldwin, you will be able to go in all honesty and bow the knee before King Guy.'

'Not on this earth!' Baldwin of Ramleh shouted. 'I say here and now, I will be the first to leave the country, rather than submit to that broken pair. Mark what I say. You will not find me in the Kingdom of Cornfield Lusignan!'

'Brother,' Balian growled, 'don't be so hasty. We'll find other ways.'

'Oh, yes, and probably as feeble as those we have already found.

It's as our Lord Regent says, each choice is as unworkable as the other. No, brother, don't soften me. My mind is set.'

'You are a man of courage,' Raymond said. 'It would be no little thing to leave your lands at Ramleh. But defection cannot help rid us of Guy and his party. Now, if the first is too much, hear the alternative. It is for us to hold Seneschal Joscelin to his word and for you to make me king. When Sir Conrad of the Hospital came to Tiberias and told me that I, and you Balian, and you Baldwin, were all supposed to have laid a claim to the throne I was shocked that such a brazen lie could be believed. But when he further informed me that the people of Jerusalem were giving credence to the Patriarch's story that I had begun a march on the capital I came near to losing my mind. Yet, my lords, if I am made king, we must do just that. You will all have to assemble your forces, gather with mine and march with me against Jerusalem. We are fully agreed, I think, that in such a situation brutish strength must triumph. I accepted Joscelin's offer in good conscience, but I will not cut a bloody swathe through my own people to reach the throne. I tell you this alternative, although my heart was never in it.' He stood silent for a moment, then drank and wiped the wine from his lips.

Walter of Caesarea said, 'You raise and lower that second choice, as you must. And I am still in agreement with you. You should be king, yes, but you cannot take that path. Yet what have we gained from this night-long discourse? We do not wish to make submission to Guy, nor to take up arms against him, nor to follow our Lord of Ramleh into exile. We are tethered, neither palfrey, nor destrier.'

'Not yet,' Raymond told him. 'I have a fresh scheme, one we passed over hours ago.'

Baldwin snapped, 'This is no time to remind us of our shortcomings. If you have unearthed something we overlooked, show it to us and let us pass an opinion on it.'

'Very well, Baldwin, assess the plausibility of this. If we, who have no claim by lineage, are unable to compete with Guy, we must find someone who is. Someone—' pointing through the smoke '—like him!'

They stared at Humphrey of Toron, who struggled to his feet. He gasped, 'Me? You would set me against——'

'And why not?' Raymond demanded. 'Like Sibylla, your wife is King Amalric's daughter.'

'Yes, but Sibylla takes precedence. We could not alter that fact.'

'We will not attempt to. Sibylla was only the ladder by which her husband reached the throne.'

'Lord Regent, are you saying that by using my wife Isabella——'

'I am saying that the queen has Agnes of Courtenay for a mother, and a shake-kneed Poitevin for a husband. Guy of Lusignan has no history in this land, whereas you, the fourth Humphrey of Toron and grandson of the warrior Constable would be welcomed with open arms by all those who mistrust Guy, to my mind the majority of the people. Remember, the crowd in Jerusalem was kept in ignorance of the truth. They did not know that Guy would be crowned. Good God, he himself did not know it until the end! He was foisted upon them, and I tell you, Humphrey, they will quickly grow cool toward him.' He turned to the other barons and remarked, 'Why, we may even draw some support from our sternest rivals. After all, Humphrey is Stephanie of Milly's son. To think, if we had the Lord of Kerak on our side!'

Balian was cautious of this dawn optimism and spared a thought for his step-son. He said, 'If that's the sum of it, let's first hear from Lord Humphrey. The responsibilities of kingship are not to all tastes.'

'Thank you, sire,' Humphrey responded, 'but I must speak my mind on this. I am totally surprised by my Lord Regent's proposal, and Princess Isabella has yet to hear it. However, this much I can say, even before I speak with her. I would rather not be king.'

'And I would rather be so!' Raymond stated. 'How else to shore up our sagging defences?'

'Seneschal Joscelin was right in one thing. It is you, Lord Regent, who merits the throne. For me, Toron is as great an area of land as I care to encompass. I beg you, all of you, search on until you find some other plan.'

Raymond frowned, then rubbed the lines away with a wine-stained hand.

'It is too late for us to suit ourselves,' he said. 'I would be king, but cannot—you say you would rather not be, but you must. I see no other way by which we can depose Guy and cleanse our condition. I suggest you sleep on this, Humphrey, then tell us on the morrow if you are still fearful of the throne. But I advise you to bow to the inevitable. You remain our only hope in this matter.' He saw Baldwin and Walter nod uncertainly, told the barons they would continue the discussion at midday and went out, his shoulders stooped with fatigue.

Balian then made an error that he was to regret all his life. Humphrey came across to him and said, 'Please, sire, tell me what position you hold. Can you really say that the Regent's scheme is composed of aught but hope and ideal?'

'In all truth,' Balian yawned, 'my thinking is warped for want of rest. I'll tell you my views to-morrow. Forgive me, young Humphrey, but I think our conversation would stand better on a foundation of sleep.' He turned his head toward a corner of the chamber and muttered, 'Good night to you, Ernoul. Or is it good day? Whichever, don't stay transcribing your notes until you drop.' He pushed himself from the chair, nodded at Reginald and Walter, then went out with his brother Baldwin.

When the barons had gone, Humphrey said, 'Ernoul, listen to me.'

The squire had moved to a small side table and was crouched over it, writing fast before his memory failed. He gestured to Humphrey to wait a moment, then sighed as his friend insisted, 'This cannot wait.' Laying his pen across the parchment, so that the sheet curled and prevented it rolling, he straightened and rubbed the base of his spine.

'Have some mercy,' he reasoned. 'Lord Balian has common sense on his side. We should first lay a foundation of——'

'I could not fall asleep now, unless I was drugged. Anyway, I won't keep you talking here. I've already decided what to do.'

'God, my back aches. Well, what have you decided?'

'Do you have the strength to stay on a horse?'

'To stay on—What in heaven's name for? You mean now?'

'Yes, now.'

'Dog's vomit, Humphrey, what riddle——'

'Yes or no? Are you too infirm, or will you ride with me?'

Ernoul clicked his tongue and glanced through the window at the flesh-coloured sky. 'Where would we go? Do you merely need the air, or is this tied to your decision?'

'Questions, questions!'

'Yes, questions.'

'It should not matter where! You are supposed to be my friend—'

'So I am, and that's why it matters. Whatever you say, you are pallid with fatigue. I, likewise, and if I'm to go charging out with you at this hour of the morning——'

'Jerusalem.'

'—then I have the right to know how far—*Jerusalem*?'

'Where else? After what was said in here to-night, where else would I ride? For once, your master and my step-father has denied us his advice, so I must act on my own accord.'

'But of all places, why Jerusalem?'

'Let me finish. I don't know how seriously you take Count Raymond's suggestion, but I'm certain that when he wakes later it will have hardened into a command. You heard him say what he would and would not do to become king. He limits himself on his own behalf, because he has no claim by lineage. But I have!'

'No. It's Princess Isabella——'

'Ah, don't be such a pedant. Isabella or Humphrey, what difference when we both must occupy the throne? And don't think I speak only for myself. I told Lord Raymond that Isabella has yet to hear of it, but I can answer for her now.' Pleading with Ernoul as though the chronicler held the power of yea and nay over him, Humphrey continued, 'We do not want the throne! I say it now and will repeat it every day of my life. I do not seek to be king; Isabella has no desire to be queen. We have discussed such things— not this present threat, but similar ones—and we are clear in our minds. We will serve the Kingdom as long as we may, but we will not lead it. That is the truth.'

Very gently, Ernoul asked, 'Why do you shun the crown?'

Humphrey took a slow, deep breath and moved across to the window. He gave some thought to the question, then said, 'For the first seventeen years of my life I remained at Kerak. I saw power wielded there, absolute power, sometimes used well, more often employed corruptly. Do you know, Ernoul, there is a dreadful satisfaction to be derived from the misuse of power? I'm confused about it, but I see it as a release, a breaking of the bonds of sense and responsibility, an opportunity to advance beyond all borders of restraint, yet ever in the knowledge that one's decisions cannot be gainsaid, nor one's actions thwarted.' He turned abruptly from the window. 'Am I clear to you, my friend?'

'If we speak of Reynald——'

'Yes, yes, we do! I have seen him acting the honest man, and as such he is so—ordinary. But when he is the true Reynald, using *himself*, then he is like a god.'

'More like a demon.'

'Of course a demon, but with such unrestricted power, razing this, murdering those, placing as little value on his words as he would on a string of wooden beads! Don't you see where I lead?'

'You think that if you became king you would also become corrupt?'

'I don't know. That's the truth, Ernoul. I don't know. But because I have seen such corruption employed, because I have lived with it, and learned that there is no man strong enough to defeat it, not one anywhere in the Kingdom, I will not risk following such an uncurbed path.' He sighed again, then smiled quizzically at the young chronicler. 'Do I sound too pious to be believed?'

'You sound deeply disturbed,' Ernoul answered, 'yet it is one of the most honest things I have ever heard a man say. You fear that power may use you, rather than you controlling it.'

'Not as master of Toron, but as King of Jerusalem, yes, I do fear it.'

'And with the mention of that city, you clearly do not think yourself strong enough to resist Raymond and the others.'

'That's so. That's why I must leave here before the council reassembles.'

'Then why do you not return straightway to Toron? The barons won't ride that far north to pester you.'

'Perhaps not, but I must first see my unreal sister-in-law and tell her that whatever she hears to the contrary, I have no wish to act in conflict with her.'

Ernoul frowned. 'You know, this might not be interpreted in your favour. For example, what will the Regent say when he hears that you have treated with his rivals? Also, there's a good chance you'll be killed.'

'We,' Humphrey corrected. 'If there's any killing, we'll both meet God. You don't imagine the queen would save your scrawny carcass, do you?'

'I am sure she would not, though I have still to say I will come with you. If the truth is told, I doubt the wisdom of this move.' He reached out a hand, said, 'Humphrey——' then let the hand fall. 'Hell's sting, I may as well ride alongside. And hope you break your neck on the way.'

They approached St Gilles, fifteen miles south of Nablus. They had kept silent most of the way, but now, terrified of what Lord Balian would do to him for having deserted—and there was no other way of describing their hasty exit from the castle—Ernoul said, 'Hold up a minute, Humphrey. We cannot risk our lives without saying farewell to our women.'

Humphrey reined in his horse and glanced scornfully at the scribbler. 'In truth, is that your fear?'

'What else?'

'Lord Balian, for something else. You're more scared of him than of Sibylla's brutal guards. That's why you want to go back.'

'You insult me,' Ernoul protested. 'I just want to bid farewell to Idela, is that so much? This way she will wake, find us gone——'

'And learn why. While you were arranging for the horses I dug old Fostus from his sleep. He knows what we're about and he'll tell Isabella and Idela when he sees them.'

'Oh. Well, that's set right then. Was he angry at being awakened?'

'He was rabid. He must be aging, because it was after dawn. Now, is your mind at ease?'

'I suppose so.'

'Then spur your mount, or we'll never get there.'

They rode on, passed the tiny roadside stronghold called Baldwin's Tower and, farther south, the small lay fortress of Bethel. Then they could see Ramallah, perched high on its hill, a reminder that they were less than ten miles from the capital.

Humphrey said, 'Let's take a rest here. We're not so pressed for time.'

'I'm not weary,' Ernoul told him. 'I thought you wanted to reach Jerusalem with all speed.'

'So I do, so I do. But I've been thinking. Once inside the walls, Sibylla, or more likely Joscelin or Amalric, might be loath to let us free.'

'Well, you've climbed down a step or two. In the castle you were busy promising me an audience with God. Now you're worried that we'll be held captive, a much better fate than a blade in the belly.'

Humphrey winced at the thought. 'You're too descriptive. And *you* faltered long enough back at St Gilles.'

'I admit it. But I'm not wavering now. You were right before; we must get there and see what happens.'

'I know that. I don't need you to tell me. I'm the one at risk!'

'We,' Ernoul murmured maliciously. 'You don't imagine the queen would protect my scrawny carcass, do you?'

They rode on again. Before they had halved the distance to Jerusalem they were halted by a road patrol. Humphrey recognised the riders as Constable Amalric's men, and they recognised him. Unceremoniously, they took his sword from him and escorted the pair as far as the city, handing them over to the Templars who manned the Gate of the Column of St Stephen.

Sibylla had decided to change her personality, as befitted her change in station. The rigours of monarchy required a more serious turn of mind, she decided, a more precise use of words, a more impressive demean. She was tired of being regarded as a frivolous child—she was twenty-eight years old, had been twice married and was now queen—and she was determined to bring credit to her position as first lady of the Kingdom.

But for all her resolution she remained a shallow *ingenue*, who attempted a part for which she was badly mis-cast. The result was embarrassing, but, like the poor actress she was, Sibylla was the last to condemn her own performance.

She waited in the Royal Palace beside the El Aqsa Mosque, in a room that was near, but not too near the throne room. In this room, named by Agnes of Courtenay the Queen's Chamber of Audience, a special throne had been installed, carpets laid and the walls painted in Sibylla's favourite colour, water blue. Together, Agnes, Joscelin and Amalric of Lusignan had managed to separate Sibylla from the decisive events of government, yet convince her that her Chamber of Audience was in every way as important as the throne room where King Guy presided. From time to time she was encouraged to wrestle with a problem of minimal consequence, and she was showered with inordinate praise, no matter what solution she reached.

This morning Guy was in town, so the Templars took Humphrey and Ernoul directly to the Chamber of Audience.

Setting eyes on Sibylla for the first time in four years, Humphrey found her as pretty as he remembered her, and, as before, dressed for a pageant. She seemed self-possessed, almost withdrawn, but he soon realised that she was attempting regality. She nodded at him, slowly, her head tilted a little to one side, then raised her eyebrows and gazed inquiringly at Ernoul.

'Humphrey,' she said, 'I had almost forgotten I had a branch of the family so far north. I take it that this young man is your squire.'

'No, Queen, he is my friend, Ernoul, squire to Lord Balian of Ibelin.'

'Don't you have one of your own?'

'No, and I'll wait until I find one as companionable as Ernoul.'

'It seems very strange to me,' she said, 'lending and borrowing squires. Surely you can tax Toron sufficiently for you to purchase your own man. Ah, well, companionship is to be treasured, I understand that.'

Humphrey said, 'I might well inquire about the financial situation here, too. Is this the proper throne room now?'

'We have two. My husband the king sits in the old throne room. This, the Chamber of Audience, is mine.'

The two men glanced round the room. Humphrey pulled down the corners of his mouth. Ernoul slid his tongue over his teeth. They were both exhausted, so found it easy to visualise a brocaded bed in the feminine chamber.

Sibylla did not like their expressions and queried, 'Did you ride

from Toron, or wherever you reside now, in order to inspect the
furnishings of the Royal Palace?'

'No, Queen, we are not yet so desperate for diversion. We came,
at least *I* came to tell you that I have been proposed as king, and
that Regent Raymond, with some support, would have Princess
Isabella and I crowned in opposition to you and Guy of Lusignan.'

The detachment of Templars had returned to St Stephen's Gate,
so Sibylla put her head back and screamed, 'Guards! Guards!
Quickly!'

Humphrey and Ernoul stood their ground as men-at-arms invaded the chamber. The stillness of the scene surprised them, and
they looked from their queen to the visitors, then to Sibylla again
for guidance.

'Find the King,' she commanded. 'Or the Seneschal. Or Amalric.
I don't care who. Tell them we hold Lord Humphrey of Toron
here and that he is planning to——'

Humphrey clapped his hands, pleased with the loud report, and
snapped, 'Tell them nothing. The Queen is presumptuous. I have
not yet finished speaking. Queen, for God's sake, draw off your
men!'

'Search them,' Sibylla said. 'They are no friends of ours, these
two.'

Patiently, Humphrey remarked, 'We have been searched. Three
times, as it happens.'

'Search them again.'

The soldiers went about their work with heavy-handed zeal.
Ernoul's cloak was torn, and, at the last moment, Humphrey
clutched the silver brooch that Isabella had given him, freely cursing
the guard who had tried to steal it. No weapons were found and
the men stood back, disappointed. Sibylla resettled herself and
waved them out. 'But be near,' she called after them. 'I may need
you again.'

Ernoul suppressed a sudden desire to laugh. He had spent the
previous day writing, or talking with Humphrey, the entire night
in council with the barons, the morning on horseback, and he was
now in the presence of an artless hysteric, while all the time men-at-
arms pawed him in search of concealed weapons. He was as tired as
a hunted buck and as hungry as the hunters. It was really very droll.

Sibylla said, 'You have little to smile about, borrowed squire!'

Bubbling dangerously, he nodded and murmured, 'Forgive me, Queen. My emotions are worn thin.'

'I know how that is,' she sweetened. 'We are not all crass beasts. Very well then, I do forgive you. Now, Humphrey, unless I am to summon the guards again, I suggest you make a true presence of your explanation—ah, I mean, a true explanation of your presence here.'

I am going to laugh, Ernoul told himself. She will have me killed, but it can't be helped. Look at her, preening and patting, trying this face and that. Oh, God, a true presence of his explanation . . .

The Lord of Toron took a deep breath and continued, 'I was saying that there are those who would have me crowned. I would have said earlier what I say now. I do not wish to be king.'

'Why not?'

'Why should I? I am not particularly well-fitted for the post. And I am not that ambitious. I simply do not covet the throne.'

'That's a poor excuse, Lord Humphrey. I don't believe you.'

'It is no excuse, Queen. It is a good reason, and you should believe it. You enjoy sitting there, I would say. For my part, I would not.'

Sibylla was bewildered. 'Why do you tell me this?'

'Forgive me if I grow impatient, but I'd have thought that the news explained itself. You have my word for it that I do not intend to be made king. Therefore, should you hear the rumours that will undoubtedly fly, you may feel it safe to ignore them. I don't like King Guy, that's well known, and I am certain that I could not do a worse job of governing the realm than he——'

'Insult! You talk treason!'

'No,' Humphrey said wearily, 'I talk to my wife's half-sister, and I talk about your husband, who rules because you are a Princess of Jerusalem. Well, so is Isabella. Thus I am in a comparable position with Guy. If I ruled it would be because of Princess Isabella, not because my qualifications were so exact. However, I repeat, I have no such ambition. Toron is enough. Am I clear?'

'You really don't want——'

'No.'

'You'll have to tell the King.'

'Willingly.'

'Do you think I make a good Queen?'

'What?'

Straight-faced, Ernoul said, 'You show a rare understanding of the important issues at hand, Queen. You can see that Lord Humphrey speaks the truth. A lesser woman might doubt such modesty of ambition, but you judge the situation for what it is. Lord Humphrey seeks to prevent unnecessary bloodshed, here and in Toron and eventually throughout the Kingdom. Is that not to be commended?'

'Well,' Sibylla smiled, basking in the light of the tribute, 'I see why Lord Humphrey keeps you with him. Yes, all in all, it is to be commended. Then, Humphrey, speak with my husband and I will assure your safe passage from Jerusalem.'

'To Nablus,' he corrected. 'Constable Amalric's men patrol the roads.'

'As you say.' She stood up and nodded graciously. 'Lord Humphrey? Squire Ernoul? Will you wait here while I apprise the King?'

Back at Nablus, the young men paid the price of their truancy. Raymond of Tripoli made Humphrey accept the judgement of his peers. Balian spoke in his defence, but Baldwin and Walter and Reginald all agreed that the Lord of Toron was weak and selfish, and that thanks was due to God that the plan had proved abortive. It was better that they had learned his nature now, rather than on some crucial future occasion.

Humphrey insisted that, even if he had desired the throne above all things, Guy and his faction would have defended their position to the end. They would have raised an army within the Kingdom, one as good as or better than that which the Regent could recruit. They would also have appealed to the rulers of the West, who would surely have supported Sibylla's claim. So far, King Guy had done nothing for which he could be condemned. He could not be deposed on the grounds that he was a fool; he would first have to do something foolish.

'It was an unreal plan, Lord Regent, hatched in desperation, too late at night. It would have stood us in the wrong and stained the Kingdom with Christian blood. I am sorry I left without due warning, but I feared you would all force me to act against my own dictates.'

'You are weak as a baby,' Raymond said. 'The Princess Isabella might have chosen better material.'

'That's an unfair observation,' Balian told him. 'My step-daughter is well pleased with this man.'

'Good. Then let him return with her and guide the petty fortunes of Toron.'

'That,' Humphrey snapped, 'is what I said at the first. I'll govern Toron as its rightful suzerain. But I will not snatch at Jerusalem when my claim there is somewhat less substantial than the handsome Poitevin's. Now, my lords, if you are finished with me, I am ready to go home.' He strode out, to find Ernoul waiting in the corridor.

They talked together for a few moments. Ernoul asked, 'Will you wait until they have dealt with me?'

'You know I will, my friend. Don't worry, they cannot be so hard on you.'

'Lord Balian can.'

'Tell them I forced you to travel with me.'

Ernoul shook his head. 'They won't accept that.'

'Then say you went along to keep a rein on me.'

'Well, in a way I did.'

'Shall I go back and speak for you? I could tell them how you softened Sibylla——'

'No, you've had your turn. Stay out of it now. They will only start on you again.' He jumped as Raymond called, 'Squire, you are wanted here.'

Humphrey touched him on the arm, waited until he had entered the Council Chamber, then pressed his ear against the closed door.

Inside, Raymond said, 'You are of no concern to us, Ernoul, but we will hear how Lord Balian regards your desertion.'

'With some severity,' Balian commented. 'Though I would make it clear that, in your state, I, too, would have kept Lord Humphrey company. However, I would not have sneaked away to tell my rivals what my allies were still propounding. I know what you did, and why, but the manner of it was deceitful. Have you anything to say?'

'No, sire. Under the circumstances I did what I believed was right, that's all.'

'You look grey in the face. You have been awake too long. I suggest you get some rest and then be punished.'

Ernoul trembled with fear and fatigue. He mumbled, 'Sire, with your permission, I will take the punishment now. I won't sleep if it's unresolved.'

Balian looked round at the barons. God, he thought, what stony countenances. One would think my skinny squire had sold us into slavery at Damascus. Faced by these men, I wouldn't sleep either.

'Very well,' he said. 'You'll be beaten in your rooms. Twenty stick strokes. And to ensure that the lesson is learned, Constable Fostus will lay on. Go up and wait for him.'

Ernoul swallowed hard, nodded and shuffled out. He heard Reginald of Sidon say, 'It should be witnessed,' and Raymond retort, 'If it's Fostus, I'm satisfied.' Then he closed the door and stared at Humphrey.

'You heard?'

'Yes. I'm sorry. It's so unjust. I dragged you into it. It should be my back.'

Ernoul wholeheartedly agreed with him, but said, 'I'll join you as soon as possible.'

Humphrey made a vague gesture of sympathy and watched his friend move, diminished by fear, to the stairway.

Ten minutes later Fostus entered the bedchamber, carrying a broken spear shaft.

'For a clever young man you're a fool,' he growled. 'If Lord Humphrey had not jerked me awake, babbled about the women, then hurried away again, I would have told him he was heaping trouble for you. He had nothing to fear, a baron of the realm, but you gain no such privileges.'

'Forgive me, Fostus. I did not think Lord Balian would give you this job.'

'Well, he has.' Speaking slowly, he continued. 'His orders were quite clear. I am to lay on twenty strokes and not stay my arm. Bare your back. Lean forward and place your hands on the wall.'

'Fostus——'

'Keep silent. Lord Reginald has sent a man to stand in the

corridor. Listen to me now, foolish Ernoul. Whatever you do, do not make a sound. Do not cry out at the first cut, you hear me?'

The stupid old bully, Ernoul whimpered. How can I not make a sound when he thrashes me with that stinking pole? What does he think I am, stone?

He pulled off his tunic and leaned shivering against the wall.

Fostus hit him with the stick. The force of the blow sent him reeling. He could feel the pain streaming left and right across his back. His tongue bled where he had bitten it, but he had forgotten to cry out. He stared at Fostus and was shocked to see the squat warrior grinning happily.

'You bastard!'

Fostus lashed out again and again. The bed shook repeatedly. Two chair legs snapped on impact. The planks on the floor were pitted in five places. Ernoul stood against the wall wide-eyed, his skin throbbing from the single blow.

As the sound of the twentieth crack died away, Fostus grated, 'There, you've been beaten. Nobody told me where to lay on the strokes. Now get some rest, while I send Reginald's spy away content.'

Ernoul's jaw hung slack and he moved like a dream-walker toward the well-thrashed bed. He managed, 'Fostus, you're the noblest man I ever . . .' and then he sank down on his side, deep in sleep.


Guy was King. It was done and could not be undone, nor made over. As good as his word, Baldwin of Ramleh refused to remain within the Kingdom. He left his lands in trust for his son and settled in Antioch, viewing developments from afar. Raymond of Tripoli also declined to submit to Guy and went home to Tiberias. Humphrey returned to Toron. Balian stayed in Nablus. The other local barons kept to their own fiefs, waiting to see what the King would do, or what Raymond could do to usurp him.

Even those nobles who had helped Guy and Sibylla left them to govern as best they could. Seneschal Joscelin rode north to Acre, while Reynald of Chatillon resumed his place in Kerak. November came and went. The treaty with Saladin held firm and, little by little, Guy mastered the ways of monarchy. He was lonely, more so, perhaps, since his only powerful friends in Jerusalem were Agnes of Courtenay, his brother Amalric, Patriarch Heraclius and Grand Master Gerard of Ridefort. These four watched his every move, assessed his development, criticised his decisions and kept up a constant barrage of comparative advice. If Reynald were king, he would not have done it this way. If Joscelin were on the throne he would have phrased it differently. Guy made the appropriate responses, while Sibylla continued to play the queen in her Chamber of Audience.

Then the worm in Reynald's brain that had instructed him to carry out his infamous Red Sea raid moved again. Captain Azo reported that a Moslem caravan was passing through Moab on its way from Cairo to Damascus. It was the largest train any of the patrol had ever seen, boasting several hundred camels, fully laden, and strings of fine Arab horses. Reynald did not hesitate. He ambushed the caravan north of Shaubak, killed every armed Moslem, plus some unfortunate merchants, rounded up the livestock and, with prisoners and booty, returned in triumph to Kerak.

As after the Red Sea expedition three and a half years earlier, Sultan Saladin demanded to know why the truce had been broken, and whether or not the King of Jerusalem could obtain compensation and a full and abject apology from the one called the Red Wolf of the Desert.

As in 1183, Reynald told his king to get on with the business of the Kingdom, whilst he settled the affairs of Oultrejourdain.

But since the sinking of the pilgrim ship Saladin had grown strong. He had become master of Syria and Egypt, and was Commander-in-Chief of the armies of Aleppo, Damascus, Emesa, Edessa, Mosul, Baalbek and Mardin. He called now, not for an attack on Kerak, nor for the lightning raids that had marked the extent of his previous displeasure, but for a concerted move by Islam against the Kingdom of Jerusalem. He called for a Holy War, the *Jihad*.

There were border raids, of course, emanating from east of the Jordan. Some of these flying columns penetrated deep into the Christian territories, into the seigneuries of Nablus and Beisan, and the Principality of Galilee.

During one of these raids Raymond of Tripoli was forced to hide under a fish stall to elude capture.

In another, three Templars were caught and dissected alive beneath the walls of their fortress at Safed.

In a raid farther south the Saracens came sweeping through the outskirts of Nablus. They fired hundreds of their deadly, black-tipped arrows and slashed indiscriminately with their curved and decorated scimitars. Eight of Lord Balian's soldiers and more than sixty civilians were killed within the space of ten or fifteen minutes. Among the dead was Ernoul's woman, Idela, who had been to the market to shop for herbs.

# CHAPTER FIFTEEN

# Jerusalem, Tiberias, Galilee

## January, May 1187

It took time for Saladin to assemble his forces.

Within the Kingdom, Guy appealed to his suzerains for unity and reconciliation. Some of the minor barons responded, and his hopes were raised when Balian of Ibelin made curt submission to him. Both men understood that there was no personal unison involved, but Guy was pleased that he had added to his list one of his most powerful erstwhile adversaries.

Having secured Balian, he next went after Raymond of Tripoli. But for once the long-nosed Regent had placed his own aspirations before those of the Kingdom.

Not long after he had been crowned, Guy had insisted that Raymond give a full account of his financial expenditure from the time he had replaced the Poitevin as Regent, some four years earlier. Raymond had refused to account for a single dinar, and, as Guy had formerly barricaded himself within the city of Ascalon, so now Raymond remained inside the borders of his own County of Tripoli and his wife's Principality of Galilee.

Guy retaliated by taking from him the city of Beirut. This had been given to Raymond by King Baldwin IV to help off-set his expenses as Regent. Guy mistakenly believed that by taking the city from him he would bring Raymond to heel. Instead, the disendowment increased his animosity. Within a few weeks of Reynald of Chatillon's caravan raid, the Regent announced that he had contacted Saladin and had made a treaty with him, safeguarding the territories of Tripoli and Galilee. This treaty was to hold good, even if conflict spread throughout the rest of the Kingdom. Furthermore, the Lord of Tiberias let it be known that he regarded any portion of the Kingdom that was safe from Saracen attack as being more sensibly directed than those areas that spurned all attempts at appeasement.

To Guy and his supporters it smacked of treason. Was Raymond advocating a totally passive attitude toward an enemy who had sworn time and again to drive the Christians into the sea? Was it his intention to become the first vassal of Saladin? Did he really believe that the armed might of Islam would stay east of the Jordan when the Frankish Kingdom was ready to crumble? If he did believe all this he was a traitor and a fool, and Guy's party acknowledged that the Regent must be brought down before he gulled others into adopting his creed.

In April, 1187, the Grand Master of the Temple, Gerard of Ridefort, sought permission to lead a force against Tiberias. He put his case to the King and the assembled barons in the Royal Palace in Jerusalem.

'God knows,' he pressed, 'if we don't reduce or capture that stronghold, he is capable of giving it over to Saladin. What then, King? A separate treaty for each hill and village? Each man swearing for you, or for the Sultan? I say let me raise an army without delay and show all true Christians how we deal with malefactors, be they robber or Regent! King?'

Balian was present, and stepped forward to block Gerard's path.

'You approach this like the insensitive man you are. We need Raymond. We need his abilities and his men.'

'In hell we may need them, Ibelin!'

Speaking now to Gerard and the barons who stood around him, now to the flushed, uncertain monarch, Balian said, 'We need that man, I tell you, alive and well and on our side. You, Grand Master, who fears that the Regent will sell us to Saladin——'

Purpling like a bruised melon, Gerard exploded, 'I fear nothing! I know it for a fact.'

'I doubt you, but suppose it were so. Where would we be then, set against all Islam, plus the strength of Tripoli and Galilee?'

'And that's why I say we must take the situation in hand and crush this traitor! Hear yourself! You are as ready as any of us to admit an alliance between Raymond and the Moslems. I say crush him.'

'I admit the possibility. Raymond is the proud protector of his lands and most of you here are as unwelcome on them as any Moslem.' That brought a gasp of anger from the barons, but Balian continued, 'Too many of you think you can diminish a problem by cutting it to pieces with your swords. King, I appeal to you. You have already lost my brother Baldwin, one of the finest knights in the land. As you know, like Raymond, Bohemond of Antioch has made his peace with Saladin. Several of our lesser peers are with Bohemond, or have returned to Europe. So far you have alienated Count Raymond, but if you now strike out against him, the Kingdom is indeed in jeopardy.'

Guy did not much mind if Grand Master Gerard came under attack; the sullen, round-faced Templar frightened him. But now it seemed that he, himself, was being admonished. Pitching his voice too high, he queried, 'You blame me personally for all this, Lord Balian?'

'We are all at fault, King, though the responsibility for our condition rests with you. When you accepted the crown——'

'Yes, yes, that's all very well, but with regard to Raymond, what else can we do?'

'Let me visit him. I'll speak with him on your behalf and attempt a reconciliation.' Ignoring the sneers of distrust he asked, 'What may I offer him in return for his submission?'

'Nothing,' Gerard intruded. 'Offer him nothing, King. He deserves nothing from you. I would not even leave him with breath in his body.'

'No, I will offer him nothing,' Guy echoed. 'You may tell him that if he presents himself here and swears fealty to me I will take no further measures against him. But that's as far as I'll go.'

The Grand Master nodded vehemently, then said, 'I want to be on this mission. The Lord of Nablus is a friend of Regent Raymond. It would balance the scales better——'

'Then come,' Balian told him. 'And we will also take your brother Grand Master with us. That, too, would balance the scales better.'

'I shall want to know how many Hospitallers he intends to bring.'

'You will be told.'

'I insist on having an equal force of Templars.'

'You shall have them,' Balian sighed. 'One for one. And you may lead.'

'So long as it's understood.'

'It is, Grand Master, it is. You have a way of making yourself understood.'

Gerard took that as a compliment. 'I've always been forthright, if that's what you mean. I don't dance with my words, like some.'

Balian turned to Guy, who nodded quickly, hoping the two men would not come to blows until they were outside. 'Yes,' he said, 'go and see Raymond, that's the thing to do.'

On 29th April, Balian of Ibelin, accompanied by Fostus and Ernoul, the Grand Masters Gerard of Ridefort and Roger of Les Moulins, Archbishop Josias of Tyre, twenty Hospitallers, twenty Templars and thirty foot soldiers donated by King Guy, left Jerusalem for Tiberias.

They spent the first night at Nablus. Even now, four months after Idela's death, Ernoul found himself looking for her in the bailey, listening for her footfall on the stairs that led to their rooms. No. His rooms. They were his again now. His, alone.

Balian and Maria Comnena had watched, helpless, during the initial period of anguish. For a week the young squire had roamed the castle, inconsolable. Then, when he could no longer hold back his tears, he had shut himself away, cursing God for a foul fiend, and Mohammed for being worse than the worst that was known to man. They had conspired together. One had killed her, while the other had let her be killed. They were of no use to him, these imperfect deities.

But when the first waves of torment had subsided, Balian asked his constable to take Ernoul in hand. Fostus badgered and bullied him, sent him on errands which he invariably insisted were of great importance—'No, not to-morrow! To-day! I want that message delivered and you back here before dusk'—then made Ernoul teach him chess and the rudiments of spelling and reading.

Once Ernoul snapped, 'Why don't you leave me alone? I'm tired of your ugly——' but went no further, for Fostus slapped him hard on the side of the face, then growled, 'Too bad. You're roped to me for a time, so get used to it.'

Later came the time when Fostus was able to loose the rope and send Ernoul back to his suzerain. He was fully recovered, save that he still thought of the girl and looked and listened and avoided the small castle cemetery where she was buried.

The next day, 30th April, Balian stayed at Nablus to comfort Maria, who had caught a spring chill, and to deal with a dozen outstanding claims for compensation brought by the townsfolk as a result of the Saracen raids. Gerard of Ridefort refused to kick his heels in the castle, so Balian sent the party ahead, proposing to rejoin them on 1st May at the small fortress of La Feve, thirty miles to the north. He told Fostus and Ernoul to take their rest during the afternoon, as they would be riding on through the night.

That evening, at Tiberias, Regent Raymond received an unexpected emissary. He had made his treaty with Saladin in good faith, so was surprised to have his word so quickly put to the test. His visitor, a wiry, dark-skinned young man who moved with the grace of a high-born woman, was the Sultan's eldest son, the Prince, called the Malik, al-Afdal. He had brought with him an interpreter named Hakam, a wizened old Syrian with the bones of a bird and a glance that darted this way and that, suspicious of everything, missing nothing. The two men were conducted to Raymond's private chambers in the keep and left in an anteroom there.

Al-Afdal was nervous and Hakam attempted to put him at his ease with a topical riddle he had saved for the occasion.

'Listen to this,' he said, 'and see if you can find its meaning. Who spends one sixth of their time gorging free fruit, one sixth drawing no music from the sweetest instrument in the world, one sixth all but naked, one sixth slapping themselves, one sixth raising their knees as they walk, and one sixth wriggling in their beds?'

Al-Afdal shrugged. 'Explain it to me. I'm not in the mood to guess.'

Hakam was disappointed, but he grinned, showing rotted teeth and said, 'Why, the people of Tiberias! Their year is divided into six parts. One is when they go out on to the lower hills and eat the ripe wild fruits. Another is when they chew on the sweet sugar cane. Then in the summer months they strip off their clothes. Then the flies come and they are forever slapping at them, or crushing them in their hands. Then it's the advent of the rains, when the roads become rivers of mud, and they have to step high as they walk. And finally, the fleas hop and the people squirm beneath their covers. Have you not heard the saying, "The Flea King rules in Eastern Galilee"?'

'I may have.' With sudden urgency he said, 'What if the Lord Raymond does not believe us?'

'Be assured, Malik, he will.'

The young prince put his hands to his head and adjusted the black cord—the *agal*—that secured his dusty head cloth. Then he brushed at his robes and stood, still and silent, watching the arch through which Raymond or his steward would enter. He thought, he must believe what I tell him. I must make him believe it.

Before long they were collected by Anselm, the diminutive Constable of Tiberias, and taken to a long, L-shaped room that was divided to make Raymond's study and private chapel. Two narrow, unglassed windows and a row of arrow-loops drove wedges of light across the cluttered study. An Armenian rug covered most of the floor, while sombre tapestries hung from roped bars on the windowless north wall. Raymond sat at an unimposing plank table, littered with seals and pots of wax, parchment rolls, pens, inks and a jar of sand. He came from behind the desk as al-Afdal and Hakam were ushered in. Anselm went away, then returned with a tray on which stood glasses filled with crushed lemon, a jug of sour milk, called *liban*, and a pewter dish containing small raisin cakes. The Constable slid the tray on to the desk, disturbing the row of pens, and bowed himself out.

Al-Afdal was not alone in his nervousness. The Lord of Tiberias realised that Saladin would not have sent his son at this stage unless he wanted something, but could not imagine what it might be. However, they were uneasy allies, so he masked his suspicion.

Offering them refreshment, he welcomed the men to his castle. They were surprised to find that he greeted them in their own tongue. They had forgotten that for eight years the Regent had been held prisoner at Aleppo. It was there that he had first studied the Arabic language and the *mores* and traditions of Islam. He did not parade his knowledge, though he derived some satisfaction from moments such as these.

With a gesture of apology he said, 'Forgive me, Prince, but I have exhausted all conversation with those few here who speak Arabic.'

'There is nothing to forgive. We should have remembered your mastery of our language. Please do not be insulted by the presence of my interpreter. Usually, when in discussion with a Christian——'

'Yes,' Raymond said. 'We are more lazy than you. Of course, the interpreter may stay.'

Al-Afdal bowed, then said, 'You speak Arabic as one who enjoys it. Who knows, in future you may have the opportunity to converse more often.' With an innocent smile he added, 'In fact, for as long as the treaty is honoured.'

'It will be, Malik, while I have a say in things. Now, may I ask why a Prince of Islam chooses to visit me?'

'A small thing. A formality. My father is on his way south from Banyas with some men——'

'Some men?'

'Yes,' the young Moslem smiled again, 'some men from Emesa and Damascus.' He held up a hand, palm forward. 'They are soldiers, but they need not frighten you. You are protected by our treaty. However, the advance party will be at Gadara, on our side of the Jordan——'

Testily, Raymond said, 'I know where Gadara is. These "some men" of yours——'

'Of my father's.'

'Whosesoever they are, they fit with the rumours we have heard of armies raised in Emesa and Damascus.'

'They will not trouble you, Lord Raymond. My father has other reasons for bringing them south.' He sipped the unsweetened lemon juice and continued. 'The advance party will reach Gadara late to-morrow. They must be fed. Your hills are alive with wild goats. As our ally you will not, I am sure, object to a hunting party——'

'You want to hunt in Galilee?'

'You grow good lemons here, too.'

'I said——'

'Yes, Lord Raymond, with your permission. The party will, of course, stay beyond the Jordan until dawn and return to Gadara before dusk. You won't miss a few goats, will you?'

Raymond knew he would have to agree. In one way, it was not so much to ask, and if it helped strengthen the treaty—

'Very well. But I must have your assurance that not one house will be fired, nor one field razed.'

The young prince looked at Hakam and both men nodded.

'You have it. And my father's gratitude. You are as we believed, Lord Raymond, the most honourable of allies. You will find that we, too, abide by every letter of every word. Now I must return and tell our cooks the good news.' He stood his glass on the tray and bowed low, touching a hand to his forehead and his heart. Then, with the unneeded interpreter still glancing left and right, he retired from the study.

Raymond stayed where he was for a moment, pulling abstractedly at his nose. Something . . . Some omission . . . A question unasked, so left unanswered . . . It seemed a reasonable enough request, and yet . . . No, perhaps not. Perhaps he was growing suspicious of every man, Frank or Moslem. He shook his head. Let them get on with it. Let them have their scrawny goats.

Then he remembered the question he should have put.

Balian did not rejoin Gerard at La Feve. He left Nablus a few hours after Raymond's conversation with al-Afdal and headed north, following the route taken by the Grand Masters and their knights. Flanked by Fostus and Ernoul, he had covered less than six of the thirty miles when he remembered that to-morrow, 1st May, was the feast day of St Philip and St James the Less. Each had been one of the Twelve Apostles, and St James was regarded by the Christians in the East as the first Bishop of Jerusalem. St Philip, equally revered, had carried out his evangelical work in Phrygia and Syria and, like St James, had been martyred for his beliefs.

Balian intended to celebrate the fête, but realised that Archbishop Josias was beyond reach at La Feve. He told Ernoul and grinned when his squire came promptly to the rescue.

'Even though we will not catch the Archbishop, sire, the next town, Sebastia, is a bishopric. We'll be there before the Saints' Day begins.'

'God bless you, you're right. He will say mass for us. I have not missed this Saints' Day in many years, and I have more to pray for this time than most. Speed up, Fostus! We'll make room for you in the church, somewhere.'

They reached Sebastia, the town in which the Patriarch's mistress Pashia de Riveri had once lived with Lambert the harness-maker, and made their way to the Bishop's palace. He offered them lodging for the night, though he and Balian stayed awake, discussing the state of the Kingdom. In the morning the trio heard mass, then rode northward again.

La Feve was a rarity among the fortresses of Frankish Palestine, for it was one of the very few to be under the joint control of both the Military Orders. At this time it contained some fifty Templars— Commanders, Knights and Sergeants—and forty or so Hospitallers. Gerard of Ridefort did not object now that the scales dipped in his favour, but used the slight numerical advantage to assert himself as leader of the expedition.

'When Lord Balian overtakes us, he may resume his command. Until then I will give the orders.'

'Tell your own men what to do,' Roger of Les Moulins retorted, 'but do not presume to tell mine.'

'As you say, brother, though I'm moving on from here at first light to-morrow.'

Mistakenly, Roger said, 'You won't be held back. Lord Balian will be here sometime after dark as he promised. I must say, I admire your zest for this mission of peace.'

'Make mockery of it if you will. I want it said and done, that's all. Either the Regent comes back with us penitent to Jerusalem, or he does not. We can get our answer to that without first waiting for Lord Balian to conclude his business at home, then to come puffing after us here. No, Master Roger, I intend taking my men on at first light.'

The Crusaders ate their evening meal in the castle, the Templars at four long tables, the Hospitallers at three. It was an uneasy affair, made worse by the presence of the dissident Grand Masters. If they had not been there the knights might have started throwing bread, then gone on to exchange jokes and stories. As it was, they sat quiet, the Knights of the Temple on one side of the long hall, the Knights of St John on the other. Gerard of Ridefort and Roger ot Les Moulins were seated facing each other in the centre of the room. They felt ridiculous and by tacit agreement hurried the meal.

Gerard was about to rise when Roger looked past him at the man who hurried through the main door and along the hall. Gerard turned as the man came level with him. He wore no badge of rank, though his mud-spattered clothes showed him to be more than an artisan or a farmer.

Thinking he was a local shop-keeper, Gerard said, 'What brings you unannounced in here? You are among the Military Orders. We don't deal with civil——'

'Are you the leader here, sir knight?'

Gerard glanced quickly at Roger, who watched him, expression-less. Then he nodded, 'Yes. I'm the Grand Master of the Temple, Gerard of Ridefort. Who on God's earth are you?'

'I am Lovel, the brother of Anselm, Constable of Tiberias. Praise heaven you have so many of your men safe here with you.'

'What nonsense are you spouting?'

'My Lord Raymond of Tripoli has sent me out to contact the garrisons of La Feve, Nazareth and Sepphoria. I'm to warn you that during the daylight hours to-morrow there will be a Moslem hunt-ing party abroad in Galilee. They have Lord Raymond's permis-sion to catch some wild goats, and they have given their word that they will not——'

'Where are they now?'

'At Gadara. They'll cross the Jordan at dawn and probably hunt in the valleys between Tiberias and Nazareth. My Lord Ray-mond——'

'Yes, well, thank our Lord Raymond for his timely warning.'

Roger growled, 'Finish what you were saying, Lovel.'

'He is finished,' Gerard said. 'What more?'

Lovel blinked his gratitude at Roger and went on, 'My Lord Raymond wishes it to be made clear that the hunting party is not to be molested——'

'That will do,' Gerard murmured.

'—and that it would be better if no patrols were sent into that area——'

'I said that will do.'

'—for fear they should antagonise the Moslems.'

'You talk, but you don't listen! I said it would do! You've given your message. Now get on to wherever it is. Get on!'

Lovel bowed briefly and hurried out.

Roger inquired, 'Why this boiling over, brother Gerard?'

'Shush! I'm thinking.'

'And I know the route your thoughts take. You would like to descend on the goat hunters.'

Gerard hunched forward over the small, central table. His round face was bathed in a sweat of pure excitement. He was no politician, but he had worked out something that would, that would——

'Listen!' he hissed. 'Why not descend on them? If we do so it will be as though Raymond himself had attacked them. God's eyes, don't you see it? It will break the treaty and force the Regent to side with us. We will kill fifty Moslems and bring all Galilee back into the Kingdom!'

'There may be more than fifty.'

'Fifty, a hundred, two hundred, what matter? Saladin will never trust Raymond again.'

'I am against it.'

'Aah, you are against every lifted finger. You are made more bulky, but in every other way you are like our tardy Lord Balian.'

'And you stand comparison with Reynald of Chatillon. With him it was a caravan raid to break the truce. With you some goat hunters.'

Gerard smiled. 'Do you think you insult me? Not so. I'll stand comparison with Prince Reynald any day. He is the only one who fights on for Christ.'

'You mean for his coffers. But we're straying from the point. I say we must wait for Lord Balian.'

'No.'

'You will not hear reason?'

'I have just expounded it. We *have* reason for this venture. If you wish to keep your black-and-white men huddled in here——'

'You know that won't do.'

'Then why the dispute? If you want Regent Raymond within

our ranks again——' He shrugged. It was clear to him, so it should be clear to Roger. He stood up, called for silence and gave the news to the one hundred and thirty assembled knights.

Later, they learned that the Marshal of the Temple, Jakelin de Mailly, and a detachment of Templars and lay knights were in the area. These were summoned to La Feve and arrived in the early hours of the morning, 1st May.

Roger of Les Moulins sent five Hospitallers south across the Plain of Jizreel to see if there was any sign of Lord Balian. There was not.

*He remembered the question he should have put.*

Anselm woke the Lord of Tiberias at dawn and pulled him by the arm towards the window of his bedchamber. 'Look,' he said. 'The hunting party.'

For a long time Raymond stared down at the road that ran below the south wall of the castle. As he watched, the blood drained from his face and his knuckles whitened under the taut skin. He whispered, 'Oh, my God, Anselm. Oh, my God.'

Gerard had not yet finished recruiting men. It was his avowed intention that not one member of the hunting party should escape. Whether they were fifty or five hundred he wanted them wiped out, so that the Moslems at Gadara would spend anxious hours wondering at their disappearance. As the first light of May flooded the Plain of Jizreel, the Grand Masters led their knights from La Feve, trotting northward toward Nazareth.

Gerard and Jakelin commanded one hundred Templars and rather more than sixty lay knights, while Roger rode at the head of a further sixty Hospitallers. Among these were the Commander of Knights, Sir Conrad, Cesarini the Italian and Matthew of Dorset, the three who had been with the Lord of Nablus at the Dead Sea four years earlier, and who had ridden from Jerusalem to warn Regent Raymond that the crown would go to Sibylla.

The garrison of La Feve was reduced to just two men, both lying jaundiced in the infirmary.

Of these two hundred and twenty mounted knights, the most impressive was Jakelin de Mailly. He was a tall, vain man, with yellow hair that he had allowed to grow unnaturally long in defiance of the precepts of his Order. Furthermore, he rode a white destrier and wore a polished silver hauberk. On several occasions in the past the Saracens had fled from him, convinced that he was St George of Cappadocia, the slayer of dragons and the personification of Christian chivalry. Jakelin was aware of his reputation and had pursued every reference to St George.

The expedition reached Nazareth in good order. Further recruiting took place and another forty lay knights, together with some foot soldiers and a mob of mercenaries were added to the column. The Archbishop of Tyre, who had kept to himself since leaving Nablus, chose to stay at Nazareth until the fighting was over. Gerard was not sorry to be rid of him; Josias would certainly have bewailed the Grand Master's intended ruthlessness.

Anticipating the direction in which the hunting party would move, Gerard of Ridefort led the column, now swelled by the few hundred infantry, toward the crest of the hill above Nazareth. He guessed that the Moslems would be somewhere in the narrow valley beyond the grassy ridge. The leaders rode abreast, Gerard of Ridefort, Roger of Les Moulins, Jakelin of Mailly, Sir Conrad and five or six others. The hunting party was where the Grand Master of the Temple had thought it would be. But what Raymond of Tripoli and all the mounted knights had failed to ascertain was the true strength of the Moslem incursion.

Shocked and slack-featured, they gaped into the valley.

Later, independent Arabic and Frankish calculation would reveal that the Moslem hunting party, led by Kukburi, Emir of Harran, was composed of seven thousand battle-hardened warriors, the regular soldiers called Mamlukes . . .

Balian entered La Feve. From some distance back he had sensed that the castle was deserted, and he was now astonished to discover that the great main gates were not even closed. Dogs ran barking about the empty yard and kites circled lazily above the towers. Fostus and Ernoul drew up on either side of him and the three men sat, squinting up at the windows, their ears tuned to any human sound, a step, a cough, anything.

'Hell in hell,' Balian breathed. 'Where have they all gone?'

Ernoul turned in his saddle, earning a frown from the others as the leather creaked. He said, 'There's no one on the walls. Shall I look inside?'

'Yes, do that. Search those buildings over there. Fostus, see to the keep. I'll make a circuit of the castle. This is beyond belief. And for members of the Military Orders to have left it thus.' He shook his head, gestured quickly at the keep and the out-buildings, indicating that his companions were to start the search, then rode out through the gate and alongside the wall.

He found nothing.

Fostus found the smoking remains of a fire, but nothing more.

Ernoul moved through empty galleries and dormitories, up and down stairways, along echoing corridors and passageways until, starting nervously, he heard a weak voice call, 'Almighty Christ! Bring us some water.'

He found the two jaundiced Crusaders in the infirmary, fetched a deep basin of water for them and asked them where the garrison had gone, and why, and how long ago. They told him what they knew, that word had come of a Saracen invasion of Galilee and that every able man had gone to do battle near Nazareth.

'But they wouldn't!' Ernoul exclaimed. 'They are not given to breaking treaties.'

'I don't know what you're talking about, lad. A Saracen is a Saracen, and a stain on Christ's Kingdom.'

The young squire would have stayed to argue, but he heard Balian call from the yard. He placed the basin where both men could reach it and ran down the nearest staircase, emerging at the same moment as Fostus.

'They've gone to Nazareth!' he shouted. 'They heard that the Saracens had invaded Galilee. It doesn't seem possible.'

'Mount up,' Balian ordered. 'God will we are not too late.'

An incredible scene was being enacted on the ridge above Nazareth. The Moslem host had noticed the line of Christian leaders, but, as yet, they were content to improve their position in the valley.

When the size of the enemy force had impressed itself upon their stunned minds, the Crusaders voiced their conflicting opinions.

Roger of Les Moulins and Sir Conrad proposed an immediate withdrawal to Nazareth, from where detachments would be sent to regarrison La Feve and to strengthen the nearby castles at Burie and Mount Tabor.

Gerard, true to his character, advocated a straight charge down the hill.

The three who had spoken then turned toward Jakelin de Mailly.

'I say we should retreat. We are out-numbered ten or twenty to one. That is no band of goat hunters down there. I say retreat, and quickly.'

Gerard gazed down into the seething valley. Without glancing at Jakelin he said, 'The thing is, you love your blond hair too much to risk losing it.'

For an instant Jakelin did not realise he was being addressed. When he did, he roared, 'When I lose it, it will be in battle, and when I die it will be like a brave man! It's you, I think, who will flee like a coward!' Without another word he wheeled his horse, rode back to where the Templars waited in a mass and yelled, 'With me! Deus vult! For St George!'

Gerard howled with pleasure, dragged his horse in a tight circle and led a second mass of knights over the ridge.

Suddenly, it had gone too far to be stopped. Templars, Hospitallers and the rest were sweeping up to the ridge and over it into the valley. None of them had seen what lay below. By the time they saw the enemy they were among them. The Grand Master of the Hospital and his Commander of Knights found themselves at the rear of their own men. They had no choice but to follow. The foot soldiers scrambled after the cavalry and within moments the ridge was devoid of Crusaders.

Roger of Les Moulins was killed in the fight.

Jakelin of Mailly was killed, and his weapons, clothes and armour taken for souvenirs of St George.

Sir Conrad of the Hospital was killed, and with him Cesarini the Italian and Matthew of Dorset.

Every Templar and Hospitaller who was not killed in battle was executed on the spot.

The lay knights who survived were taken prisoner and dispatched to Damascus.

Every foot soldier was murdered out of hand.

Of the two hundred and sixty knights, two hundred and fifty-seven were killed or captured. Of the three who escaped, one was Gerard of Ridefort.

# CHAPTER SIXTEEN

# Nazareth, Jerusalem, Palestine

## *May, June 1187*

His face was lacerated, his hands thrust into crimson gauntlets woven from his own blood. One of his companions had been hacked so deeply above the left wrist that it was clear he would lose the hand. The third rider clutched the shaft of an arrow that had entered one side of his neck and emerged on the other. The wooden shaft blocked his air pipe and each breath required a greater effort. The three horses were webbed with cuts, though none had been hamstrung or pierced by arrows. Slowly, favouring their injuries, they carried their riders round the base of the hill and on to a road that led back to Nazareth.

Balian saw them from the crest of the ridge. He also saw the carnage in the valley, the stripped bodies of the dead Crusaders, the ruined horses and the milling host of Saracens, while here and there stood the taller figures of their few Frankish prisoners. In turn, the Mamlukes saw Balian and Fostus and Ernoul, but, as before, they made no attempt to storm the hill. A few moments passed, and then, as though responding to an order, the Saracens started eastward along the valley, and Balian turned west to intercept the three Christian survivors.

Gerard heard the horses approach and peered in agony toward the sound. He recognised the Lord of Nablus, raised a bloody hand and flapped it:—leave me be, leave me be. But Balian was already level with him.

'You bastard!' he roared. 'You foul iniquity! This is your doing! I *know* you! Oh, God, you have had your way with us. You have maimed us now, and I am going to kill you for it. Aah, Gerard, you *bastard*!' He twisted clumsily in his saddle and unsheathed his sword.

Gerard flapped his hand. 'Leave me be,' he croaked. 'You stayed away, so you can't know how it was.'

'I know, filth, and I am going to kill you.' He jerked his horse round to keep its head clear of the blade, then swung the sword. There was a clash of steel. The weapon shuddered in his hand. He looked to his right and saw that Fostus had drawn his own sword and parried the blow.

'No, lord, or it makes you like him. I could kill him ten times over——'

'Move back, Constable.'

'No, sire. You would favour him to kill him——'

'For the last time, because I love you. *Move back!*'

Quick, Ernoul told himself, say something. Christ, they will cut each other. Say something. Oh, Jesus, quick.

'That man dies,' he gabbled. 'Over there, the one with the arrow. Look, he's going.'

It was true. The Crusader slid from his horse and fell head first, snapping the arrow as he landed. Terrified beyond thought, Ernoul forced his way between Balian and Fostus. It was an instinctive movement and he sat, his eyes closed tight, waiting to be cut from right or left. All the while Gerard flapped his hand and mumbled, 'Leave me be. You can't know the way of it. Leave me be.'

Fostus waited, scarcely aware of the shivering obstacle hunched in his path. Lord Balian must decide how it would go.

Balian held his position, then suddenly reversed his sword and sheathed it. 'Yes,' he sighed. 'It's as you say. It would make me like him.' Looking up sharply he asked, 'Would you have cut me?'

'I would have disarmed you, sire.'

'You think so? You think you could have done it?'

'I could.'

Balian grinned, his fury dissipated. 'I think so, too. Hey, Ernoul, you can stop playing the barrier now.' He leaned across and touched him on the shoulder.

Fostus growled, 'That's the way to get your head lopped off, fool.'

'I know,' Ernoul said, 'but you wouldn't have done it.' Then, still trembling, 'Would you?'

Fostus chose not to answer. The three men accompanied Gerard

and his remaining companion to Nazareth, and left them in the care
of local physicians. Then they collected Archbishop Josias and,
unescorted, set out to complete their ill-fated mission. Now it
seemed certain that King Guy and Regent Raymond would be
reconciled.

The Lord of Tiberias had already heard the news and reached the
same conclusion. Ironically, al-Afdal had kept his promise, as he
had said, abiding by every letter of every word. The hunting party
had entered Galilee with the light and would be back at Gadara
before nightfall. Not a house had been fired, nor a wheatfield razed.
The fact that the Moslem prince had not specified the size of the
party did not mark him as a liar, though the result of the day's work
made a mockery of the treaty.

Without hesitation, Raymond disowned all allegiance with
Saladin and, leaving his wife Eschiva to organise the defence of
Tiberias, he rode with Balian and the others to Jerusalem.

He was, in many respects, a broken man. His desire for the throne
had been thwarted, his attempt to have Humphrey of Toron made
king had proved abortive, and his treaty with the Sultan had been
short-lived. He despised himself for having failed to discover the
size of Emir Kukburi's hunting party, and the ride south was a dis-
mal, uncommunicative affair. He was now prepared to do whatever
King Guy commanded, and to take whatever punishment the
monarch meted out. At one stage of the journey he did speak, but
it was only to remark that the Kingdom of Jerusalem was no place
for a man of good intentions.

Later, addressing no-one in particular, he mused, 'I have always
believed in the rightness of my actions. And in the future of the
Christ's Holy Land. Perhaps, if I had been born a Joscelin of Courtenay, or a Reynald of Chatillon, I might have served the Kingdom
better. Not as them, but with some of their cunning.'

Riding next to him, Balian said, 'Nobody may condemn you for
following your beliefs. It's not cunning we lack. God knows,
we have some fine practitioners of that. It's unity. We have never
faced the same way long enough to see the truth. Now, if God
wills it and the King is not too vengeful, we may at last all stand
together.'

'I hope so, Balian. One more single mistake and we are all lost, you know that. By the way, do you think Gerard will die?'

'If Fostus here had not baulked me, our Grand Master would already be meat for the worms. As it is, I don't know. The Templar looks like a pig, but he has the strength of a wild boar. I would not bury him too soon.'

Fostus stated, 'He'll be on the field in a week or two.'

Conversation flagged and they continued in silence on their one hundred and twenty mile journey from the black rock shore of the Sea of Galilee to the two thousand foot heights of the capital.

The King's patrols warned him of the approach of Regent Raymond. With rare good sense Guy summoned his brother Constable Amalric, Joscelin of Courtenay, one representative of the Temple and one of the Hospital, and told them to ride with him and greet their contrite Regent.

'You won't wait for him in the palace?' Amalric queried. 'You should make him come to you.'

'No. This is a gesture we can afford. Balian was right. We need Raymond, now as never before.'

Astride a magnificently caparisoned horse, he led them out of the city and along the road toward the Ramallah fork.

The two groups met a mile south of the fork. Guy nodded at Raymond and Balian and Archbishop Josias, and was about to dismount when Amalric hissed, 'Not yet! Let the Regent show willing.'

'Oh, your pride will bring us down,' Guy grumbled. 'Does it matter who puts their foot on the ground first?' Nevertheless, he stayed in the saddle until Raymond had climbed from his horse.

'Now,' Guy said, 'is that sufficient for us, brother?'

'It's done better this way—King.'

Raymond came forward alone. When he was a dozen feet away Seneschal Joscelin challenged him.

'Do you come here in peace, Regent?'

Raymond opened his hands. He was face to face with the man who had promised him the throne, then tricked him as though he were a child begging sugar stalks. He despised Joscelin more than he despised himself and he made no attempt to hide his feelings.

'That's a foolish question, Seneschal. I would not have come this far to cause trouble at court. There are enough of you here for that.'

'Still swollen with self-esteem, eh, Tripoli?'

'No, Joscelin. Still Regent of the Kingdom.'

'Oh, come,' Guy appealed. 'I wish I'd left you all in Jerusalem. Raymond, tell me, will you make submission to me? If only for the sake of my prideful companions.'

'I will,' Raymond nodded, 'but not for their sake. I'll do it for the Kingdom, naught else.' With that he lowered himself to his knees in the dusty road.

Guy dismounted and hurried to him. 'No, no, this won't do. On your feet, I pray you. Here, embrace me. That's it, that's better.'

Turning to make sure that Joscelin and Amalric could hear him, he said, 'You've made your peace with me, Lord Regent. Now I'll make mine with you. With regard to my coronation, it was ill-conceived and I am sorry for it. The Moslem world still look on you as the true Christian leader, as do the weight of our own people. However, what's done is done.'

Amalric glared at him, while Joscelin glanced at the Hospitaller and the Templar to see how they were taking it. The Templar seemed confused. The Hospitaller was too busy slapping flies from his face to listen.

Guy leaned down and brushed the dust from Raymond's clothes. Then he said, 'Be with me. I need good advice,' and walked back to his horse. The two groups mixed and returned in some kind of unity to Jerusalem.

Reynald of Chatillon's caravan raid had affixed the seal to the Moslem *Jihad*. The massacre at Nazareth had done as much for Christendom. It was time to face the enemy in strength and to hear which cry came louder, 'Allah Akbar! La ilaha il' Allah!' or 'Christus vincit! Christus regnat! Deus vult!'

Humphrey of Toron prepared to leave for war.

He spent the last evening at the castle alone with Isabella. They ate early, and then, while Constable Pola checked the final condition of men and materials, they retired to their bedchamber. For a while they sat like shy, would-be lovers, warming their hands at a small fire that burned in a hollow in the outer wall. Then Isabella moved away and brought wine and two of her best glasses, a gift from her mother Maria Comnena.

She passed a full glass to Humphrey and he looked up, startled, showing the fear in his eyes.

'What? Oh, I'm sorry, my love. My thoughts were miles away.'

She sipped her wine and said, 'I wrote about you again yesterday.'

'Mmm? In your diary?'

'Yes.' She smiled over the rim of the glass. 'In the code you unravelled so quickly.'

'I hope you found something good to say.'

'Oh, I did, love. Oh, yes, I have always found good to say about you.'

He started to speak, but drank his wine instead, then flicked drops of wine into the fire to hear them hiss. The drops became Moslem horsemen and he found that by dipping four fingers into the glass he could annihilate an entire spray of Saracens . . .

He stopped playing and murmured, 'Isabella, we are on the threshold of a decisive battle, I believe. We cannot lose, for we are stronger, if not in numbers then in the power of our knights, better equipped and desperate to preserve our lands. But in any battle there will be casualties——'

'Not you.'

'I pray not, though if God choose to take me——'

'Ah, dear husband, don't torture yourself. I may be the youngest châtelaine in the Kingdom, but I know where my duties lie. This must be said, so let me say it. If you die, or are captured in the coming fight, I will continue to govern Toron as I have seen you govern it. And as for the ransom, I'll raise that in a week.'

'There'll be no ransom if I'm dead. You will then have to find a man.'

'In time, yes. But whoever he is, he'll never replace you. Not in my heart, nor my mind, nor in my bed.'

'That would be unfair.'

'No, no, for I would not let him compare with you. He would be —a different man, that's all.' She laughed gently. 'I hope you would approve of him, though you would probably think I had chosen badly.'

Humphrey said, 'Your uncle, Baldwin of Ramleh, he'd do.'

'Hmm, that type of man, perhaps, but not Lord Baldwin. He's too tempestuous. And he drinks to excess.'

His fears diminished, Humphrey raised his glass. 'To your next husband, then,' he grinned, 'though I trust we won't need him for many years.'

'We won't,' she said, adding, 'nor do we need him to-night.'

They let the fire burn on and undressed by its light. They lay quiet in the wide bed, allowing their thoughts to probe the future, then return to the warmth of the soft-lit bedchamber. They moved together and gave love unhurriedly, the twenty-year-old master of Toron and his fourteen-year-old princess. They lay quiet again and Isabella slept in his arms. Later, he slid from the bed, dressed and spent the dawn hours in prayer in the private chapel. While he prayed he laid one hand flat on the silver brooch she had magicked for him.

In the morning he led his Constable, knights and foot soldiers away from the castle, then south-west across the Aamel Mountains toward Acre. He left Isabella eighteen men with which to defend Toron.

With the death in the valley near Nazareth of both Grand Master Roger of Les Moulins and the Commander of Knights, Sir Conrad, the Order of the Hospital elected a new leader. This was a husky, dedicated Hospitaller named Ermengard de Daps. Ermengard was in many ways akin to Roger, so the election did nothing to dampen the rivalry between the Hospital and the Temple. Throughout the month of June, the black-and-white knights emptied their castles, among them those of Markab, Château Rouge, Bethsour, Beth Gibelin, Recordane Mills and L'Assebebe, and made their way to Acre.

Reynald of Chatillon prepared to leave for war.

He celebrated his departure by releasing several merchants

taken prisoner during his attack on the caravan the previous winter. At first he had insisted that they obtain their freedom by paying an exorbitant ransom. But since the massacre of the Crusaders at Nazareth he had decided not to wait for the merchants' families to raise and send the money. Instead, he released the men—minus their hands.

It was his way of showing Sultan Saladin that he welcomed the approaching conflict and wished to be regarded—as he had always claimed—as the enemy of enemies.

With her own money Stephanie of Milly bought him a present of forty European mercenaries, each fully outfitted and armed and all bearing shields inscribed with the words of his seal—RAINALDUS PRINCEPS ANTIOCHENUS—SANCTUS PETRUS SANCTUS PAULUS. These men, together with all but forty of the garrison, allowed him to leave Kerak with more than sixty knights, some twenty-five of whom were from the neighbouring fortress of Shaubak, and close on three hundred foot soldiers. He left as Stephanie wanted him to leave, unashamed of the past and confident of the future. He told her he would send word to her from Saladin's palace in Damascus, for that was surely where the battle would end.


The Grand Master of the Temple and architect of the defeat at Nazareth recovered from his wounds and set about recruiting his own contingent. More than one quarter of the Templar knights— and these the elite—had been lost in the massacre, so that most of the money King Henry II of England had sent in lieu of his presence in the Holy Land was appropriated to pay for more mercenaries. A number of likely-looking soldiers were given the buffet of knight-hood, and the ranks were further swelled by the exodus of Templars from Jericho, Maldouin, Château Pelerin, Le Chastellet and Safed.

Gerard of Ridefort was regarded as a hero by the members of his Order—who but a Templar would have dared attack seven thousand Mamlukes?—and their adulation helped convince him that he had acted with courage and honour. They missed their friends and the chivalric Marshal, Jakelin de Mailly, though their deaths injected the remaining knights with fresh determination. They would meet these Mamlukes again, but this time the massacre would go in favour of the Temple.

Joscelin of Courtenay prepared to leave for war.

His sister kept him from his bed until the early hours, repeating advice she had offered on a hundred past occasions.

'Watch the Regent, brother. I am not persuaded that he has finished with Saladin. The treaty can be remade, and, if it is, if all our Christian leaders are caught in the same trap, then you can be sure that sweet Raymond will emerge unscathed. For all we know, the Sultan has given orders for his long-nosed ally to be left alone. So study what he says and agree to nothing until you are certain that he will not derive some special benefit from it. Do you see where I lead?'

'Now as ever. But you need not reiterate what we all know so well. He will be watched, and you will be informed of the progress of things.'

She treated him to a thin smile, then quickly stole it back. Joscelin was like a dancing bear, and it was fun to poke him with verbal sticks. 'I know I will. I have enough of my own representatives in the army. They will furnish the news for me, and it will be the unpainted truth.'

It was Joscelin's turn to show a brief, wintry smile. Thinking of her bony body and insatiable appetites he said, 'I am sure you have your informants, from men-at-arms to leaders of the realm. In fact, we may come to rely on you for a report on our progress.'

'Why not?' she asked. 'You always have, and you always will. Now go to bed and dream of how you will save the Kingdom.'

She watched him make his way to his room at the rear of the house. Then she crossed to a small, badly-hung door and opened it without knocking. Light from the main room fell across the face and chest of a young, well-muscled manservant. Agnes hissed, 'Are you awake, Cobert?'

The man groaned and muttered, 'Half awake, half asleep.'

'Well, rouse the dormant half. I have some loose coins spilled on the floor upstairs. They'll belong to whoever collects them.' She gazed at the flat nipples and the curled hairs on his chest, then left the door open and went up to her own chambers.

The self-exiled nobles of Antioch were slow to respond to Guy's plea for men. They held fire until both Balian of Ibelin and Raymond of Tripoli had appealed to them to lay aside their personal feelings toward the Poitevin and to come to the defence of the Kingdom. Reluctantly, they agreed to re-enter the land they had forsworn, but only until the Moslem force had been eliminated. Bohemond of Antioch had no quarrel with Saladin, so would not come in person. However, he sent his son, together with a strong force led by Balian's brother, Baldwin of Ramleh. This contingent left the principality during the middle days of June.

Guy of Lusignan prepared to leave for war.

His people would have been greatly disturbed could they have seen their king during the final days at Jerusalem. He had lost his appetite, yet suffered bouts of vomiting, hollow retching that skinned his throat and turned his voice to an arid whisper. All the while, Queen Sibylla hung round his neck, imploring him to stay in bed and delegate the leadership.

'Let the Regent take them on! He was once so greedy for the crown, why don't you let him have his way? Oh, Guy, you are marked out there. The Saracens will ride directly against you. It's *you* they'll kill!'

'Please,' he gasped, 'desist! This talk won't stiffen my resolve.'

'I don't want you stiffened, for the stiffness of courage precedes the stiffness of death. Look, you cannot even trust your own nobles. There's Raymond, Balian, now his brother Baldwin again. They would all like to run a knife into you. How will you be safe?'

Guy remembered the time when the Leper King's pallet had been ringed by armed men, ostensibly to protect him from assassins, more sensibly to hold back his unfaithful friends. Now, according to Sibylla, it was his turn.

She prattled on, unaware that the whine in her voice had increased in pitch. He sat on a bench normally used by the court secretary, set midway between the west wall of the throne room and the throne itself. Sibylla had followed him this far from their private quarters and now moved back and forth in front of the bench.

He knew his wife loved him, but, as he listened, he realised that there was more to her entreaties than a woman's concern for her man. There was self-pity, mingled with the insecurity that stalks in the shadow of the vain. Now that she was queen, with her own throne in her Chamber of Audience, she did not want to be widowed, then married off to some strong interloper, then reduced to being his lady and nothing more. To be queen alongside Guy was one thing, but suppose her next husband was a real man? No, it was Guy's bounden duty as she saw it to avoid danger and minimise risk. He could wear the trappings of Commander-in-Chief of the Christian army, but he had no right to fight.

'—enemies on every side,' she continued. 'And we need employ no deceit. You *are* ill. You may take to your bed with a clear conscience——'

'Stop!' he rasped. 'This once, listen to me and say nothing. I am not ill. I vomit and hiss and move like a ghost because I am near panic.'

'No, you're not.'

'Yes, woman, yes! I am! I am terrified. I can't describe to you how I feel, even the words are in hiding. I am a coward, and my fear makes me sick. I recognise my weakness, but that makes me vomit the more. So don't try putting me to bed. I will lead the army. I must, for what else is there?'

'You're delirious, husband——'

'And you are spoiled. You are, in all, a vain, shallow-brained child, selfish and weakening. Damn your coloured hair, I need to be put on a horse, not under your covers. I'm an uncertain man, I grant you that, but by God I am yet a man! Now go back to your chambers. You've sapped enough of my blood.'

'You don't know what you say,' she told him. 'Ill as you are, something must be done——'

'Get out!'

'Husband?'

'Out! Stay away from me. You're killing me quicker than a Saracen arrow. Please, just leave me alone. Just leave me alone.'

Sibylla guessed that he was more ill than he knew, because he had never spoken to her in such a way before.

The malaise was not contained within the walls of the Royal Palace. Patriarch Heraclius was also unwell, and had already taken to his bed. His own physicians were in some doubt as to the exact nature of his disease, but those Crusaders who had visited him and asked him to carry the True Cross into battle settled for an immediate and unanimous diagnosis. Heraclius was a coward, from cap to boot. There was nothing wrong with him that Pashia de Riveri and the comforts of Jerusalem could not cure.

So the True Cross was placed in the hands of Bishop Rufin of Acre and Bishop Bernard of Lydda, while Heraclius raised a limp hand from his mattress and blessed the enterprise.

Balian of Ibelin prepared to leave for war.

He had managed to spend three nights with Maria at Nablus, but now his contingent was ready in the fields, waiting for him to lead them north to Acre. Maria walked with him to the barbican gate.

On the way she said, 'I put forward no complaint, Balian, but twenty-three men is pitifully few with which to hold your castle. Could you not leave Constable Fostus with me?'

'I would leave you another fifty men, if it were possible. Though even then I could not include Fostus. Half the army at Acre will have heard of him, and his presence there will be of immeasurable benefit to us. With Roger of Les Moulins gone, and Jakelin of Mailly and my old friend Sir Conrad, the Christian heroes have been sadly depleted. Would it comfort you if I were to send back another ten from the field?'

'It would, of course.'

'I'll do it in a moment. Do you understand why we must have Fostus with us?'

'Yes,' she smiled. 'Give me the extra ten and I'll stop pestering you.' She waited for him to mount his palfrey, then rested a hand on his thigh. 'For God's sake take care, my lord. And do what you can to keep Ernoul in one piece, will you?'

He grinned down at her and placed his hand over hers. 'So it emerges at last, eh? Do you look so favourably upon my skinny squire?'

She was too sad to play out the joke. 'He's a good man, but no great thing, I would say, in a battle.'

'Fear not, I'll watch him. Though, in return, you must do something for me.'

'Whatever you ask.'

'Regardless of events in the north, you may be subjected to fleeting Saracen raids. If you could preserve my window, the one in the library——'

'Oh, it's done,' she laughed. 'It has already been packed away. I could not face you, if your precious window had been damaged.'

'Well,' he said, 'that's that. I'll return the ten to you.'

'God speed, my lord.'

'God bless you, Maria.' He leaned down, drew her to him and kissed her. Then she stepped back, a tall, regal figure in a tasselled grey kirtle, and he turned his horse and rode out through the barbican gate.

A few moments later ten men-at-arms entered the castle, slouching to show their displeasure at being kept back from the battle. To the north-west, dust rose above the fields as the contingent began to move. Maria watched the fine cloud until it had dispersed in the direction of Sebastia, then thought of how best to deploy her thirty-three defenders.

At Tubanie, nearly four years earlier, Reynald of Chatillon had criticised the inaccurate estimates made by the Frankish scouts when they had returned from viewing the rows of Moslem tents ranged across the plain. The criticism still held good, though this time it was the strength of the Christian army that was in dispute. Some reports listed 1,500 knights, twice that number of mercenary cavalry and upwards of 10,000 foot soldiers. Others put the number of lay knights at a thousand, with a further sixteen hundred Templars and Hospitallers, more than thirty thousand infantry and three or four thousand mounted Turcopoles.

Ernoul made his own assessment and allowed that the camp at Acre contained from ten to twelve thousand foot soldiers, one tenth as many lay knights, a similar number financed by the

Military Orders, and some three thousand Turcopoles. Thus he estimated the Christian army at between fifteen thousand and seventeen and a half thousand men, the most powerful force that had ever assembled around the Royal standard of Jerusalem.

However, with leaders such as Guy, Reynald, Joscelin, Amalric, Gerard, Raymond and Balian, the Frankish body sprouted a gorgon's head.

# CHAPTER SEVENTEEN

# Acre, Sepphoria

## 1st, 2nd July 1187

On Wednesday, 22nd Rabi II., 583 A.H.—being the five hundred and eighty-third year after the *Hegira*, the flight of the prophet Mohammed from Mecca to Yathreb, later called Medina—Sultan Saladin invaded the Kingdom of Jerusalem. He crossed the Jordan at the Bridge of Sennabra, just south of the Sea of Galilee. The bulk of the Moslem army was composed of mounted archers, most of whom disdained to wear armour, and infantry, called *Harbieh*, equipped with reed lances tipped with iron, scimitars, or stolen Frankish swords, small circular shields and the inevitable daggers. There were also a number of the dreaded *Naffatin*, foot soldiers who carried catapults and wicker baskets filled with naphtha balls. These would be placed in the catapults, set alight and hurled deep into the enemy ranks. The flaming missiles were all but inextinguishable and they burned fiercely on whatever surface they touched.

The army of Islam was divided into three sections, the centre commanded by Saladin himself, the right by his nephew Takedin, the left by the man who had led the hunting party to Nazareth exactly two months earlier, Kukburi, Emir of Harran. The force that crossed the bridge at Sennabra numbered between eighteen and twenty thousand men. This, too, was one of the largest armies the Moslems had ever sent against the Crusader Kingdom.

At first light on Thursday, 23rd Rabi II.—2nd July by the Christian calendar—Saladin took his six thousand men as far as Kafr Sebt, a village that lay some five miles west-south-west of Tiberias. Takedin led his column parallel with the western shore of the Sea of Galilee, but stayed two miles from the water. Kukburi moved directly against Tiberias, fired the town and laid siege to the castle. The army was now positioned to Saladin's satisfaction. The castle was under attack, the wide valley to the west was blocked and the main Acre-Sennabra road was cut. The Sultan waited to see if the Crusaders would ride to the defence of Regent Raymond's wife, Princess Eschiva of Bures.

News of the invasion and the siege was immediately sent by carrier pigeon to the coops at Acre. The messages were in Eschiva's own hand, and King Guy wasted no time in convening a council of his leaders. The council was held in Joscelin of Courtenay's palace, and the majority of barons came with their opinions already hardened. Because it was the Count of Tripoli's castle that was the object of Kukburi's attack, he was invited to open the discussion.

Pacing the blue and purple mosaic floor, moving so that his compeers had to turn their heads to follow his progress, he said, 'I heard this news less than an hour ago, though it has been in my head for some days. Also, I know what is in your heads at this moment, so I would say this to you. The weather will be as hot to-day as at any time this year. The sun is hardly clear of the hills as yet, but you may take my word for it, I know the climate in these parts. In hand with that is the fact that we are more than forty marching miles from Tiberias. To start now would take us through the noon hours, and by nightfall we would still be ten miles or more from my castle. The men and animals will be exhausted, but more than that, we could not march those ten final miles in the dark——'

'Why not?' Gerard of Ridefort gibed. 'Does the darkness frighten you?'

'—without the risk of falling into an ambush. No, Grand Master, but the thought of defeat does.'

'What? Surely you, of all nobles, should not have such a thought in your head. Saladin has already bought you, and what he has bought he will protect.'

'That accusation is unjust! I am not his man and never was.'

'You say!'

'My lords,' Guy pleaded. 'Must we have another round of re-crimination? Tiberias stands besieged, and whatever our Regent may or may not have entreated with the Sultan——'

'He's Saladin's man,' Gerard insisted. 'We've no doubt of it.'

'You!' Balian snapped. 'Will you hold your silence until the king has finished?'

Somebody at the rear of the group muttered, 'King-lover,' and Gerard nodded emphatically.

Guy had lost the direction of his thoughts and asked, 'Where was I? Ah, yes, I was saying that whatever transpired between Regent Raymond and the Sultan is buried in the past. What we must now decide is whether or not to go straightway to the relief of Tiberias and the courageous Princess Eschiva.'

Reynald of Chatillon dragged a hand irritably through his thick red hair, then elbowed his way forward until he was standing almost toe to toe with Guy. He had tried this manœuvre many times before and had found that it usually intimidated lesser men. It certainly intimidated King Guy, who moved back until he bumped against Balian and Baldwin of Ramleh. These two barred any further retreat, and although he derived some comfort from their proximity, he was unable to look Reynald in the eye.

'Decide?' Reynald bored. 'There is nothing left to decide. Some might think you would keep us here, discussing events until we hear that Tiberias has fallen and that we are therefore no longer needed. I'll make no point of it; suffice it to say that some might well think it of you, King.'

Rushing his words, Guy protested, 'Then they'd be wrong, quite wrong. If you honestly believe that it would be to our advantage to press on toward——'

'Not ours,' Joscelin of Courtenay interposed. 'Princess Eschiva's. Her husband seems loath to save her, but we are not.' He glanced at Reynald, who blinked, giving him the floor.

'Great God!' he continued, 'you have around you the mightiest army Christendom has ever seen, yet you still bring us here to argue this way and that——'

'Not argue. I didn't say argue.'

'—while the black pigs of Islam snuffle against the walls of Tiberias. I say we must go and rescue the ladies of that citadel.'

'And I,' Reynald echoed.

'And I,' from Gerard.

Constable Amalric led a chorus of assent from the lesser barons. Guy was convinced and turned to his Regent. But Raymond strode away until he was isolated from his heavy, sweating peers, then spun round and stabbed a finger at them. He was not usually given to such dramatic gestures and they stopped voting. The shiny mosaic added a bluish tinge to his skin, so that his friends thought him sick with concern, while his rivals recognised the colour often used to depict Satan in religious frescoes.

'Before we take one more step,' he said, 'set your minds back to the October of four years past. We were then at Tubanie. You were there, Reynald, and you, Amalric, and you Joscelin. We were led at that time, as now, by Guy. We were all there, and I remind you of it for one reason only. *It is now as it was then.*

'The Saracens are on our borders. Before a week is out they will be forced to feed themselves from the country. This time the heat is greater, so their desire for water must be more strong. If they advance it will be into arid country. If they remain where they are they will soon grow hungry. So I say, if you are set on approaching them, let us go as far as Sepphoria. But, my lords, not one mile farther. We know from the last time that our position there is defensible, and that we, ourselves, will not go short of food and water. Moreover, we will be able to control the valleys to the north, and the Plain of Jizreel to the south. I would rather we stayed here and let the enemy tire, but as a compromise, will you accept it?'

Reynald replied for his party. 'We'll accept anything that takes us closer to Tiberias. But we warn you, Regent, Sepphoria may only satisfy us for a very short time. We, you see, are eager to glimpse the enemy.'

The alarm was sounded throughout the Christian camp and by mid-morning the army was on its way along the convenient road that curved south-east to Sepphoria. Among the fifteen thousand and more soldiers there were only eighteen casualties during the march. Three horsemen were injured when they raced each other, veered too close and collided. Five were smitten by the heat, while a number of others fell or were pushed under the wheels of baggage carts. Two men were wounded in knife fights. Two were drowned during an unnecessary attempt to ford a stream that ran below the Templar castle of Le Saffran, and one hanged himself for undisclosed reasons in a wood near the village of Saka. So far as the leaders were concerned, it was a dusty, uneventful march.

By the time the sky had dimmed above western Galilee, the Crusaders were safely encamped at Sepphoria. Raymond of Tripoli knew that Saladin expected him to ride to the rescue of Eschiva, and he told Balian, 'If you have any regard for me, do not let me accede to his wishes. The trap is as obvious as earth and water. I love that woman above all else, save the land we have sworn to defend. Will you stay with me this night?'

Balian nodded, imagining how it would be if Tiberias were Nablus, and Eschiva were Maria. He acknowledged that he, too, would need a friend close by.

Reynald of Chatillon did not make empty threats. An hour after dusk, he, Amalric, Joscelin and Gerard called for a further conference with King Guy. So for the second time that day the barons assembled before their monarch, only now the mosaic of the palace gave way to the grassy floor of Guy's scarlet tent.

Even alongside the Constable of the Kingdom, the Seneschal of the Kingdom and the Grand Master of the Temple, the Lord of Kerak remained the principal spokesman.

He said, 'We have discussed the situation amongst ourselves, King, and we are united in our belief that if the castle of Tiberias is to be saved, and with it the Princess of Galilee, then we must make our move now.'

'Oh, this is too much,' Guy exploded. 'You let the entire army pitch camp, patrols have been sent in all directions, guards posted by the hundred, and now you say you want to go on again. Well, you can't. I am your Commander and I say you can't.'

'King,' Reynald menaced, 'there's a whole world moving between what a man says and what he is heard to say. In Jerusalem now, they might hear it as the beating of a faint heart. We *can* go on. You know we are able. When you say we can't, are you really commanding us not to go against the enemy?'

Guy looked at his brother, but could see he would get no help there. He turned to Raymond, thinking as he did so, whenever I am pressed I run to him or Balian. If only they could have made one of them king and had done with it.

'In essence,' Raymond said, 'the king's command is as you suggest. For the moment, for the hours of darkness, we are not to move against the unseen enemy. Only a madman would take any army out there to-night.'

'Are you saying we are mad?' Reynald demanded.

One who had not spoken at the earlier meeting, young Humphrey of Toron, now rekindled his step-father's enmity by replying, 'A whole world moves between what we say and what you hear, Lord Reynald.'

There were smiles and chuckles of approval, but Reynald was not so easily deterred.

'Wit at this hour is out of place, kinsman. And if it is second-hand, it is already tarnished. Now, either make some constructive comment, or get to bed. You are still not yet full grown.'

His supporters enjoyed the riposte and Humphrey was forced to hear the cruel laughter of his elders.

Then Gerard steered the discussion back on to its original path with an impatient outburst. 'Talk the night away, if that's your taste, but I have been out on patrol since we arrived here—Oh, yes, Regent, I thought that might surprise you—and I have received several reports from more recent patrols. They confirmed what I surmised. There are no Saracens in the area. None. But I doubt that I could say the same in the morning. While we stand here rooted like fruit trees the Saracens creep closer to reap the harvest. I grant you, we have nothing to lose by remaining here. Nothing except the fortress and town of Tiberias, and most of Galilee!'

'You impertinent adventurer!' Raymond roared. 'Who in hell's jaws will lose most? It is *my* castle, *my* town, and these are *my* lands! Stretch your eyes, Gerard of Ridefort, and try to see more than your splintered corner of the picture. I would rather my town and castle were taken and laid waste, rather my wife and soldiers and all my possessions were lost for ever, than see the entire Kingdom destroyed. I know that if we advance, you, for one, but not you alone, will be captured or slain. With you will go the army, and if that goes, who defends the Kingdom? You smirk, but I will tell you why you are lost out there. There is one spring, just one, between here and Tiberias. It's called the Spring of Cresson, and if it can assuage the thirst of one hundred men I shall be surprised. What are we? Eh, Gerard? Ten, twenty thousand? And what if your creeping Saracens have reached it first? It will be of little use to them, but not even you will get a drink there. Most of us will die of thirst, while those who survive will fall mewing to the Saracens. As for my wife, Eschiva, I will ransom her later. As for my fortress, I will retake it later. But for the present I will do nothing to save what is mine, but set my mind to safeguarding what is God's.'

There was a long, impressed silence. Then Guy said, 'We will stay here the night.'

Balian, Humphrey and Raymond exchanged glances with their allies. It seemed that good sense had triumphed at last.

Ernoul explored the Christian camp. There was no symmetry in the arrangement of tents; each Commander had set up his own defences, so the camp bulged at the northern end, where the ground was flat, and tailed away to the south. The first contingents to arrive at Sepphoria—those in the van—had naturally chosen the best places. Gerard's Templars and hired mercenaries had brought up the rear of the column, and Ernoul could see the lights of their fires on the northern slopes of the Hill of Nazareth. Gerard's tent was pitched less than half a mile from the valley into which he had led the suicidal charge against Kukburi. The young squire did not know whether the Grand Master had chosen the site intentionally, or was there because it was one of the last available. But his present position befitted his character. Like a thief, he seemed drawn to the scene of his crime.

In the centre of the northern bulge, Welsh and Irish mercenaries mingled with Bretons, Venetians, Danes, Navarrese and local-born Franks. The Moslem mercenaries—the Turcopoles—kept to themselves, and neither they, nor the pale-skinned Crusaders would have much to do with the dark, big-boned half-castes called *Pullani*, lawful or illegitimate offspring of Frankish-Syrian unions.

Wandering from group to group, Ernoul caught snatches of conversation and eavesdropped shamelessly on the more interesting titbits. One red-bearded soldier had gathered a large audience of leering night-owls around him and was entertaining them with a repertoire of licentious stories. He had just concluded one tale with the words '—so the priest convinced the silly woman that the child would be born malformed unless she allowed him to remedy the situation with his own pure seed. So far as I know he's still at it with any woman he hears is pregnant!'

The audience made appropriate comments about the faltering standards of the clergy, then nodded at red-beard to begin another.

He cleared his throat, winked at them and said, 'Here's one I heard when I was in Brabant. I won't vouch for the truth of it, but it's a pretty story.'

The listeners were not at all concerned with the veracity of such anecdotes. Who cared if they were true, so long as they amused?

'You were in Brabant,' they said. 'Go on from there.'

'Yes, well, this took place in a small town, I forget exactly where.'

You cunning old devil, Ernoul thought. You say that so each man may picture his own town.

'There was this married woman who had been consistently un-faithful to her husband——'

'Aren't they all?' one of them intruded. 'I know mine is!' He looked round and repeated, 'I know mine is, God rot her!'

'Let him tell it. Unfaithful to her husband. Go on.'

'Then don't interrupt. As I said, a small town, and in fact she had seen the ceiling over the shoulder of a knight who was garrisoned at a nearby castle, the constable of the town, and a young lawyer who had taken up practice there.'

'Taken up practice where, eh? Huh?'

'Shush, let him tell it!'

'Well, you need to know that her husband had had some work done in the house, but had not paid for it. The man who'd done the work had complained to the constable, and the husband knew the constable was out to question him. Of course, he didn't know that the constable was also bread on his wife's plate. Anyway, one after-noon the husband was in town, while the wife was being charged down by her knight.'

'Charged down!' they grinned. 'And with his lance well-couched, eh?'

'Just so,' red-beard snapped. 'But before he had quite struck home, the husband returned. The knight leapt from his horse——'

'Leapt from his horse!'

'——and hid in a large wooden cupboard. The husband entered the bedchamber, surprised to see his wife laid so low at that hour of the day, though not entirely sorry she was there. Like a good man he joined her and they drew closer and closer, until——'

'Yes? Get on! What then?'

Ernoul acknowledged that even if the story was a pack of lies, the soldier knew how to hold his audience.

'What then? Oh, well, there was a knock on the street door and the constable announced himself. Naturally, the husband had no wish to be taken for questioning, so he told his wife what to say and hid where she indicated, in a linen chest.'

'And then the constable came in, didn't he?'

Glaring at the speaker, red-beard intoned, 'And then the constable came in. Listen, if you're better equipped to tell the story——'

'No, no. You tell it.'

Wishing to be helpful, somebody else murmured, 'The constable. He's just come in.'

'Yes,' red-beard grated, 'the constable came in and asked the wife where her husband was. She said what she'd been told to say, that he was away from there on a visit. So the constable, being her lover anyway, carried on from where the husband left off. But that's not the end of it, for the husband had already talked over the problem of payment with his wife, and she had sent him to the young lawyer. Being a thorough man, the lawyer spent hours writing out advice, and, it so happens, he chose that very afternoon to present his ideas to the husband at home.'

Unable to remain silent, one of the listeners howled, 'There's a knock on the door! It's the lawyer!'

'That's quick of you,' red-beard spat. 'You're right, there *was* a knock and it *was* the lawyer. Now shut your mouth.'

Ernoul shook his head. Red-beard was clearly losing his grip on their ears. He would have to think of something fresh to catch their interest.

The same thought had already occurred to the soldier and he hurried on. 'Like the others, the constable had no wish to be discovered, so he sheathed his sword and hid under the bed. The lawyer gets in with the wife, but he has only had time to dip his quill when there's a terrible hammering on the street door, then feet on the stairs, then more hammering on the door of the bedchamber. The lawyer takes his advice with him behind a high-back chair, and the wife bids the lastcomer enter.' He risked a short pause, then said, 'It's the workman, with three of his strongest friends. "I didn't get paid for my work," he says. "I'm the best carpenter this town is ever likely to see, and I've talked it over with my friends, and I've decided to take back what I did until I see some money." Whereupon he consulted a list and announced, "We're taking away one plainwood cupboard, one linen box, one large bed and one high-back chair. Better clear out the contents, missy, or I'll give them to my wife." At which point the woman climbs out of her busy bed and laughing says, "No, rope everything and take it as it is. I am in a generous mood to-day, and your wife will appreciate what I'm giving her!" '

The audience roared and produced wine for red-beard. They hoped he would not be killed in battle for such story tellers were rare outside country fairs and the courts of the nobility.

While the army slept, four of its leaders stayed talking until an hour before midnight. Then, having reached agreement, one of them made his way through the camp, halting when he was challenged by the guards around the royal tent.

The caller identified himself, stepped forward into the light of the pitch torches, and was recognised by the guards. They told him the king was asleep.

'Then wake him. I haven't come here to sell unripe oranges. What I bring won't improve with keeping. Go on, man, rouse your king.'

Reluctantly, a guard entered the tent and shook Guy awake. He stirred himself with equal reluctance and was about to drive the guard away when his visitor ducked in under the canopy.

'Oh, God,' Guy groaned. 'Is there some plan to exhaust me to death?'

'No, King, but extreme circumstances demand extreme measures.'

'Granted, though you never put it in such a way before. Who loaned you that phrase?'

'It's time to get things done.'

'Ah, that's better, that's in your style. Why, are we attacked?'

'No.'

'A fire then? Has some section deserted?'

'No.'

'Then what, for God's sake? Is dawn far off?'

'Yes, far off.'

Guy nodded, not quite sure why he had asked the question. Then he told the guard to set a light in the bracket of the tent pole and dismissed him. Pushing his legs over the side of his cot, he leaned forward and grumbled, 'It's cold. Pass me that mantle. There, beside you. Hell's teeth, mine are set to knock themselves from my mouth. Ah, it's warmer with the fur turned inward. Now, what brings you from your bed?'

'It's the opinion of many of your leaders that the army should march on to Tiberias——'

'Oh, my God, we've talked this out!'

'Too sparsely for some of us. We want to go on.'

'Very well, we will go on. In the morn——'

'To-night.'

'This damned mantle is too short. The cold makes my legs ache. To-night? No, impossible.'

'A vote was taken.'

'Indeed? Then I imagine you are here because your proposal found favour with my other leaders.'

'Yes.'

'How many cast their vote?'

'That's of no account, King. What is important is that if you do not give the order to move——'

'How many took the vote?'

'——certain sections will leave the army——'

'How many—Oh, no matter. My legs are like dungeon stones.'

'——among them the majority of the mercenaries. Moreover, I know that the Military Orders would rather relinquish their vows than allow the Lady of Tiberias to fall into the hands of the enemy. The army waits for you to lead them into battle, that's the sum of it.'

'I'm too cold to argue, *that's* the sum of it.' He wrapped his arms round his body and thought, if I say no and send him away, he'll speak further with his friends, and then he or they will return to plague me. And as for saving Tiberias, my leaders were in favour, all save Raymond and Balian. Suppose the Regent is wrong this time; he could be, he's no more than human. What would the army think of me then, ignoring the advice of ten to follow one who has already tried to make his peace with Saladin? His castle or no, Raymond could be wrong, and Balian with him.

He shivered and said, 'I don't like your methods, but I am persuaded that if it is what my leaders believe to be right——'

'It is, King, I know it.'

'Then put the word about. Let the alert be sounded in the camp. Oh, before you go. Pass my boots over. I'm too stiff to move.'

The visitor did as he was ordered, then went out to spread the ripples of wakefulness through the camp. When he reached his own tent again one of his companions inquired brusquely, 'How did it go between you?'

'It went well, Reynald. We'll be at Tiberias with the light.'

The Lord of Kerak looked at Amalric and Joscelin, then clapped his friend on the shoulder. 'You're made of my stuff, Grand Master. Tell me, why did he accede so quickly?'

'He was cold,' Gerard of Ridefort whined, mimicking the king. 'The night wind chilled his manhood.'

The four men grinned at each other, then left to rejoin the stirring mass of soldiery.

# CHAPTER EIGHTEEN

# Sepphoria, Hattin

## 3rd July 1187

By dawn the massive Christian army was strung out along the bare hills of Eastern Galilee. Raymond of Tripoli, feeling much as he had felt when he had learned that Sibylla and not he was to be crowned, rode in silence at the head of the army. He was accompanied by Reginald of Sidon and Walter of Caesarea, neither of whom were able to dispel the mood of black pessimism that had settled over him.

The centre of the army was commanded by King Guy, who rode with his brother Amalric and Seneschal Joscelin. Behind them, protected by a phalanx of infantry and a triple line of lay knights came the most precious of all Christian symbols in the East, the True Cross. It was coated with red gold, set with pearls and rubies, and contained a chip of wood purporting to be from Christ's own cross. The True Cross was carried in turn by Bishop Rufin of Acre and his fellow-cleric Bernard of Lydda.

Some fifty yards farther back another detachment of horsemen and foot soldiers formed a solid wall around the Kingdom's greatest secular emblem, the Crusader Standard. Where the True Cross could be seen by only a handful, the Standard was designed as a signal to the entire army. The flag-pole itself stood as tall as a ship's mast. It was made from prepared sections, and each joint was bound with a high hoop of iron. From the top of the pole flew the Royal Banner, while the base was fixed to a huge, four-wheeled platform. Twenty guards from Guy's household stood on the platform, and the entire structure was drawn by eight deep-chested shire horses.

The importance of the Standard to every Christian soldier was inestimable. The Moslems had long known this, so made ceaseless attacks upon it. They knew that while it reared above the battlefield, while a Crusader might look up and see the Royal Banner floating out from the topmast, he would gain fresh heart and fight on, whatever the odds. But they knew, too, that if the platform could be overturned, or the pole cut down, the Franks would assume that their leaders had been defeated and would promptly lose heart. They had learned from past example that the Standard was all things, good and bad, to the soldiers of Christ.

So the True Cross and the Crusader Standard were afforded the fullest protection, and the morale of the army rose with the sun.

The rear of the column, acknowledged to be the most vulnerable position, was under the collaborative command of Reynald of Chatillon, Balian of Ibelin, and the Grand Masters Gerard of Ridefort and Ermengard de Daps. Humphrey of Toron shunned his step-father and rode with Balian, while Baldwin of Ramleh kept company with the Grand Master of the Hospital.

The minor peers attached themselves to one of the three main sections, and the Christian host wound eastward toward the black basalt Hills of Hattin, beyond which lay the sunken waters of the Sea of Galilee. Tiberias stood between the Hills of Hattin and the sea, and Guy expected to reach the citadel during the early hours of the afternoon.*

He no longer complained about the cold. As if in answer to his prayers the sun warmed the ridges of the hills. By mid-morning the heat had become uncomfortable; the army sweated and grew thirsty and the infantry dragged their feet, halving the speed of the advance. Scouts were sent to inspect the Springs of Cresson. They returned to report that the entire area was swarming with Moslem cavalry, and that anyway the springs appeared to have dried up.

The army continued at a snail's pace. Guy vacillated and sought the advice of Regent Raymond.

'You know what I will say,' Raymond snarled. 'Lead us back to Sepphoria before it's too late. We will shortly be midway between there and Tiberias, at the farthest point from water. Why do you trouble to ask me now, when you allowed Gerard to persuade you last night? Christ in Heaven, King, will you for once take my advice and hold to it, or will we be halfway back when you spin again?'

* See map p. 9.

The heat was beginning to dry the sweat on Guy's face, so he poured water on a hand towel and wiped his eyes with it. 'Please,' he said, 'you know I cannot retreat when I have not yet seen the enemy! There must be water hereabouts. In the valleys perhaps?' He offered the towel to Raymond, who waved it away.

'All you will find in the valleys are Saracens. Can't you see, we are shuffling into a trap!' His face livid with anger, he shouted, 'I told you at Acre! I told you at Sepphoria! I tell you again here, on this blasted hill—Saladin's sole purpose is to draw us away from the water! He all but succeeded when we left the coast. Then we settled at Sepphoria and I pleaded with you to stay there. But no, you were intent on giving him the second chance. Well, with Gerard's help you have given him that chance. We are at last without water, while every step takes us farther into his embrace!'

'I still say there must a spring, a river——'

'You fool! I know these lands. Many of the Saracens know them. But how can you know, when the workings of your own mind are foreign to you? There are no springs, save Cresson. There is no river, save that feeble thing we skirted to reach Sepphoria. How many times must I tell you? Now turn the army and take us out of here, or I promise you—we are lost.'

He had hardly finished speaking when the first black-feathered arrows thudded into the column. Men fell to the ground. Horses reared and threw their riders. Christian crossbowmen ran to the perimeter of their sections, peering down the slopes of the hills at the thin lines of Moslem horsemen who wheeled their mounts, sped parallel with the Crusaders, fired once, twice, three times, then turned away again out of arrow shot.

The army came to a halt. Balian prepared to repulse an attack on the rear and, while he and Reynald formed their men into a defensive half-circle, the Templars and Hospitallers charged left and right toward the Saracens. The superior weight of the Christian knights smashed the enemy lines and the surviving archers fled into the valleys.

The Military Orders reformed and rode back slowly to the ridge. Many of them carried hacked-off Moslem limbs. Others grinned, prickly with embedded arrows. The army moved forward again, yelling triumphantly. There was now no turning back. The invaders had struck and the Crusaders had retaliated. The battle was joined.

Saladin was overjoyed to hear that the Christians had left Sepphoria. He sent word to Takedin and Kukburi and, leaving two hundred men to continue the siege of Tiberias, the rest of the Moslem army advanced along the valley that Takedin had previously blocked. The army halted at its northern end, sealing the valley like a stopper in a jar.

The Sultan's scouts informed him that if the Crusaders continued on their present path they would reach the Moslem position via the ridge that separated the valleys of Batuf and Tur'an. The only sources of water were in Saracen hands, so if the Christians could be halted, then driven north against the steep hillside, they would have to repulse not only the assaults of Islam, but the intolerable agonies of thirst.

Saladin listened to the volunteered advice, gazing directly at each man who spoke. By Western standards he did not seem physically equipped to lead an army of such magnitude. He was of average height, but with a spare frame, thin wrists and fingers, and the face of a scribe, or an ascete. He was bearded, the hair starting high on his cheeks and growing down, grizzled, to his chest. Like all Moslems, he took care to keep the beard clean and well-combed; not for him the lice-ridden growth of the Crusader. The upper half of his face was unremarkable; brown eyes and a hooked nose, and dark skin that was wrinkled over narrow cheek bones. Even in repose his expression was grave. He would smile gently, as a father to his child, but in anger there was none of the blazing intensity that seared the Frankish countenance.

The Crusaders knew him to be a brilliant general, though they themselves would never have followed such a reedy scholar.

When his scouts had finished, he said, 'Then we must contain them between the valley we are in and those two pinnacles of rock. If they should break through us here, they will find water at that village——'

'It's called Lubieh,' one of the scouts told him.

'Yes, at Lubieh. We must prevent that, and we must also ensure that they do not escape between the peaks and so reach Tiberias

and the sea.' Nodding at the scout who had named the village,
Saladin asked, 'What does one call those two pinnacles, do you
know?'

'I do, Sultan. The Franks call them the Horns of Hattin, after
Kafr Hittim, the Wheat Village.'

'So. Then we will do all we can, under Almighty Allah, to impale
the enemy on those horns.'

He gazed at the twin peaks for some time, acknowledging that
not even Allah and walls of rock were sufficient, by themselves, to
defeat the Crusaders. He therefore made his own preparations. By
noon the Saracens had constructed eighteen hundred arrow shelters,
set up seven hundred and fifty weapons points, from where the
archers could draw arrows, and the infantry collect spears and lances.
More than four hundred sheaves of arrows were held in reserve and
sixty-six camels were set aside to carry them about the field. So far
five hundred horsemen had been sent out to harry the enemy. This
number was now doubled, and dust rose up to fill the valley
of Tur'an as the cavalry galloped west toward the approaching
army.

The Christian advance was being seriously hampered by the
irregular fire-and-flee tactics of the Moslem archers. During the
hours that straddled noon Reynald of Chatillon made eight sorties
against them. He emerged unscathed from all but the last, when his
horse was brought down with a lance in its flank and he was thrown
heavily on to the grass. Heaving himself to his feet, he retrieved IN
NOMINE DOMINI, aware that this was the third time in his life that
he had lost his grip on the sword. He stayed where he was beside
the stricken horse, waiting for the Saracens to recognise their most
hated enemy.

Before long three horsemen rode at him. They fired five arrows as
they spurred in, but their enthusiasm impaired their aim. Two of
the arrows flew above his head and the other three fell short. Exchanging their bows for scimitars they closed in on him. He chose
the nearest rider—one who had moved well ahead of his companions—and lumbered to the left, swinging the great sword. At
the final instant the Moslem saw that Reynald had timed the swing
to perfection. He jerked the reins, but he was too late to pull clear

of the near-five-foot-blade. His own scimitar was more than a foot and a half from Reynald's red-bearded face when IN NOMINE DOMINI cut him in half at the waist. The Arab stallion carried its rider past, then ran off, toppling the torso. Reynald was knocked flat by the impact of the blow. He twisted away from the sound of hoofbeats and glimpsed the other two riders as they thundered by. Astonished that they had not killed him, he dragged himself to his knees.

Having seen what the Red Wolf of the Desert had done to their companion, the pair had banished all thought of a sword-fight. Instead, they determined to trample him beneath their horses' hooves. In his mind, each had decided to say later that he had used an animal to kill an animal.

They brought their mounts in line again and charged. Reynald's left wrist was broken—perhaps when his destrier had thrown him, perhaps when he had slashed his first Moslem—so he stayed on one knee, jammed the hilt of the sword against his hip and let the blade rest on his raised left arm. IN NOMINE DOMINI angled up like a lance. He realised that if he jerked aside in time the first horse would take the blade in the chest and stumble on, clear of him. But if he was too slow, the hilt would be driven back, smashing his hip bone. He gave no thought to what the second horseman might accomplish.

He snarled at them as they came toward him. 'Come on, pigs, come on, come on——'

Then suddenly there were three horses.

The Saracens were less than twenty feet away when the third horse slammed into them. There was a flurry of bodies, one bearing the Templar cross, and the Saracens were hurled aside, their horses crashing down on them. The heavy Norman destrier staggered and recovered, and Gerard of Ridefort reached down, yelling, 'With me, Prince! With me!'

Reynald jammed his sword into his belt, missing the sheath so that the blade cut deep into the leather, then snatched at Gerard's arm and hauled himself up behind the saddle. The two Moslems lay crushed under their mounts. Gerard spat at them and took his friend back to the column.

Reynald's wrist was swollen, so Garrison Captain Azo bound it with wet leather. When the leather dried it would shrink and hold

the wrist firm. The Lord of Kerak would be in constant pain, but
he would be able to wield IN NOMINE DOMINI.

Ernoul was put to work winding cross-bows. Both Balian and
Fostus were accomplished shots, so the young squire worked
without respite. His fingers bled, and when he had loaded and re-
loaded a hundred times or more he threw aside the arbalest and
begged for a cloth to wrap round his hands. It was Balian's weapon
that he had failed to prepare, so it was Balian who dealt with him.

'Pick it up! What are you, some sulky girl? Pick it up, and hurry
about it.'

'My hands——'

'Damn your hands! Men are dying here. Look! Knights and
soldiers fall by the score.'

'I only want a rag, my lord.'

In a voice Ernoul had never heard, Balian said, 'Pick-it-up. Wind
it, load it, then hand it to me. *Now, boy!*'

Ernoul stooped and gathered the cross-bow. Balian glared at him
while he loaded it, then snatched it and strode back to the perimeter.
When he had gone Fostus shook his head and growled, 'You're
lucky, skin-and-bone. In his mind your action bordered on desertion. If he did not hold you special——'

'Oh, Christ, Fostus, I only wanted to cover my hands.'

'Wind on, or we'll have the Saracens among us. Then you won't
have any hands to cover.' He collected the loaded cross-bow, took
careful aim and sent a Saracen flopping from his horse. Ernoul
opened his mouth to congratulate him, when he saw Balian bringing his arbalest back for reloading. Lowering his gaze and mutter-
ing childishly, the young squire reached out to take the weapon
from him. Instead, he felt a sharp sting on the palm of his hand and
looked up to see a pair of gauntlets draped across it.

'Wear them,' Balian said, 'and let's have no more nonsense from
you.'

'Yes, sire, thank you. I'll be able to work much fas—— *Christ!*
*Down, down, down!*' He threw himself on his face. Balian dropped
as though his legs had been cut from him. Fostus had already dived
under an arrow cart. Nearby Crusaders heard the warning and took
cover, or looked around, or fired one last quarrel. Of those who

stayed on their feet, three were instantly immolated by Greek fire, while others were splashed with the ghastly flaming substance. Grass, flesh and armour were set alight, each burning as briskly as the other. Ernoul gagged on the stench, then pulled on the gauntlets, loaded Balian's bow and yelled, 'There! Those four on horseback! They're filling the slings again!'

Balian did not bother to rise. He grabbed the bow, fell forward on his elbows and fired. The *Naffatin* threw up his arms and slid sideways from his horse. Working faster than he thought possible, Ernoul tossed Fostus a loaded bow, grabbed Balian's from him, wound it, rammed in the quarrel and sent it skidding forward across the grass. The Lord and Constable of Nablus fired together. Fostus hit his man before he could light the naphtha ball, but Balian's target was already swinging his sling when the bolt thudded home. He screamed with pain and lost his hold on the sling. Still containing the flaming naphtha, the sling rose straight in the air, slowed, then fell back beside the fourth man. The horse bearing the last *Naffatin* sprang aside like a doe, but the rider was less agile and fell into the searing morass.

Ernoul leapt in the air, mindless of the enemy archers. 'Well shot! Well shot! Those bastards, look how they burn!'

Balian and Fostus glanced at each other. The young scribbler who had complained that his hands were cut had become a vicious animal, thirsty for blood. Like them, he was now just another soldier, fighting for his life.

The army continued its interrupted advance toward Tiberias. They came down from the hills and skirted the southern edge of the valley of Batuf. The Hospitallers were detailed to remain on the ridge. The Templars took over from the lay contingents commanded by Balian and Reynald, and defended the rear of the column. Neither Military Order could claim they had the more difficult task. The black-and-white men of the Hospital suffered severe casualties clearing the Saracens from the heights. Edouard de Cavanne was killed up there, as were Denys and Thomas the Wanderer and eighteen or twenty more. Then, when the Saracens retreated from the ridge, it was only to harry the army on the floor of the valley. Keeping them from the centre of the column, the

Templars Honore the Tiger, Simon FitzNigel and Hubert of Bonneville were slain. Gerard of Ridefort was stabbed in the foot, but so long as he stayed on horseback the wound would not hinder him.

When the army was still two miles from the eastern end of the valley Grand Master Ermengard de Daps appealed to Guy to withdraw the Hospitallers.

'It is not our way of fighting up there, King, and I am losing too many of my knights. If they are to die it would be better that they did so in the turmoil of a real fight, not swatting flies on the ridge.'

'Can they see what lies ahead?'

'Yes. The ground slopes some way on. Beyond the end of the ridge is a wide plateau. On our side are the two peaks of Hattin. So far as we can tell, the Moslem army is massed on the far side of the plateau and across it's southern extreme. But no doubt Saladin has sent men behind the peaks to stop us marching straight to the sea.'

'Which route would you take, Grand Master?'

'I'd continue on as we are. Whichever way we move we'll have a fight on our hands, but if we keep in the direction of that low hill ahead, I think it's called Arbel, we'll come out above Tiberias.'

'Then you don't favour a standing fight on the plateau.'

'Not if we press on with all speed now. Drive the army forward for the next few hours and we'll pass straight by most of the Moslem force. On the other hand, they will soon fill the gap between Hattin's Horns and Arbel. Once that's done, we're bottled in the valley.'

Guy nodded. 'Bring your men from the heights. I'll weigh your advice until you return.'

Although the losses were heavy, the army moved inexorably toward the sea. If the pace was speeded up, the vanguard would pass north of the Horns of Hattin within an hour. Then they would fight their way south-east and, as Ermengard had said, emerge between the hill of Arbel and the besieged fortress of Tiberias.

Thirst was now acute among the foot soldiers; they had pushed their bodies hard through the hottest hours of the day, and since dawn they had moved under an unbroken pall of dust. Some of them slunk to the sides of the valley, or scrambled up to the heights, seeking clearer air, but finding only certain death from a reed lance or an ostrich-feathered arrow.

Raymond of Tripoli had assessed the reports of his own scouts and rode back from the vanguard to make sure that Guy would not waver at this crucial point in the march. Now that it was too late to turn back, the army must be made to go on, until each man had soaked his feet in the Sea of Galilee.

The King assured his Regent that he had every intention of continuing the advance.

The army had shortened the distance to Tiberias by another mile when Humphrey of Toron galloped to the head of the column to inform Raymond that there had been a change in plan. His face was rimed with dust, his lips cracked and swollen. He looked twice his age, and when he spoke it was with the voice of a juiceless old man.

'It's beyond belief, Lord Regent! They took him to the rear to show him the carnage——'

'Calm yourself. Who took whom? Put some names to these people.'

'I'm sorry, it's just unbelievable, that's all.'

'So you said. Move aside, let that wagon through. Now start again, slowly.'

'Gerard and Reynald,' the young noble rasped. 'The Templars were being horribly mauled at the rear, so the Grand Master and my damned step-father went to see the king. Gerard said his men could not go on, that the king should call a halt to the advance.'

'What?'

'Yes! And then they made Guy ride back with them to view the extent of the Templar losses. You can imagine what happened. Between them, Gerard and Reynald convinced that bloody weakling to turn on to the plateau. Balian sent me straightway to tell you. Look! Can you see back there? They're already turning short of the horns.' He guessed what Raymond was thinking and let his breath out in a dusty sigh. 'No, Lord Regent, you won't get him to bend your way again. The army welcomes a halt. We're set on the plateau now, like it or not.' He hesitated, then said, 'I know how you feel about me for deserting your council at Nablus. If I had known things would come to this I would have let you make me king. God forgive me, but how was anyone to know?'

Staring at where the dust cloud divided, Raymond said, 'I don't feel badly toward you, Lord Humphrey. It was a poor enough idea. Though I must say, both you and I would have stood more firm than that corn stalk we call king. Well, tell Lord Balian that I will bring my men back on to the plateau.' Shielding his eyes from the sun, he looked along the ridges and peaks of the Hills of Hattin. The skyline was alive with Saracens.

Emir Kukburi's entire force of six thousand men was moving north between the head of the Christian army and the hill of Arbel. Takedin's troops clung to the horns and sealed the eastern end of the plateau. Saladin had positioned his six thousand across the plateau so that they formed a human wall, with the village of Lubieh at their backs. In his wildest dreams the Sultan could not have imagined that the entire Christian host would shuffle open-mouthed into such a perfect trap. But not in his wildest dreams could he have imagined that the Crusaders would hand such responsibility to a man like Guy of Lusignan . . .

As the light of 3rd July dimmed above Eastern Galilee, upward of thirty-three thousand men assembled on the plateau and on the Hills of Hattin and on the steep rise to the north-east of the grassy field. This natural barrier was known as the Hill of the Multiplication of Pains.

# CHAPTER NINETEEN

# Hattin

## 3rd, 4th July 1187

Some of Joscelin of Courtenay's men found a well. It was a crude, low-walled structure, probably dug by shepherds and shared by them and their sheep. The soldiers who had spotted it howled with relief and plunged toward it. It was filled with rocks to within six feet of the surface.

So there was no water.

The army made its stand at the farthest point from the enemy archers. The Moslems were ranged along the Tell, or saddle of rock that joined the twin Horns of Hattin. They fired high into the air, but the arrows fell short of the Frankish perimeter. As the light faded, men advanced from both camps, the Crusaders to scout for water, the Moslems to wreak havoc among the forward positions.

Raymond of Tripoli, after so many arduous years as the backbone of the Kingdom, finally gave himself up to the lassitude of total surrender. He rode through the camp, like some bowed, long-nosed gargoyle, moaning, 'Alas, great God, the war is over before it is begun. We are all dead men now. The Kingdom is finished.'

One of the soldiers, who knew nothing of the politics that had brought him there, shouted, 'Damn you, Regent! If it was not for your wife we would be well clear of this hole!'

Raymond heard him, smiled foolishly and murmured, 'It is my fault, all mine. I have killed the Kingdom. God have mercy on me, I have killed it.'

Baldwin of Ramleh saw his condition and took pity on him. Riding alongside, he eased the reins gently from Raymond's grasp and led him, still moaning, to where Balian waited at the western edge of the camp.

'Here, brother,' Baldwin said. 'Our Regent's mind is broken. It would be best to put him in one of our tents and get a physician to him. If he rides around like this he'll bring us all down, or get himself killed.'

'Killed,' Raymond murmured, 'yes, it is killed now. The war is over and we are dead. We are judged by God, all of us, and I above the rest am found wanting. God will slay me now for what I have done.'

Balian wiped a hand over his face and told Baldwin to help lower Raymond to the ground. Then they half led, half-carried him to the nearest tent and laid him on a sagging, leather-bound cot.

'Keep this to yourself,' Balian said. 'We'd lose half the army if they believed Raymond was finished. God will that he'll sleep and wake sane again.'

'It is finished,' Raymond mumbled. 'All the Kingdom is gone now, all gone, all gone . . .'

The barons left the tent and stood listening to the sounds of battle that came from the south and east. Humphrey of Toron appeared with the news that the Grand Masters had at last agreed to co-operate and would combine their Orders in one impressive cavalry unit.

'Thank God for that,' Balian said. 'It comes late in the day, but at least we have one strong fist.'

'I wouldn't count on the infantry,' Humphrey warned. 'Some of them have already turned themselves over for water.'

'I never do rely on the infantry. They're a scrappy lot at the best of times. They have their uses, though they never won or lost a battle yet. It's the cavalry who must organise.' Touching his brother on the arm, he said, 'The Grand Masters have given me an idea. What if we extend their alliance and put Reynald with Joscelin and Amalric, while you and young Humphrey and I gather our own knights under one banner? That will give us three fists. Guy's knights and those of the other barons will make a fourth. Then we'll charge and charge again until we smash a hole in their line.'

Baldwin rolled his head from side to side. 'It's possible, but we're all boiling in our armour——'

'It'll soon grow cooler.'

'—and I'm as thirsty as any man.'

'Then fight for your drink!' Balian snapped. 'Otherwise, we're here all night and taken in the morning. Now, what do you say?'

'I'm for it,' Humphrey assented. 'I'll go and put it to my step-father.'

'God knows, it's all we can do,' Baldwin sighed. 'But what of Raymond's knights?'

'We'll put them with those of Sidon and Caesarea. It'll give us a fifth unit.'

They made ready, and the combined weight of Hospitallers and Templars charged out with the last flicker of day. Led by Gerard and Ermengard, they thundered south towards Lubieh. For two hours the Military Orders ploughed into the enemy lines, decimating them in one of the bloodiest contests any of the knights could remember. They advanced to the outskirts of Lubieh, but barred by black stone walls and restricted to the narrow streets, they were forced to retire again. They rode back into the Christian camp, not grinning this time, too weary to bring back trophies or souvenirs.

Reynald, with the Constable and Seneschal of the Kingdom, led the next charge. They were not as successful as the knights of the Military Orders and were halted several hundred yards short of the village. It was now full dark and the horsemen stayed in close formation, not wishing to be separated. The Moslem archers used fire arrows, while the *Naffatin* continued their deadly work. The night sky was etched with flames, and the knights glimpsed not only the enemy, but many of their own foot soldiers stumbling unarmed toward the Moslem lines.

By the end of 3rd July, more than one third of the Frankish infantry had surrendered.

By the end of 3rd July—24th Rabi II.—the prayers of the Faithful had risen throughout Islam to Allah, Lord of Creation, Judge of the Last Day.

'You alone do we worship, and to You alone do we pray. Guide us to Your straight way, the way of those on whom You look with favour, not of those who have angered You, nor of those who have strayed from Your way. All praise be to You, Almighty Allah, the Compassionate, the Merciful.'

'*La ilaha il' Mohammed rasul Allah!*'
'There is no God but Allah, and Mohammed is His Prophet!'

On Balian's orders, one of the army physicians had administered a powerful sleeping potion to Raymond. The physician had not been able to say with any accuracy how long the effects of the potion would last, but he thought until dawn, or even full light. He was wrong, for by the middle of the third hour of Saturday, 4th July, the Regent had woken, calm but listless, and had sneaked out of the tent and made his way to his king.

Guy had never been so pleased to see his erstwhile rival.

'Where in hell were you? I've had men scouring the camp!'

'How is our situation?' Raymond intoned, blinking as though every movement of his eyelids was premeditated. 'Are we holding?'

'Don't you know? Isn't it obvious to you? Our situation is grave and no, we are not holding. Listen to me now. I make no pretence of the fact that many of my leaders are beyond my control. If you had been with me when Gerard and Reynald took me back to see——'

'Are we holding, King?'

'—the extent of the injuries sustained by the—What? I've told you once, no, we are not. What is it? Are you unwell?'

'The situation is grave, King. I make no pretence of that fact.'

Guy frowned at him. 'I just said that. Why do you blink in such a way? What's wrong with you?'

'In a while I will ride out of here. It's too dry.'

Thinking that the Regent was suffering from excessive fatigue, Guy snatched at this last opportunity to use him. Raymond was still the best tactician in the army, and he was still the man the soldiers looked to as their true leader. Fatigued or not, he must be put to work, rallying the Crusaders.

'Yes,' the king pressed, 'that's it, you ride out. Take Reginald of Sidon and young Raymond of Antioch with you. The sea's only five miles distant. Take all the men you need and break out to the east.'

'It's dry here.'

'Don't worry, Princess Eschiva will give you water.'

'Eschiva?'

'Your wife, Regent. Ride to her. Hew a path for us and we will all follow.' Struggling to find words to which Raymond would respond, Guy said, 'It's dry *here*, but not at Tiberias. Your wife waits for you with jars and baths of water. If you lead us, the army will follow.'

'If only I were king.'

'Well, you're n—— Yes, yes, you are all but king now. Save us to-day and the crown is promised to you.'

'The sea is only five miles away.'

'Exactly. What is that to a man like you?'

'Hmmm?'

'It's nothing, is it?' He swallowed and said, 'You can lead the army five miles, whereas I could not take it fifty yards.'

'I'll ride out of here,' Raymond repeated. 'This is not a good place to stay.'

Guy put a hand on his arm. 'Sit here in the king's tent for a while. I'll raise some men for you.' He led Raymond into the scarlet cone and left him seated in a small chair. He was about to leave when a thought struck him and he poured Raymond a glass of wine, then placed his simple gold coronet on the Regent's head. 'There,' he said. 'How does it feel to be king?'

'Dry,' Raymond told him. 'I'll soon ride away from here.'

Reminding himself to reclaim the coronet before Raymond led the charge toward Tiberias, he went out, whispered to three of his guards to humour the Regent, but to keep him inside the tent, then hurried through the camp in search of Reginald and Walter and anyone else who would join the charge.

Constable Pola of Toron was killed by a sling-shot whilst in conversation with Humphrey near the south-west perimeter of the camp.

A few moments later, Bishop Rufin of Acre was hit in the chest by an arrow and fell dying, still clutching the True Cross. Bishop Bernard of Lydda was quickly summoned and prised the cross from Rufin's hands.

The smell of burning that already pervaded the field became stronger, and smoke began to drift across the camp. Before long the Crusaders realised that the Moslems had fired the grass and bushes on the plateau. The acrid smoke rolled in with the light wind, adding to the confusion and sharpening their desperate desire for water. More foot soldiers surrendered, but the knights held their ground, many of them divested of their heavy armour.

Bohemond of Antioch's son and the Lords of Sidon and Caesarea were located, their knights assembled and Raymond of Tripoli led, minus Guy's coronet, to his horse. As was the way, the leaders rode together in advance of their men. The object of the attack was to break Takedin's line between the eastern Horn of Hattin and the northern edge of the Hill of the Multiplication of Pains. If this was achieved, the entire Christian army would stream eastward in their wake and thus break out in the direction of Tiberias.

The other leaders were occupied elsewhere, so only Guy and Bishop Bernard were present to wish Raymond well.

As the first faint dawn light hued the sky the foot soldiers on the eastern perimeter moved aside and the cavalry trotted out. Raymond's thoughts were muddled. He was not sure whether Guy had promised him the crown if he reached Tiberias, or if he was expected to collect water from Eschiva and bring it back so that the king might bathe. Whichever, he was determined that neither Reginald, nor Walter, nor Bohemond's son would beat him to the crown, so he spurred forward without warning his compeers, or preparing the knights for a charge.

The wiry Emir of Hamat saw him approaching through the smoke, sensed that something was amiss, and shouted to the nearby soldiers, 'That's the Regent of the Kingdom! What is it about him?'

'He has no sword!' they said. 'He's traded it for a lance.'

For a moment Takedin stared at the man all Islam held in high esteem, then gasped as he saw the fault in Raymond. *He was holding the lance the wrong way round.*

Clearly, the Regent did not realise it, for the lance was couched properly, the shaft tucked against his body, the blunt end protruding alongside the horse's head. But the leaf-shaped tip was already cutting into the animals croup, like some devilish spur. Takedin waited for him to correct his error and reverse the lance. When he did not, and when he refused to acknowledge the shouts of warning from his Christian companions, the Moslem knew that a madness had overtaken him. Waving his men aside, he shouted, 'Let him through! Let that man go by! Wait for the others!'

At that moment Raymond's three fellow barons drew level with him, and their knights were subjected to the incredible sight of the Lords of Tiberias, Sidon, Caesarea and Antioch, plunging along an open corridor between the enemy lines. A few disobedient archers fired, hoping to hit one of the three sane leaders, but it was over too quickly and Takedin was screaming at them to close their ranks again.

With the Christian army trapped on the plateau, Saladin had sent word to Emir Kukburi to withdraw his men from the valley of Batuf and to bring them round to reinforce his and Takedin's contingents. So the Regent, Reginald, Walter and Raymond of Antioch found themselves free, almost as though they had been evicted from the battle. They rode on as far as the hill of Arbel, then reined in, shattered by Takedin's tactics.

There was nothing they could do. There was no possible way by which they might re-enter the plateau. They were free men, free to live with the knowledge that they had been forced to desert their knights and had failed to strike a blow against their mortal enemy.

It was Bohemond of Antioch's son who leaned over to reverse the Regent's lance.

Raymond said, 'Thank you,' and then, 'take heart, my lords, I will be made king in a day or two.'

They headed north, were given food and water at the Templar castle of Safed, and rested there before riding on to Raymond's county of Tripoli.

At dawn the Saracens on the Hills of Hattin carried out a critical inspection of the plateau below. The grass was still burning, though more than half the field was now blackened. The Christian perimeter had shrunk and the onlookers were astonished to see that less than three thousand men were left inside the lines. More than three-quarters of the infantry had capitulated, and there was an obvious shortage of horses within the camp. But the Crusader Standard was still erect, and Guy had moved his tent on to a low mound, where it could be seen by all who were prepared to fight on. The plateau was a charnel-house of bodies, some moving, most of them stiffened.

The Moslem generals had encircled the camp on three sides, while the archers on the peaks that formed the fourth side waited for the Crusaders to retreat toward them. Once they came within arrow-shot the battle would be over.

Standing midway between the camp and the walls of Lubieh, Saladin reviewed the scene. His eldest son was with him, witness to the changing emotions in the man who many thought too calm for feelings.

'They will make two charges,' Saladin mused. 'Then their force will be depleted. You know their Regent escaped with a number of other leaders.'

'I know,' al-Afdal said. 'I am glad Emir Takedin allowed Ray-mond to go. I found the man's sincerity worthy of respect. I'm glad he eluded us.'

Saladin nodded, not taking his eyes from the scarlet tent and the fluttering Standard. 'I, too. Have your troops found any trace of the Red Wolf yet?'

'No. He must still be out there. Now there's a beast of a different stripe. We will not let *him* ride away.'

'I feel personally about him,' Saladin said. 'I should not allow it, but I wonder how long I would hesitate before I raised my own sword against him.'

'None would blame you for it if you did. By all that's just he should have been cut down long ago.'

'Would you kill him, my son?'

'I would, and Allah would put strength in my arm! Give him to me and you'll see.'

'It may go that way, though first we have to—— Look! They are ready to charge.'

'Their first attempt,' al-Afdal said. 'Like you, I give them one other.'

The Crusaders had reached an obvious conclusion. The two and a half thousand knights and three thousand Turcopoles who had left Acre had been reduced to six hundred Templars and Hospitallers, between four and five hundred lay horsemen and less than seven hundred Moslem mercenaries. This was tragic enough, but only half the survivors had horses to ride.

So the nine hundred who were still able to do battle were divided into two sections, one led by King Guy, Reynald of Chatillon, Gerard of Ridefort, Constable Amalric and Seneschal Joscelin, the other by Balian of Ibelin, Baldwin of Ramleh, Humphrey of Toron and Grand Master Ermengard de Daps.

Balian was ordered to mount the first charge, but the direction of it was left to him.

'We will ride directly at them,' he said, 'then turn west before we come into arrow range.'

'You won't do battle with them?' Baldwin demanded. 'By God, I've come too far to flee now.'

'You may have more years in you than I, brother, but I ride in command to-day. As for your battle, do you really think we will make an impression on them?'

'I don't care what impression we make, so long as we break their bones!'

'Doughty as ever, but as short-sighted. When we are killed or captured, who is left to raise another army? No, brave Baldwin, we'll do things my way and see who rides safely out of here. You'll have enough fighting on your hands just breaking free. Now clasp mine and we'll say farewell. Now you, Grand Master. I think the Hospital is well-pleased that you should have been chosen to succeed the valiant Roger of Les Moulins. And now you, Humphrey. You have made my step-daughter happy and been a good husband to her. I note that you wear her silver brooch. She told me once that she had bled on it and slept on it for you.' He smiled wearily. 'It's strong magic from a young woman. I pray it keeps you safe.' He gripped Humphrey's hand, then raised his arm in the air and waved the knights forward.

They streamed out of the shrunken camp, riding a little east of south toward Lubieh. The Saracen cavalry advanced to meet them head-on. A few stray horses and camels ran to the edges of the fast-diminishing gap and then there was nothing but the black, corpse-strewn plateau separating foe from foe . . .

Balian watched where the Moslem arrows fell, then waved repeatedly toward the entrance to the valley of Tur'an and wheeled to the west. A moment later Islam and Christendom collided, both sides fighting with unprecedented ferocity. Blood founted in the air, and the hills rang with the screams of men and horses. Fostus carved a path, hoping Balian would follow, but it was Ernoul who stayed close behind, while the Lord of Nablus made his own way on another part of the field.

Baldwin of Ramleh shouted for support. Twenty knights rode to him, then found themselves hemmed in by a hundred grim Saracens. Baldwin's sword was dashed from his grasp and he felt a dozen hands dragging him to the ground.

Humphrey joined Balian and fought alongside him, as each moment brought the valley entrance a yard nearer. They saw Ermengard, with the remnants of his Hospitallers, and Humphrey turned, thinking Balian was still with him. The Lord of Toron was between Balian and the Grand Master when a Saracen threw his shield at him, sending it spinning flat like a discus. It caught Humphrey on the rim of his helmet and knocked him cold. The dark-skinned horsemen swooped on him and pitched him from his saddle.

By now Fostus had been singled out for immediate dispatch. He had done too much damage and looked set to do more, so a group of Saracen archers marked him as their target. Eager to make up in his glance what he lacked in muscle, Ernoul yelled, ''Ware bowmen!' and charged at them. It was an instinctive movement, as when he had ridden between Balian and the Constable at Nazareth, and it irritated the Saracens. They had no time to waste on this skinny Frank. He was unimportant and could be easily cut down later. But at the moment he was in their way, blocking their view of the hairy monster who continued to bedevil them. If he didn't turn aside soon——

Suddenly realising what he was at, Ernoul tugged at the reins and fled. The archers raised their bows, then screamed imprecations. The warrior-ape had gone, cutting a swathe through to rejoin his master.

Because Balian's unexpected manœuvre had given the Crusaders a few moments advantage, a number of them reached the valley of Tur'an. They did not stop there, but put five good miles between themselves and the Horns of Hattin. Twenty lay knights arrived first, then a handful of Hospitallers, then a further thirty knights, then Ernoul, then a mixed dozen, then Fostus, Balian, eight more who wore the split-pointed cross, and Grand Master Ermengard. They waited for some time and were joined by another sixty horsemen.

At a rough count, Ernoul estimated that somewhat less than one hundred and fifty had escaped, leaving twice that number dead or captive on the field. Balian searched for his brother and young Humphrey, but too many survivors had seen them fall. It was poor consolation to know that they could be ransomed, so were probably still alive.

Al-Afdal shouted, 'Look! They make their second attempt!'

This time the knights did not veer east or west, but rode straight at Lubieh and the Sultan. They paid dearly for their guileless courage, and within the first few moments of combat Hugh Embriaco, Lord of Jebail, was taken, and the king's brother Amalric, and the Lord of Botrun. Then, as the knights retreated to the slope below Guy's tent, the aged William III, Marquis of Montferrat was dragged, none too gently, from his horse. William was the grandfather of Queen Sibylla's sickly son, the late Child King Baldwin V, and the Saracens who led him back to their lines were confident of gaining a good price for him.

Now Saladin and his son watched as the Moslems made their final assaults on the camp. Twice they attacked and twice they were beaten back, the last time bringing them dangerously near their Sultan. Each time the Moslems reached the low hill al-Afdal shouted, 'We have them!' and each time Saladin replied, 'Be silent. They are not yet finished.'

Then Takedin and Kukburi waved their men forward and Saladin watched as the mighty Crusader Standard teetered and fell, while the royal tent disappeared with a last flash of scarlet. Spilling tears of joy, the Sultan sank to his knees and made obeisance to Allah. Then he climbed to his feet again, his expression as grave as ever and said, 'Bring their leaders to my tent. I will speak with them there.'

Al-Afdal nodded. He could not believe that the battle was over. But it was over, all save the final reckoning.

Leaden-limbed and smeared with blood the Christian overlords were herded down the slope and across the razed field. The True

Cross was taken from Bishop Bernard. Rumour had it that an officer in the Moslem cavalry took it with him to Damascus where he tied it to the tail of his horse and dragged it through the gutters of the city. True or not, it was never seen again by the Christians of Palestine. When they reached the Sultan's tent, Guy was briefly reunited with his brother, then the Lusignans, Baldwin, Humphrey, Joscelin and Reynald were led before their victor.

They expected many things, but not a gentle greeting and an invitation to be seated on scattered cushions. Indicating that King Guy should sit at his left and young Humphrey at his right, Saladin then extended the gesture to include Balian's brother, the Seneschal and Constable of the Kingdom, and the Red Wolf of the Desert.

Guy moved to bend his legs, but they buckled and he sprawled on the cushions. Affecting not to notice, Saladin sensed that the king was almost paralysed with fear. His yellow hair was matted, his face streaked with blood and dirt, his hands twitching without control. Pained that Guy should harbour such fear in his presence, the Sultan nodded to one of his servants, who turned aside to set jugs and glasses on a tray.

Baldwin sat erect, his legs crossed in the Arab manner, his blood still racing with the will to fight.

Amalric let his head hang forward and rested his hands, palm uppermost, on the carpeted ground.

Reynald looked at Saladin, then turned away, as though the leader of all Islam was some bow-backed dog.

Humphrey sat quiet, his fingers crooked around Isabella's brooch. He wondered if Ernoul had escaped, or if his friend was lying out there, dead on the field. He murmured a prayer, then stopped as Saladin glanced at him.

The servant placed a tray before his master and Saladin poured rosewater into a glass, rubbed ice against it and handed the glass to King Guy. The Poitevin steadied it in both hands and drank greedily. The glass was a little less than half full as he passed it on to Reynald. Couching his broken left wrist, the Lord of Kerak reached for it with his good hand.

'One moment,' Saladin said. 'Do any of you speak my language?'

'A few words,' Humphrey stammered. 'Though I could not converse——'

'Ah, but you understand my question well enough, Lord Humphrey. So if you understand me now, please tell that man that his king gives him water to drink, not I.'

'You mean——'

'I mean that man there.'

Humphrey relayed the message to Reynald, who mouthed, 'Water's water. What difference who gives it?'

Saladin nodded at Humphrey and the young noble found himself with the unenviable task of interpreting between the leader of Islam and his hated step-father.

Speaking directly at Reynald and hardly giving Humphrey time to translate, Saladin remarked, 'It makes the greatest difference, Lord Reynald. It is the custom of our people—as you know full well—that if a stranger is given food or drink he may not be harmed. You are no stranger to me, but the tradition applies.' He clapped once and his servant dispensed rosewater to Baldwin, Joscelin and Amalric. Saladin himself passed a glass to Humphrey.

Reynald growled, 'If you intend harm, get on with it. You don't see me trembling.'

'No, but you should tremble, with the debt you owe. It sullies my mouth to say it, but I am bound to spare you should you embrace Islam.'

'Embrace it?' Reynald said. 'I'd first rub the contents of my bowels on it.'

Guy clenched his hands around his glass. Amalric glanced up sharply, one eye sealed with dried blood. Humphrey breathed with his mouth open, deaf to any sounds beyond the tent.

Quietly, Saladin asked, 'What did that man say?'

'I—I didn't hear clearly.'

'What did he say, Lord Humphrey?'

'Nothing of moment, Sultan. Nothing that bears repeating.'

'Who are you to judge?' Reynald demanded. 'Tell the pig what I said. Tell him I squat with a bare arse on his Faith. Tell him! Tell him!'

With a curious mixture of terror and relief, Humphrey translated Reynald's boast. His head hurt from the spinning shield blow, and he found it difficult to focus. As he spoke, Saladin rose like a blurred phantom beside him. Even on his feet, the Sultan seemed thin and ineffectual among the taller, heavy-boned Crusaders. But as Humphrey's voice trailed away he said, 'You twice broke the treaty. You sank a pilgrim ship. You murdered civilians. You sacked caravans. You threatened the holy places of Islam. You tortured prisoners until they were maimed. And now you would defile our religion.'

'What of it? Kings do all you say, and I am only a prince. You're lucky I didn't do worse——' The final sibilance was still on his lips as Saladin drew his sword and hacked downward. The blow cut halfway through Reynald's neck. He rose from the floor, eyes and mouth stretched wide. Then, with his lips pulled back, exposing his great stained teeth, he fell back again in a welter of blood. He tried once more to rise, but his left wrist failed to support him and he splashed over on his side.

His one-time companion, the Sicilian corsair Camini, may have turned his own ravaged face from the agonies of Hell and felt avenged, for Bloodhead was dying with a whistle on his lips.

Although his enemy of enemies was not yet dead, Saladin would have no more to do with him. He was satisfied that he had not hesitated to raise his sword against this Godless monster, and now motioned to his servant to drag the thing away. Humphrey's last sight of his step-father was of his massive head flapped over to one side as he was hauled out to be butchered on the burnt grass.

Guy broke the glass he was holding and jerked like a hanged man. Saladin placed his sword behind his cushions and murmured, 'Be calm, Guy of Lusignan. That perfidious creature went beyond all measure, but you have nothing to fear. It is not written that a king shall kill a king.'

Now it was over.

Saladin commanded that every Templar and Hospitaller be executed on the field, and went so far as to purchase them from their captors. Then, having paid a generous sum for them, he put them with the others, to be beheaded. Only one member of the Military Orders was reprieved. This was the Grand Master of the Temple, Gerard of Ridefort.

The lay knights and barons were taken fettered to Damascus, to be held for ransom.

The Turcopoles were murdered for being traitors to their race, though some, who had become Christians, turned back to Mohammed and were spared.

The Frankish infantry was led away in droves, and since so many had surrendered without a fight it was soon possible to buy a prisoner for three dinars, or a string of six for twenty.

To further impress the citizens of Damascus, cart-loads of heads were hauled through the city and were passed out freely to any with the stomach for such a souvenir.

It was over. Yet for Salah ed-Din Yusuf, the Great Saladin, surnamed al-Malik un-Nasir, the Victorious King, and for the Moslem world, it had only begun.

# Palestine

## *July, September 1187*

Next day, 5th July, Tiberias surrendered. Princess Eschiva was afforded every courtesy and was given safe conduct to Tripoli.

Saladin's brother, al-Malik al-Adil, captured Jaffa on 9th July.

On the following day Acre was taken. Shortly after, Nablus fell and, within two weeks, Toron.

With little or no difficulty the Saracens occupied Nazareth and Sebastia and, on the coast, Haifa, Caesarea and Arsuf.

The fortresses of Recordane Mills, Sepphoria, Duburieh, Calansua, La Feve and Beisan were subdued.

Reginald of Sidon sought refuge in his castle of Beaufort, so on 29th July his city was taken without bloodshed.

One week later, Beirut surrendered.

A few days more and, on Hugh Embriaco's orders, Jebail yielded. For this he was set free.

Saladin swept south and took Jamnia, Darum and Ramleh.

Toward the end of August, Raymond of Tripoli wasted away and died—assuredly of remorse.

After bitter fighting, Ascalon was occupied on 4th September. Meanwhile, other Moslem contingents had seized Latrun and Beth Gibelin.

The Templars at Gaza laid down their arms in return for their lives and the release of their Grand Master. Saladin kept his word and Gerard of Ridefort was set free.

The Saracens failed to take Tyre, Tortosa, Beaufort, the impregnable Hospitaller stronghold of Krak des Chevaliers, and its equivalent, Kerak of Moab. But the rest of Palestine was in Moslem hands and on 20th September Saladin pitched camp before the walls of Jerusalem.

The Christian capital in the East refused to surrender. At that time there were only two knights within the walls, and of the two obvious leaders, one was of doubtful mettle. He was the Patriarch, Heraclius, up from his bed. So it was to the other that the population of merchants, women and youths looked for deliverance. And Balian of Ibelin was determined that they should not look in vain.

The major events in this story are based on established historical record. Reynald of Chatillon's Red Sea raid happened, and Saladin personally killed or mortally wounded him. The Sultan's surprise attack during the wedding at Kerak, and the massacre of the Military Orders in the valley near Nazareth, are true. Gerard of Ridefort was indeed one of three survivors, and was the only Templar spared at Hattin. Pashia de Riveri existed, along with all the listed characters with the exception of Fostus. Many of the recorded incidents have been embellished in an attempt to put flesh upon the bones of those who have lain for more than 700 years beneath the surface of that tortured Holy Land.

The Story of the Houses of Ibelin, Lusignan and Toron, and of the other leaders of Frankish Palestine, plus the advent of Richard Cœur de Lion, Philip Augustus and Frederick Barbarossa, is continued and concluded in The Kings of Vain Intent.

G.S.